RUMI AND THE RETRIBUTION

A GABRIEL MCKNIGHT THRILLER

RUMI AND THE RETRIBUTION

YOU ARE
WHAT YOU SEEK

POONEH SADEGHI

ROGUE
RIVER

An imprint of Roan & Weatherford Publishing Associates, LLC
Bentonville, Arkansas
www.roanweatherford.com

Library of Congress Cataloging-in-Publication Data
Names: Sadeghi, Pooneh, author.
Title: Rumi and the Retrubition/Pooneh Sadeghi | Gabriel McKnight #1
Description: First Edition | Bentonville: Rogue River, 2024.
Identifiers: LCCN: 2024939992 | ISBN: 978-1-63373-946-8 (hardcover) |
ISBN: 978-1-63373-947-5 (paperback) | ISBN: 978-1-63373-948-2 (eBook)
Subjects: BISAC: FICTION/Thrillers/Espionage | FICTION/RomanceAction & Adventure
FICTION/Mystery & Detective/International Crime & Mystery

Rogue River trade paperback edition December, 2024

Cover Design by Casey W. Cowan
Interior Design by Michele Jones
Editing by Staci Troilo

To my father who taught me the magic and power of words. I miss you every day!

CHAPTER ONE

PARIS, JULY 14, 1997

Dying for your loved ones is a noble sacrifice, yet outsmarting a killer before you die—it's a sweeping triumph! That's what Shiraz Rahman thought as she rushed out of the Trocadero metro station on a balmy summer evening.

The sun had begun its descent, making way for midnight blue skies. Paris dressed in lights, welcoming all to its various restaurants and cafés. Shiraz's gaze darted around as she turned into the Delessert Boulevard. Her posture was stiff, her pace fast, and her breath labored.

Up ahead, the Café Delessert bustled with activity. Waiters rushed about delivering trays of food. The aroma of coffee and French cuisine drifted in the air. Parisians and tourists clustered around the tables lined by the sidewalk, their carefree laughter carrying into the night. Shiraz recalled the days when she, too, laughed freely, unaware of the evil surrounding her.

A loud clatter broke through the night. Shiraz bit back a

scream and jerked around. A waiter had dropped a tray on the sidewalk. He bent over to pick it up. Shiraz clutched her purse and hastened her pace. Every so often, she looked back to make sure she wasn't being followed.

The Delessert Boulevard swarmed with people. It was no surprise. This area offered the best view of the Eiffel Tower. Each year, thousands of people gathered here to celebrate and watch the dazzling fireworks display from the Eiffel Tower and the Trocadero gardens.

It seemed like a normal night, and by all accounts it should have been, but Shiraz knew better. *I will die tonight.* Beads of sweat formed on her upper lip. *I'm not afraid. I'm prepared.* After all, her daughter's life depended on it.

Noor, my sweet Noor! Shiraz rubbed her chest as she considered her options another time. There was one way to keep Noor safe, and when the time was right, Noor would know the truth. Shiraz had made sure of it.

She approached her bookstore and risked another glance over her shoulder. A shiver ran up her spine. The killer was in the crowd, waiting for an opportunity to strike. She squared her shoulders. *Come and get me. That's all you'll get.*

She entered her bookstore and let her head fall against the door. The scent of worn leather, polished wood, and new books were welcoming and familiar.

Jean Luc, her friend, and the bookstore's sole employee, sat by the reading nook.

Shiraz pasted a smile on her face. "Why are you working when you should be outside celebrating with the rest of the country?"

Jean Luc placed a book on a shelf close to the armchair he occupied. "Cheri, we have a splendid view. I can watch the celebration from here."

Shiraz placed her hands on her hips and furrowed her brows into a mock frown. "It's Independence Day. Go drink wine, celebrate your freedom, and flirt with someone nice. I'll close the store tonight."

"Come with me," Jean Luc pleaded. "We'll find two delicious men and party all night."

Shiraz snorted. "The only man I'll ever love is Parviz." She rushed on before Jean Luc could say anything. "I know my husband died years ago, but what Parviz and I had was unique. Something like that happens once in a lifetime." She made shooing motions with her hands. "That's why I'm closing, and you're leaving. It's your turn to find your soulmate."

A movement outside of the window caught her eye. For an instant, Shiraz saw a familiar figure standing in the crowd outside of her store. She gripped the armchair and craned her neck to get a better look. The Trocadero gardens overflowed with people wearing France's national colors. Its fountains switched from red to blue and back. The Eiffel Tower shone tall and proud. Her heart thudded wildly. "Why did it take me so long to figure out the truth?"

"Shiraz, are you all right?" Jean Luc asked, concern evident in his ruddy round face. "You were mumbling to yourself."

Shiraz studied her hands. Her knuckles had gone white. She let go of the armchair and relaxed her features. "I'm fine. I was just thinking, that's all."

Jean Luc looked uncertain. "Are you sure you want to stay here?"

Shiraz bobbed her head. "Yes, Noor and I have plans. Go enjoy your evening."

Jean Luc finally gave in and left the store. Shiraz shut the door behind him then poured herself a cup of tea. She sat behind the counter and picked up a volume of Rumi's poems.

"Life is a multitude of patterns that rise, fall, and flow together. You taught me that." She traced her hands along the book's spine. "It's Noor's turn to find her place and purpose in life.

I know you'll guide her as you did me." Shiraz opened the book and lost herself in Rumi's compelling verse.

The sound of chimes announced a newcomer. Footsteps echoed in the silent store. The grandfather clock ticked in the corner, counting every second that remained of her life.

Shiraz closed the book and stared into the stone cold eyes of a killer.

The killer aimed a gun at her. "I put the 'Closed' sign up. Let's go to the back of the store."

Shiraz grimaced, revulsion evident in her face. "I can't believe it. All the lies, and the betrayal. How could you do it?"

The killer spoke with a coldness Shiraz had never heard before. "Easily. Now move. I don't have all night."

She rose and headed toward the small office at the back of the store.

Her enemy held the gun at her back and pushed her into the office.

She stumbled and straightened herself. "I know why you're here. You shouldn't have come."

"Where is the package?"

Shiraz raised her chin. "I don't know."

Her enemy slapped her with enough force to knock her head against the bookshelf behind the desk. Shiraz stumbled and straightened herself. She spat blood, and at that moment the future of her daughter was all that mattered. Her face flushed. There was a moment of stillness on both sides, then Shiraz charged her foe. She was no match for her opponent's strength, but it took her assailant off guard.

They fell to the floor in a struggle. Shiraz kicked her opponent as hard as she could and struggled to rise to her feet. Outside, voices rose as thousands of Parisians sang their national anthem.

The murderer grabbed Shiraz's ankle and dragged her back down. Shiraz reached out and grabbed the volume of Rumi's poems. She knocked her assailant over the head with the book.

"Argh!" her assailant grunted, nonplussed.

Shiraz wobbled to her feet. Her breath hitched as she forced her shaky limbs to move. She made it halfway to the exit when the murderer grabbed a fist full of her hair and dragged her back to the office.

Shiraz's chest heaved, and her lungs burned as she gulped air.

The killer aimed the gun at her. "I'm in no mood to play games. I'll ask one more time. Where is the package?"

Shiraz met her foe's gaze defiantly, and for an instant, her mouth turned up. "You'll never find it."

Nostrils flared. "Then you're no use to me."

Gunshots echoed in the store just as the fireworks at the Trocadero started. Shiraz blinked. She felt nothing for a few seconds, then fell to the floor as pain gripped her body.

She tried to rise. Her body didn't cooperate. It twitched and convulsed as blood drained from her wounds. She flung her hand out, trying to reach for the telephone cord a few feet away. Her vision grew blurry, and her breath came gasps.

She didn't know how much time had passed when footsteps approached her. A man bent over her. Shiraz squinted through the haze of pain. It was Morris, her late husband's friend.

Morris pressed his hands over her wounds, trying to stop the bleeding. He shouted something, but a tremor shook her body, drowning out his words.

She coughed blood.

Sweat formed on Morris's upper lip. "Hold on." He tore strips of his own shirt to bind her wounds.

The pain began to ease and grow distant. A bright haze filled her vision. Shiraz felt light, as if she was floating. She looked up and blinked.

Her late husband, Parviz, stood by the doorway of her office. He gazed at her lovingly, then opened his arms.

No, not yet! Shiraz mustered all her strength and gripped Morris's arm. "Noor," she whispered.

Morris's eyes glistened with tears. He nodded grimly. "I'll keep her safe. You have my word."

Satisfied she'd done everything she could for her daughter, Shiraz Rahman took her last breath and stepped into her husband's arms.

CHAPTER TWO

"It's time we tend to you.
We will convert you into a house of fire
A raw gem hidden in the earth's maze
Your polished self will dazzle in the flames of the blaze."
—Rumi

NEW YORK CITY, NINETEEN YEARS LATER

Gabriel McKnight exited the limousine and inhaled the crisp winter air. What a wonderful day! He adjusted his tie and stepped toward the red carpet at Radio City Music Hall.

The old theatre had spruced up for the movie premiere. Large posters surrounded the red carpet. Spotlights centered on the guests, and fans lined up on both sides of the theatre. Security guards and police officers stood stoically watching the crowd, while photographers snapped photos of glamorous stars and attendees.

The couple in front of him posed for several pictures. Gabriel shifted, turning from the cameras, a habit he hadn't shed. He relaxed his shoulders and forced himself to smile as he made his way through the throng of guests gathered for the event.

He spotted CJ Anderson, the brilliant actor who played the role of Jason Van. CJ grinned and winked at him. Gabriel waved in return. Several photographers asked him to pose for pictures with CJ. He obliged them.

A reporter approached him and stuck a microphone under his nose. "Mister McKnight, how does it feel to have another one of your novels adapted to the silver screen?"

Oh, right. Harvey mentioned the press would speak with him. Gabriel widened his smile. "Thank you. I feel excited and grateful."

The reporter tilted her head back. "Hoorah, as Jason Van would say."

Suddenly, the hair on his neck prickled, and his muscles tightened. Years of training taught him to stay calm while he scanned the crowd, trying to pinpoint a threat. All he saw was the throng of fans gathered outside the theatre.

The reporter leaned closer. "Your main character, Jason Van, is a former Navy SEAL, and so are you. Are the novels based on your life? Are you Jason Van?"

Gabriel glanced at the reporter's name tag. "No, Marcie, Jason is charismatic and adventurous. I'm an introverted writer. As for the novels, I try to provide readers with entertaining stories that bring forward real-life issues, like the lack of human rights in certain countries. I hope it will make us all think of ways to better our world." Gabriel answered more questions and proceeded down the red carpet.

The hair on his neck prickled again. He studied the buildings across the street. No threats there. He searched for a warning sign, a movement—anything—and found nothing. The crowd roared when CJ Anderson approached the fans lined up by the theatre. That's when he spotted the man.

Standing over six feet tall, the guy wore a grey suit and stood in the crowd, sizing him up. His gaze met Gabriel's, and he smirked.

Gabriel approached the crowd of fans lined up on the sidewalk. People shoved pieces of paper in front of him. He greeted the crowd and signed whatever they gave him while searching for grey suit, but he'd disappeared. Gabriel shook a few hands and turned back to the red carpet.

Radio City Music Hall had several theatres and an enormous grand foyer with a large staircase, balconies, and mirrors. The theatre's plush burgundy carpet and orange-red art deco design gave visitors the impression of walking into a sunset.

Inside the theatre, an attendant escorted him to a reception lounge. He searched for Harvey Cornwall, his agent and friend.

Harvey was talking to one of the film producers. He spotted Gabriel, and his craggy face split into a huge grin. He shook hands with the producer, then joined Gabriel.

For a heavy man, Harvey was incredibly light on his feet. "Gabe, I finished reading your manuscript. It's brilliant!" Harvey blotted his face with a handkerchief. "The twist at the end was a surprise. I didn't see it coming."

Gabriel kept his eyes on the entrance and reached for a glass of water set up by the drinks. "That's the whole point. I don't want to be predictable to readers." Another ripple of tension streaked through his body. He searched the crowd, trying to find his brother Michael. No luck.

Harvey's forehead wrinkled. "Why aren't you mingling with the guests or talking to the press?"

He turned back to Harvey. "I wanted to see if you liked the manuscript. Your opinion matters. Besides, I've already talked to the press. You arranged it, remember? Maybe you're getting old, and it's affecting your memory. Maybe I need a new agent."

Harvey scowled. "You know what I dislike most? Writers who are mouthy outside of a manuscript. Keep it for the books!"

Grinning, he clapped Harvey on the shoulder. "I love you too,

Harv." He spotted Mom and Dad and was about to greet them when two women approached him for a picture. He posed for the picture and excused himself.

Harvey fell into step with him. "What is it with you and women? They gather around you like bees attracted to honey, and you run them off."

"I don't run women off."

"Oh, yeah?" Harvey cocked his head. "What happened to the last gal you were dating? She was nice enough."

"Kate was very nice." Gabriel lifted his shoulders. "We didn't have a real connection."

Harvey stepped closer to him, the lines on his face deepening. "Gabe, you reach out and connect to your readers in the best way possible. Why can't you do it in real life?"

"Gabriel, honey, we're so proud of you!" Mom rushed over to hug him and therefore saved him from answering Harvey. Mom's trim figure and cobalt blue eyes made her look younger than her age.

Gabriel kissed her cheek. "Thanks, Mom. I'm glad you're here."

Dad was debonair in his suit. He embraced Gabriel. "We wouldn't miss it for the world, son."

Mom beamed at Harvey. "Harvey, are you losing weight?"

Harvey blushed. "I'm working on it." He excused himself on the pretense of talking to someone and scampered off.

Lily, Gabriel's sister, stood on tiptoe to kiss him. Gabriel tugged on her hair and shook hands with Ethan, his brother-in-law.

Dad craned his neck to see past the crowd. "Have you seen Michael? It's not like your brother to be late."

"No, I haven't." Gabriel's cell phone rang. He noticed the blocked number. "This must be Michael." He answered the call. "Where are you, Mike?"

"Gabriel, is that you?" The voice was familiar, yet he couldn't place it. "This is Nolan Jameson, Mike's team lead."

Gabriel froze, rooted to the floor. Cold sweat gathered on his neck. He lowered his voice. "Is Mike all right?"

Several moments of silence ensued. "Mike's missing. Jonathan Smith, the assistant director, is in New York. I hear he's a family friend. He can meet you in an hour. Where are you staying?"

Gabriel took a deep breath to steady his pounding heart. "We're all at the Ritz Carlton. We're on our way."

Mom stepped forward. "What's wrong, sweetheart? You look pale."

Harvey rushed over and grabbed his arm before he could answer. "Gabe, you need to come with me."

Gabriel pulled away. "Sorry Harv, I—"

Harvey tugged on his arm. "Listen to me."

Two men approached them. Both wore rumpled suits. One of them was grey suit.

Harvey glanced at the men and tugged at his shirt collar.

Grey suit stepped forward. "Are you Gabriel McKnight?"

Alarm bells went off in Gabriel's head. He ignored them and turned toward the exit. "I'm sorry, I can't talk right now."

Grey suit put a restraining hand on Gabriel's arm. He lowered his voice. "Mister McKnight, I'm Detective Denton from the Washington D.C. Police Department, and this is Detective Mason from the New York City Police Department. We don't want to cause a scene. Please come with us."

Gabriel blinked. "Why?"

"Gabriel McKnight, we're taking you in for the murder of Asra Madison."

CHAPTER THREE

W*hat?!* Gabriel narrowed his eyes. "Is this some kind of joke?" Christ, he didn't have time for this. He needed to get back to the hotel. Why was Mike missing? Gabriel prayed he was all right.

Detective Denton's expression hardened. "I'm afraid not. If you come quietly, there won't be a scene."

The one named Mason stepped closer and flanked Gabriel's other side.

Gabriel ran a hand through his hair. Every passing moment was the difference between life and death for Mike. He glanced at the reception lounge.

Actors, Hollywood bigshots, and the press clustered in groups. The crowd flowed through the lobby and spanned toward the main theatre resembling a bird spreading its wings. Conversation and laughter echoed in the lounge.

He forced himself to stand still. Causing a scene would attract unnecessary attention and, more important, delay him. "There must be a misunderstanding. I don't know what you're talking about."

Denton's grip tightened on his arm. "Please come with us."

A sudden ripple traveled through the crowd. Lights flashed, heads turned, and the noise level increased several notches.

"Gabriel! It's so good to see you!" A willowy brunette approached the group and embraced him, enveloping him in a cloud of perfume.

Eva Mesda was Hollywood's latest flame and the actress who played Jason Van's current love interest. Eva linked her arm through his and struck a pose, preening at the attention the press bestowed on her.

Denton kept his hold on Gabriel's arm and turned his head, avoiding the cameras. Mason scowled and stood straighter.

Gabriel met Denton's stare. "I need a minute," he mouthed.

Denton's mouth tightened into a thin line. He nodded.

Gabriel exchanged greetings with Eva and introduced her to Harvey.

Not one to miss a cue, Harvey guided Eva to a group of producers.

Dad waited until Harvey and the actress moved away. His voice shook when he spoke. "What in God's name is going on?"

"This is a misunderstanding," Gabriel said. "Go back to the hotel with Mom. Jonathan Smith will meet you there. It's urgent." He turned to Ethan. "Will you go with Mom and Dad?"

"Yes." Ethan bent to murmur something to Lily.

Mom paled at the mention of Jonathan Smith's name. Her hand traveled to her throat, uncertain what to do.

Gabriel gave her an encouraging nod. "Go on, I'll catch up with you."

Mom nodded and rushed off with Ethan and Dad.

Gabriel's eyes traveled to Denton's hand. "Are you arresting me?"

"We have questions," Denton said.

He kept his voice low. "Am I under arrest?"

"My partner spoke hastily," Mason interjected. "What he meant was we'd like to ask you some questions."

Gabriel yanked his arm free. "That's different from taking me in. You of all people should know you must be clear. I'm busy. Call me next week."

Mason stepped closer. "You're a person of interest in a woman's murder, Mister McKnight. We'd like to ask you some questions at the precinct."

Gabriel ground his teeth. "In case you haven't noticed, I'm at the movie premiere of my book. I'll answer your questions later."

Having left Eva with a group of producers, Harvey scurried back and stepped in front of Gabriel, blocking him from prying eyes. "There's a conference room in the hallway by the reception lounge. If Gabriel decides to speak with you, it'll have to be brief. He can come to your precinct later if you need to have a longer discussion."

Gabriel glanced at his watch. "Fine. You have five minutes. Let's get this over."

"I'll join you," Lily said.

Mason stepped in front of Lily and shook his head. "No."

Lily lifted her chin. "I'm my brother's legal counsel. I'll go with him."

Mason exchanged a look with Denton and shrugged.

Harvey guided Gabriel, Lily, and the two detectives across the lounge and into the main hallway. The group turned into a secluded corridor and arrived at a set of double doors. Harvey held the door open.

Lily pulled a notepad from her purse. She scribbled something on it and handed it to Harvey. "This is the number of a defense attorney. Please call him and give him my name. Ask him to meet us here. Then please go to the Ritz Carlton. Mom and Dad are meeting with someone by the name of Jonathan Smith. It's important you tell Mister Smith Gabriel is talking to Detectives Denton and Mason."

Harvey took the note. He straightened his five-feet four-inch frame and glared at Denton. "You are barking up the wrong tree, sir. I've known Gabriel for many years. He's honorable and decent. I won't allow you to damage his good name and reputation." Harvey turned on his heels and marched off.

Gabriel stalked into the office and glowered at the detectives. "I don't have much time, so I'll make this brief. I don't know who Asra Madison is, and I haven't hurt or killed anyone."

Detective Denton motioned to one of the leather chairs. "Have a seat."

Gabriel sneaked a glance at his watch. He'd give the detectives ten minutes. He took the chair closest to the door. Lily sat by him, while Mason stood in the corner.

Denton pulled a photograph from his coat pocket. He placed it in front of Gabriel. "Do you own a 2023 black Nissan Murano with this license plate?"

Gabriel picked up the photograph. Yep, it was his car and his license plate. "Yes, but—"

Denton leaned forward. "We found the body of a woman, Asra Madison, in your car, by the Potomac River." He placed another photograph on the desk.

A woman lay sprawled across the front seat of Gabriel's car. Her dark hair covered half of her battered face. Her glazed eyes stared ahead, lifeless. One of her arms fell over the steering wheel. Her mouth was pulled back in an expression of horror, and her midsection lay open, exposing the insides of her stomach. It was as if a wild animal had attacked her. Blood covered Gabriel's front seat and was spattered across the windows.

Lily paled and knotted her hands together.

Gabriel clenched his jaw and studied the photograph, aware of Denton's scrutiny. When he spoke, his voice was hoarse. "I'm sorry for what happened to this woman, but I don't know who she is and how she wound up in my car."

"Is this the only car you own?" Denton asked.

"No, I also own a BMW. I drove it to New York."

"When is the last time you saw your Murano?"

Gabriel didn't hesitate. "Last week, when I was in D.C."

"Does anyone else have access to your vehicles?"

Yes, my brother Michael has access to everything I own. Gabriel cleared his throat. "No."

Lily sat up straight . "When did you find the body?"

"Yesterday. The medical examiner placed Miss Madison's time of death a week ago today anywhere from five p.m. to midnight," Denton said.

Lily nodded. "That's last Sunday. My brothers and I were at my parents' home for dinner. We stayed late and watched movies."

Denton rubbed his chin. "Can you confirm they were there until midnight?"

Lily smirked. "I'll answer that when you provide us with a more accurate time of death."

His gaze narrowed on Gabriel. "Is it true that you and your brother Michael are identical twins?"

"Yes."

Denton tilted his head. "Is it true that you and your brother spent your childhood in Iran?"

Gabriel blinked. "What does that have to do with this woman's death?"

"Answer the question, please."

Gabriel bit back a retort. "Yes, our father was a diplomat stationed in Iran before the Islamic revolution in 1979."

Denton rubbed his chin. "Asra Madison was an Iranian-American. She became a U.S. citizen six years ago."

Gabriel raised a brow. "I don't see the relevance."

Denton tapped his fingers on the desk. "Where is your brother, Mister McKnight?"

Gabriel said nothing.

"Where is Michael McKnight?"

Gabriel ran his hand through his hair. "I don't know."

"Gabriel doesn't keep track of Michael's schedule, and neither do I," Lily said. "If you want to speak with Michael, I suggest you contact him."

Denton placed another photograph on the desk. This one had a bloody hunting knife on it. "We found the weapon in the trunk of your car. The fingerprints on the weapon match the ones that are all over the car. They're your and your brother's fingerprints."

"A moment please." Lily touched Gabriel's arm. "Is the knife yours, Gabe?"

"Yes."

Lily nodded. "Since the knife belongs to my brother, it's not a surprise his or Michael's fingerprints are on it. Your so-called evidence is circumstantial."

Gabriel studied Denton. "How do you know the prints are mine?"

"We subpoenaed your records from the military."

The vein in Gabriel's temple throbbed. He resisted the urge to massage his temple. "Detective, I'll say this for the last time. I don't know an Asra Madison, and I sure as hell don't know how my car wound up by the Potomac River. I've been in New York for the past week."

Denton rose and loomed over Gabriel. "There are two sets of fingerprints in your car—yours and your brother's. That tells us you and your brother were present when Miss Madison died. It doesn't look good for either of you."

"Detective." Lily's tone held a note of warning. "As stated, your evidence is circumstantial and weak. My brother answered your questions, and unless you have a warrant to arrest him, we are leaving. You may call us if you have further questions."

Denton sneered. "If you want to get technical, the fingerprints on the knife are all I need to bring both of your brothers in."

Mason's phone beeped. "The car is waiting at the back entrance. We can take Mister McKnight and his legal counsel through the back doors."

"Let's go," Denton said.

Lily scowled. "That's not how it works, Detective."

"Ma'am." Denton rose. "We want to clear your brother's name and cross him off our suspect list as much as you do. Let's get this over so you can return to your premiere."

Gabriel rubbed his chin. This was all wrong, and he'd been so preoccupied with Mike's disappearance, he hadn't noticed until that moment. He nudged Lily. They followed the men back to the hallway. Voices from the reception carried into the hall. Gabriel waited until they reached a back exit and paused. "I'd like to see your IDs please."

"Are you stalling?" Denton growled.

"Show me your IDs first."

Mason reached into his vest and pulled out a gun. "Move or I'll shoot your sister!"

Years of training kicked in. Gabriel landed a roundhouse kick in Mason's groin. The man hit the floor. "Run!" Gabriel warned Lily as Denton slammed his head into Gabriel's stomach, throwing him to the carpeted floor.

Denton and Gabriel rolled around, each trying to overpower the other. Denton used his weight to pin Gabriel down and put his hands around his throat. Gabriel jabbed his finger into Denton's eye.

"Argh!"

Gabriel shoved his knee in Denton's stomach.

Denton grunted and rolled over.

Gabriel sprinted to the reception lounge. He caught up with Lily and grabbed her hand.

Lily's voice shook. "What's happening?"

Gabriel put his arm around her. "They weren't cops. Mike's disappearance put me off my game. I should have asked for their IDs earlier."

Lily's mouth fell open. "Mike's missing?"

He guided them to the main hall. "Smile and follow my lead.

They can't hurt us in public." They mingled with the guests as Gabriel guided them toward the main entrance.

Lily shivered and leaned closer to Gabriel. "Who were they?"

"I don't know. I think it has to do with Mike." Outside, Gabriel raised his hand and motioned for the valet. "We'll talk about it at the hotel."

A car appeared, and the valet rushed to open the door for them.

"Go to the hotel and stay with Mom and Dad."

Lily grabbed his arm. "Aren't you coming?"

"No, I want to find out who these men are."

Lily opened her mouth to say something.

Gabriel nudged her toward the car. "I'll catch up with you. Go to the hotel."

Lily climbed in and gave the driver directions.

Gabriel shut the car door and headed back into the building. He circled the theatre and the lounge. No one was there. He ran to the back doors of the theatre and checked the parking lot. The men were gone.

CHAPTER FOUR

Gabriel entered the code to his hotel suite.

Mom sat on the living room couch, her hands clasped. Lily rocked her infant son. Ethan had his arm around Lily's shoulders, and Harvey occupied an armchair, his mouth pressed into a thin line. Farther off, Jonathan Smith, Mike's director, stood by the fireplace with Dad. Jonathan was talking on his cell phone.

Mom spotted Gabriel and sprang forward. "Oh, thank God!"

"I'm all right, Mom."

Dad threw his arm around his shoulder.

Gabriel disengaged himself from Mom and Dad's embrace and went to Lily. "Are you all right?"

"I'm fine." Lily nuzzled the baby. "How did you know they weren't police officers?"

"Their timing was off. They told me they got my fingerprints from the military. It takes the military weeks to provide you with copies of records."

Jonathan Smith pocketed his cell phone and pursed his lips. "Seems like you've had quite the evening."

Gabriel caressed the baby's head. "It sure as heck wasn't what I expected."

"Were you able to find out who the men were?"

Gabriel straightened and gritted his teeth. "No, by the time I went after them, they were gone."

"I gave the descriptions of the fake cops to the local police. They're on a lookout," Johnathan said.

Gabriel took his coat and tie off and grabbed a bottle of water from the fridge. "Can CIU work with local law enforcement?"

Jonathan nodded. "We have jurisdiction across all agencies."

Harvey's forehead creased. "What's CIU?"

Jonathan glanced at Gabriel.

Harvey noticed the look and jumped up from his seat. "I'm glad you're all right, Gabe. This is a family matter. I'll be on my way."

Gabriel put a restraining hand on Harvey's shoulder. "Stay, Harv. You're family."

Harvey adjusted his glasses and sat back down.

Gabriel turned to Jonathan. "I trust Harvey."

Jonathan nodded. "CIU is short for Clandestine Investigations Unit. CIU is a branch of The Bureau of Counterterrorism. The agency has the power and authority to work with and across various government entities such as the FBI, the CIA, the NSA, and local law enforcement. Michael works for CIU."

Harvey straightened his glasses. "I see."

Mom threw her hands in the air. "Will someone please explain what's going on? Why were Gabriel and Lily in danger? And where is Michael?"

Gabriel went to Mom and put his arm around her shoulders. "I got a call before the fake cops showed up. Mike is missing."

Mom blinked several times. "Missing? What do you mean?"

Jonathan took a tentative step toward Mom. "For the past six months, Mike has been working closely with one of our agents. He requested time off last week. The next thing we know, he jumps off a helicopter in the Persian Gulf, and our other agent, Asra Madison, is found dead in a car by the Potomac." He homed in on Gabriel. "No, the car wasn't yours."

Jonathan paused, measuring his words. "The helicopter was high up. The odds of Mike surviving the jump aren't great."

Mom burst into tears.

Dad paced up and down the room. "I don't understand. What was Mike doing in the Persian Gulf?"

"My son isn't dead!" Mom sobbed.

Jonathan softened his tone. "We have search parties looking for him, Moira. We won't give up."

Gabriel scrubbed a hand over his face. "Is this woman's murder connected to Mike's disappearance?"

"I didn't think the incidents were related." Jonathan scratched his chin. "I have to consider the possibility after tonight's events."

"Why did those men go after Gabriel?" Lily asked, rocking the baby.

Gabriel sighed. "They wanted leverage."

"I'm sorry," Harvey interjected. "What does that mean?"

"The fake cops wanted Mike, not me. They planned to kidnap me to get to Mike. The real question is, why were they looking for Mike?"

Jonathan checked his watch. "I must go. I'll keep you updated on the search for Mike."

Gabriel accompanied Jonathan to the door. He shut the door in the hallway and lowered his voice. "Mister Smith, if Mike is alive and stuck in some country, I'll get him out."

"I know, son." Jonathan waited a beat. "There's one more thing. I didn't mention it because your parents have enough on their minds. They found a note in Asra Madison's pocket. It had your and Michael's names scribbled on it."

Gabriel clenched his fists. "Neither one of us had anything to do with that woman's death."

"I know that, but the police don't." Jonathan put a hand on his shoulder. "Two detectives, real ones, will land on your doorstep. CIU gave them an official report. That won't stop them from reaching out to you."

Gabriel nodded. "I appreciate the heads up." He bid Jonathan good night.

Back in the suite, Harvey grabbed bottles of water from the fridge and handed them out to everyone.

Gabriel shoved his hands into his pockets. "I'm sorry I dragged you into this, Harv."

Harvey waved his hand, dismissing the apology. "Like you said, we're family."

"Thanks." Gabriel turned to his family. "Get some rest. I'm driving back to Washington."

GABRIEL TURNED the car into his driveway a little after midnight. He didn't get out of the car. Where was Mike? What did the fake cops want with him? Why was Mike's colleague murdered? And why were his and Mike's names on the body of a murder victim? "So many questions and no answers."

He let his hands fall from the steering wheel and felt the blood rush back into his fingers. He went inside, and after a quick shower, fired up his laptop. Gabriel checked foreign news stations to see if the stations reported a body found in the Persian Gulf area. The news stations reported nothing. He rose and paced the room. He knew of one person who could help. He grabbed his cell phone and dialed an overseas number. The phone rang several times.

"Well, well, this is a surprise I wasn't expecting." The woman's voice was sensual and throaty. It invoked images of satin sheets and moonlit nights. *"To what do I owe this pleasure, handsome?"*

"Hi, Sheila. I need a favor."

Sheila's laugh was husky and melodic. *"Don't we all."*

"Can you find someone for me?"

Silence. *"Who are you looking for?"*

Gabriel ran a hand through his hair. "My brother, Michael. He was last seen jumping out of a helicopter close to the city of Bushehre, in the Persian Gulf."

More silence. *"I need time,"* Sheila said.

Gabriel thanked Sheila and hung up. It was after three in the morning. There wasn't much more he could do at this hour. He stretched out on the couch in his study and drifted to sleep.

CHAPTER FIVE

A loud peal penetrated the fog of Gabriel's mind. He grimaced, trying to block it. Another peal sounded and reverberated in his head. Ugh. The doorbell. He squinted at his watch. It was six thirty in the morning. The doorbell rang again. Gabriel stumbled to the window.

Two people stood on his doorstep—a man and a woman. The police had arrived.

He splashed water on his face and descended the stairs to open the door. A tall, barrel-chested man stepped forward and produced a badge. "Mister McKnight, I'm Detective Ryan Robin." He motioned to the slender Asian-American woman standing by him. "This is my partner, Detective Sue Hood. We'd like to talk to you."

Biting back a smile, Gabriel held the door open for Detectives Robin and Hood. "Come in. I'll make coffee."

The detectives followed Gabriel to the kitchen. He studied them while pouring ground coffee beans into the coffeemaker. Detective Robin's posture was straight, and his entire persona screamed efficient. His blond hair was cut in a no-nonsense buzz, his clothes were immaculate and pressed, and his shoes were polished. The man was former military, a marine no doubt.

Detective Hood wore a pair of washed out skinny jeans, a rumpled forest green sweater, and converse shoes. She'd pulled her dark glossy hair back into a haphazard ponytail, and her eyes were bloodshot, indicating she wasn't in the habit of early morning interviews.

Gabriel poured coffee into three cups and took them to the kitchen table.

Hood took the cup with a grateful smile.

Robin pulled out a notebook and in a voice that would have made a drill sergeant proud cried, "Detective Hood and I are investigating the murder of Asra Madison. We're working with CIU on this case."

Hood snorted and took a long sip of her coffee. "Our captain ordered us to play nice with CIU. We didn't have a choice."

Robin cleared his throat. "Assistant Director Smith gave us a summary of what transpired in New York last night. We—"

Hood cut him off. "What my partner is trying to say is we wouldn't dream of asking you to tell us what happened in New York since CIU gave us an official report. However, if you want to tell us, we won't stop you," she finished with a smile.

Robin's shoulders slumped.

Gabriel's mouth twitched. Robin the jarhead had his hands full with Hood the rebel. "I don't mind telling you what happened." He recounted the previous night's events from the moment he set foot on the red carpet.

Robin took meticulous notes. "Do you know why the fake detectives came after you?"

"No."

Robin glanced at his notepad. "When is the last time you saw your brother?"

"A little over a week ago."

Robin scribbled on his notepad. "Do you know where your brother is?"

"No, I don't."

Robin scribbled more. "Childhood impressions are strong. You and your brother spent several years in Iran. Do you have a fondness for the country?"

Gabriel's brows furrowed. "How is that relevant to last night's events?"

"Please answer the question."

"Iran is an exotic country with a rich culture, so yes, we are fond of the country."

Robin studied him the way scientists study lab rats. "Would it be correct to say you are loyal to Iran because of your fondness for the country?"

Gabriel clenched his jaw. "One can be fond of another country and still be loyal to one's own country and government."

Robin raised an eyebrow. "Did you know Asra Madison?"

"No."

"But your brother knew her, correct?"

Gabriel met Robin's gaze head-on. "Ask my brother."

"We found a note in Miss Madison's pocket. It had both your name and your brother's name along with your addresses on it. Can you tell me why Miss Madison would have your information?" Robin asked.

"No, Detective, I can't."

Robin's smile was that of a predator closing in on its prey. "You admit that you like Iran. Miss Madison is an Iranian-born government agent. Someone murders Miss Madison, and the police find your and your brother's names on a note in her pocket. That's a lot of coincidence."

"You forget, Detective." Gabriel put an emphasis on *Detective*. "Michael is a government agent. He also spent a little over a decade serving our country in the armed forces, as did I."

Robin was about to say something, but Hood threw him a warning glance and leaned forward. "What my partner means is your brother's disappearance may be connected to Miss Madison's death. We all want the same thing. Do you have any idea where your brother could be?"

Gabriel almost rolled his eyes at the good cop bad cop routine. "I'm sorry, I don't."

Hood pulled a card out and placed it on the table. "If you hear from him, will you please contact us?"

Gabriel picked up the card. "Certainly."

The detectives rose to leave. Gabriel walked them to the door.

Robin turned around and bared a row of white teeth. "We advise you to not leave the city while we are investigating Miss Madison's death."

Gabriel raised an eyebrow. "Really, and why is that?"

Hood intervened again. "It's standard procedure in case we have more questions."

Gabriel smirked. "That won't be a problem. My agent always knows where I am."

A deep flush covered Robin's face, and the veins in his neck stood out. "What does that mean?"

"I explained what it means. Have a good day." Gabriel shut the door on a surprised Robin. He leaned against the door. "Christ, what a mess."

His cell phone rang. Gabriel ran up to his study to answer it.

"Gabe, it's Harvey. How are you?"

Gabriel snorted. "You mean aside from my brother missing and me being a murder suspect?"

"What?" Harvey's voice rose to a high octave. "I thought that was a bunch of bogus?"

"No, the police think one of us murdered the woman, and the other one is an accomplice. I'm not sure which one of us is guilty of which crime though."

"Jesus! What will you do?"

A silver frame sat on Gabriel's desk. He picked it up. It was a picture of him and Mike taken when they were six. Both wore identical grins.

"Gabe, are you there?"

Gabriel put the photograph back down. "I'm here."

"What will you do?"

He straightened his shoulders. "I'm going to find Mike."

CHAPTER SIX

WASHINGTON, D.C.

G abriel exited CIU and turned west. His posture was
stiff, and the vein in his temple throbbed. "Unbelievable," he growled, quickening his pace.

He turned into Twenty-third Street and walked toward the
Lincoln Memorial. Anger swirled in his stomach like a ball of fire.
He swallowed another oath and crossed the street leading to the
memorial park.

He expected more from Jonathan and Mina Delany. Heck,
Mina had recruited Michael. *She believes Michael is dead.* Gabriel
raked a hand through his hair. Michael wasn't dead. He knew it.
He felt it deep in his chest. How could he explain that to CIU?

Gabriel's thoughts were so occupied that he didn't notice the
SUV barreling down the street until it screeched to a halt
beside him.

Two men exited the car. Both had wide shoulders that looked
out of place in their dark suits. Both sported the vacant expressions seen on statues. It didn't take a genius to figure out they
were government agents.

The first one approached Gabriel. "Mister McKnight, please come with us."

Gabriel raised an eyebrow. "And if I don't?"

The man's jaw clenched. "I'd rather not use force, sir."

A part of him welcomed the challenge, knowing he could grapple and overcome the man. His muscles tensed ready for the fight, while the rational part of his brain kicked into gear. He couldn't think of anyone who wanted to speak with him. He'd stormed out of the meeting with CIU, and if Mina or Jonathan wanted to speak with him, they could call his cell phone. Curiosity propelled him to give in. "Fine."

The man's shoulders relaxed. He held the car door open for Gabriel and got in after him. The agent nodded at the driver, and the SUV pulled away from the curve.

There was no point in guessing where he was going. He'd find out soon enough. Gabriel leaned back in his seat and stared out the window.

The car wound through the highways toward the forest surrounding the Potomac River. The Washington sky was a deep shade of grey, indicating upcoming rain. The trees loomed above them, blocking the outside world. The wind howled, and dark clouds rolled in. Lightning streaked across the skies.

As the trees took on hues of silver and grey, a childhood memory surfaced. Gabriel was playing hide and seek with Michael on a day like this one. It was his turn to find Michael, and he'd searched everywhere, unable to find his brother. Thunder roared, and the first drops of rain fell, sending a young Gabriel into a panic. Desperate and fearful he'd lost Michael, Gabriel called out to his mother.

Michael sprang from a bush and hugged him. "You can't lose me, Gabe. I'll always tell you where I am, even when I'm hiding."

Where the hell are you, Mike?

The SUV stopped by a clearing, jolting Gabriel back to the present. The rain had started, splashing pellets of water on the window. A house sat in a clearing surrounded by trees. Smoke arose from its chimney. Firewood lay in neat stacks on the porch by the entrance, and a wooden shed sat to the right of the structure.

"Go ahead, sir." The agent tilted his head in the direction of the house.

Gabriel climbed out of the car. The mingled scents of wet grass and firewood drifted in the air. Icy rain poured over his face. He pulled his collar up and strode toward a stone path leading to the house. He entered without knocking.

A short hallway led to a rectangular space where a brilliant fire crackled, spreading warmth throughout the room. The scents of pinewood and tobacco lingered in the air. A snoring hound raised its head and studied Gabriel.

"It's all right, boy." A lanky man with silver hair patted the dog's head from an armchair, then rose. He was dressed casually in a pair of jeans and a thick burgundy sweater. The wire-rimmed glasses perched on his nose didn't conceal the shrewd amber eyes summing him up.

Gabriel blinked. He knew this man. He'd met him at a fundraiser several years ago. Arthur McMillan was the former director of CIU and a legend in the intelligence community. He had also been an advisor to the secretary of state. McMillan was retired, or so Gabriel thought.

McMillan's mouth turned up. "Thank you for accepting my invitation."

Gabriel didn't recall having a choice in the matter. He didn't move.

McMillan's eyes twinkled as if reading his thoughts. He motioned to the other armchair. "Please have a seat."

Sighing inwardly, Gabriel strode to the other armchair.

The dog watched him under heavy-lidded eyes. Sensing no threat from Gabriel, it dropped its head and went to sleep.

"Would you like a drink?" McMillan offered.

"No, thank you."

McMillan settled back into his chair. "You are wondering why you are here."

"The question comes to mind."

McMillan sipped his drink. "I'm sorry Michael is missing. He was a good agent."

Gabriel ground his teeth and said nothing.

McMillan's golden eyes bore into Gabriel. "Do you believe Michael's dead?"

"No." Gabriel didn't trust himself to say more.

McMillan furrowed his brow in consternation. "I hope to God you are right. Not only for obvious family reasons, but for our nation's security." He reached out and added a log to the fire. The flames rose and cackled, throwing shadows on the opposite wall. "I occasionally consult for our government." The furrows in his brow deepened. "CIU categorizes threats into four levels. A level one threat is handled by local law enforcement. When a level two threat occurs, national agencies step in to assist, and it escalates from there." McMillan paused. "A level four threat has global impact. CIU assigns a select group of agents to neutralize level four threats. Michael was one of them." He swiveled his head to face Gabriel. "The information I'm going to share with you is known by less than a handful of people. It must stay that way."

Gabriel nodded.

Satisfied, McMillan continued. "Your brother called me the night of your movie premiere. He claimed he had identified a level four threat."

Interesting! Mike had called McMillan, not Jonathan or Mina. Gabriel kept his face impassive and waited for McMillan to continue.

"We planned to meet after your movie premiere." McMillan waved a hand. "You know the rest."

Gabriel pursed his lips. "Was Asra Madison involved in this?"

McMillan sighed. "The timing of her death suggests it."

"Why am I here?" Gabriel asked.

A gleam entered McMillan's eyes. "Michael reached out to me. Not his colleagues, and not our partnering agencies." He steepled his fingers. "You know Michael best. You know how he thinks and operates. If he's alive, you can find him and bring him home. If he's dead, I want you to find the threat Michael identified and eliminate it."

Gabriel tilted his head and studied McMillan. "You have an army of capable agents. Why ask me?"

McMillan leaned forward. "If Michael was here, and I asked him whom he trusted most, he would say you. That's why I'm asking you."

The anger Gabriel labored to keep at bay rose in his chest. CIU had stopped the search on Michael, yet this man had the gall to ask him for help.

Reading his thoughts again, McMillan raised a hand. "CIU protocol requires they stop the search after several weeks. If they go out of protocol, it will attract attention. It's best not to raise suspicion."

"Best for whom?" Gabriel growled.

"Best for all parties involved, and that includes Michael," McMillan said. "If Michael's alive, his chances of survival are better with others thinking him dead."

Damn McMillan for his politics and manipulation. He knew damn well Gabriel would do anything to find Michael. Gabriel ran a hand through his hair. "I'll do it."

McMillan nodded. "You'll be on your own. The police will hound you, and Michael's enemies will come after you. Can you handle it?"

Gabriel shrugged. "Do I have a choice?"

CHAPTER SEVEN

GEORGETOWN, WASHINGTON, D.C.

G abriel unlocked the door to his house, and the tension in his body eased. No matter the circumstances, coming home gave him a welcoming rush.

He'd always wanted a house in Georgetown and couldn't afford one on his military income. He'd lived from paycheck to paycheck back then. He bought the house after his third book was published. Mike had taken time off work to help him with the renovations. They'd kept the house's historical exterior and turned the interior into an elegant modern home.

The memory brought a pang to his heart. Where should he look for Mike? What had led Mike to the Persian Gulf? Why the Persian Gulf? Gabriel threw his keys into the crystal bowl by the console and jogged up the stairs to his study.

How to proceed? He needed a plan. Gabriel rubbed his chin. He'd planned and plotted thrillers. He was methodical and thorough at research. He'd studied the psychology of murder, and a killer's need to hunt. As a SEAL, he'd seen the dark side of human nature. Finally, he wasn't active, but he'd kept in shape. He would use everything in his arsenal to locate Michael.

The enemy hunted Michael, which meant they knew him and would come after him. The hunt had started with Asra Madison's death. Someone had framed them? Why? Was it because of the threat Michael had identified?

"Or is there another reason?"

The way to find out would be to retrace Michael's footsteps before he disappeared. Gabriel made a list of places and people to search. First on his list was Michael's apartment. Next, he made a list of his own vulnerabilities. He wrote his routines, the people he interacted with, and the places he frequented. He'd change his schedule.

How to turn the tables on their foe while he searched for Mike?

A floorboard creaked.

Gabriel froze. He tilted his head, ears straining. Yes, someone was in his house. He reached for the letter opener on his desk and turned off the lights.

Footsteps sounded on the stairs.

Gabriel hid behind the study door.

Thud, thud. Two men entered the upper floor.

The first, a man with a beaky nose, darted to his bedroom. The second intruder, a beefy man with gorilla arms, crept into his study. Gorilla carried a gun.

Gabriel waited for him to enter, then knocked the gun out of the gorilla's hand.

Gorilla arms grunted and bumped into the desk.

Gabriel landed a punch in gorilla's jaw.

His head snapped back, and he went down.

The sound of their scuffle brought beak nose to the study. Beak nose carried a bat. He charged Gabriel with it.

Gabriel ducked the blow and moved behind the desk.

Beak nose followed him.

A hand grabbed Gabriel's ankle causing him to stumble. Gorilla had gained consciousness.

Gabriel kicked him.

The bat smacked Gabriel between his shoulders.

"Omph!" He ground his teeth, then landed a roundhouse kick in Beaky's knee.

Beaky stumbled and dropped the bat.

Gabriel drove the letter opener into Beaky's thigh.

"Aargh!"

Reaching for the gun, Gabriel shifted and turned the lights on.

Gorilla was out cold. Beaky sat on the floor holding his thigh.

He grabbed the baseball bat.

Beaky cringed and held his hands up. "Don't!"

Gabriel's shoulder felt like it was on fire. "Who are you? And why are you here?"

Beak nose gulped. "I'm supposed to get the whereabouts of the goods from you."

Gabriel raised the bat. "What goods?"

"I don't know," Beaky cried. "I must take the goods from Michael McKnight."

Gabriel grabbed the man's collar. "Who hired you? What goods?"

Beaky wiped the blood from his nose. "I don't know. The job came through the mail."

The doorbell rang. Beak nose swiveled his head.

Someone pounded on his door. "Mister McKnight, this is the police. Please open the door."

Gabriel glanced out the window.

Four police cars sat along his driveway. Detectives Robin and Hood stood on his doorstep.

"You'll have to explain to the police why you are here."

Gabriel exited the study and locked the two men in. He grabbed a backpack he'd prepared and crept down the stairs into his back-yard. He took the back alley to Montrose Park and ran to the cab station.

CHAPTER EIGHT

Gabriel unlocked the door to Mike's apartment. Mike lived on the fourth floor of a luxurious condo. The place was high enough to keep intruders out, and low enough to escape if need be.

The apartment offered a generous view of the Potomac River. An open spaced rectangle housed the living room, dining room, and kitchen. A stone fireplace sat in the center, and a corridor connected to the bedrooms.

Gabriel went from room to room and checked everything. He searched behind mirrors, in the bathrooms, and in every bedroom. He searched through Mike's files and clothes. He checked the walls and searched the floors for hidden areas. Nothing!

What next? Gabriel paced the living room. His gaze fell on the open bar in the living room.

A bottle of scotch stood at the open bar. Mike didn't drink scotch.

He picked up the bottle. *Expensive.* "Who were you trying to impress?" He put down the bottle and raked a hand through his hair. "What am I missing?" By two a.m. he'd searched the condo three times. Exhausted and sore, he lay down on Mike's couch, and fell asleep.

A BLARING ringtone jolted Gabriel awake. He reached for his phone, blinking against the sunlight filtering through the windows.

"McKnight."

"*Good morning, sweet thing.*" Sheila's voice was as bright as the sunlight blinding him.

He groaned. "Don't you sleep?"

Sheila tsked. "*Sleep is for the dead. Besides, I have information for you.*"

Gabriel sat up and held his breath.

"*None of my people found a body by the shorelines.*" Sheila paused. "*Don't get your hopes up. It's not unusual considering the circumstances.*"

Gabriel exhaled. "Thank you, Sheila."

"*No need for thanks. You saved my life, literally, and I've never thanked you for it.*"

"I have to go." He hung up and leaned back on the couch. "They didn't find a body!" He rose and headed to the bathroom.

Sunlight bounced off the bottle of scotch sitting on the open bar. It exposed a scratch by the plaque on the bottle. The scratch was etched into the bottle and ran under the plaque.

He took the bottle to the kitchen and used a knife to yank the plaque off. Someone, Mike most likely, had etched a series of figures into the glass under the plaque. Gabriel tilted the bottle.

Liquid filled in the scratches. Six numbers appeared on the bottle. 030497.

He put the bottle down and searched the open bar. His heart pounded, and his pulse raced. He ran his hands along the bar's surface, searching for hidden levers. He searched under the bar and found a dent in the board. Gabriel pushed at the dent, and the board slid aside, revealing a hollow space with a safe.

He punched the numbers in with clammy hands. The safe popped opened, then he withdrew a large manila envelope. Inside, he found a file with a note. Mike's slanted handwriting stood out.

Gabe,

I stumbled onto something important, and I'm in trouble. It's no use asking you to stay away. I know you'll come for me. The information in the envelope will help you. Be careful. You're being watched!

Mike

Gabriel opened the file and pulled out two maps. The first was a map of Tehran, Iran dated 1979, and a newer version printed in 2019. Next, he pulled out three newspaper clippings, a torn photograph, and a note with a name and address scrawled on it.

Gabriel studied the newspaper clippings. The first one was an article about Tehran's Central Bank, the second one was the obituary of a General Parviz Rahman, dated 1978, and the third one was the obituary of Mrs. Shiraz Rahman, dated 1997. He scratched his chin as memories from his childhood in Iran rushed back.

Mike had scrawled the name Noor Rahman and an address on the note. He would find out who Noor Rahman is. He picked up the photograph. Someone had torn it from the middle and noted "Tehran, July 1978" at the bottom. The photo showed a group of people at a dinner table. Smiling faces looked into the camera. His parents were in the photo.

He raked a hand through his hair. "What the hell is going on?"

Gabriel pulled out his cell phone and dialed a number.

A baritone voice answered. *"Yo Fa, please tell me you're using the chip I gave you."*

Gabriel snorted. "I wouldn't call your private line without it."

Billy Mason, Gabriel's former navy SEAL teammate and friend grunted. *"What's up?"*

Gabriel hated to involve his friend yet he had no other choice. "Can you meet me at Mike's place?"

Thirty minutes later, a low tap sounded on the door. Gabriel checked the peephole and opened the door for his friend.

Billy Mason, aka Dotts, carried six feet three inches of pure muscle. He wore faded jeans and a black sweater that couldn't hide his sinewy frame. A ball cap covered his shaggy blond hair.

Billy's hawklike gaze scanned the apartment. Satisfied there were no threats, he turned his attention to Gabriel. "You look like hell."

Gabriel's smile didn't reach his eyes. "Gee, thanks."

"I call it as it is. What is it they say about the truth?" Billy tapped a forefinger on his lips. "Something about liberation." He huffed. "Crock of bull, if you ask me. Truth is the truth, end of story." He crossed his arms over his chest. "What's wrong?"

Gabriel shoved his hands in his pockets. "The short version is Mike's former colleague was murdered. Someone's making it look like Mike and I killed her. Mike is missing, and the police are on my doorstep."

"Shit!" Billy grimaced, making the freckles that had earned him his nickname in the SEAL teams more pronounced.

"Yeah."

"When did Mike go missing?" Billy asked.

"Around the time his colleague was murdered."

Billy raised an eyebrow.

Gabriel gritted his teeth. "He didn't kill her."

Billy scratched his chin. "I'm not saying he did it. I'm saying it doesn't look good he's missing. Do you have any leads?"

Gabriel motioned to the newspaper clippings and photo on the dining room table. "Mike left me a note. He stumbled onto something that goes back to when my father was stationed in Iran. The Rahman family were my parents' friends. That picture was taken at the Rahmans' home. We used to go there when we were kids."

Billy picked up the newspaper clippings. "You're the linguist. What do the articles say?"

"Not much. There are two obituaries and an article about a Tehran's central bank."

Billy grunted. "How can I help?"

"Get my parents and Lily to your restaurant. I'm calling a family meeting. I also need two burner phones."

CHAPTER NINE

"You're certain someone's watching us?" Dad asked.

Gabriel nodded. His family had gathered in the private dining room of Little Italy, the restaurant Billy and his wife, Leah, owned.

Mom's aquamarine eyes clouded with concern. "I don't understand. First, Mike disappears, then the police show up on our doorstep looking for you."

"I found something," Gabriel said. He told his family about the envelope in Mike's apartment. "It's why we couldn't find anything on Mike. He's gone dark, and I think he's done it to protect us."

"How is this related to the murder of that poor woman?" Lily asked.

The furrows in Gabriel's brows deepened. "I think the people searching for Mike framed us for the murder."

Mom paled. "But why?"

Gabriel pursed his lips. He had to be careful what he shared with his parents. "Mike found something that threatens them."

"How can we help?" Dad asked.

Gabriel leaned forward. "I was a child when we were in Iran. Tell me about the Rahman family."

The lines around Dad's eyes tightened. "Our time in Iran was one of the happiest and saddest experiences in my career. The Pahlavi's reign was controversial and tumultuous."

Mom nodded, patting his arm.

"It wasn't a long dynasty," Gabriel said. "It lasted two generations."

Dad nodded. "That's correct. General Reza Pahlavi founded the dynasty in 1925. He overthrew the former monarchy and took over the throne. The fifty-four years of the Pahlavi reign impacted Iran significantly. The country expanded its infrastructure and developed significant industrialization and economic moderniza-tion." Dad paused and accepted the cup of coffee Mom handed him. "Reza Shah's son, Mohammad Reza Pahlavi, took over the throne in 1941 when Britain and the Soviet Union forced his father into exile. The new Shah ruled Iran differently, yet he shared many of his father's ambitions for the country.

"Mohammad Reza Shah continued the modernization efforts his father had started. He aligned himself with the west and advocated reform policies, which included land reform, the extension of voting rights to women, and eliminating illiteracy." Dad sipped his coffee. "The Shah vowed to be a constitutional monarch who would yield to the power of the parliamentary government, yet he involved himself in governmental affairs and opposed or thwarted strong prime ministers and politicians. He also maintained full control over the military force.

"The United States became Iran's closest ally, and Iran's Impe-rial Air Force was unrivaled by all but a handful of the world's most powerful air forces. Jonathan Smith and I were assigned to Iran to strengthen the Iran-USA relations." Dad paused, staring into his mug. "General Parviz Rahman was one of the highest-ranking generals commanding the Imperial Iranian Air Force in the 1970s. He was a trusted advisor to the Shah, a strong leader, and an honorable man. I considered him a friend." Dad stopped as if measuring his words. "Many criticized the Shah for subservience to the U.S. Others saw the Shah's leadership style as autocratic and lavish, and the changes he instituted provoked religious leaders who feared they would lose their traditional authority.

"The Shah's goal was to develop Iran into a powerful country in the region. Those loyal to the Shah believed in him, but they couldn't stand against the widespread discontent and riots." Dad heaved a sigh. "It was a difficult climate. The people blamed the Shah and wanted him gone, and President Carter's government withdrew their support of the Shah."

Gabriel leaned forward. "What about General Rahman? What was his stance?"

"Parviz did his best to keep the riots under control," Dad said. "Knowing Parviz, he had a strategy to stop the riots, but his hands were tied. The Shah didn't want to fight the people. He wouldn't allow it." Sadness creeped into Dad's voice. "I offered help, but Parviz"—Dad cleared his throat—"Parviz wouldn't abandon his country. He died trying to control a riot."

"General Rahman was a good man." Mom's gaze grew distant. "His wife, Shiraz, was my friend. She was intelligent, kind, and beautiful. Most people believed Shiraz married the general for his money. It wasn't true. She loved him."

A ghost of a smile appeared on Gabriel's lips. "I remember her. She was a language teacher at the school Mike and I attended."

Mom's nodded. "Shiraz was pregnant when the general died. She moved to Paris after his death and gave birth to a little girl."

"I researched the daughter," Gabriel said. "Noor Rahman is the only child of Parviz and Shiraz Rahman. Noor was born and raised in Paris. She was eighteen when a thief killed Shiraz Rahman in her bookstore. After her mother's death, Noor moved to the USA with her grandmother and aunt. She lives in Oklahoma City. She was an investigative reporter for a decade. She started her own business several years ago and is a well-known author coach and editor. She has a team of editors working for her. She's single, and the sole heir to the Rahman fortune."

Dad rubbed his chin. "Michael's note points to Parviz's daughter. How does she fit into whatever this is?"

Gabriel had asked himself the same question. "I don't know, but I intend to find out."

Dad scowled. "I won't sit back and do nothing. I want to—"

"I have a plan," Gabriel interjected. "The best way you can help is to keep doing what you've been doing. Keep looking for Michael. If the police ask you about me, tell them you haven't heard from me." He rubbed at a sore spot behind his neck. "I won't be in touch for a while."

"I'll come with you," Ethan said.

"No." Gabriel clapped Ethan on the back. "Lily and the baby need you."

Billy stepped into the private dining room, his eyes hard. "A cop car just parked outside of the restaurant."

Lily grabbed Gabriel's arm. "Don't go. We'll prove you didn't kill Asra Madison."

Gabriel's mouth curved into a humorless smile. "We're running out of time. I must go."

Mom took hold of his arm. "Where are you going?"

"I'm going to Oklahoma City. I need to find Noor Rahman."

"What about the police?" Lily asked.

"Harvey will talk to them and buy me time."

"The office has an apartment in Oklahoma City," Ethan said. "We use it when we travel to meet clients. You can stay there." Ethan was an international attorney. He had clients all over the U.S. and outside of the country.

"Thanks."

Mom leaned up and kissed his cheek. "Be careful, sweetheart."

CHAPTER TEN

"In confidence I asked a wiseman
to not withhold the mysteries of the universe.
Gently he whispered in my ear, be still
it should be learned, not revealed."
—*Rumi*

OKLAHOMA CITY, OKLAHOMA

Noor Rahman jogged past two runners and followed the trail circling the Oklahoma River, a seven-mile stretch of the North Canadian River. The river transformed into to a series of river lakes bordered by landscaped areas with running trails, recreational facilities, and a row of iconic boathouses with water activities. The pounding of her feet on the concrete was both rhythmic and soothing.

She took the trail to a wooded area. Up ahead, lavender plants bloomed in the sun. Their sweet floral scent evoked memories of Parisian summers and a terrace brimming with lavender plants. Mom's laughter echoed in Noor's mind.

Mom! Noor blinked back the tears. Mom was her hero, her

support, and her world. On the heels of her grief came anger. The anger was as familiar to her as her own skin. She'd learned to keep the anger at bay, but it was there like the ashes of a fire, quiet and simmering. She could handle the anger. In fact, she'd become an expert at containing it. It was the grief she couldn't handle. The overwhelming sucker punch of pain, leaving her weak and hollow.

Noor ran faster, pushing her muscles. The pain in her chest loosened. She turned into the trail close to the river and completed her last round. She went from run to jog, and from jog to walk. By the time she reached the Chesapeake Finish Line Tower, her breathing had returned to normal.

The Chesapeake Finish Line Tower was a dramatic four-story glass structure overlooking the Oklahoma River. It stood as a symbol for the iconic boathouse district and pulled the park, boathouses, and the spirit of water sports together.

Rainbow colors bounced off the Chesapeake tower's glass walls, while sunlight turned the river into shimmering shades of blue and turquoise. Two teams of rowers raced toward the finish line, their paddles creating circular patterns on the river. Farther off, a woman kayaked. The movement of her upper body and arms were a graceful dance to the river's music. Behind her, tall buildings stretched into the sky, greeting the sun.

A strangled sob worked its way up Noor's throat. *Damn it!* She rubbed her face with her hands and headed toward her car.

I might as well get something for breakfast. They'll all be there. She drove to Elemental Coffee and ordered six lattes and a box of croissants. When she arrived home, she put the coffee and croissants on the kitchen table and ran upstairs to take a shower.

"I will not cry. Crying changes nothing. I am strong." Noor sank to the shower floor and repeated the phrases over and over, pushing the fiery ball of pain to the deep recesses of her soul.

After her shower, she pulled on a fluffy bathrobe and sat on her bed, staring out the window. The photo frame by her bed glinted under the sunlight. It was a picture of her and Mom on her eighteenth birthday. Noor brushed her fingers over the picture.

People claimed time was healer of all wounds. They told her the pain of loss would gradually decrease, and she'd learn to accept Mom's death. They were wrong. Time hadn't offered magical relief. The pain was sharp as ever, and her anger was just as fierce. "She didn't deserve to die like that!" Noor banged her fist on her thigh.

She picked up the volume of Rumi's poems and held it close to her chest. The book belonged to Mom. Reading Rumi's work gave her comfort. It made her feel closer to Mom. She turned to a bookmarked page.

"My will lies discarded at the door.
In favor of my lover's forevermore."

"I'm trying to accept," she whispered, clenching her fists. "It's hard to accept when I don't know why she died." A tear streaked down her cheek. She brushed it away, knowing she must dress and face her family.

She did several deep breathing exercises to settle herself and rose to dress for the day. She brushed her long hair and applied makeup to her face and eyes. She went into her closet and chose a simple black dress with matching pumps. She fastened Mom's favorite pearls and glanced at her reflection in the mirror. Satisfied with her appearance, Noor descended the stairs to greet her family.

"We are not dating. Boris is a friend," Noor's grandmother, whom she called Grand-mere, explained.

"I want to be you when I grow up, Missus Navid." Brodie's reverent tone filled the kitchen.

"Hah!" Aunt Roshi's throaty laugh sounded welcoming. "Good for you, Mom. I wish your granddaughter would take a page from your book."

"Her granddaughter and your niece are right here," Noor announced, entering the kitchen.

"Oh, sweetie, you look lovely!" Grand-mere exclaimed, hugging her. Her eyes didn't have their usual gleam, and her mouth was slightly pinched.

Noor kissed her grandmother's cheek and grabbed a latte. "I'm fine, Grand-mere. Please don't worry." She blew air kisses to Uncle Morrie and Brodie. Counting to three, she pasted a smile on her face. "So, you and Boris are not dating?"

"We are not dating," Grand-mere said. "Boris is my friend. End of story."

Brodie's eyes twinkled. "A friend who brings her flowers and calls her sweetheart. By the way, where did you meet this friend?"

Grand-mere sniffed. "At my book club."

Brodie Sinclair was the first friend Noor made in Oklahoma. He'd studied performing arts at the same college she attended. Brodie did a few stints at Broadway and realized he preferred to read dramas rather than act in them. When Noor started her business, she offered Brodie a job as an editor. Brodie's keen intelligence, wit, and movie star good looks made him popular with clients and business associates.

"There's nothing wrong with being careful," Uncle Morrie, her father's friend, grumbled as he sipped his latte.

Noor raised both of her hands. "I appreciate the love and concern; however, my private life is not up for discussion."

Aunt Roshi pulled Noor into a hug. "Ignore our banter, love. How are you feeling?"

Noor leaned into the hug. "I'm fine."

Uncle Morrie snorted.

Grand-mere approached her and cupped her cheeks. "Baby girl, we're all hurting today. We are here for you."

Tears prickled Noor's eyes. "You lost your daughter, and Aunt Roshi lost her sister. I'm here for you." Noor hugged her grandmother and aunt then addressed the group. "Enjoy breakfast.

Brodie and I have a conference to attend. I'll see you tonight for dinner." She linked her arm through Brodie's. "We have a private family memorial for my mom each year. You are family. Are you coming?"

Brodie shook his head. "I wish I could, but I have dinner with a client."

"No worries. I'll bring you some leftovers tomorrow. Whoever leaves last please, lock the door," Noor called out as she and Brodie rushed out the door.

GABRIEL TURNED INTO SHERIDAN AVENUE. The Oklahoma City Writers' Conference was at the Cox Convention Center. The convention center was on the east of the Myriad Gardens, a seventeen-acre botanical garden and park.

Gabriel had never visited Oklahoma City. The city was clean, with open spaces and a charming downtown area. It wasn't Georgetown, yet it was appealing.

Like most convention centers, the Cox Convention Center had signs pointing to different conference halls in its lobby. Gabriel took the stairs to the second floor and found the writers' conference hall.

Booths representing literary agencies and publishing houses lined the hallway all the way to the entrance of the conference room. Aspiring writers, current writers, agents, publicists, and editors occupied the conference tables. A large stage sat at one end of the room. The media was also present, taking photos and interviewing the writers. Gabriel pulled his ball cap lower and weaved through the crowd.

Noor was the first speaker at the conference. If he moved fast, he'd catch her before her talk. Gabriel crossed the conference hall, avoiding the press, and found a small hallway on the side of the stage. The hallway led to a pair of double doors.

"Can I help you?" A pimple-faced kid blocked his way.

Gabriel was about to answer when the kid's eyes widened. "You're Gabriel McKnight! I didn't know you were on the guest list, sir." The kid fidgeted, jingling the set of keys in his hand. "I've read the entire Jason Van series. He's a badass." The kid's ears turned red.

Gabriel's lips twitched. "Thank you."

"Are you a speaker, sir?"

Gabriel smiled. "Not today. I came to see Miss Rahman."

The kid bobbed his head. "Yes, of course." He unlocked the doors and motioned for Gabriel to enter. "Miss Rahman is backstage with the host."

Gabriel handed the kid a tip and headed backstage. A woman was talking to the host. She had her back to him. He took his time checking her out. She was of medium height. Her dark hair was thick and glossy. It fell to her waist like a silk curtain. She wore a simple black dress that did nothing to hide her long shapely legs. *Nice!*

The host shook hands with the woman and proceeded to the stage. The woman turned around, and he did a double take. *Wow!* She had an oval face, creamy skin, luscious full lips, and a pair of dazzling green eyes that were emphasized by the bangs covering her forehead. Her body was all delightful curves, the kind that made a man want to run his hands all over it.

He was about to introduce himself when her eyes lit up. "Mister McKnight, what a wonderful surprise! You said you couldn't make it."

Huh?!

CHAPTER ELEVEN

G abriel froze as Noor Rahman approached him. It took a few seconds for him to realize Mike had met this woman pretending to be him.

He forced himself to speak. "Hi. It's good to be back."

Noor's mouth turned up. "This city has that effect on people. I think it's the red dirt. Are you the surprise guest speaker?"

Having lost his ability to form a coherent sentence, Gabriel shook his head.

Noor beamed. "How long are you staying in Oklahoma City?" Her eyes were a vibrant green like emeralds or spring leaves after rain.

Gabriel cleared his throat. "I'll be in town for two days. I was hoping we could talk."

Her smile widened. "We should have lunch. I'd like to introduce you to the rest of my staff."

A blond, muscular man walked up to Noor. He hugged her and wished her good luck. Gabriel wanted to push the Thor lookalike away.

"Brodie, wait." Noor turned to Gabriel. "This is my best friend and associate Brodie Sinclair. Brodie, meet Gabriel McKnight, author extraordinaire."

Gabriel grudgingly shook hands with the man.

Brodie beamed. "Mister McKnight, you must tire from hearing this, but I'm a great fan."

"Thank you." He worked hard to keep his tone even.

Noor placed her hand on Brodie's arm. "Mister McKnight and I talked a while ago. He wants us to be editors for his new series. It's about a former Navy SEAL who spent the first decade of his life in Iran. It's based on his own life." Noor must have seen the shock on his face because she hurriedly said, "Brodie is a trusted colleague. He won't tell anyone until your current editor retires."

What the hell, Mike! Gabriel clenched his jaw. "Of course, I trust your judgment." He made a mental note to call Harvey for damage control. "Miss Rahman, do you have time to talk today?"

"Sure, my team is vetting potential clients. Would you like to talk here or somewhere else?"

Gabriel ran a hand through his hair. "I don't know the city. Are there any coffee shops nearby?"

"Yes, we can take my car." Noor turned her face up to meet his eyes. Her bottom lip was full and inviting. She bit her lip, waiting for his answer.

Gabriel looked away from her mouth. "That sounds good."

Noor checked her watch. "Okay, I'm up. We'll leave after my talk."

Once her talk was over, Noor guided Gabriel to her car. She kept a steady flow of conversation on the drive to the coffee shop. Gabriel was silent most of the drive.

She parked the car. "We're here." She pointed to a sign that read "Elemental Coffee."

The coffee shop itself was a small batch roastery and café. The place was simple and understated. They placed their order and sat at a table in the corner of the café. The barista had their coffee ready in no time.

Gabriel took a sip of his espresso and closed his eyes, allowing the unique taste of the Brazilian coffee to settle on his tongue.

Noor watched him with a knowing smile. "You know they have an interesting philosophy here. Their goal is to deliver coffee as it's intended to taste. They never try to enhance or alter the coffee's natural existence. The coffee may taste a certain way one day, and it may be different on another. Either way, it always tastes good."

Gabriel raised an eyebrow. "I would have pegged you for tea aficionado."

"I was raised to appreciate both," she said. "My Iranian heritage appreciates tea, and the years spent in Paris taught me to appreciate coffee."

"Makes sense. I was raised to appreciate both, too."

Noor's eyes traveled over him and lingered on his face. Women liked his physical appearance. He had Dad's dark hair and athletic build, along with Mom's blue eyes. Interestingly though, his own heartbeat picked up. In another place and another time, things would've ended differently.

Noor's brows furrowed. She searched his face perplexedly as if searching for something.

"Do I pass?"

Two spots of color appeared on her cheeks. "I'm sorry, I didn't mean to stare. It's just that you seem different."

"Really, how so?"

"You seem more," she bit her lip, searching for the right word. "Settled."

"Settled?" Gabriel raised an eyebrow.

"Y-yes," Noor stammered as a flush of pink spread over her cheeks. "Last time you seemed restless, and this time you seem settled. That's the best way I can describe it."

Impressive. There weren't many people who caught the subtle

differences between him and Michael. He studied her intently, wondering where to start.

Noor opened her mouth to say something.

He interrupted her. "Miss Rahman."

"Call me Noor."

"Very well, Noor, I want to discuss something important with you."

She cut him off. "If you're worried about our services, I assure you we are very good. We specialize in working with authors who write multi-culture series. I offered to provide you with references last time. You declined. Let me give you the references."

Gabriel raised his hand. "I don't doubt your team's skills. That's not what I'm here for."

"Oh?" Noor's eyes widened a fraction. "Why are you here?"

Gabriel massaged the back of his neck. *Where to begin?* "What I'm about to tell you is confidential." He launched into the reason for his visit.

Noor said nothing for several seconds. She gaped at him, her mouth hanging open.

Gabriel scrolled through the pictures on his cell phone. He found a photo of him and Mike at Christmas and showed it to her. "This is a picture of me and my brother this past Christmas. There are a few more with my family. Scroll through them."

She scrolled through the pictures, studying them for a long time. She finally raised her eyes to his. "Mister McKnight,"

"Call me Gabriel."

"Very well, Gabriel, I am sorry for what you and your family are going through." She lifted her shoulders. "I don't understand what it has to do with me."

"I don't either. All I know is my brother was researching your family when he disappeared." Gabriel raked a hand through his hair. "Mike came to Oklahoma City to see you because you're somehow involved in this. Knowing Mike, he pretended to be me to keep you safe. Can you tell me when you met him and what you talked about?"

Noor stared into her coffee cup. "He called my office back in February. You can imagine how surprised I was to receive a phone call from Gabriel McKnight. He told me he wanted to meet with me to discuss the new series he was working on. He wanted to know if I would work with him on the series. He said his agent recommended me." Noor looked up. "I guess I can safely assume there is no new series, correct?"

Gabriel let out a harsh breath. "I'm sorry, Noor, I—"

"It's not a problem. Really, it's okay." She paused. "Your brother was researching Iran for his new series. He inquired about my family's past in Iran."

"What did you tell him?"

Noor spread her palms. "The truth—I know little about my family's life in Iran. My knowledge comprises of memories my mother shared with me."

"Memories are a good starting point. I'd appreciate anything you can share with me, memories, family albums, whatever you know." Gabriel leaned closer. "Please, my brother's life depends on it."

Noor stared at the window for several seconds. "Iranian revolutionaries killed my father. My mother...." Her voice trembled. "Mom died nineteen years ago, today."

Gabriel felt a tug in his chest. He softened his tone. "I remember your mother. She was beautiful and kind."

Tears glistened in Noor's eyes. "Yes, she was."

Gabriel touched her hand. "I'm sorry for your loss."

"Thank you." Her eyes locked with Gabriel's. She seemed to consider something and bit her lip. "We hold a memorial for Mom every year. My family comes over for dinner. We cook her favorite foods, look at albums, and share our favorite memories of her. The people at the dinner know about my parents' life in Iran.

I don't know if it will be helpful, but you're welcome to attend. Plus, the food is great."

Gabriel exhaled. "Thank you, Noor." He glanced at his watch. He promised Dotts he'd check in with him. "I must get back to my hotel."

She nodded. "I can drive you."

"What time would you like me to be there?"

"We'll eat at seven o'clock. Would you like me to pick you up?"

"No, I have a ride. I didn't bring it to the convention."

She held out her hand. "Let me type my address into your phone."

Gabriel handed her his phone. "One more thing. We can't tell your family the reason I'm attending the dinner."

Her forehead wrinkled. "Why not?"

"It's dangerous. We don't know who or what we're dealing with. You don't want to put your family in unnecessary danger."

Noor's expression tightened. "No, I don't."

"Good, we'll keep it as close to the truth as we can. Our parents were friends back in Iran. I've come to Oklahoma City for a conference and called on you. You invited me to dinner."

Noor nodded. "Okay."

CHAPTER TWELVE

G abriel parked Ethan's Harley Davidson in a boulevard lined with oak trees.

He studied Noor's house. Mom believed a person's home offered insight into who they are. Noor's home was a two-story red brick structure in the historical area of Oklahoma City. Her lawn was neat and manicured. A flight of stairs led to a painted wraparound porch. Rows of bright flowers lined both sides of the house and filled two big pots on her porch. The effect was elegant and welcoming.

Holding a bottle of wine in one hand, he rang the doorbell.

The door swung open.

"Hi." Noor had ditched the dress for a pair of tight navy-blue pants and a loose white shirt. She had tied her hair back into a ponytail and applied makeup to her eyes, making them glitter.

Gabriel's mouth went dry. "Hi."

"Come in." She motioned for him to enter.

Gabriel handed her the bottle of Bordeaux and followed her inside.

The house was a mix of dark wood floors, bright colored

walls, and furniture. Bookshelves lined three sides of the living room.

He went to the shelves. She liked variety. He found collections of poems and plays, mysteries, thrillers, memoirs, books on art and science, and books in different languages. He grinned when he saw the complete Jason Van collection.

She lifted her shoulders. "You must tire of hearing it, but I am a fan."

"Thank you, and I never tire of hearing it." Gabriel followed her to the kitchen, where she grabbed two large platters from the refrigerator. "What's in those?"

She pulled the lids off. "These were my mother's favorite appetizers. The first one is a vegetable dulmeh. The other one is cutlets."

Gabriel sat on one of the kitchen barstools and grabbed a dulmeh from the platter. An explosion of flavor and spice assaulted him. "Mm, this is great." He reached for another dulmeh. "Tell me about your family."

The doorbell rang. Her eyes twinkled. "They're here. You'll see for yourself." She laughed, running to the door.

Noor came back to the kitchen with a man in tow.

The man was in his late fifties. He was muscular with a medium build. His dark hair had streaks of grey and fell to his shoulders in a shaggy mane.

She shifted on her feet. "Gabriel, you remember Uncle Morrie. You met him back in January."

That was his cue, and Gabriel played along. He rose and shook hands with the man. "Yes, I do. It's nice to see you again."

Morris nodded.

TWO HOURS LATER, they were all seated in Noor's living room, drinking tea with dessert. Dinner had been a wonderful spread of

Persian dishes and kebabs. Gabriel made a mental note to jog longer the next day.

"No, no, Borris." Mrs. Navid waved her hand. "It wasn't the communists. They aren't responsible for everything. I believe the Islamic Republic of Iran killed my daughter. After all, she was the wife of a powerful general in the Shah's regime."

Noor's grandmother was a petite woman with silver hair and mocha-colored eyes. She watched every interaction Gabriel had with Noor.

Noor shook her head. "Why would the Islamic Republic kill Mom? She wasn't political. And why kill her eighteen years after the Iranian revolution? It doesn't make sense."

Gabriel agreed with Noor. It didn't make sense.

Mrs. Navid lifted her slim shoulders. "Who knows why? They never explain the reasons for what they do."

"If it wasn't the communists, and it wasn't the Islamic Republic, then who could it be?" Aunt Shahla wondered. She was an octogenarian with ebony hair that must have come from a bottle, and an angular face. She was a cousin of sorts. She waved a bony hand covered in rings. "It had to be political."

Roshi sighed. "After all these years, I still can't believe it." Noor's aunt, Roshi, was slim, with dark chin-length hair. Her playful personality was a sharp contrast to the haunted look in her eyes.

Aunt Shahla raised her beady eyes to the ceiling and ran into the kitchen. Pots and pans clanked. Loud popping sounds followed. Smoke rose from the kitchen, and the scent of burning seeds filtered into the living room.

Startled, Gabriel rose to go check on Aunt Shahla.

Noor put a restraining hand on his shoulder. "Aunt Shahla is preparing esphand."

Gabriel glanced warily at the kitchen. "I lived in Iran, but for the life of me I can't recall what esphand is."

"It's an ancient Persian custom. It originates to the pre-Islamic days. Esphand is a seed grown in Iran. Persians burn it over a small pot over a fire or charcoal. It keeps the evil eye away."

Gabriel put his teacup down. "The evil eye? Are you serious?"

Noor bobbed her head. "Yes."

Aunt Shahla rushed back into the living room. She held a small pan with a long handle. Smoke trailed from the pan. She punched each person between the shoulders while waving the smoking pan over their heads and mumbling something in Persian. When his turn came, Gabriel took the punch docilely.

Noor bit her lip to keep from laughing. "Persians believe in the evil eye. Esphand is a staple in every Persian home."

Gabriel lowered his voice. "What's the punch between the shoulders for?"

She chuckled. "I have no idea."

Roshi wrinkled her nose. "We're lucky Aunt Shahla delivers a punch with it. We used to have a nanny who would wave it over our heads, then stick her finger in her mouth and touch us with a saliva covered finger. Your mother and I would run away."

"Ugh, that's gross." Noor shuddered.

"It's all superstition," Uncle Morris said. His eyes strayed to the windows and doors, assessing threat. Uncle Morris's laid-back body language didn't fool Gabriel. The man had military training and was alert. Gabriel was certain of it.

Roshi nudged Morris. "You're awfully silent. Do you think the Islamic Government killed Shiraz, or was it a burglary gone wrong?"

"The Islamic Republic focused on eliminating the Pahlavi dynasty," Morris murmured, sipping his tea. "I don't believe they were after Shiraz."

Gabriel knew many Persians called the era before the Islamic revolution the old days. He went for what he hoped was a curious smile. "Tell me about the old days."

Aunt Shahla clasped her hands together. Her onyx eyes came to life. "Summer nights in Tehran were magical. The scent of jasmine lingered in the air. Cafés and restaurants were overflowed with people. Music carried into the night, and people were happy." Her voice lowered. "Beneath all that gaiety, a great evil simmered, and in the blink of an eye it was all gone." The room fell silent as Aunt Shahla painted a vivid picture of the tumultuous days leading to the Islamic revolution.

Roshi's smile didn't reach her eyes. "I remember your parents, Gabriel. The last time I saw them was at my sister's birthday party."

Noor brightened. "Mom told me about her birthday. She said it was one of the last happy memories she had before she left Iran."

Roshi nodded. "We all set our troubles aside for one evening. We celebrated your mother's birthday and meaningful friendships."

Noor touched Gabriel's arm. "I have pictures from Mom's birthday party. Your parents should be in them. Do you want to see them?"

"Yes, I'd like that."

An antique trunk sat at the other end of the living room. Noor lifted the lid of the trunk and grabbed an album. She flipped through the album and brought it to him.

Gabriel studied the pictures. He smiled when he spotted his parents. "They're younger than I am now." He flipped through the pages and whoa! The last photograph in the album was the original of the torn photograph Mike had left in the file.

The photo showed a group of people sitting at a dinner table. The group included Noor's parents, Roshi, two men he didn't know, a young woman, his parents, and to his surprise Michael's director, Jonathan Smith, and his supervisor, Mina Delany. Interesting that two key members of CIU were in Iran back then.

Noor sensed his interest. She gave him a questioning look.

Gabriel nodded slightly.

She took the album to Roshi. "Aunt Roshi, aside from family, who are the other people in this picture?"

Roshi put her glasses on and studied the picture. "That's Cameron Jahan. He's the young man Leila fell in love with."

"Who is Leila?" Gabriel asked.

"Leila is Noor's cousin and Parviz's niece," Roshi explained. "Her parents died in a car accident when she was a child. She lived with Parviz and Shiraz. Cameron died after Leila left the country. He was in the wrong place at the wrong time." Roshi shook her head. "Leila lost her uncle and the man she loved in two weeks."

"I had no idea," Noor murmured. She pointed to another man in the photo. "Who is this gentleman?"

"That's your mother's classmate. His name is Ash Kosha. I believe he still lives in Tehran. He runs multiple art galleries." Roshi pointed to the man sitting by Gabriel's mother. "That's Jonathan Smith and his date. Jonathan was your father's colleague and friend."

Gabriel studied the photograph. "He's still friends with Dad."

Roshi pointed to a couple. "That's Tyler Delany and his wife Mina. Tyler worked with Gabriel's father."

Mrs. Navid yawned and rose. "I'm going home, my dears. Aunt Shahla is staying with me."

Roshi put the album aside and grabbed Morris's arm. "You should walk me home. It's the gentlemanly thing to do."

Morris rose to leave with her.

Roshi wiggled her fingers at them. "Have fun, you two."

Noor rolled her eyes while she accompanied them to the door.

Gabriel was still flipping through the photos when Noor came back. "Can I take a picture of this photograph?"

"Sure."

Gabriel took a few pictures and pocketed his cell phone. "Is there anything else in this house that's connected to your mother's birthday?"

Noor pursed her lips. "There are the necklaces Mom left me and a volume of Rumi's poems. The volume contains both the DiVan-e Shams, and the Masnavi, but Mom always had Rumi's poems with her. I don't know if that counts."

"Necklaces?"

"Yes, my dad gave Mom two necklaces for her birthday. One was for Mom, and the other one was for their future daughter." Noor shrugged, "Mom was pregnant back then, and I guess Dad wanted a girl."

"And the book?" Gabriel inquired.

"It's a book of Rumi's poems."

"Can I see them?"

She nodded. "Come with me." Noor led him to the garage where she opened the door to a cabinet. A safe sat mounted into the wall. "This was Uncle Morrie's idea. He says intruders look for a safe inside a house." She put the combination in and pulled out two velvet cases.

Gabriel opened the cases. One held a ruby necklace, and the other one had an emerald necklace. He examined the necklaces and returned them to her. "Can I see the book?"

"Yes, it's in the living room."

He followed her into the living room where a large cover box sat on a coffee table. The box had intricate Persian calligraphy and artwork in bold blues, gold, and silver.

Noor pulled a large book with matching leather cover from the box. "Mom always kept the necklaces and Rumi's volume of poetry close to her."

Gabriel opened the book. A poem was handwritten on the first page in Farsi along with its English translation.

"IF YOU LINK *a hundred days together,*

My heart won't be relived of the torture.
Wise one, you laugh at my tale
But you're not crazed with love, if you're still sober."

—Rumi

HE READ the poem in Farsi.

Noor blinked. "You speak Farsi?"

"Yes, I told you I spent my early childhood in Iran. Mike and I were fluent in Farsi. When we moved back home, Dad hired Iranian tutors to make sure we wouldn't forget the language." Gabriel studied the poem. "When you look at the table of contents, there is a number in front of the title of each poem. The number shows you the page you can find the poem on. Your mother wrote a number under the Farsi version of the poem. Why would she do that if it's already in the table of contents?"

Noor peered over his shoulder. "I don't know, I never thought about it."

Gabriel looked at the number by the poem and flipped to the page where he found the poem. "Look, your mother circled certain letters and put a number on top of each circled letter. It could be a message."

Noor grabbed a pen and a piece of paper. She wrote the letters and the numbers. "I used to be good at this in school. I can play around with the letters and numbers to see if I can come up with anything." She wrote the numbers and changed the sequence. "It's not a date."

An idea occurred to Gabriel. "What if the numbers show the sequence of the letters? Then the letter with the number one would be the first letter of your word. Try that."

Noor rearranged the letters. "Safhe-aval. It says 'first page' in Farsi."

Gabriel flipped back to page one. He touched the page and held it up in the light. Nothing seemed out of the ordinary.

Noor pursed her lips. "Maybe Mom didn't mean page one. Maybe she literally meant the first page of the book."

Gabriel flipped back to the first page of the book. It was glued to the inner side of the front cover. He studied the title page, then ran his hands along the inner cover and the back cover. "The front cover of the book is slightly thicker than the back cover, and the glue at the bottom of the front cover looks newer than the glue on the bottom of the back cover." Gabriel pulled out a pocketknife. "I want to peel away the title page. I'll have your book repaired, I promise."

Noor acquiesced.

Gabriel cut a slit from the bottom of the cover to the top and gently peeled aside the title page. A sheet of paper and a postcard fell out.

Noor gasped.

CHAPTER THIRTEEN

"All the power needed for our life journey is already embedded in the heart."

—Rassouli, 2015

Gabriel placed the note and postcard on the table.
Noor picked up the sheet of paper with shaky hands.

My Darling girl, My Noor,

If you've found this note, I'm no longer alive. You've experienced loss, and I'm sorry I couldn't protect you from it. I know you, sweetheart. You'll want answers, but this road is dangerous. The problem is I don't know how much safer you will be if you ignore it. This is your journey. You are the only one who will recognize the clues. Follow them, and you'll find the truth. Be careful! I love you very much.

Mom

. . .

NOOR SANK INTO THE SOFA. Her face was ashen, and a sheen of tears gleamed in her eyes.

Gabriel went to the bar and found a bottle of brandy. He poured some into a glass and took it to her. "Drink this."

She took a sip and closed her eyes. When she spoke, her voice shook. "I knew her death wasn't a freak incident. I knew it!"

Gabriel stood back, giving her space. He waited until she regained some of her color. "I know this is difficult. I'd like to try something. I need you to trust me. Can you do that?"

She hesitated for a moment. "Y-yes."

"Sit back and close your eyes. I'll walk you through it."

Noor leaned back on the sofa and did as he bade.

"Take a deep breath and let your mind go blank." Gabriel walked her through a breathing exercise and waited until her shoulders relaxed. "I want you to go back to the day your mother died. You woke up in the morning. What did you do?"

"I took a shower, I... no, we had a late night, which is why I didn't go on a run."

"We?" Gabriel prompted.

"Mom, Grand-mere, my cousin Leila, Aunt Roshi, and me. Aunt Roshi and Leila had come for a surprise visit. We stayed out late the previous night."

"What happened next?" Gabriel asked.

"We all had breakfast in the dining room. We were planning to go to the Marais, an old district in Paris. Mom was too tired. She wanted to stay home and rest. She called Jean Luc, her assistant, and asked him to open the bookstore for her."

"What did you do next?"

Noor paused. "Grand-mere, Aunt Roshi, Leila, and I went to the Marais. We visited some art galleries and went to lunch."

"What did you do after lunch?"

Noor rubbed her temples. "Leila went to see a friend, and

Aunt Roshi went to an exhibition. Grand-mere and I went shopping."

"Was it normal for your mother to be tired after an evening out?"

Noor's eyes popped open. Her forehead wrinkled. "No, Mom rarely slept in. She was an early riser and preferred to open the store herself. In fact, she rarely switched schedules with Jean Luc. That's why I was worried."

"You knew her better than anyone else. Was she tired? Or was it something else, like anxiety or fear?"

"She seemed...." Noor bit her lip. "Preoccupied, like something was bothering her."

"Did you talk to her at all that day?" Gabriel asked.

"No." She closed her eyes. "Actually, yes, I called the store to check on her and tell her Grand-mere and I were bringing pizza for dinner."

"Think hard. Did your mother sound like her usual self?"

"She sounded different. I thought it was the fatigue." Noor ran a shaky hand through her hair. "I was wrong."

Gabriel picked up the postcard. It had a picture of the Bastille Square in Paris. He flipped it over. Shiraz Rahman had written two poems on the postcard and numbered them. She had scrawled "Be Aware" at the top of the postcard.

(1)
The messenger brings me pain
Yet the message cannot withhold the truth
The word "prison" can be written at a garden's fence
And a prison it's not, because of a word, hence. (Rumi)

(2)
You never see red, green, and reddish brown, until you
see light, prior to (seeing) these (three) colors.

Because your mind was distracted by color, the
colors became a veil to you from (perceiving) the light.
Since the colors are hidden at night, you have therefore
found (that) the sight of colors is (necessarily) due to light.
(For) without external light, there isn't (any) sight of
color. (It is) the same way (with the sight of) inward mental
colors. (Gamard, n.d.)

"Can you make any sense of this?"

"They're both Rumi's poems."

Gabriel's knowledge on Rumi was rudimentary. He made a mental note to research Rumi.

Noor rubbed her forehead. "I need to think."

Gabriel took her hand and held it in both of his. "I understand. I'll give you some privacy. Will you be all right on your own?"

She nodded.

He squeezed her hand. "Get some rest. If it's okay with you, I'll come back first thing in the morning. We can pick up where we left off."

"Okay." Noor rose to accompany him to the door.

He paused in the doorway. "Call me if you need anything."

"Thank you. Good night, Gabriel."

"Good night." Gabriel watched her go inside, and then climbed the bike, mulling over what he had learned. Shiraz Rahman's birthday party was important. Mike hid a clue telling him so. Why? And why was Shiraz Rahman killed eighteen years after the Iranian revolution? The dinner at Noor's place left him with more questions.

Gabriel parked the bike in front of the apartment Ethan's law firm owned and took the elevator with a couple locked in a tight embrace. He brushed past them to get off the elevator.

He was categorizing the information in his mind when he

noticed the door to the apartment was ajar. He glanced up and down the corridor. No one was there.

Gabriel crept into the apartment, ready to tackle the intruder. He checked the living room and opened the door to the bedroom. Someone had scattered his clothes and paperwork on every surface.

The sound of the front door slamming shut echoed in the apartment. Gabriel ran back into the hallway. The door to the exit in the stairwell slammed shut. Gabriel ran to the emergency stairwell. A man scampered down the stairs. He followed the man to the fourth-floor landing. Gabriel took the exit to the fourth-floor landing and ran up and down the hallway. Nothing! Gabriel ran to the lobby. *Damn it, I lost him!*

He took the elevator back to the apartment. He'd bet anything the intruder was after the file that Mike left him. He patted his pocket. He'd scanned the contents of the file into a USB drive and burnt the file. The USB drive was in his pocket.

The intruder must have followed him from Washington.

Gabriel froze. "And I led him straight to Noor."

Gabriel threw his clothes into his carryon and ran to the parking lot. The bike's engine roared as he sped toward Noor's home.

CHAPTER FOURTEEN

Gabriel arrived at Noor's house in record time. He ran toward the house when he saw the police cruiser parked in the front.

A police officer blocked his path. "Sir, what are you doing here?"

"I'm a friend."

The officer didn't budge. "Please give me your name. I'll let our senior officer know you're here."

Gabriel was about to sidestep the police officer when he heard Noor's voice. He exhaled. *She's okay.*

Noor walked toward the front door with another police officer and Uncle Morris. She spotted him standing outside and looked relieved. "Gabriel!"

Morris narrowed his eyes.

Noor beamed at the police officer. "It's all right. Gabriel is a friend."

The officer stepped back, allowing Gabriel to enter the house.

Gabriel went to her. "What happened?"

"My alarm tripped. It must have been a squirrel or a racoon." Her tone was bright and her smile strained. "Thank God for the

Oklahoma City police department. They were here in no time. Anyway, everything's all right."

The officer standing by her spoke to her for a few minutes.

Noor thanked him and turned to the house. "Let's go inside. I'll make tea."

Inside, Gabriel found Noor's grandmother and aunt sitting on a couch. Mrs. Navid was in a house robe, and Roshi was in a silk jumpsuit.

Noor took her grandmother's hand. "Grand-mere, it was a false alarm. Everything's all right. You can go home."

Mrs. Navid patted Noor's hand. "I'm staying with you, my dear."

Roshi spotted Gabriel and smirked. "She's got company, Mom. She'll be fine."

Mrs. Navid looked up. "Are you staying here, Gabriel?"

"Yes, ma'am. I left to get my carryon." It wasn't exactly a lie. He planned on spending the night to make sure Noor was safe.

Mrs. Navid rose. "In that case, I'll go home." She kissed Noor's cheek. "Lock your doors, baby. We're all close by if you need us."

Roshi winked at Gabriel and called out to Morris. "Are you coming?"

Morris didn't look away from Gabriel. "I want to check the house one more time. I'll stop by and check on you and Missus Navid."

Gabriel watched Noor's aunt and grandmother cross the street. "Your grandmother lives close by?"

"We all live on the same street. Grand-mere lives next door, and Aunt Roshi lives two houses down from her. Uncle Morrie lives in the house across the street." She must have read the surprise on his face because she rushed to explain. "We've lost too many loved ones. We stay close to each other."

Morris went to check the backyard.

Gabriel waited until Morris was out of earshot. "This is my fault, I—"

"You're not the other one," Morris snapped. He'd come back silently and stood with his arms crossed over his chest. "You're his identical twin, aren't you?"

Yep, Uncle Morris was no fool. Gabriel wasn't going to play games. "Looks like my brother is getting sloppy."

Morris shook his head. "No, I couldn't tell if it wasn't for Noor."

Noor's eyes widened. "Me?"

Morris spoke without looking at her. "You weren't as attentive to the other one. That's what gave it away."

The statement pleased Gabriel.

Morris scowled at Gabriel. "What the hell is going on? Why are you here? And while you're at it, explain why your face is plastered all over the news."

Noor's forehead wrinkled. "What are you talking about?"

Morris grabbed the remote and turned on the TV. He switched the channel to cable news.

Gabriel watched in horror. His photo covered the TV screen. The subtitles read, *The Washington D.C. police department announced author Gabriel McKnight is a person of interest in the murder of Asra Madison, a teacher at Washington Heights Elementary School. Mr. McKnight has disappeared. None of his family and friends have heard from him in two days.*

"No!" Noor shook her head in disbelief.

Gabriel stepped toward her then stopped when she backed away. "I haven't hurt or killed anyone." He ran a hand through his hair. "My brother works for a government agency that deals with international terrorism. Asra Madison was my brother's colleague. Someone set me up." Gabriel paused. "I realize it's a lot to ask you to trust me—"

"Damn right it is!" Morris growled.

Gabriel ignored Morris. "I've been honest with you from the beginning. Please believe I'm not here to hurt you. I'm trying to find my brother." He stepped closer to her. "If you don't believe me, I'll leave, and you'll never hear from me again." Gabriel held his breath and waited.

Noor searched his face. The seconds ticked by. "I believe you," she finally murmured.

Gabriel exhaled and switched his focus to Morris. "My brother was researching Noor's family when he disappeared. I believe his disappearance is connected to Missus Rahman's murder."

"Uncle Morrie, Mom's death wasn't a coincidence," Noor interjected.

"I know, child," Morris said, not taking his eyes off Gabriel.

"Mom left me a note." Noor rushed over to the shelf and pulled out the note and postcard.

Morris studied the letter and postcard intently. His gaze homed in on Gabriel. "Why was your brother researching the Rahmans?"

Gabriel lifted his shoulders. "That's what I'm trying to find out."

Noor touched Morris's shoulder. "You were my father's friend. You knew about Mom and Dad's life in Iran. Why would anyone want to kill Mom?"

Morris set the letter and postcard down. He opened his mouth to say something and cursed. He motioned to the sofa. "Sit down, it's time I told you a few things."

Noor blinked several times but did as he asked.

Morris sat beside her and scratched his chin. "For the record, I wasn't your father's friend. I never met your father."

"What are you talking about?" Noor rubbed her temples. "You told Mom you were a friend, Dad's friend."

"I am a friend," Morris huffed. "And I never claimed such a thing. I helped your mother leave Iran when she was in danger. Your mother assumed I was your father's friend, and I never corrected her."

Noor's mouth hung open. "But why? Why did you help Mom?"

"Your mother was innocent. We wanted to protect her."

"We?" Gabriel prompted.

Morris glared at him, then turned back to Noor. "The people I work for protect the innocent. I helped your mother because she was innocent. I was certain she would be safe in Paris, and I was right until the night she died." Morris looked away. "I'm sorry I wasn't able to save her."

Noor was silent for several moments, digesting the information. "We've been a family for nineteen years. Why didn't you tell me the truth?"

Morris massaged his neck. "I wanted you to be safe. I never believed your mother's death was a random incident. The less you knew, the better."

Noor raised her chin. "Did your boss or whoever you work for tell you to stay close to us?"

Morris shook his head. "No." He didn't offer an explanation.

Two spots of red appeared on Noor's cheeks. She jabbed a finger in Morris's chest. "I want to know why!" *Woah!* The woman had a temper.

Morris fidgeted, looking uncomfortable. "I made a promise to the girl—I mean your mother, or at least that was why initially."

Noor crossed her arms and waited.

Morris gave in. "I grew attached. You're like my child."

Noor studied Morris for several seconds then hugged him. "Uncle Morrie, that's the most sentiment you've shown since I've known you. I love you, too."

Morris awkwardly returned the hug.

"And just because I love you doesn't mean I'm not angry at you." She tilted her head. "Are you a government agent like Gabriel's brother?"

"What? No!" Morris sputtered.

Gabriel decided it was time to intervene. "Who do you work for?"

Morris scowled at him. He caught Noor's expression and rushed to explain. "I won't tell you who I work for, not because I don't trust you. I want to keep you safe. That's all you need to know. You'll have to trust me."

Noor sighed. "I trust you, Uncle Morrie."

Gabriel didn't. He let it go for now. He'd keep an eye on dear Uncle Morris.

Morris scratched his chin. "We have a few things to discuss. Let's start with the break-in. I assume it's related to your visit."

Gabriel told them about the break-in at the apartment."

Noor jumped up from the couch. "Oh my God! You could have been hurt."

"I'm fine. I should have known they would follow me, and I hate I led them straight to you." Gabriel shoved both of his hands in his pockets. "I have a theory. I think your mother discovered something important. Something that goes back to the final days of the Shah's regime in Iran. My brother was looking for the same thing."

Noor's forehead wrinkled. "What did Mom find?"

"I don't know. Whatever it is, someone else is after it. I believe it's why your mother was killed, and it's likely why Mike is missing."

Morris pursed his lips. "Noor's father was one of the king's advisors. We know he was guarding something. Maybe Shiraz discovered what the general was guarding."

Gabriel pointed to the note and postcard. "Missus Rahman left Noor the clues, and Mike left me a few leads. The combined information will give me direction. I'll follow the clues."

"Great. I'm coming with you," Noor announced.

Gabriel shook his head emphatically. "No, you're not."

Her brows furrowed. "My father was guarding something valuable. Someone murdered my mother for it. I'm part of this.

Besides, Mom's note says I'm the only one who will understand the clues. I can help."

Gabriel gritted his teeth. "No."

Noor crossed her arms across her chest. "Fine, I'll search for answers on my own."

Didn't she realize her life would be in danger? Gabriel took hold of her arms. "This isn't a treasure hunt. These people are killers. Besides, every cop in the country is after me. You can't come with me."

Noor pounded on her chest with her fist. "For nineteen years I wondered who killed my mother and why. For nineteen years I've had a hole burning in my chest. I won't stop until I find justice for Mom." Her eyes grew misty, their color reminding Gabriel of forest ferns after a rainfall.

He was about to object when Morris interjected. "Some distance from Oklahoma City is a good thing. The people who killed her parents may think she knows something. They will come after her."

Gabriel ran a hand through his hair. "It's too risky."

Morris glared at him. "It's riskier for her to stay here."

Indecision made Gabriel pause. If he went alone, he had himself to worry about. Problem was, he didn't know if Morris could keep Noor safe, and his concern for Noor would distract him. Gabriel couldn't afford distractions.

He blew out a breath. "Fine, but you do what I tell you. It's the only way I can keep you safe. Deal?"

A dimple appeared in her cheek. "Deal. What do we do next?"

"Your mother was killed in Paris. I—" Gabriel corrected himself. "We should go to Paris to follow your mother's movements on the day she died. You can take a commercial flight. I'll make other arrangements."

Morris smirked. "Isn't this your lucky day? I can get you both out of the country." He shook his head before Noor questioned him. "No questions. I'll get you to Canada. You can take a commercial flight from there." He studied Gabriel. "Do you have the means of securing a firearm in Paris?"

Gabriel went through a mental list of people he could reach out to. "I don't want to attract attention by reaching out to the people I know."

Morris nodded. "I'll make the arrangements. In the meantime, there's an apartment you can stay at downtown. I'll give you the address. You two better get moving."

"Why must we go downtown?" Noor asked.

Morris jerked his thumb at Gabriel. "It won't be long before those officers recognize his face." He turned to the door. "Wait here. I'll be back with the keys to the apartment."

Noor took the stairs two at a time. "I'll pack an overnight bag."

Gabriel waited in the living room. He reached into his pocket and pulled out a small lapis lazuli stone. The azure stone was smooth and covered with streaks of sky-blue. He gripped the stone in his fist while memories flooded his mind—the nip of the morning wind, mountains peaked with snow, a pair of moss green eyes lit with humor. He scrubbed a hand over his face and shoved the stone back in his pocket.

"I'm ready," Noor announced, carrying a small duffel bag.

CHAPTER FIFTEEN

"When Rumi and his family were departing from a visit to the famous mystic Persian poet, Attar, young Rumi walked closely behind his father. Attar turned to one of the dervishes and said, 'Look at this peculiar situation. There goes a sea followed by an ocean.'"

—Friedlander, 1975

GABRIEL SETTLED into the plush leather seat of the private jet Morris had arranged for them. True to Morris's word, the captain and crew didn't ask them for their IDs.

Noor studied the luxurious interior of the plane and furrowed her brows. "Uncle Morrie didn't tell me who this plane belongs to."

"Could it be his plane?" Gabriel asked.

"No." Her mouth tightened. "I mean, I don't know. I thought I knew everything about my family. I was wrong."

Her vulnerability tugged at his heart. Gabriel took her hand. "Do you trust your family?"

She didn't hesitate. "Yes."

"Do you believe they love you?" Gabriel asked.

Humor lit her eyes. "Yes."

He squeezed her hand, then let it go. "The rest is mere details. Nothing a conversation can't solve."

Her mouth curved upward. "Thank you." She buckled her seat belt and leaned back in the seat as the plane prepared to take off.

Gabriel grabbed his laptop to take notes. The people chasing them knew he'd contacted Noor. If these people had researched Gabriel, they would expect him to travel alone. He'd use that to his advantage.

He glanced over at Noor. She had fallen asleep. Her lashes fluttered as she shifted her position, clutching the book of Rumi's poems.

Gabriel's knowledge of Rumi was rudimentary. It was time to change that. He began to research Rumi.

Jalal ad-Din Mohammad Rumi, also known as Mowlana or Mevlana, was a philosopher, spiritual leader, jurist, theologian, scholar, poet, and Sufi. His poetry and doctrine had been widely known and appreciated in both the eastern and western hemisphere.

Rumi was born on the eastern shores of the Persian Empire in the city of Balkh, which is Afghanistan today.

When the Mongols invaded central Asia, Rumi's family traveled west.

Rumi eventually settled in the city of Konya, which was the western territory of the Persian Empire back then, and in Turkey today. By then Rumi was one of Persia's best scholars. He was a respected teacher and judge.

Noor stirred and opened her eyes. "What are you doing?"

Gabriel shifted in his seat. "I'm educating myself on Rumi. Who was the dervish Shams?"

Noor sat up and rubbed her eyes. "Rumi was serious and scholarly until the day he met a man named Shams.

"Shamsudin of Tabriz, or Shams, was a wild and wandering dervish. A dervish was a holy man who lived a simple existence like a monk. Stories claimed Shams and Rumi were very different on the surface. Rumi was educated and refined, whereas Shams was a rough, uneducated man with a fierce temper.

"When Rumi met Shams, something awakened deep within him. Shams preached the possibility and necessity of direct communication with God. He spoke of love for God and joining the beloved. Overnight, Rumi went from soberly preaching Islam and the law to someone filled with passion and love for God. From then on, Rumi spent most of his time with Shams. Rumi became the student, the disciple, and Shams the mentor.

"Rumi's radical change and behavior shocked and concerned his family and friends. They became resentful of Shams and disliked his influence. One night, Shams disappeared and never came back."

Gabriel leaned forward. "What happened to Shams?"

She lifted her shoulders. "No one knows. Some stories claim Rumi's supporters and family killed Shams. Others say something else. Either way, Shams's departure caused Rumi immense grief. He composed a series of poems in honor of Shams. Rumi named his collection of poems *Divan-e-Shams*. After the *Divan-e Shams,* Rumi spent twelve years composing six volumes of poems. The poems provide wisdom while entertaining the reader. The book is called *Masnavi*."

Gabriel turned back to his computer. "The general theme of Rumi's work centers on union with God or the Beloved, correct?"

Noor nodded. "Rumi believed spiritual maturity comes from learning that our true self is a reflection of God, and until we learn to love God, we live in an unenlightened human state where ego takes over." She paused. "The journey to enlightenment is a journey of spiritual growth where the spirit gradually matures and frees itself from the ego. Love plays an important part in this journey." She smiled. "Rumi believed the divine essence is in everything. He believed we must learn to look for more than the outer surface to see the inner pearl. As we grow, we shed the ego and learn to love God. We become the drop of water that unites with the ocean. That's the essence of Rumi's work." She handed Gabriel the volume of Rumi's poems. "Look for yourself. When you read Rumi's poems, his spirit touches your heart and soul. His work is passionate, powerful, and moving."

Gabriel opened the volume and began to read.

CHAPTER SIXTEEN

WASHINGTON, D.C.

Noor followed Gabriel through Georgetown's historic district. Brick and frame row houses lined the cobble-stoned streets. Restaurants, shops, and jazz bars populated the waterfront area. Old-fashioned streetlamps threw shadows over the brick buildings. The trees by the canal glimmered with fairy lights, and jazz music drifted into the night. The entire area was captivating, yet she couldn't shake off the menace she felt looming over them. It drifted in the night's breeze and taunted her, ruffling her hair. Noor glanced warily around her and shivered despite the warm weather.

Someone had followed Gabriel to Oklahoma. *Why?* Was it the same person or people who killed Mom? Were the killers following them right now?

Sensing her fear, Gabriel tightened his hold on her hand. "We're almost there." He guided her to an alley and stopped at the back door of what used to be a large colonial home. "My friend Billy and his wife inherited this place. They turned it into a restaurant."

Noor grabbed his arm. "Are you sure this is a good meeting place? What if someone recognizes you?"

"They won't." Gabriel tapped on the door.

A petite blond with bright blue eyes opened the door and embraced Gabriel. "Are you all right?"

Gabriel kissed the woman's cheek. "I'm fine." He placed his hand behind Noor's back and nudged her inside. "This is Leah Mason. She runs this place and keeps Billy in line. Leah, meet Noor Rahman."

Leah took Noor's hands in both of hers. Her cornflower blue eyes were warm and friendly. "Any friend of Gabriel's is our friend."

"Thank you." The woman's sincerity warmed Noor's heart.

Leah sighed and shook her head. "You'd better fix this mess, McKnight."

"I'm working on it."

Leah opened a door on the right. "We'll go this way. There's a hidden staircase behind this door." She guided them up the staircase into an oval room with a pair of French doors facing a balcony. A large dining room table sat at the center. She had piled the table with trays of cannoli, appetizers, and sweet cakes. "You can't run on an empty stomach. Have a seat, and I'll get you something to drink. We have a good wine selection if you care for wine."

Noor's mouth watered. She hadn't eaten anything in twenty-four hours. "I'll take carbonated water please."

"I'll have the same thing," Gabriel chimed in.

Leah shook her head. "You found your soul mate, McKnight. I'll tell Billy you're here." She sauntered off, her blond ponytail bouncing from side to side.

Noor watched Leah walk away. "What was that about?"

Gabriel smothered a laugh. "I rarely drink. Leah says I'm crazy to eat Italian food without wine. Billy, on the other hand, has a soft spot for fine wine."

"I have a soft spot for beautiful women and fine wine," a man drawled, stepping into the dining room.

Noor blinked. Gabriel's friend was tall, with a massive chest and sinewy arms. He looked like he could bench press a refrigerator.

Gabriel gave the man a one-armed hug, then introduced her.

Billy's eyes twinkled. He took Noor's hand and kissed it. "Noor is Persian for light, isn't it?"

"Yes, it is."

"An appropriate name for a beautiful woman," Billy said. "Every man needs light in his life."

Gabriel elbowed Billy. "Stop flirting."

Billy clapped Gabriel on the shoulder. "I can't help it if us southerners are perfect gentlemen."

Gabriel scowled.

Billy's smile widened.

Noor laughed. Billy Mason was all charm.

Billy grabbed a chair and straddled it. He tilted his head to the side. "So, how did you get pulled into Fa's mess?"

"Fa?" Noor's brow furrowed. "Why do you call him Fa?"

"It was his nickname when we served in the military," Billy explained. "Gabe and Mike are identical, so we nicknamed them Alpha and Beta, but then we shorted their names to Fa and Be."

She giggled. "That's horrible!"

"Yes, ma'am, we were a bad lot." Billy shared a look with Gabriel, silently asking a question.

Gabriel grabbed an appetizer and finished it in two bites. "You can talk in front of Noor."

Billy nodded. "My contact in Dubai has a nephew in the fake ID business. They'll contact me if they hear anything. What are you going to do?"

"Noor and I are going to Paris. I want to research Missus Rahman's death."

"That's a good starting point," Billy said, glancing toward the kitchen. "I gotta help in the kitchen. It's a full house tonight. Your parents should be here any minute. Leave through the back door when you're done and call me if you need anything."

"Thanks, Dotts," Gabriel said.

Billy waved the thanks off and took Noor's hand. "It was nice meeting you. I hope you'll come visit us again."

Noor bid him good night. She watched him leave through the staircase, amazed that a man Billy's size could move so nimbly. It reminded her of Gabriel. He moved with the ease and grace of a jungle cat. *A beautiful jungle cat.*

Gabriel handed her a plate. "Dig in. The food is great."

Noor's stomach rumbled on cue. She resisted the urge to moan when she bit into the tortellini. "When did you and your brother start pretending to be each other?"

Gabriel blinked. "I think we were five when we realized we looked identical. We experimented a few times and perfected it as we grew older." The corners of his eyes crinkled. "We'd play tricks on each other. During our junior year at high school, Mike got detention. He pretended to be me, so I had to spend the next day in detention. I got back at him."

"Really?" Noor took another spoonful of tortellini. "What did you do?"

He smirked. "I flunked his French exam for him. He had to take it again."

She chuckled. "Your poor mother. I can't imagine what she went through."

Gabriel's eyes softened. "Funny, Mike and I never fooled Mom, no matter what crazy scheme Mike came up with."

She heard the emotion in his voice. "You're close to your brother, aren't you?"

"Mike's my brother and my best friend."

"Now that she's started, she couldn't stop asking questions. "When did you decide to become a writer?"

He considered her question. "I wouldn't say it was a decision.

Words are a powerful arsenal. Words have the power to penetrate hearts and liberate the soul. They inspire and ignite emotion. Every revolution and movement for freedom begins with words." He waved his fork in the air. "I had words and stories floating in my mind, and for the longest time, I was happy to keep them there. I got to a point where I needed to write them down. I wrote my first novel when I was in service, and the rest is history."

"That's the difference between a true writer and someone who likes to write," Noor mumbled in between bites. "Writers need to write. It's that simple."

Gabriel sipped his drink. "Why did your mother leave you answers in Rumi's poems?"

She bit her lip, considering how to best answer his question. "It has to do with culture. Persians are very proud of their culture and heritage. Persian literature is the heart and soul of the Persian culture. Iran has many poets who are masters of speech and wisdom. Persians cherish the work of these masters and raise their children with the ancient wisdom."

Gabriel nodded. "What is a Sufi? I ran across the term when I was researching Rumi."

"Sufism is about being with God through enlightenment and love. Mystics believe this journey requires introspection and heart. It's a way of life." She set her fork down. "My parents believed in the individual journey to enlightenment. They studied the works of our master poets, especially Rumi. The poet and mystic Freydoon Rassouli said it best. Rumi's love is human love transcending the earth and becoming divine. When we focus our attention on what we love and not what we dislike or hate, we are allowing our love to expand and become divine." She blew out a breath. "Mom started reading Rumi to me when I was ten. His doctrine was woven in the fabric of our lives. That's why she left me the answers in his poems. She knew I'd understand."

Gabriel had stopped eating during her explanation. He tilted his head as if trying to look into her soul.

She was very aware of those azure eyes. Her mouth went dry, and her stomach did a little flip. She put her fork down, knowing she couldn't eat another bite.

The door to the dining room swung open, and an older couple joined them.

CHAPTER SEVENTEEN

Noor stood back to give Gabriel and his family privacy.

Gabriel spoke to them in hushed tones. He gently disengaged himself from their embrace and took hold of her hand, pulling her forward. "Mom, Dad, meet Noor Rahman. Noor, these are my parents, Moira, and Carl McKnight."

Gabriel's mother was a petite woman with expressive blue eyes. She embraced Noor. "My goodness, you look so much like Shiraz."

Noor felt the tension ease from her shoulders. Moira McKnight had a kind of inner light that reminded her of her own mother.

Gabriel's father was tall with a thick mane of silver hair, kind eyes, and a pronounced jaw. He smiled warmly. "You look like your mother, but you have some of Parviz in you."

"It's her eyes. She has her father's eyes," Moira declared, patting Noor on the shoulder. "Your mother and father were decent and kind. What happened to them was tragic."

Noor's smile was genuine. "Thank you."

Moira's eyes filled with tears. She grabbed Gabriel's arm. "You can't hide like this. Come and talk to the police. There must be a misunderstanding."

Gabriel put an arm around Moira's shoulders. "We don't have time for that."

"But—"

Gabriel didn't let his mother finish. "Mike needs my help. That's what matters right now."

Moira blinked back the tears gleaming in her eyes. "How can I help?"

Gabriel motioned to the dining room table. "There's coffee and dessert. Have a seat."

Moira and Carl joined them at the table.

Gabriel pulled his cell phone out. "This is a picture of Shiraz Rahman's birthday back in 1978. Mike left me a torn copy of this picture. It's important. What can you remember from that night?"

Carl took the photo and studied it. "Those were tough times. Parviz and I struggled with the decisions our superiors were making. Iran was in turmoil. That night was a reprieve for all of us. That's what I remember."

"What about the people in this photo? What do you remember about them?" Gabriel asked.

"I remember Jonathan and his date, Benita," Carl said. "She was an administrative assistant at the embassy. There was Parviz's young niece, Leila. She'd fallen for an architect. The kid seemed decent." Carl paused. "Aside from the disagreement with Shiraz's friend. It was a pleasant night."

Gabriel stiffened. "Who had a disagreement?"

Carl shrugged. "It wasn't important. Parviz had a few words with Shiraz's classmate. Tyler Delany knew more about it than I do."

Gabriel's brow furrowed as he digested the information. "Did General Rahman argue with anyone else that night?"

"Not that I know of," Carl said.

Gabriel showed Moira the picture. "Do you remember anything out of the ordinary that night?"

Moira bit her lip. "I remember Roshi impressed us with her knowledge about gems. Now, what was the name of that unique diamond? Do you remember, Carl?"

Carl poured himself a cup of coffee. "Yes. Aside from his usual responsibilities, Parviz was also responsible for keeping Iran's treasury of national jewels safe. One of the treasury's valuable jewels was a unique diamond that had been part of the Iranian royal collection for centuries."

"I had no idea," Noor breathed.

Carl poured creamer into his coffee. "I assume it was confidential. I think your cousin Leila blurted it out unintentionally."

Moira clasped her hands together. "Oh, now I remember. It was Leila who started the conversation. She boasted she was proud of Parviz because he held many responsibilities, including guarding the treasury of national jewels. Then she talked about some undisclosed items in the treasury's secret vault."

Startled, Noor's eyes flew to Gabriel.

Gabriel turned his attention to his mother. "What are you talking about?"

Moira lifted her shoulders. "I don't know. Leila claimed there were rumors that Iran's national treasury had a hidden vault full of undisclosed jewels, artifacts, and documents. She may have talked about the rumors. That's all I remember."

Noor set her coffee cup down. "What was my father's reaction when Leila mentioned the vault?"

Carl pursed his lips. "Now that you mention it, Parviz blew it off."

Gabriel pulled his phone out and typed, and a moment later he gave his phone to Moira. "Is this the diamond Leila was talking about? Was it the *Darya-e-Noor*?"

Moira examined the picture on the screen. "Yes, that's it. But what does this have to do with Mike? Or Noor?"

"I don't know," Gabriel murmured.

"What will you do?" Carl persisted.

Noor realized her hands were shaking. She clasped them tightly in her lap.

Gabriel put an arm around her shoulders. "Noor and I are going to Paris."

CHAPTER EIGHTEEN

G abriel guided Noor through the back alley to the rental car.

She touched his arm. "Your parents are sweet."

Her comment pleased Gabriel. He held the car door open for her. "Thank you. They liked you, too."

He drove around the block to make sure they weren't being followed. He had been careful since the incident in Oklahoma City.

Noor stared out the window. "Do you think there's any truth to what Leila claimed?"

He'd been asking himself the same question. "There must be some truth to it, or Mike wouldn't have left a picture of your mother's birthday."

Gabriel turned the car into Massachusetts Avenue. A black sedan had been following them since they turned into the highway. Wary of the sedan, he turned into the first exit. The sedan followed. Gabriel turned into Independence Avenue and sped up to a cluster of cars farther ahead.

Noor glanced at him. "What's wrong?"

Gabriel checked the rear-view mirror. "We're being followed. I'll try to lose them."

The sedan sped up and went into the lane on their right. The window rolled down. A man with a gun leaned out.

Gabriel swerved the car. "Get down, Noor!"

Shots rang out. The window behind Noor shattered.

Gabriel pushed on the brake and swiveled the car around. The sedan made a circular motion and followed them. He passed two red lights and prayed the police would show up. The sedan slammed into them from the back.

"Hold on." Gabriel pushed the accelerator. The car shot forward. He turned into an alley just before the sedan could slam into them again. He drove toward a side road close to the river. "There's a construction site a few blocks away. It'll give us cover."

Gabriel turned left into D Street then looped back onto Fourteenth Street Southwest. The construction area came into view. He turned into it and parked the car behind a large metal cylinder. He turned the headlights off and turned to check on Noor. Her face was pale, but she was all right. "We'll wait here for a while."

Several moments later, the sedan approached the construction area.

"Duck!" Gabriel pulled Noor down as the sedan drove by.

Several seconds passed. "Are we safe now?" Noor whispered.

"Not yet. They may turn back."

The sedan circled back around and slowed down by the construction area. It stopped by the construction site for a moment then drove away.

Gabriel waited several moments. "Wait here. I'll check if the coast is clear." He got out of the car and ran toward the road. The sedan was gone. He ran back to the car and opened the door. "They're gone. I don't want to take any chances. We're not driving home in this car." He opened the trunk of his car and pulled a gym bag. Gabriel rummaged through the bag and pulled out running shorts and two T-shirts. "Here, change into these." He handed Noor a pair of elastic shorts and a red T-shirt. He looked around the construction site and pointed to a large metal cylinder. "You can change back there."

Noor took the clothes he gave her and ran toward the cylinder. When she came back, he had changed and was pulling running shoes out of the gym bag.

Noor glanced down at her shoes. "Good thing I wore my flats tonight."

Gabriel held his hand out. "I'll put your clothes in the bag. Billy can pick the car up tomorrow." She handed him her clothes. He put them in the bag and pulled out a ball cap. "Can you put your hair up?"

Noor rummaged in her purse and found an elastic band. She pulled her hair into a ponytail.

Gabriel handed her the ball cap. "Put this on." He took hold of her hand and steered her toward Fourteenth Street. "Slow down. We don't want to attract attention." He spotted a white Toyota Camry by the second spotlight. "That's our Uber cab." He waved at the driver, then nudged her toward the car.

The cab dropped them off by a series of brick buildings close to the historic waterfront. Gabriel guided Noor through an alley to the back door of a commercial building. "I bought this place several years ago. I come here to write when I need inspiration."

He punched in a code, and the large metal doors swung open. A crate elevator sat at the far right of the ground level. Gabriel punched in another code, and they took the elevator to the second floor.

An open-spaced apartment greeted them. The wraparound porch offered a beautiful view of the city, and a flight of metal stairs led to a loft.

Noor went to the dining room table and collapsed into a chair, dropping her head on her arm.

Gabriel squatted in front of her. "I'm sorry I got you into this."

She raised her head. "Don't apologize. This is not your fault. I was born into this mess."

He studied her ashen face and wondered if she'd rather stay behind. "We've rattled someone's cage. It's a good thing because it means we're getting closer. I'll understand if you want to stay here and not go to Paris. I can arrange for you to be safe."

"No!" She took a deep breath. "I want to find answers as much as you do. Plus, I feel safer with you."

Warmth spread through Gabriel's stomach. He didn't recognize what it was but it felt good.

CHAPTER NINETEEN

"When a person becomes aware of the possibility of becoming as infinite as an ocean, why would anyone want to be only a drop?"

—Rassouli, 2015

The apartment was Gabriel's private sanctuary. He came here to distance himself from the world and think. He hadn't brought anyone here. Only Mike had seen the place.

The main floor boasted a silver and grey fireplace. Old pipes lined the ceiling, and the walls were original brick whitewashed. Floor to ceiling windows opened onto a large terrace, offering a generous view of the waterfront. He'd hung a few pieces of ceramic art on the walls. The furniture was sparse and white. He wondered what Noor thought of it.

As if reading his thoughts, her mouth turned up. "It suits you. I like it."

Gabriel exhaled. "Make yourself at home." He tilted his head in the direction of the loft. "It's a comfortable and private space."

Noor dragged her carryon to the stairs leading to the loft. "Thank you. I'll take a shower and unwind."

Gabriel watched her climb the stairs and grabbed his own carryon. The master bedroom was on the ground floor. A king-size bed sat in the middle of the room facing the TV mounted on the wall. Gabriel stripped his clothes off and stepped into the shower.

He let the water work its magic on his sore muscles and tried to make sense of what he'd learned. Shiraz Rahman was killed because she discovered something important. *What did she discover?* Mike left him half of a photograph from Shiraz Rahman's birthday party. Jonathan Smith, Mina Delany, and Tyler Delany were in it. Was Mike suspicious of Jonathan and Mina? Is that why he didn't call them when he ran into trouble? Or did he believe they knew something? Either way, it was time to talk to Jonathan. Gabriel finished his shower and dialed Jonathan's secure line.

He answered on the first ring.

"It's Gabriel, sir. Can you meet with me tomorrow at noon?"

"Where?"

"The Westend Bistro. I'll be at the last booth."

"Got it." Jonathan disconnected the call.

Satisfied with his plan, Gabriel went to the kitchen to make tea. He was pouring hot water into two mugs when Noor rushed into the living room. She wore a long summer dress. Her thick hair was still damp. Her feet were bare, and her cheeks flushed.

"I figured out the first clue." She waved the postcard in front of him.

"Great." Gabriel took both mugs out to the terrace. "Let's go sit outside while you tell me about it."

Gabriel placed the mugs on a coffee table and lit a small lantern. Two lounging chairs sat on each side of the coffee table. They sank into the plush cushions. Neither one of them spoke, allowing the calm to wash away the unpleasantness of the evening.

The Washington sky was a blanket of midnight blue streaked with stars. A warm breeze brought the scents of summer flowers. The waterfront's music blended with the sounds of rustling leaves and night creatures, creating a melodic symphony. What was it his Scottish grandmother used to say? Something about the day having eyes while the night had ears.

Noor's skin glowed under the lantern's soft light. Her silky hair framed her face, and her eyes, though tired, held a spark of resolve.

Gabriel wanted to reach out and touch her. He wanted to ask about the postcard. Instead, he said, "Tell me something you've learned from Rumi."

A soft smile tugged at her mouth. "One of the first stories Mom read to me was from the *Masnavi*. There was an elephant brought over from India for an exhibition. The elephant was placed in a dark stable. People went to see the creature. The stable was dark, so they used their hands to identify the elephant.

"The hand of one fell on the elephant's trunk and said, 'It's like a drainpipe.' Another one touched the elephant's ear and found a fan, one touched the elephant's leg and found a pillar, while another touched its back and discovered a throne. There were others who interpreted it as different shapes. If they had a candle, they would see the elephant's real shape." She paused, and her brow furrowed. "Our general perception sees parts of the whole, not the entire whole. Rumi believed it's not the eyes but the heart and spirit that perceive truth. Mystics believe the heart connects to the spirit. Open your heart to love, and your spirit grows." She sighed. "I learned not to take anything at face value. I learned to listen and observe with my eyes, my reason, and my heart."

"You enjoy reading Rumi."

"I do," she said. "Rumi shattered the status quo and

denounced outdated social norms. His poetry is not a gentle caress. It's vibrant, timeless, and powerful. His poems grab your heart and twist it." She leaned closer to him. "It makes you think and contemplate till your head hurts and your spirit awakens." She paused, self-conscious. A blush tinted her cheeks. She looked away. "Sorry I got carried away."

Gabriel bit back a smile. "Tell me about the postcard."

She cleared her throat. "The first step in the spiritual journey is awareness. People get to a point where religion isn't enough. They seek more and want enlightenment." Noor bit her lip. "The 'Be Aware' Mom wrote at the top of the postcard was her way of saying this is the first step in finding the truth." She read the first poem.

> *"The messenger brings me pain*
> *Yet the message cannot withhold the truth.*
> *The word 'prison' can be written at the garden's fence*
> *And prison it's not, because of a word, hence."*

"The word 'prison' is mentioned twice in the poem, and the post-card is from the Bastille Square. I knew Mom was referring to the Bastille area, yet I couldn't figure out why. Then it hit me. For most people, the Bastille is a reminder of the prison and the role it played during the French revolution. Mom and I loved that area because of the Promenade Plantee. Have you been to the Promenade Plantee?"

Gabriel recalled his previous trips to Paris. "No, what is it?"

"The Promenade Plantee is an elevated tree-lined linear park built on top of an obsolete railway infrastructure in Paris's twelfth district. It's about two point eight miles long. Mom and I used to walk it every weekend. Mom wants us to go there. That's the first clue."

Gabriel grinned. "Excellent work. What about the second poem? Have you figured out what it means?"

She lounged back in the chair. "Not yet. The second poem is from Rumi's *Masnavi*. It has layers. I've worked out the first two lines. I'm uncertain about the rest."

"Let me see the poem." Gabriel held out his hand.

She handed him the postcard.

کی ببینی سرخ و سبز و فور را ** تا نبینی پیش از این سه نور را

لیک چون در رنگ گم شد هوش تو ** شد ز نور آن رنگها رو پوش تو

چون که شب آن رنگها مستور بود ** پس بدیدی دید رنگ از نور بود

نیست دید رنگ بی‌نور برون ** همچنین رنگ خیال اندرون

"You never see red, green, and reddish brown, until you
see light, prior to (seeing) these (three) colors.
Because your mind was distracted by color, the
colors became a veil to you from (perceiving) the light.

Since the colors are hidden at night, you have therefore
found (that) the sight of colors is (necessarily) due to light.
(For) without external light, there isn't (any) sight of
color. (It is) the same way (with the sight of) inward mental
colors." (Gamard, n.d.)

He rubbed his chin. "Your mother underlined the word 'light' three times."

Noor pursed her lips. "I'm certain the word 'light' means something different in each line. I believe that light in the second line literally means while there is light. That would be the early afternoon when the sun is at its peak. Then there are the three colors mentioned in the poem. When you walk the promenade, there are trees and flower patches on your path. Mom wants us to be there when all three colors are visible. That means when the flowers bloom, when the grass is green, and when the flower patch dirt is past being fresh so that it's reddish brown. That's anytime from June to August in Paris. I haven't worked out the rest."

Gabriel studied the delicate lines on her face. "Do you know why your mother wants you to go there?"

She sighed and turned to face him. "No, and I don't know how it's related to your brother's disappearance."

"We won't know till we get there." Gabriel raked his hand through his hair. "We're meeting with Jonathan Smith, Michael's director, tomorrow. I'll tell him we're investigating your mother's death to see if it's connected to Michael's disappearance. For now, we keep the clues your mother left and our trip to Paris to ourselves."

"Okay." She opened her mouth to say something, then looked away.

"What's wrong?"

Noor chewed on her lip. "I've had these clues for nineteen years. They've been right under my nose. How did I miss them?"

"You were eighteen," Gabriel reasoned. "A trained operative could have missed it." He noticed the hollows under her eyes and softened his tone. "You should get some rest."

She yawned. "Aren't you going to sleep?"

"I'll go to bed in a bit."

She rose and pulled the terrace door open. "I'm glad I don't have to deal with this alone. I would have, but I'm glad you're with me." She turned and went inside.

Gabriel reached into his pocket and pulled out the lapis lazuli stone, gripping it in his palm.

CHAPTER TWENTY

Noor slid into a booth at the Westend Bistro. The Bistro was on the ground floor of the Ritz Carlton. It wasn't what she expected. The restaurant's warm tones and cherry wood furniture were a complete contrast to the hotel's formal decor. "This is an interesting place. It's both classy and casual."

Gabriel smirked. "That's why I like it. It's a surprise. Plus, the food's great."

Their booth was in a secluded alcove in the back of the restaurant. It offered a nice view of the main street.

Gabriel wore a ball cap and sat at an angle where the booth's wooden panel covered his face. "Don't worry. We're safe."

She stared at the windows. Men and women in business attire rushed by, immersed in life's daily routine. Noor considered her own life. So much had changed since the day she met Gabriel McKnight.

Gabriel tilted his head to the side. "What are you thinking?"

"I was thinking how life pulls the rug from underneath you. There's no warning bell or transition. Your world turns upside down in an instant, like yours was when your brother disappeared."

"And yours was when your mother died," he finished.

"Yes." Noor noticed the blue stone in his hand. "You carry that stone with you. What is it?"

Gabriel went still. He opened his palm and showed her the oval stone. "It's a lapis lazuli. A friend gave it to me."

She studied the stone. Its smooth surface was streaked with shades of cobalt the same color as Gabriel's eyes. "It's lovely. Where is your friend now?"

Gabriel's eyes flickered with emotion. The lines around his mouth tightened. "My friend died." His fist closed around the stone.

Her stomach dropped. She knew the signs. Gabriel had lost someone he cared about. She of all people understood loss. Her eyes filled with tears. "I'm sorry, Gabriel."

The air between them felt heavy, making it hard to breathe. Gabriel cleared his throat. "Yeah, me, too."

She decided to change the subject. "Tell me about Jonathan Smith."

His eyes softened at her tactic. He rose and threw her own words back at her. "He's here. You'll see for yourself."

Jonathan Smith was a man of average height. His silver hair was combed back from his forehead. His jaw and shoulders were square, and his eyes were a pale watery blue reminding her of the ice serpents she'd read about as a child. He wore a designer suit that emphasized his trim frame and carried himself with confidence. His eyes narrowed when they landed on her. A shiver worked its way up Noor's spine. This was not a man to trifle with.

Gabriel made the introductions.

Jonathan's mouth curved into a smile that didn't reach his eyes. "You're Parviz and Shiraz's daughter. It's nice to meet you." He shook her hand, holding onto it a little too long.

"Thank you." Noor pulled her hand away.

Jonathan's cold gaze washed over her. She tried not to fidget.

"You look just like your mother, well except—"

"My eyes," Noor finished. "I have my father's eyes,"

Jonathan's voice carried no inflection. "Your father was a good man."

"Thank you."

Jonathan's attention shifted to Gabriel. "CIU is talking to the local law enforcement. They don't have evidence you were involved in Asra Madison's murder. I can't help with the press, but I've made it clear you're not a murderer."

"Thank you, sir."

"Talk to the police," Jonathan pressed.

To his credit, Gabriel didn't flinch. "I'll talk to them when I find Mike."

Jonathan sighed. "I knew you'd say that. Problem is I agree with you, or I'd have hauled you in myself." He drummed his fingers on the table. Every tap pounded in Noor's head. "Why is Noor here?" he asked.

Gabriel kept it as close to the truth as possible. "I found Noor's name in Mike's apartment. I researched her past and uncovered two significant events in her life. The first one was her father's death. General Rahman died before she was born. I don't think there's a connection there. The second incident is Missus Rahman's death. The French police called it a random incident. I'm researching Missus Rahman's death to see if there's anything that could lead us to Mike."

"I see." Jonathan rubbed his chin.

"We must be on the right track." Gabriel told Jonathan about the sedan that followed them the previous night.

Jonathan's voice hardened. "Do you know who followed you?" he asked.

Gabriel ran a hand through his hair. "I wasn't able to get a license plate."

Jonathan turned to her. "I'm sorry you were dragged into this. The last thing I want is for you to get hurt."

Noor clutched the edge of the table. "I appreciate your concern. For the record, no one dragged me into this."

Gabriel lowered his voice. "Mom and Dad said General Rahman was responsible for the safety of Iran's treasury of national jewels. They learned it at Missus Rahman's birthday party back in Tehran."

Jonathan narrowed his eyes. "What does Mike's disappearance have to do with Shiraz's birthday or Parviz's responsibilities?"

The furrows in Gabriel's brow deepened. "I can't say it has anything to do with either. I'm checking every lead." He paused. "I must try."

Jonathan quit drumming on the table. "I understand."

"What do you remember about Miss Rahman's birthday?" Gabriel asked.

Jonathan stared at the pedestrians crossing the sidewalk. "Parviz had organized a small gathering of friends and family for Shiraz's birthday. It was a good break from the stress we were all under. I went to the party with a friend. She died several weeks after the party."

"How did the Darya-e-Noor diamond come up?"

Jonathan blinked and rubbed his chin. "Parviz's niece said something about how proud she was of her uncle. The diamond was part of the royal jewelry collection Parviz kept safe." He pursed his lips. "Do you have a safe place to stay at?"

"Yes," Gabriel said.

"Be careful and keep me updated."

Gabriel nodded. "I will."

Jonathan reached out and took Noor's hand in both of his. "I look forward to seeing you again."

Noor forced herself to relax as she bid him goodbye. The waiter arrived with their lunch as Jonathan rose to leave. Her eyes stayed on his back until he blended in the crowd. She couldn't pinpoint what it was about Jonathan that made her cringe. He seemed genuinely concerned for them. Or was he?

Gabriel nudged her. "What's wrong?"

Noor grimaced. "He just seemed overly protective."

"Running a counter-terrorism unit for over a decade can make you a bit"—Gabriel paused looking for the right word—"intense."

She snorted. "Yes, Mister Smith is definitely intense."

Gabriel checked his watch. "Do you mind if I have one more meeting?"

"Of course not." Noor glanced around the restaurant. "Who are you meeting with?" she asked.

"My agent. Harvey should know what's going on."

CHAPTER TWENTY-ONE

"A learned man once said there is a certain tree in India from which whoever eats the fruit, he will never become old or die. A king heard this tale and sent his envoy to find this tree. The envoy wandered about India for years searching for this tree unsuccessfully. People mocked the envoy for his search and gave him false directions. Exhausted and discouraged from his quest, the envoy decided to return to the king and set out shedding tears of despair. Along the way he met a wise man who asked the envoy why he was so despaired. The envoy related his trials. The wise man laughed and explained that he was seeking the tree of knowledge. The tree of knowledge is very high and grand, and it contains the water of life from the Sea of God. 'You have searched for the form of the tree and not the essence....'" —Rumi, Masnavi

Harvey lumbered into the Bistro after lunch. He spotted Gabriel and quickened his pace. He noticed Noor and raised an eyebrow.

Gabriel introduced Noor to him.

Harvey's face mirrored the multitude of questions on his

mind, however he was a gentleman. He shook Noor's hand and engaged her in conversation. "I admire what you've done with your career," Harvey said. "Your team of developmental editors help first time and veteran writers, correct?"

Noor beamed. "Yes, we coach writers and help them achieve their maximum potential."

Gabriel's burner phone rang. He answered the call.

Billy's voice boomed through the phone. *"I got your message, frogman."*

"I put an envelope in your mailbox," Gabriel said. "There are six names in the envelope. They have high-level security clearance. Can you check their whereabouts on the dates listed in the envelope without them knowing about it?"

Billy snickered. *"The short answer is yes because it's me and not your average tech junkie. I won't give you the longer version."*

Gabriel thanked Billy and disconnected the call.

Harvey raised his eyebrows, making the lines in his forehead look like crevices.

Noor grabbed her purse. "Please excuse me. I must call my grandmother." She touched Gabriel's shoulder. "I'll wait for you in the lobby." She bid Harvey goodbye and left to give them privacy.

Gabriel watched her leave the restaurant and turned back to Harvey. "Thank you for driving down. Order something, and I'll bring you up to speed."

Harvey folded his arms across his protruding stomach and glared at Gabriel. "Please do. The suspense is killing me."

Over coffee and dessert, Gabriel relayed everything that happened from the moment he found the folder in Michael's apartment.

"Incredible." Harvey rubbed his temples. "This stuff happens in manuscripts, not in real life."

"Unless you're a McKnight, then it happens in real life,"

Gabriel said. He leaned back in his seat and studied Harvey. "Thank you."

Harvey scowled. "What are you thanking me for?"

"For not asking about my past, and for not asking if the Jason Van stories are my life story."

"Would you tell me if I did?"

"Nope."

"That's why I don't ask." Harvey leaned forward. "What if the clues in Miss Rahman's book have nothing to do with your brother's disappearance? What then?"

Gabriel massaged his neck. "I don't know. I haven't thought far ahead."

Harvey lowered his voice. "While you and I know you're not a killer, the police still consider you a murder suspect. I've done everything humanly possible to convince the publisher and the movie producers that it's all a misunderstanding. If you leave the country, you could lose everything you've worked for." He straightened. "Lawyer up and talk to the police. Let Miss Rahman go on her own. She's the only one who can make sense of the clues anyway. If she finds anything connected to Mike's disappearance, you can make different plans."

Gabriel scowled. "I'm going to find Mike, and I won't abandon Noor. She could be in danger."

"We can hire a private security firm to make sure she's safe," Harvey exclaimed.

"I'm going with her, Harv."

"You're risking everything for a woman you barely know."

Gabriel pointed at himself. "I went to Oklahoma City. I led the people behind this to her doorstep. It's my fault."

Harvey's mouth tightened into a thin line "Why risk your life and career for Noor's safety?"

Gabriel stared mutely at Harvey.

Harvey threw his hands in the air. "Talk to me, Gabe."

Gabriel gripped the lapis lazuli stone. Memories pushed

down on his chest like heavy boulders. The pain intermingled with darkness. He loosened his grip on the stone. When he spoke, his voice was low. "Years ago, I made a mistake, and it cost someone her life." He transferred the stone to his left hand. The pain in his chest shifted to his heart. "In my early military years, we had a mission in Afghanistan. There were rumors that one of the Taliban leaders held meetings with his generals and enforcers in a certain village. We were deployed to the village to get information on the whereabouts of the leader.

"The locals were wary of us at first, but in time, they accepted our presence. We helped them establish and maintain a safe environment.

"One day, Mike was about to step into an alley full of mines. A girl called out to us. She led us away from the minefield and showed us where the dangerous areas in the village were. The girl's name was Baran. We didn't know what she looked like. She wore a burka. All we knew was Baran was eighteen years old and had green eyes.

"We soon learned that Baran was the village outcast. Local superstition believed green eyes brought bad luck. They avoided her like the plague.

"Baran lived with her elderly father. He was the village schoolteacher. The village tolerated her because they respected her father." Gabriel rubbed his neck. "She was smart, Harv. Baran was independent and hungry for knowledge. I lent her books, and in time we became friends.

"Baran picked up the information about the Taliban meetings while shopping in the village. The information was valuable, and she shared it with me. We carried out several successful raids, yet we couldn't capture the main leader.

"One day, Baran told me one of the Taliban enforcers would name the time and place of the next Taliban meeting at a village wedding. The main leader planned to attend the next meeting.

"I talked to my superior officer and got permission for Baran and her family to seek asylum in the U.S. in exchange for helping us catch the Taliban leader. Baran was excited. She looked forward to starting a new life in the U.S. She removed her burka when Mike and I visited their home." Gabriel took a long sip of water. "Two nights before the village wedding, my superior officer received intel it was a setup. He told me to make sure the wedding was not an ambush. I talked to some villagers and confirmed the wedding was real. All Baran had to do was show up and get the time and date of the next meeting.

"My gut told me to get her away from the village. I sent her a warning note.

"On the day of the wedding, the Taliban attacked the village. I drove to the village with Mike." Gabriel wiped a hand over his face. He was back in Afghanistan, back in the village cradled between the mountains. Patches of green poked out of the snow. Grey clouds obscured the sun, and the wind nipped at his skin.

He'd driven to the village and stormed out of the jeep. There was no smoke coming out of the village homes, and no children running to greet them. The eerie silence made his skin crawl. He remembered the hammering of his heart as he ran toward Baran's home.

Gabriel brought himself back to the present. His throat was raw, and his mouth felt like it was full of sawdust. He swallowed. "The village was deserted. We found an old man crying in an alley. He told us what happened.

"The Taliban knew the villagers were friendly with us. They wanted to teach the villagers a lesson. They also knew Baran was bringing us information. They captured, beat, and tortured Baran in the village square. They killed her and her father and opened fire on the villagers. The remaining survivors left the village for good.

"I went to the square and found—" Gabriel couldn't stop the tremor in his voice. "I found Baran's body in pieces. They'd cut her up and scattered her remains all over the square. Mike

helped me gather what was left of her, and we buried her."
Gabriel swiped at the tears streaming down his face. The images
were imprinted in his mind and soul. "I could have stopped it
from happening. I made a bad call, and Baran died because of it.
She'd be alive today if it weren't for me."

Harvey's eyes brimmed with tears. "You couldn't predict what
would happen."

"Don't!" Gabriel snapped. "Don't make excuses for me."

Harvey took his glasses off and wiped them with a napkin.
"Now, there's another brave woman in danger." He put his glasses
back on and sighed heavily. "You know they're looking at loca-
tions in Paris for the next Jason Van movie. I'm thinking the
director needs your input on the Paris scenes. I'll call the studio
to confirm it, and I'll do what I can to convince the police you'll
be back."

Gabriel felt a rush of affection for the man, his mentor, business partner, and friend. "Thank you."

"How are you going to leave the country or get past airport
security?" Harvey asked.

"We'll drive to Canada," Gabriel said. "I'll carry a fake ID.
We'll fly to France from Canada."

Harvey put his glasses back on. "Go find your brother. Go
keep the girl safe, and while you're at it, redeem yourself."

CHAPTER TWENTY-TWO

PARIS, FRANCE

The cab exited the Charles De Gaulle airport as the sun began its ascent into the skies. Rays of orange and gold shone down Paris's tree-lined boulevards. The Eiffel Tower stood gracefully against the skyline, and small ripples skittered across the waters of the Seine River, where boats nestled against the docks.

Noor sat upright, her eyes alight with pleasure and something else. *Guilt?* She caught Gabriel watching her and lifted her shoulders. "I love Paris. Every time I come back, it's like I've been away from home. I love Oklahoma City because that's home, too, and there's my Iranian heritage. It's confusing."

Gabriel watched the sunrise, making a mental note to use the backdrop in one of his scenes. "I spent the first seven years of my life in Iran. We immersed ourselves in the language and the culture. We loved being there and still miss it. I felt the same way for years. I realized later that loving another country didn't mean I wasn't loyal to my own. It gave me a better understanding of the world."

The lines around Noor's eyes softened. She reached out and squeezed his hand. "You know, Paris only sleeps during a short interlude between the night and sunrise. It's my favorite time of the day. You'll see what I mean."

The cab turned into Ranelagh Street, and for the next thirty minutes, Gabriel watched Paris's sleep-leaden eyes flutter open as the cafés and bakeries opened their doors to the first wave of customers.

They turned into a wide tree-lined boulevard in the sixteenth district, or *arrondissement* as the French called it. The Delessert Boulevard was lined with elegant grey stoned buildings. Cafés and boutiques occupied the corners of every stoplight. The cab stopped in front of a four-story stone building.

Noor's home was the only apartment on the top floor. She unlocked the door and grinned. "Welcome to my home."

Gabriel followed her into a marble foyer with a large circular staircase on the left.

"The staircase leads to the second-floor suite," Noor said. "The view is stunning. I recommend you take that room."

She gave him a quick tour. The foyer led to a spacious living room lined with three sets of windows offering a view of Paris. A stone fireplace covered one end of the living room, and the wall on the other end had a built-in bookcase the color of white sand. Farther off, an archway connected to a dining room and a large kitchen. The other end of the living room opened into a library and a hallway connecting to the bedrooms.

In the library, Gabriel stopped to look at the framed pictures on the shelves. There were pictures of Noor and her mother at different stages of Noor's life. One picture made him grin. Noor stood in front of her mother with Roshi and Mrs. Navid. Another woman stood to the left. She held a big patch of cotton candy, and a huge smile covered her face. "Who is the woman on the left?"

"That's Leila, my cousin," Noor said. "I'll call her and let her know I'm in Paris." She checked her watch. "We have plenty of time. Do you want to rest?"

Gabriel grabbed his carryon. "I'm not tired. I'll just unpack and take a quick shower."

An hour later, they were sitting in the living room sipping coffee with a large basket of freshly baked croissants and an assortment of jams.

Gabriel bit into his second croissant, enjoying the flaky, buttery flavor. "Can I ask you a personal question?"

"Sure."

"You inherited a fortune. Why did you go after a career?"

Noor pointed to a shop across the street. "That used to be my mother's bookstore. She bought it when I started school and turned it into a profitable business. Mom believed in being independent and living a rewarding life. I feel the same way. I enjoy helping authors, and I like running a successful business."

Gabriel picked up another croissant. "I can understand that. Writing gives me a sense of satisfaction and achievement." He tilted his head in the bookstore's direction. "Do you still own the bookstore?"

"No, Mom's assistant, Jean Luc, bought it after she died. He still owns it."

Gabriel searched her face. "I need to talk to him. I can go on my own if it's difficult for you."

"No," Noor said. "I want to be there. Besides, I always stop by the store when I'm in town."

Gabriel glanced at his watch. "Let's head out shortly. We'll go talk to Jean Luc first. Then we'll meet with a friend of mine. He's a detective in the French police. He'll bring us a copy of the police report from your mother's death. After that, we'll head to the Promenade Plantee."

The doorbell rang, making Noor jump.

Gabriel took hold of her arm. "Wait here." He went to the door and looked through at the peephole. A gangly teenager stood in the stairwell with a package in his hand. Gabriel opened the door.

"This is a package for *Monsieur* McKnight. Are you *Monsieur* McKnight?"

"Yes."

The kid handed him the package. "Mister Morris took care of the tip."

Gabriel thanked the kid and shut the door.

Noor came into the foyer. "Who was it?"

Gabriel peeked in the package. He found a gun and ammunition. "Your uncle sent me a package. Let's head out."

CHAPTER TWENTY-THREE

Jean Luc was a short and stocky man with a bulbous nose and rosy cheeks. He spotted Noor and did a jump of joy. "*Cherie, ca fait longtemps que je n'ai pas eu de tes nouvelles!*" He rushed around the counter to greet Noor. The guy was agile.

Noor kissed Jean Luc on the cheeks three times, in the French fashion. "I'm sorry I haven't been in touch. I've been very busy."

Jean Luc glanced appreciatively at Gabriel. "Mm, I can see that, *cherie.*"

Noor rolled her eyes. "Gabriel, meet my friend Jean Luc. He owns the bookstore."

Gabriel held out his hand. "It's nice to meet you," he said in fluent French.

Noor's mouth formed into an O.

"McKnight? As in the writer of the Jason Van series?" Jean Luc squealed.

Gabriel bowed his head.

Jean Luc rubbed his hands together and boomed, "Spot on, bud!"

His imitation of Jason Van's famous gesture and exclamation made Gabriel smile.

"*Dieu*, I'm a huge fan, *Monsieur* McKnight. I've read all your novels and seen the movies. It's an honor to meet you." He ran to the counter and grabbed the first Jason Van novel. "Will you please sign this book for me?"

Gabriel gave Jean Luc his most winning smile. "I'll sign a few others for you if you'd like to sell signed copies."

Jean Luc fisted his hand in the air. "Hoorah!" This was another one of Jason Van's gestures.

Noor bit her lip to keep from laughing.

"I cannot thank you enough. Please come sit down. I'll make coffee, and my assistant will bring several copies for you to sign." Jean Luc turned to the back of the store and addressed a young woman. "Francine, please bring us ten copies of the latest Jason Van novel."

The bookstore was spacious. An arch separated the reading nook from the chocolate-colored bookshelves. The earth-toned furniture and scent of leather and new books made one want to linger in the store.

Jean Luc ushered them to the reading nook. Wiggling his eyebrows, he said, "I'm pleased to see that Noor has found a good friend." Subtlety wasn't Jean Luc's strong suit.

Gabriel sat in an armchair and leaned back. He'd let Noor lead the conversation.

Jean Luc brought coffee and settled beside Noor.

"Remember the summer I opened the store?" Noor said. "You and I had breakfast together every morning. You had a crush on one of the clients."

Jean Luc's eyes twinkled. "He was handsome, wasn't he? But then—" Jean Luc threw Gabriel a flirtatious wink—"he wasn't as handsome as your man."

Gabriel's lips twitched. He didn't comment.

"Your mother encouraged me to go talk to the customer." Jean

Luc shook his head, and his hazel eyes filled with tears. "Shiraz was a wonderful woman. I miss her every day."

"Me, too!" Noor took hold of Jean Luc's hand. "What do you remember about the day Mom died? Did anything out of the ordinary happen?"

Jean Luc angled his head to the side. "What do you mean?"

"Was Mom her usual self?" Noor asked.

Jean Luc waved his hands in animated gestures that would put an orchestra conductor to shame. "*Cherie*, what difference does it make? She's gone, God rest her soul."

Noor bit her lip. "Mom's been on my mind a lot lately. I can't help thinking about that day."

Jean Luc's lower lip trembled. "I think of her every time I place a new book on the shelves. Shiraz was like the sun. She spread warmth and comfort to everyone around her." He stared into his coffee cup. "She didn't work the shift that day. She arrived just before the fireworks at the Trocadero started."

Noor narrowed her eyes. "Really? Did she say why she was late?"

"She said she had errands to run. She seemed pleased she'd accomplished all her errands."

"Did she tell you what her errands were?" Noor asked.

"No, she was preoccupied. I remember I had to ask her questions twice. I guess her friend from the past brought back too many memories."

Ah! Here we go. Gabriel shifted slightly.

Noor gripped Jean Luc's hand. "Wait, are you saying Mom had a visitor that day?"

Jean Luc bobbed his head.

"Do you know who her visitor was?"

"No, Shiraz took the evening shift the night before she died because I had a doctor's appointment. I called her after my appointment to see if she needed me at the store. She told me she was with an old friend from the past and the store wasn't busy. I figured her trip down memory lane was the reason for her preoccupation. She sent me home early that night." A tear flowed down Jean Luc's ruddy cheek. "If I had stayed, I could have prevented her death."

"I'm glad you weren't there," Noor said. "The thief would have killed you, too." She squeezed Jean Luc's hand.

Jean Luc wiped away his tears. "No more talk about sad memories. The famous Gabriel McKnight is visiting us." He turned to Gabriel. "Can I ask you a question?"

Gabriel stifled a sigh. "Sure."

"Are you Jason Van? Are the books based on your own life?"

Gabriel knew too well Jean Luc wouldn't believe him. "No, aside from serving in the Navy, I have nothing in common with Jason Van."

"Bah." Jean Luc chuckled. "You are being modest." He leaned forward and rubbed his ear. "Spot on!"

Gabriel was proud he didn't grimace.

Jean Luc's assistant brought copies of the Jason Van books for Gabriel to sign.

Gabriel signed the books and took a few pictures with Jean Luc. He and Noor bid Jean Luc goodbye and left the store.

CHAPTER TWENTY-FOUR

"Wasn't Jean Luc's imitation of Jason Van cute?"

Gabriel raised his brows. "That's one word to call it."

Her brow furrowed. "You don't like it when people imitate Jason's mannerisms?"

"It's not that." How to explain? "I don't understand it. He's a fictional character."

"Yes, one that people like." She didn't say anything else.

They were on a bus headed toward the Bastille Square. Gabriel stared out the window as the bus trudged through the cobblestoned streets of Paris. They passed the Pont Alexandre III, the most ornate bridge in Paris. Gleaming gold, bronze, and copper statues of nymphs, cherubs, winged horses, and angels adorned the bridge, while classic lamps ran along its parapet. Tourists stood by the bridge, taking pictures. An artist drew a sketch of the river, his hand stroking the canvas. A picture formed in Gabriel's mind. Like the artist's work, Gabriel's picture was incomplete.

He turned away from the scene and caught Noor studying him. Her brow puckered.

"Something wrong?" Gabriel asked.

"Some men look rumpled with a five o'clock shadow. How do you pull it off?"

Christ, she was staring at his mouth. His own eyes roamed her face and settled on her plush lips. The deep curve on her lower lip drove him crazy. A streak of heat zinged through his body. He leaned forward. The bus jolted, bringing him back to his senses. *Hell!* He turned away and turned his attention back to the scenery.

Oblivious to his reaction, Noor glanced around, making sure no one overheard their conversation. "How do you know a French detective?"

Gabriel kept his gaze on the bridge. "He used to be in the French military. I met him during an exercise."

She nudged him. "And?"

Gabriel turned toward her. "That's it."

Noor scowled. "That's it? That's all you have to say?"

"Yep."

"Do you speak any other languages aside from French and Farsi?" she asked.

"Yep."

Flecks of gold flashed in her eyes. "Are you going to tell me what other languages you can speak?"

Gabriel's chin quivered. She was easy to bait. "Aside from Farsi and French, I can speak Arabic, German, and Russian."

Noor chewed on her lip. "Is there anything else that I don't know about you?"

"Plenty."

She threw her hands in the air. "How am I going to know more about you if you don't share information?"

Gabriel chucked her under the chin. "You'll just have to stick around and figure it out."

She snorted. "You're impossible, Mister McKnight."

He grinned. "So I've been told, Miss Rahman."

The bus came to a halt.

"We're here," Noor announced.

He craned his neck to see past the passengers. A series of maroon brick arches housed trendy cafés, art galleries, and high-end boutiques. He descended the bus and followed Noor to the side of the arches.

Noor pointed to the stairs leading to the top of the structure. "We're at The Viaduc des Art. This used to be a railroad that traveled from Paris to Bastille and Vincennes on a high and long bridge. The French government converted it into a promenade."

They climbed the stairs to the top of the Viaduc. Gabriel guessed they were about thirty-two feet above the ground. The walkway was narrow and flanked by greenery. He was surprised he'd missed this in his past visits.

He took her arm. "Did you bring the postcard?"

She handed it to him.

Gabriel read the first two lines of the poem out loud.

"You never see red, green, and reddish brown, until you see light, prior to (seeing) these (three) colors. (Gamard, n.d.)

"If your interpretation is correct, the first underlined 'light' literally means daylight. We have the correct time of the day." Gabriel scanned the promenade. "Let's find a spot where we can see all three of the colors mentioned in the poem." They walked the promenade till they arrived at the end of the first section.

"Look over there." Noor pointed to the end of the first section. Trimmed bushes and patches of grass lined the walkway. Clusters of red peonies gleamed under the sun. "The dirt is reddish brown. This should be the right place."

They stood where the first strip of the promenade ended and the second section started. The scenery in the second section was entirely different. A few feet ahead, the path was a simple concrete surrounded by tall buildings with art deco statues on the outside.

Gabriel read the next two lines on the postcard.

"Because your mind was distracted by color, the
colors became a veil to you from (perceiving) the light.
(Gamard, n.d.)

"The first part doesn't seem too hard. The poem says we shouldn't focus on the area with the three colors because the colors are a distraction that obscures the 'light.' What do you think the word 'light' refers to this time?"

Noor bit her lip. "In Rumi's poem, the word 'light' refers to knowledge and divine wisdom, and the colors could be distractions that obscure knowledge. Rumi believed the goal of our human existence is union with God, and union with God illuminates us with divine intellect. I don't know how it applies to the promenade, but the answer must be here."

Gabriel checked the buildings surrounding them. The building on the right was a five-story stone structure. Art deco statues covered its top two floors. There were seven statues altogether. They stood in line, one after the other. Each statue had its left arm raised above the head, while the right arm rested on the statue's rib cage.

Noor gasped.

Gabriel spun around. "What is it? What's wrong?"

Noor pointed to the buildings on their right. "Look at the stone building with the statues. Look at the last statue."

He studied the building. The upper torso of the last statue ended by an apartment with two large windows. The corner window of the apartment fell into a line of shade. An old lantern sat behind the window. Someone had turned the lantern on. Its light flickered in the shade.

"The lamp has several interpretations in Persian literature.

Many Persians interpret the lamp as a symbol for guidance," Noor whispered.

Gabriel read the next two lines of the poem.

"Since the colors are hidden at night, you have therefore found (that) the sight of colors is (necessarily) due to light."
(Gamard, n.d.)

"ONE INTERPRETATION IS that you can't understand what distracts and distances you from God unless you have the knowledge and wisdom to identify the distractions," Noor said.

Gabriel pointed to the poem. "Your mother underlined nothing in these two lines."

Noor kept her eyes on the building. "Maybe Mom wants us to overlook them. What do the next lines say?"

Gabriel read the next two lines.

"(For) without external light, there isn't (any) sight of color. (It is) the same way (with the sight of) inward mental colors. (Gamard, n.d.)"

She ran a hand through her hair. "There are a few interpretations to these lines. One being just as you can't see an assortment of colors in our physical world without light, you cannot see the various layers of your own ego without internal light or love of God."

"Your mother underlined the words 'light' and 'color' in these lines. What could they mean?" Gabriel closed his eyes and repeated the verses. What was Noor's mother alluding to? The answer had to be close, and it hit him. He laughed. "It's brilliant! The answer is standing in front of me." He nudged her. "It's you."

She stepped back. "I'm sorry, I don't understand."

"Your name is Noor, and Noor means light. The poem says

without external light there isn't sight of color. The 'external light' mentioned in the poem is you, and the word color refers to the answers we are looking for. Translated, you're the only one who can get the answers."

"I don't know." She bit her lip.

Gabriel lowered his voice. "It's clear your mother wanted you to come here. She left clues pointing to that specific apartment. Let's go find the apartment."

Noor grabbed his arm. "Gabriel, wait! We could be wrong. Even if we find the apartment, we can't just knock on someone's door. What would we say? They'll think we're crazy. Heck, I think it's crazy."

Gabriel's body vibrated with tension. He pried her fingers from his arm. "It's the only solid clue we have."

"But—"

He looked her in the eye. "My brother's life is on the line. I must try."

She let out a deep breath. "Fine."

He took her arm. "Let's go."

They found the building with the statues and took the elevator to the top floor. Two apartments sat at opposite ends of a narrow corridor.

Gabriel motioned to the apartment on the left. "It's this one." He went to the door and rang the bell. There was no answer. He rang again.

"Coming," a voice called out from behind the door. They heard the shuffling of feet, and the door cracked open. An elderly man opened the door. His skeletal frame was bent over, and he leaned on a cane. A white yarmulke—or skull cap—covered his silver hair. Charcoal eyes peered up at them and rested on Noor.

Gabriel opened his mouth to speak.

The man raised his hand, silencing him. He leaned back. "Father Pierre," he called over his shoulder.

"Coming, Rabbi," another voice answered.

A priest joined the old man. He was tall and wide with springy silver hair. His tanned skin and creased face were a contrast to the rabbi's pallor. The priest's ice-blue eyes zeroed in on Noor. He stared at her for several seconds, and his craggy face split into a warm smile. "I thought you'd never show up, child. Come in." He held the door open for them to enter.

CHAPTER TWENTY-FIVE

"The opposition (among) people takes place because of names.
Peace occurs when they go to the real meaning."
—Rumi, Masnavi (Gamard, n.d.)

G abriel stepped in front of Noor. "Wait here." He pulled his gun out and stepped inside the apartment.

The apartment was small and immaculate. The living room was neat. A small open kitchen sat behind the living room. The lantern sat on the kitchen windowsill.

Another man sat by a table on the left. He rose as Gabriel entered. He was tall and broad-shouldered. A long shirt hung over his trousers. The man smiled, and a row of white teeth gleamed against his brown skin.

Gabriel turned to the priest. "Are there other rooms in here?"

The priest motioned to the right.

Gabriel followed the narrow hallway to a bedroom and a bathroom. There was no one in the bedroom. He holstered his gun and walked back to the living room. "Come in, Noor. It's safe."

Noor entered the apartment. The three men studied her with varying expressions. The priest looked on kindly. The rabbi wrinkled his nose and studied her the way scientists study lab rats. The third man chuckled to himself and stroked his beard as if enjoying a personal joke. All three stayed clear of Gabriel.

The priest cleared his throat. "Now that this gentleman has checked the premises, allow me to make the introductions. I'm Father Pierre." He tilted his head toward the rabbi. "This gentleman is Rabbi Abarron, and—" he motioned to the tall, dark man—"this is Mustafa." Father Pierre spread his arms and beamed. "We are friends of your mother, Noor. Shiraz told us you would seek us some day, and here you are."

As strange as the situation was, Noor handled it well. "I'm pleased to meet you. This is my friend, Gabriel McKnight."

Gabriel nodded his head in place of a greeting. The men stared at him in silence.

The one named Mustafa grinned. "You're the writer, aren't you?"

Gabriel nodded again.

Abarron's bushy brows furrowed. "Writer, eh? What does the boy write?"

Boy?

"Thrillers. He's good, too," Mustafa pointed out. "I've read a few of his books. They are quite entertaining." He rubbed his palms together. "Spot on." He beamed. "That's what Jason Van says."

"Pft," Abarron scoffed. "Look at what writing has done to the boy. He's running around with a gun."

Gabriel crossed his arms across his chest. It seemed best to remain silent.

Noor touched the priest's arm. "How did you know my mother?"

Father Pierre was about to answer when Abarron pounded his cane against the floor. "Are we going to stand on our feet all day? My arthritis is acting up."

"Sit down, Abarron." Father Pierre pulled out a chair for the rabbi. "In fact, let's all sit down. Mustafa makes great tea. Would you be kind enough to make us tea, Mustafa?"

Mustafa rose with a chuckle and headed toward the kitchen.

"I want honey and lemon in mine," Abarron barked.

"Yes, yes," Mustafa's deep voice boomed. "I know how you like your tea. We've been drinking tea together for decades."

Gabriel pulled a chair out for Noor and sat beside her. For the second time that day, he forced himself to relax. *I keep this up, and I'll become a Zen master.*

Father Pierre beamed. "I first met your mother when she was pregnant with you. She visited the church I serviced. In time, we developed a friendship. She told me about her life in Iran and everything she had been through. She was brave."

"Bah," Abarron interjected. "You only speak of yourself. We were all her mother's friends." He leaned forward. "We had tea with your mother once a week. She told us all about you." He pulled out a pair of wiry glasses and peered closely at her. "You look very much like her." He leaned back and raised his voice. "Did you hear me, Mustafa? The child takes after Shiraz."

"Yes, I can hear you," Mustafa called out, laughing. "I'm only a few feet away, not in the next continent."

Gabriel met Noor's bewildered gaze. A glint of humor shone in her eyes.

Mustafa brought a tea tray to the table. He handed Noor a cup. "You must think, what do these men have in common, eh?" He didn't wait for an answer. "We are different on the surface. We each come from a different culture, a different religion, and a different trade. However, contrary to the general population, we focus on what we have in common versus our differences. We all have a deep love for God and want to help our fellow humans.

Although," Mustafa added with chuckle. "Some of us are more pleasant than others."

"I appreciate and respect that, but how is this related to my mother?" Noor asked, unable to mask her bewilderment.

Father Pierre reached for a cup of tea. "Your mother was a friend. Throughout the years, I, no, we"—he pointed to himself, Abarron, and Mustafa—"offered your mother counsel and friendship."

Abarron bobbed his head. "Shiraz would consult us when she needed advice. We spent many afternoons discussing theology with her. She was intelligent, God rest her soul."

"Gentlemen," Father Pierre intervened. "Please let me finish." He turned back to Noor. "Your mother came to us the day before she died. She left a package here for you. She told us you would seek it when the time was right."

Gabriel was done being patient. He loomed over the priest. "Where's the package?"

"It's in a safe in the other room." Father Pierre rose and went to the bedroom. He returned holding a large sealed envelope and handed it to Noor.

Gabriel studied the priest. "Did Noor's mother say anything else when she gave you the package?"

"Yes, she mentioned that she'd found the answer to a question she carried in her heart for many years." Father Pierre's voice softened. "Your mother would light up at the mention of your name."

Noor clutched the envelope. "Thank you, Father. May I ask you a question?"

"Of course."

"Why do you have a lamp on your windowsill in broad daylight?"

Father Pierre's mouth twisted into a lopsided smile. "That lamp is a beacon for anyone who needs help. It tells them I'm here. I travel for mission work half of the year."

"I see," Noor murmured. "I travel to Paris often. If it's all right with you, I'd like to come and visit you, all three of you."

Father Pierre took Noor's hand. "We look forward to that. I'll give you my contact information."

"What do you mean, we look forward to it?" Abarron growled. "Just tell the child she will have us in her life." He glared at Noor. "Get used to it."

Noor bit her lip to keep from laughing. "Thank you."

Gabriel and Noor bid the trio goodbye and left.

Noor tried to open the envelope in the elevator. "I can't wait till we get to the hotel."

"We can go to a café and see what's inside," Gabriel said, feeling the same sense of urgency.

Once they were outside, they turned into Rue Saint-Antoine. Up ahead, the Café Français came into view. The sun was out. Parisians and tourists occupied the café's outdoor tables.

Gabriel headed toward the café. "Let's stop here."

They chose a booth inside where it was less crowded. The booth sat in a corner close to the kitchen and faced the entrance to the café.

Gabriel sat with his back to the kitchen where he could monitor the café's entrance. "Christ, that was weird. And I thought I'd seen everything."

Noor giggled. "It felt like an alternate reality. I can't believe Mom didn't tell me about them." Her smiled dimmed. "I'm glad Mom had friends to lean on when she needed it." She tore the envelope open and pulled out another envelope. The words "Lose yourself in order to find yourself" were written on the envelope.

"Do you know what the phrase means?" Gabriel asked.

Noor nodded. "Part of the Sufi's journey is to lose the ego to become one with God. You lose yourself to find your true self in God."

Gabriel noticed the slight tightening of her mouth. "You disagree with that?"

She pursed her lips. "I don't believe in annihilating the ego. I believe in mastering it. Mastering our ego develops spiritual growth and maturity. We begin to know our true self as we grow." Noor paused. "What Mom wrote on the envelope tells me our real journey is here. This is where the answers are." Noor tore the envelope open and pulled out a newspaper clipping. "It's an article titled Tehran's Black Friday. That's when a massive demonstration turned violent back in 1978. My father died on Black Friday." She handed the newspaper clipping to him.

Gabriel read the article and handed it back to her.

Noor pulled out another piece of paper. "Here's an article on my father's death. The obituary is here, too."

"This is one of the documents Mike left me," Gabriel said, reading through the article.

Noor pulled out another piece of paper. She turned it over. "It's an article on Tehran's Treasury of National Jewels. Did your brother leave you this, too?"

Gabriel skimmed the article. "Yes."

She pulled out a dried white rose in a small plastic tube, and her face lit up. "I thought I'd lost this."

"What's significant about the rose?" Gabriel asked.

Noor placed the plastic tube on the table. "Mom picked it from a rose bush she loved when she left Tehran. I don't know what the rose has to do with anything." She reached in and pulled out a picture and a postcard. Her eyes softened when she saw the picture. "It's Mom and Dad."

Gabriel leaned in to examine the photo. Shiraz Rahman and the general stood beside a series of rose bushes. The general had his arm around Shiraz's shoulders. A gazebo stood in the background. A ghost of a smile hovered over his lips. "It's your parents' home. Mike and I used to play hide and seek behind the gazebo."

Noor brushed her fingers over the photo. "They look so happy." She turned the photo over. "Mom wrote a note."

"On the surface you will see lifeless faces,
All the way from Rome to Khorasan.
What you refer to, references itself
to see the human ocean, look at yourself."

—Rumi

Gabriel leaned over her shoulder. "Another Rumi poem?"

"Yes." Noor reached into the envelope and pulled out a post-card. Her brow wrinkled. "It's Rumi's tomb in Turkey." She turned it over and read her mother's note.

"An old friend of mine, Banu, owns a gift shop by Rumi's tomb.
She'll show you the nameless grave."

She handed the postcard to Gabriel.

Gabriel's brow furrowed. He rubbed his neck. "Do you know someone named Banu?"

"No."

"What about the nameless grave? Do you know if it's real or some type of code?"

Noor shook her head. She reached in and pulled out a small notebook. She opened the notebook. Tears filled her eyes. "Mom kept a journal!" She reached in and pulled out a photo. "Look, it's the same photo from Mom's birthday."

Gabriel compared the photo with the one on his phone. He turned it over. Shiraz Rahman had written a note in Farsi.

Someone in this picture murdered your father.
Mom

CHAPTER TWENTY-SIX

"How can we search for (true) knowledge? By abandoning (false) knowledge. How can we seek (true) peace? By abandoning (false) peace...."
—Rumi (Gamard, n.d.)

G abriel stared at the note in disbelief. "What the fuck?! My parents are in the photo for God's sake." Was Shiraz Rahman out of her mind? His parents weren't killers. *Someone in that picture is a killer,* the voice in his head whispered. Gabriel wanted to tear the envelope into pieces.

Noor said something and tugged on his arm. Her voice was hoarse. "This can't be true. The revolutionaries killed my father. There's a newspaper article in this envelope that says it." She turned away and jumped to her feet, trying to hide the sheen of tears filling her eyes. "I need a minute." She scurried to the bathroom.

Gabriel didn't follow her. Noor needed time to compose herself, and he needed to think.

It was unbelievable, and highly incredible, *but not impossible.* If Noor's mother was right, then everyone in that photo was a suspect in General Rahman's murder. And that included Mike's supervisors, Mina Delany, and Jonathan Smith. Was that Mike's connection to the Rahman family?

Was that why Mike left him the picture? Gabriel ran a hand over his face. The clues in the packet had the answers to his questions. They needed to get back to the hotel where he could think and research the dates in the articles.

Noor returned several minutes later and sank down beside him. "My whole life has been a lie. Someone murdered my father. Both of my parents were murdered."

What could he say? "I'm sorry," seemed lame, and "Everything will be all right," was a lie. He placed his hand over hers and squeezed it, offering comfort.

Noor raised her chin. A glint of steel shone in her eyes. "We'll find your brother, and I'll find who killed my parents. I won't stop till I do." She gripped his hand in both of hers.

"That's the plan." Gabriel pried his hand free. "I've been thinking about the connection between Mike's disappearance and your parents' deaths."

"And?"

Gabriel ran a hand through his hair. "I think it has to do with what your father was guarding."

"We don't know what—" Noor didn't finish her sentence.

A dark van screeched to a halt in front of the café. A stocky man with a leather trench coat stepped out of the van. He reached into his coat.

Instinct pushed Gabriel into action. He shoved the envelope and its contents under his shirt, grabbed Noor, and pulled her behind the booth.

Gunshots filled the air, while bullets rained down on the café like winter hail. Pandemonium broke loose. People shouted, turning tables over.

Gabriel dragged Noor into the hallway behind the booth, taking cover behind a pair of large beams. Bullets ricocheted off the wooden beams, scattering wood particles everywhere.

Three men with machine guns approached the café, blocking its main entrance. They sprayed the café with more bullets.

Gabriel placed himself in front of Noor. His heart thudded loudly. Adrenaline flooded his veins, and everything sharpened. The acrid scent of fear and human sweat filled his nostrils. The metallic taste of gunpowder flitted over his tongue. Glass crunched and crackled as people ran over the broken shards of the café windows. Droplets of cold sweat gathered on his spine, tickling his skin.

He searched the café and spotted the door to the kitchen. He dragged Noor into the kitchen. Most of the staff was running toward a set of double doors at the other end of it. Gabriel picked up a lighter and steered Noor toward the double doors at the opposite end.

They found themselves in a hallway with two doors on each side of the hallway. He opened the door on the right and found a closet full of cleaning material. He picked up a bottle of flammable cleaning solution and guided Noor toward the exit.

Gunshots exploded outside of the rear exit. Another shooter stood at the back door, ambushing anyone who tried to escape.

Gabriel poured the solution down the hallway, dragging Noor with him. They stopped by the back door. Gabriel peered through the small window at the top of the door.

A man stood outside the door, rifle in hand. He had to be several inches taller and forty pounds heavier than Gabriel.

The kitchen staff lay crumpled at the man's feet.

Gabriel's stomach churned. He pulled Noor close. "The Jolly Green Giant's evil twin is out there. When I say go, run across the street and into the metro station. Got it?"

She bobbed her head.

"Good, stand back."

Noor moved to the other side of the door.

Gabriel kicked the door open and fired his gun. Bad giant went down.

Footsteps sounded in the back hallway. The other shooters were approaching them.

He pushed Noor out the door. "Go!"

She ran to the metro station.

Gabriel threw the lighter into the cleaning solution on the floor and followed Noor. He heard the blast of the explosion as he descended into the metro station.

Noor waited for him, huddled behind a ticket booth.

"This way." Gabriel pulled her toward the trains. They boarded an oncoming train. He guided her from one train to another, until they stopped at Palais Royal, Louvre Museum station. They exited and hailed a cab.

"We're in a hurry. Can you get us home fast?" Gabriel gave the driver directions.

"Yes, *monsieur*." The driver turned into a side road and accelerated.

Gabriel's eyes skimmed over Noor. She wasn't hurt. He grabbed her hand and squeezed it. She squeezed back. He bit back a smile. The non-verbal cues for Are you all right? and Yes, I'm fine, were established.

They arrived at Noor's apartment twenty minutes later. Gabriel unlocked the door. "Wait here." He checked the apartment. Satisfied it was safe, her called out to her.

She came in and collapsed on the couch.

Gabriel massaged his neck. "This was my mistake. I attracted someone's attention when I requested a copy of the police report."

Her eyes welled with tears. "Why did they hurt those innocent people?"

"I don't know." He blew out a breath. "Someone's getting

desperate. We can't stay here. Pack a bag and grab your travel documents. We need to leave."

"Okay." She ran to her room.

Gabriel pulled out the burner phone Morris had given him and dialed.

Morris picked up on the first ring. *"Is Noor all right?"*

"Yes." Gabriel threw his things into a carryon. "Some gunmen tried to kill us."

Morris cursed. *"Do you need a safe place?"*

He threw his laptop into the carryon. "No, I have a place in mind."

Morris grunted. *"You'll need cash. Go to the Tuileries gardens at seven p.m. Sit on the second bench. A driver will bring you a rucksack with cash and another weapon."*

"Thanks."

"Gabriel."

"Yes."

"Keep Noor safe."

Gabriel hung up and ran back down.

Noor stood in the foyer holding a travel bag. "I'm ready."

Incredible woman!

CHAPTER TWENTY-SEVEN

Gabriel set their luggage on the pavement and hailed a cab.

Noor shivered. "Where are we going?"

"We're going to a hotel. The owner is a friend. No one will know we're there." He gave the cab driver the address. The cab wound through the streets of Paris and stopped at the Latin quarter near St. Germain-des-Pres.

Paris's Latin quarter was well known for its famous cafés, and universities. A myriad of crooked cobblestoned streets connect the Latin quarter's two main boulevards, boasting cafés, restaurants, shops, and museums. It was a gathering place for artists, writers, students, intellectuals, and tourists.

Gabriel guided Noor through a narrow street and turned into Rue Christine. He stopped by a stone entrance. "We're here."

They passed through the stone entrance and within seconds found themselves transplanted in the tranquil courtyard of an elegant mansion.

"My friend Celine owns this place." Gabriel put down their suitcases. "Celine is out of the country. I told her I'm traveling with a friend and needed some privacy. It was the best I could come up with."

Noor held onto his arm. "That's fine."

They crossed the courtyard and entered an elegant reception area. The receptionist welcomed them. "Your suite is ready, *monsieur*. Would you like to go to the bar for a drink?"

Noor's face was an ash grey, her eyes hollow and breathing shallow. "Can room service send over some tea and sandwiches?"

"Certainly." The receptionist signaled to a porter. "Armand will show you to your room. Have a wonderful stay."

Gabriel kept his arm around Noor's waist. They followed the porter to a hallway on the right.

"You have a garden suite per your request, *monsieur*." The porter opened the door to the suite.

"Thank you." Gabriel tipped the kid and ushered Noor inside.

The suite was spacious, with a sitting room and two bedrooms. It also had its own private garden terrace.

He ran a hand through his hair. "I chose this suite because it's in the building's eastern corner where entry isn't easy. Is it okay?"

"Yes, thank you." Noor swayed on her feet.

"Do you want to lie down?"

"No, I'll take a shower." She scurried into the bedroom and shut the door.

Gabriel raked a hand through his hair and paced the room. Someone was nervous enough to attack them in public. He cursed under his breath and pulled out the yellow envelope. The answers were in the packet. He went through the contents and took notes.

Room service had delivered tea and sandwiches when Noor came into the sitting room. She'd changed into a pair of forest green pants and a white shirt. She plopped down on the couch and sat cross-legged. Gabriel was relieved to see the color back in her cheeks.

"I was terrified," she whispered.

Gabriel handed her a cup of tea. "I was, too."

She bit her lip. "Can I ask you a question?"

He nodded. "Sure, shoot."

"How did you do it? How did you handle the violence?" She was referring to his time with the SEAL teams.

"We spent a lot of time training and preparing before an op. Plus, we knew how to destress after missions."

"Really?" Curiosity brightened her eyes. "How do you destress?"

Sex. I find a smart, willing woman and lose myself in her body. I make her burn, and I burn with her. Gabriel shrugged. "I deal with it." He picked up the envelope. "We have a series of events, time-lines, and clues. If you look at everything in chronological order, you'll see a picture.

"It all started during the final months of the Shah's regime in 1978. The Shah made your father responsible for the safety of the treasury of national jewelry. Your father was also responsible for guarding something else, something confidential and important. Your cousin unintentionally let it slip at your mother's birth-day party.

"Someone killed your father on September eighth, 1978. The authorities believed he died in the demonstrations. Your mother left the country and raised you in Paris.

"Fast forward eighteen years. Your mother's life is uneventful. One day a friend from the past shows up, and the next day a thief kills your mother.

"I'll bet anything your mother's visitor was the same person who killed her. I think the visitor was after whatever your father was guarding and probably let something slip during the initial meeting with your mom. Your mother put two and two together and realized someone other than the demonstrators killed your father.

"Knowing her life was in danger, your mother claimed fatigue the next day. She waited for when you left the house, then put together a packet for you and left it with Father Pierre." Gabriel rose and paced the room. "Nineteen years later, my brother Mike visited you to see if you knew your family's history. He realized you didn't know much and didn't contact you again." Gabriel ran a hand through his hair. "This whole time I've questioned two things. First, why was Mike interested in your family? He didn't come to see you because of a mission. He came on his own personal time. Second, what did he find?"

"How do you know Mike came to see me on his own time?" Noor asked.

Gabriel stared out the window overlooking the garden. "Mike was on leave in January. We planned a ski trip with our friends." He turned around and shoved his hands into his pockets. "I think I have the answers to both questions. Asra Madison had partnered with Mike on a mission. I think they discovered something that led Mike to your doorstep."

"They discovered the secret my father was hiding," Noor finished.

Gabriel nodded. "What's interesting is that Mike came to see you on his own time. He didn't want his colleagues to know what he and Asra had found."

Noor's brow puckered. "But why?"

Gabriel shrugged. "I don't know. Mike has a strong sense of integrity. He's gone dark for a reason."

Noor wrinkled her nose. "What does 'gone dark' mean?"

"It means he's cut all communication with anyone he knows," Gabriel said.

Noor sipped her tea. "Why would he do that?"

Gabriel pursed his lips. "For several reasons—Mike's life could be in danger, he could be protecting our family, or it could be a combination of both. Either way, Mike needs my help."

Noor swallowed. "Wow!"

"Yeah." Gabriel pointed to the yellow envelope. "The clues tell us two things. First, someone from your parents' circle of friends is a killer. Second, the killer wanted what your father was guarding."

Noor wrapped her hands around the coffee cup. "We don't know what my father was guarding."

"No, but the people who want it don't have it. I alerted them by looking into your mother's death."

Noor stared into her mug. "What do we do next?"

"We visit your cousin, Leila. She lived with your parents in Tehran. She might have seen or heard something important." Gabriel picked up a sandwich. "We can't tell your cousin why we're asking questions."

Noor dipped her head in acknowledgement. "Agreed. What do we tell her?"

Gabriel finished the sandwich in two bites and grabbed a bottle of water. "We'll stay as close to the truth as possible. We're friends. We planned to spend a day in London and decided to visit her."

"I'll call Leila." Noor put her mug down and reached for the burner phone.

"Call her when we're in London. We don't know if anyone's listening to her calls." Gabriel pulled his wallet out and produced a small chip. "This will jam any listening devices planted in Leila's home, granted there are any. I'll plant it when we visit her." He sighed. "It's the best I can do to keep your cousin safe."

Noor's eyes took on a soft glow. "Thank you, Gabriel."

Gabriel checked his watch and rose. "Morris has a package for me. I'm supposed to pick it up at seven. Are you okay if we lie low and dine here tonight?"

"Okay." A smile hovered at her mouth. "Gabriel?"

"Yes?"

She rose from the couch and threw her arms around him. It took him by surprise. He waited a heartbeat and wrapped his arms around her. Damn, she smelled like summer flowers. Something deep in Gabriel's chest settled.

He held her a little longer, then released her. "I won't be long." He rushed out of the room before he did something stupid.

CHAPTER TWENTY-EIGHT

NEW YORK CITY, NEW YORK

Morris turned into Lafayette Street. The sun had disappeared during his walk. Patches of dark grey poked out between the buildings. Skyscrapers reflected the silver and grey of the incoming clouds. A crisp wind jostled the newspaper stands on the curbside. New Yorkers and tourists rushed by, their footsteps echoing like the beats of a drum. The scents of various cuisines allured the crowds to the restaurants lining the avenue. The overall effect was a symphony for the senses.

Morris entered the Sant Ambroeus café and settled into a corner booth, removing his jacket. Images of a similar evening in Paris flickered across his mind.

The year was 1978. Nightfall had settled in, and the city of lights had come to life. Le Petit Cluny café was animated and warm. Waiters with large white aprons wove through the crowd, delivering trays of drinks and French cuisine. A trio of musicians played outside the café, evoking images of a bohemian Paris.

No one noticed the three men sitting in the café's corner. They looked like a trio of friends enjoying a drink on a cold evening.

The men were powerful, each well known in his business circles. None of them used their real names. Morris's employer was the most powerful and underrated of the three. Morris approached the table.

"Ah, Morris is here." The Frenchman motioned to a vacant seat. "I want to speed up the timetable. We can't lose this opportunity."

The one known as the American frowned. The American had a deceivingly wholesome looking face. "Everything's ready on my side. All I need is the go ahead."

Everyone turned to Morris's employer, also known as the Iranian.

"Well?" the Frenchman demanded. "Are we still on?"

The Iranian stared off into space, drumming his fingers on the table.

The Frenchman exchanged a look with the American. The Frenchman didn't know he was playing with fire. The Iranian's youth and good looks made it easy for people to underestimate him, and he preferred it that way.

Several seconds passed in silence. The Iranian leaned back in his chair. "Gentlemen, while my objectives differ from yours, we must collaborate to pull this off. I need more time." The Iranian held up his hands as the other two protested. "I need three months."

The Frenchman pouted. "Why?"

The Iranian's smile tightened. It was the only sign of his irritation. "If you want the right outcome, you must be patient." He motioned to the waiter for the bill.

The American's eyes gleamed, reminding Morris of a frozen lake close to his childhood home. "I'm okay with a three-month delay."

The Frenchman studied the men warily. "Are you certain?"

The Iranian bowed his head. "Yes." The waiter arrived with the bill. The Iranian reached into his pocket and placed cash on the table. "Wait for my message. When you receive it, all timetables apply."

Later that evening, Morris accompanied the Iranian to the Marche Aux Puces, Paris's flea market. Being the largest of its kind, the market held fourteen submarkets, indoors and out, upstairs and down, in alleys, streets, and passages. Its streets and alleys boast cafés, shops, vendors, and antique treasures. The Marche was deserted at night.

The Iranian led Morris to the back door of a small shop. He motioned for Morris to pick the lock and followed Morris inside. They were at the back of the shop. The room had a square table, two chairs, and a telephone.

The Iranian turned on a flashlight. "Don't turn the lights on. We don't want to attract attention."

A tap sounded at the back door. The Iranian opened the door.

The American joined them, gun in hand. "I came prepared."

The Iranian checked his watch. "It won't be long."

They waited in silence. The menace in the air was tangible, weighing down on them. Morris didn't know if it came from the American or if it was the general atmosphere of the shop.

Several minutes later, the front door to the shop opened, and footsteps echoed in the store. The door to the storage area swung open, and a shadow loomed in the doorway. A hand reached out for the light switch.

"I wouldn't do that if I were you," the Iranian said.

The figure froze and cursed in French.

The Iranian took a step forward and aimed his flashlight at the Frenchman. "Turn around."

The Frenchman turned.

The Iranian tilted his head. "I knew you would betray us. I was hoping I was wrong, but then, I'm rarely, if ever, wrong."

The Frenchman's breathing grew shallow. "Wait," he panted. "There's no harm done. I have informed no one. Let me fix this. You can take half of my share."

The Iranian snorted. "I already explained that my objectives differ from yours."

Feet shuffled in the room. The American stepped out of the shadows and raised his arm.

The Frenchman raised his arms in front of his face. "No! Listen —" He never finished his sentence. He was dead when he hit the floor.

The American unscrewed the suppressor from his gun. "What do we do next?"

The Iranian shone his flashlight over the Frenchman's body. "We follow the original plan."

The sound of footsteps interrupted their discussion. The American screwed the suppressor back onto the gun.

The Iranian lay a restraining hand on his arm. "My men are here to take care of the body. Leave. Go through the back door."

The American turned to leave, then stopped. "I'll see you in Tehran."

Morris saw the flash of fury in his employer's eyes. It disappeared as quickly as it had appeared. "No, you won't. This is the last time we meet."

Morris waited until they were on a train headed back to their hotel. "Do you trust the American?"

The Iranian pursed his lips. "As much as I trust any government agent." His mouth turned down. "General Rahman will protect what's in the vault at any cost."

Morris nodded. He wasn't surprised. The general was loyal to the Shah.

The Iranian rubbed his chin. "The general's wife is innocent. She'll need our help. Go to Tehran and keep an eye on Shiraz Rahman. Make sure she doesn't get hurt."

"Hello, Morris."

Morris snapped back to the present. The Iranian set his umbrella by the table and pulled out the chair in front of him. He wore a fitted grey suit, white shirt, and a silk tie. His thick hair had streaks of silver and was combed back from his fore-head. Time, the cruel creature that sucked youth and vitality out of most, had been generous to the Iranian. He was in shape, no belly fat for him, and the fine lines on his face enhanced his aristocratic features. He looked more like an actor than the powerful business mogul he was.

The Iranian wiped a speck of lint from his coat sleeve and scanned the café. "This is a pleasant change. You don't like to leave Oklahoma City."

"Thank you for coming. It's urgent," Morris said.

"I assumed that was the case." The Iranian signaled the waitress. "Two lattes and some coffee cake please."

The waitress stopped, blushed, and tripped over herself. She rushed off to get his order.

Amused, the Iranian turned his attention back to Morris. "What's the emergency?"

Morris leaned forward. "Shiraz Rahman discovered something before she died. She left Noor a series of messages and clues." Morris told his employer about Gabriel's visit and the letter Shiraz left for Noor.

The Iranian bent his head and steepled his fingers together, taking in everything Morris said. When he raised his head, his eyes gleamed. "This is an interesting development, very interesting. Are you certain this Gabriel McKnight is telling the truth?"

Morris rubbed his chin. "Yes. I've checked his background. He's clean. His brother is a CIU agent. He was researching Noor's family. I think the brother knows what General Rahman was guarding. Something must have happened to him because he disappeared."

The Iranian pursed his lips. "It's that, or he's smart enough to hide before he has a target pinned on his back."

"There's more," Morris announced. "The brother, Michael McKnight, worked with an agent named Asra Madison. Someone murdered her. Both brothers are persons of interest for the murder."

The Iranian leaned back in his chair. "They're being framed?"

"Yes."

The waitress arrived with their order.

The Iranian smile and tipped her.

The waitress stammered a thank you and rushed off.

He picked up a coffee cup. "This becomes more interesting by the minute. Where are the children right now?"

Morris swallowed the bubble of fear that had formed in his stomach since Gabriel's phone call. "They're somewhere in Paris. They ran into trouble. They're on the move." He ran a hand through his shaggy hair. "It's a matter of time before they wind up in Iran. McKnight is capable. He can keep her safe while they're in the west. I'm worried about Iran. They'll need help there."

The Iranian sipped his coffee. "The odds won't be in their favor if they go to Tehran. Too many people are interested in the vault. We must be discreet until we are certain they have the answers." The Iranian paused. "I say we even the odds for them. Do you agree?"

Morris exhaled. "That's why I wanted to talk to you. I don't think the average muscle will do."

A ghost of a smile hovered on the Iranian's mouth. "You're right. We need the services of a professional. Call Sheila."

Morris grunted and pulled out his cell phone.

Sheila's husky voice answered on the second ring. *"Hello, Morris. To what do I owe this pleasure?"*

"My employer has a request."

"What can Sheila do for the Iranian?"

"The Iranian wants to ensure two people enter and leave Iran safely," Morris explained.

The Iranian held his hand out.

"Hold on." Morris handed his cellphone to the Iranian.

"Hello Sheila." The Iranian chuckled. "Ah, that voice of yours reminds me of warm honey." Pause. The Iranian chuckled again. "The two individuals Morris referred to seem capable. I don't want to interfere in their mission. I'd merely like to tip the odds in their favor." Silence. "Yes, thank you, Sheila. Morris will transfer your fee to the usual account." The Iranian handed the phone back to Morris with a smile.

"What are their names?" Sheila inquired.

"Gabriel McKnight and Noor Rahman. The girl, she... she's family," Morris finished.

"I understand," Sheila murmured. *"Do you know where they are?"*

Morris ran a hand through his hair. "They're somewhere in Paris. They'll be in Iran soon." Morris disconnected the line.

SHEILA STARED VACANTLY at the computer monitor. This was an interesting development. "What have you gotten yourself into, Gabriel?" Sheila hit the central intercom. "Please come to my office."

Several moments later, a knock sounded on the door.

"Come in," Sheila called out.

Ari—short for Ariana—stepped into the office.

"Tell Aram to get the plane ready. We're going to Paris, then Tehran."

Ari bowed her head. "When would you like to leave?"

"Tonight."

If Ari was surprised, she didn't show it. Ari was the quintessential assistant. "I'll make the arrangements."

CHAPTER TWENTY-NINE

Shiraz Rahman's Journal

Tehran, July 1, 1978

We are in the land that gave birth to mystics like Attar, Rumi, Hafez, and Nezami. Mystics who believed the path to God is through the gateway of the heart. When did we become hateful? When did we lose our way?

Iran has changed. There's no light, no joy, no celebrations. Instead, there's darkness. The people, the streets, the air I breathe, it pulses with negative energy. Parviz works day and night to keep our cities safe, yet the demonstrations grow like a damned cancer.

Yesterday, Leila, Roshi, and I took a walk. We stumbled on to a group of protestors and found ourselves confined by a wall of protest, all with their fists in the air. All crying for a regime change. It turned violent quickly.

I took three showers today, and the sour scent of rage still clings to my skin.

Tehran, July 28, 1978

Parviz made my birthday memorable. He invited our closest friends to dinner and stayed home. We made love all afternoon and read

Rumi's poems in bed. It felt so normal, and God knows I've forgotten what normal feels like.

Later, I went to change for the party, I wore the burgundy gown Parviz loves and left my hair down the way he likes it. I wanted to look my best for Parviz.

"You're stunning."

I swiveled around, amazed that I hadn't heard him enter the bathroom. He leaned against the doorframe, all muscles and tousled hair. Is it me? Or do all women lust for their husbands?

I leaned up and kissed him. "And you look very handsome, General Rahman."

Parviz pulled a velvet pouch from his pocket. "Happy birthday, sweetheart."

Inside lay a gold chain attached to a heart. Diamonds covered the outer side of the heart. The inside was hollow except for a large red ruby in the center. There was a matching pair of earrings.

"The heart is to remind you that my heart is yours, and the ruby is there because it's your favorite stone."

I ran my fingers over the heart. "Thank you. I love it." I leaned up and kissed him.

He pulled out another velvet pouch. "For our daughter."

I fell into a fit of laughter. I couldn't help it. Parviz believes the baby is a girl. I feel a little thrill and a little dread when I think of the baby. Here's this beautiful life growing, and then reality hits. Do I even know how to raise a child? Can I be a good mother?

I dug in the pouch. A necklace lay inside. The chain was white gold and woven in patterns like an intricate rope. The rope connected to a round diamond. A large emerald in the shape of a tear hung below the diamond.

"It's a vintage Persian design. Our daughter should have something from her country," Parviz said.

"Parviz, it's lovely. She'll love it." Oh God, will there be a bright future for us?

Reading my thoughts, Parviz tipped my chin up. "Tonight, we cele-

brate life. We put all our troubles aside for one night. That's the rule."
He held out his hand. "Are you ready to celebrate, Mrs. Rahman?"

I took his hand. "Yes."

And celebrate we did. Roshi and Leila filled the living room with candles and my favorite flowers. Parviz turned the garden lights on, making the garden an extension of the living room. Mrs. Asaad cooked my favorite foods, and my cake was a mountain of mouthwatering chocolate eclairs.

There was a strange moment though. It happened at dinner. I wish Leila hadn't mentioned the Treasury of National Jewels, but she meant well. We raised our drinks in a toast, and that was when I felt a trickle of unease. If I hadn't turned away from Parviz, I would've missed the hostility in one of the guest's eyes. It was there and gone in an instant, making me doubt I'd seen it.

Was it aimed at us? Maybe I am being paranoid. After all, the recent months have been stressful. What matters is Parviz gave me a precious memory to cherish.

~

NOOR'S BREATH caught in her throat. She dug her fingers into Gabriel's arm.

Gabriel dipped his head and studied her.

The train's speakers turned on. *"Attention passengers, the Eurostar will depart in five minutes. The destination is St. Pancras International Station, London."*

The Eurostar was a train that traveled from London to Paris and Brussels. The train crossed the English Channel through a thirty-one-mile tunnel that ran under water. Gabriel had purchased two tickets to London the previous night.

She lowered her voice. "Mom saw something the night of her birthday." She handed Gabriel the journal.

He read the passages in the journal. His brow furrowed in into deep grooves. "This confirms our theory." He pulled his laptop out of a backpack and turned it on. "I've made a list of people who attended your mother's birthday party. We need to check where everyone on the list was on July fourteen of nineteen ninety-seven. We can start with my parents." He continued before she could protest. "I know my parents aren't killers, but we must consider everyone's alibis and start an elimination process." He turned his laptop over. "Look at this picture."

She leaned closer to look at the screen. The scent of Gabriel's aftershave teased her senses. Noor forced herself to focus. It was a photo of Gabriel and his brother Michael. They wore military uniforms and stood between their parents. A young girl stood by Mrs. McKnight. Gabriel's mother had scribbled a date at the bottom of the picture. *July 13, 1997. Proud of my boys.*

"I got this from Mom. We took the picture when Mike and I graduated from Basic Underwater Demolition/SEAL or BUD/S training. We spent the week with Mom, Dad, and Lily. They couldn't have killed your mother."

Noor met his eyes. "For the record, I never suspected your parents."

Gabriel's smile was slow. It started at his mouth and traveled into his lagoon-colored eyes, making the fine lines around them crinkle.

She blinked. *Wow!* The McKnight smile was not for the weak-hearted.

"Leila and Roshi were in Paris the day your mother died. Correct?"

"Hm?" She was still reeling from his killer smile.

Gabriel repeated the question.

She resisted the urge to roll her eyes. "Yes, but neither one is a killer."

"Leila and Roshi were with you and your grandmother till lunch. Can you remember where they went after lunch?" Gabriel asked.

"Leila went to visit a friend, and Roshi was at a classmate's exhibition. His name is Joshua Arthur. He's well known for his sculptures."

Gabriel's fingers flew over the laptop's keyboard. "Roshi's alibi shouldn't be hard to check out. Ask your cousin who she went to see that day, without making her suspicious."

"Fine." Noor tried not to glower.

Gabriel studied the list pensively. "That leaves Jonathan Smith, Benita Varoujan, Mina, and Tyler Delany. I'll call Mom. She may know where Benita is. It shouldn't be hard to trace her. Jonathan and Mina will be a problem though."

"How so?"

Gabriel typed. "Mina and Johnathan work with Mike. They also have high-level security access. They'll know if anyone researches them."

"What are you going to do?"

His eyes gleamed with humor. "I've asked Billy to dig into their past. He loves projects like this." He sobered. "Your mother's journal won't have a happy ending."

"I know." Noor looked away. She could handle fury. She could handle vengeance, and she could handle the man on a mission. What she couldn't handle was his sympathy.

Gabriel's eyes softened in understanding. He turned back to his computer, giving her the space she needed.

She sighed, grateful he hadn't pushed her. That was Gabriel McKnight for you. He was strong and determined, yet kind and considerate.

Noor set the journal aside, avoiding another emotional roller-coaster. She picked up the morning paper and leafed through it. The front page covered yesterday's shooting at the Bastille. The French police were trying to figure out if the shooting was another terrorist attack. Thank God no one had caught them on camera.

The train passed the final bridge and entered the tunnel

descending under water. She gripped Gabriel's hand, trying not to panic.

Gabriel's gaze swept over her in concern. "I thought you've traveled with the Eurostar."

Noor's grip tightened. "I have." She inhaled, trying to regulate her pounding heart. "I-I don't enjoy being under water."

"Think of it this way. If you were on a plane from Paris to London, you'd be thousands of feet in the air. It can be scary either way," Gabriel said.

She forced herself to stay calm. "I must sound silly."

Gabriel's gaze bore into her. "Fear is a natural thing. Once you find the source of your fear, you're better equipped to deal with it."

"What are you afraid of?" She'd blurted the question before thinking better of it.

He grimaced. "I've never been a fan of heights. I didn't like parachute jumping. Mike, on the other hand, loved it."

Intrigued, she tilted her head. "What did you do?"

He massaged his neck. "I did my best, but I also knew that I was stronger with my teammates. In my case, Mike was better at parachute jumping, and I was better at the underwater exercises. The two of us balanced each other out."

"I guess it's good you're here. Having Aquaman with me helps."

Gabriel narrowed his eyes, a faint scowl marring his forehead. "Aquaman?"

She realized she enjoyed baiting him. "Yep."

He snorted. "You can help Aquaman sort through alibis. Feel better?"

"Yes." She realized she was clinging to Gabriel's hand and pulled hers away.

CHAPTER THIRTY

LONDON, ENGLAND

Leila's house was a classic three-story structure in Kensington Square. Noor rang the doorbell.

A middle-aged woman opened the door. The woman's birdlike gaze flew to Gabriel, then settled on Noor.

"Hello, Missus Forrester."

The woman's severe face broke into a wide smile. "Miss Rahman, this is a pleasant surprise." She fluttered her hands in gestures that Gabriel assumed was an invitation to enter. "Please come in."

Gabriel followed Noor inside. A circular staircase stood at one end of the foyer. A square console of rich mahogany sat at the center. Intricate Persian miniatures covered the top of the console. He leaned in to admire the artwork.

"Noor, my sweet, what a delightful surprise!" A tall, curvy woman descended the stairs. The tight grey dress she wore clung to her curves and flared out at the knees, making her descent look rhythmic and sensual.

At first glance, she seemed younger than the middle-aged woman Gabriel expected.

Leila pulled Noor into her arms and hugged her tightly. "I've missed you, little cuz."

Noor kissed Leila's cheek. "I hope it's all right I showed up without a call."

Leila waved a hand. "We're family. This is your home, too." Her dark eyes settled on Gabriel. A perfectly plucked brow rose.

Noor linked her arm through Gabriel's. "This is my friend, Gabriel McKnight. Before you ask, yes, he's the author."

Gabriel pulled on his "let me charm you" smile and held out his hand. "It's nice to meet you."

Leila's eyes traveled from his face to his body, and back up to his face, making him feel like a racehorse at an auction. She licked her lips. "The pleasure is all mine." She motioned to a hallway. "Let's not stand in the foyer. The drawing room is this way."

They followed her to a room more suited for a museum display rather than a drawing room. Persian rugs covered the floor. Antique furniture was spaced throughout the room. Classic paintings decorated the walls, and a series of bronze statues sat on stands at the corners of the room. The entire room was color coordinated in white and gold. Opulent and ostentatious were the words that came to mind.

Leila waved to a beige sofa. "Please have a seat. Missus Forrester will bring drinks." She sank gracefully into an armchair and crossed her legs. The move showed her legs to advantage.

Gabriel looked away.

Leila stroked Noor's cheek. "Shiraz's memorial was last week. It still hurts."

"Yes, it does." Noor shifted in her seat. "I had to be at a writer's conference with Gabriel. We flew over this week."

"I love the Jason Van books," Leila said. "Jason knows how to please a woman in bed." She tapped her finger on her mouth and studied Gabriel. "You know how to write a good sex scene. There's enough to entice the reader, but not too much detail."

Thankfully, Mrs. Forrester arrived with a tea cart and saved him from replying to the comment. She parked the cart close to the trio and left the room.

Noor intervened by changing the subject. "Do you remember Carl and Moira McKnight? Gabriel is their son."

Leila chuckled. "I do. They were good friends with Shiraz and my uncle. How are your parents?"

"They are well. Thank you," Gabriel replied.

"I believe the last time I saw your parents was at Shiraz's birthday party in Tehran."

Noor took advantage of the segue. "Gabriel plans to use Iran as a setting in his next novel. He is very interested in the political climate of the pre-revolution days. Mom's birthday fell into that period. What do you remember about it?"

Leila's smile faltered. "Why would you write about that period?"

Gabriel took the cup of tea Noor offered him. "My new series covers Tehran's pre-revolution days. I want to talk to people who were there to gain perspective on the months leading to the revolution."

Leila's mouth pressed into a firm line, and the lines around her eyes tightened. "There were riots and demonstrations everywhere. My poor uncle was under a lot of pressure, and your father was, too."

"Was my father under pressure because of the riots?" Noor asked.

Leila's eyes grew distant. She stared vacantly at the marble fireplace. When she answered, her voice was low. "Controlling the riots was only one of my uncle's responsibilities. He had much more on his plate."

Noor leaned forward. "I heard Dad was responsible for the safety of the treasury of national jewels at the Central Bank."

Leila smirked. "The Central Bank houses a famous diamond named Darya-e-Noor. Your father guarded that and more."

And that was Gabriel's cue. "Miss Ameri."

Leila batted her eyelashes. "Call me Leila."

"Miss Leila, this is great material for my book. I know the treasury holds priceless jewels. You mentioned the general guarded more. What else was he responsible for?"

Leila studied her manicured nails. "A handful of people knew my uncle guarded the treasury of national jewels. Less than a handful of people knew my uncle was responsible for the safe-keeping of something else, something secret."

"Secret?" Gabriel aimed for a mild curiosity.

"Yes, the Central Bank housed a large vault with priceless treasures no one knew existed. My uncle was responsible for the safety of that vault, too."

Leila reached for a mimosa and sipped it. "There are different rumors why the Shah kept the vault a secret. Some say the Persian monarchy wanted to keep the vault's items for itself. Others say it was because knowledge of the vault's treasures would attract the attention of other governments."

"Do you know what was in the vault?" Gabriel asked.

Leila pursed her lips. "Rumor has it the vault held artifacts, secret documents, and private correspondences between the Persian kings and other sovereigns. One rumor says the vault housed another diamond identical to the Darya-e-Noor diamond. If that's true, the twin diamond is priceless. It was all very exciting because the few who had heard of the vault believed it was a rumor. I knew the vault existed."

"How did you know?" Noor asked. "Did my father tell you?"

Leila snorted. "God no. My uncle took confidentiality to a whole new level." Her eyes grew misty. "I was young and in love. I snuck out at night to meet with Cameron, the man I loved. One night, I snuck past my uncle's study and heard him talking to a group of guards. My uncle handpicked the guards. They were responsible for the vault's safety."

Gabriel whistled. "If that's the case, then the Islamic Republic of Iran has the artifacts in the vault."

"Not all of them." Leila smirked. "As Iran grew unstable, my uncle vacated the vault and hid the artifacts from the revolutionaries." She stroked Noor's hair. "You never met your father. He was smart, honorable, and kind." Her lower lip trembled. "I lost my family because of the Islamic revolution. Noor is all I have left."

Noor took Leila's hand. "We have each other, Grand-mere, Roshi, and Uncle Morrie."

A smiled hovered at Leila's mouth. "Yes, I'm lucky to have your grandmother and Roshi." Her brows furrowed. "I'm not so sure about Morris though. You can have him."

Noor giggled. "He's not bad, Leila."

"Are you kidding? Mister Paranoid who suspects everyone and everything. But then," Leila mused, taking Noor's hand in both of hers. "I can see why Morris is paranoid when it comes to you."

Noor blinked. "What do you mean?"

"My uncle knew he wouldn't live beyond the revolution. I'm certain he told Shiraz where he hid the treasures. If anyone finds out Shiraz knew where my uncle hid the Darya-e-Noor's twin diamond, they'll come after you."

"What?" Noor practically jumped out of her seat. "What are you talking about?"

Gabriel's stomach dropped. Leila confirmed what he had feared. *Like hell!* A streak of heat shot through his chest. He wouldn't let anyone hurt Noor. He returned his attention to Leila.

Leila stroked Noor's cheek. "Didn't Shiraz tell you?"

Noor shook her head. "No."

Leila patted Noor's shoulder. "It's for the best. That diamond is nothing but trouble. Now, on to happier topics.

What are you and the handsome Mister McKnight planning to do today?"

Gabriel jumped in before Noor could answer. "It's a surprise." He spread his hands. "Sorry, sweetheart."

"Hoorah!" Leila mimicked Jason Van and winked playfully at him. "Your surprise should include a comfortable bed."

Gabriel put an arm around Noor's shoulders, praying she'd play along.

Noor scooted closer to him. "We still have the rest of the day." She beamed at her cousin. "I'm sorry. I'm spending the next two weeks with Gabriel. He has this trip planned for us. Roshi's exhibition is in three weeks. You promised to spend time with me in Oklahoma City. Are you coming?"

"Yes," Leila said. "I'm bringing some of my new pieces to the exhibition. The store shipped them yesterday."

"Aunt Roshi is coordinating a Middle Eastern jewelry exhibition at the Oklahoma City Art Museum in three weeks," Noor explained. "The curator is Aunt Roshi's friend. I'm lending two necklaces Mom left me, and Leila owns a successful jewelry design business. She's loaning some of her pieces."

"Anything for family," Leila quipped, raising her glass.

They spent the next thirty minutes talking about Iran. Gabriel signaled Noor, and they rose to bid Leila goodbye.

Leila took Noor into her arms. "It's always a pleasure to see you."

Gabriel resisted the urge to pull Noor away.

Leila leaned in to kiss his cheek. "Safe travels, Mister McKnight." The spicy scent of her perfume overwhelmed him.

He put his arm around Noor's waist and all but dragged her out the door.

Once they were outside, he strode toward Kensington Square.

Noor quickened her pace to keep up with him. "Gabriel, what's wrong? Are we in danger?"

"No." He removed his arm from her waist.

"Is Leila in any danger?"

"No." Gabriel walked faster.

Noor pulled him to a stop. "What's the matter?"

"Is your cousin always like this?"

Noor's eyes widened in confusion. "L-like what?"

"Self-centered and pretentious?"

Her mouth fell open. "That's not fair! I'll admit that Leila likes extravagance, but she has a good heart underneath it all."

Gabriel scowled. "If you say so."

Concern and hurt laced her voice. "What's this really about?"

Truth of it was Gabriel did not know the reason for his anger. He rubbed his neck and exhaled loudly. "I shouldn't have said that. I'm sorry."

Noor's eyes took on a soft glow. She reached up and caressed his cheek. "With "It's been a stressful few days, even for Aquaman."

The gentle touch was a soothing balm. His anger evaporated, and his muscles relaxed. He looked at her upturned face and let himself drown in her emerald eyes.

Her lips parted. Her tongue darted out to touch her lips, making the plush bottom lip glisten.

The simple gesture sent a ball of heat coursing through his body. His mouth went dry, and his heartbeat picked up. The air between them pulsed. Gabriel leaned closer, focused on her mouth. He wanted this woman. He wanted to bury his hands in her hair and kiss her. He wanted to drag her to the nearest hotel and explore every inch of her delectable body, and under different circumstances, he would have. But they were standing in the middle of a square like sitting ducks. *My timing sucks!*

Gabriel took hold of her hand and kissed it. "We have to keep moving."

"Huh?"

It felt good to know he wasn't the only one affected by their chemistry. He bit back a smile. "We must go, Noor."

She shook herself out of the trance. "Oh, right. Where are we going?"

"We will do what women love most."

She fell into pace beside him, her eyes brightening with interest. "Really? What's that?"

"We're going shopping."

She narrowed her eyes. "Is that a joke?"

He grinned. "Nope."

Noor scowled. "That's it? That's all you'll tell me?"

Gabriel grinned. "Yep."

She scowled. "Economy of words shouldn't apply to every situation."

CHAPTER THIRTY-ONE

G abriel glanced at the sky. The London temperature was a little chilly for a summer afternoon. Rays of sunlight occasionally filtered through the grey clouds surrounding the city. Street performers, tourists, and shoppers crowded the Fountain of Piccadilly Circus. He circled the fountain and passed a trio of artists performing a pantomime skit.

Noor buttoned up her sweater and took hold of his arm. "Seriously, what are we doing here?"

"We'll buy disguises before we head back to the train station," Gabriel said. He guided her to Coventry Street and stopped in front of a wig store opening the door for her. "You will look like a different person when we're done."

An hour later, Noor pulled a shopping bag containing a shoulder length red wig and a forest green dress over her shoulder. A flush covered her cheeks, and her eyes gleamed. "Okay, I have to admit, I can't wait to try it out."

Gabriel chuckled. "Be careful, Miss Rahman. You're getting a hankering for the cloak and dagger business."

Her eyes twinkled. "How did you know about this place?"

"You learn a lot when you spend time with filming crews," Gabriel said, scanning the immediate area to make sure they weren't followed. "I spent a few weeks in London for one of the Jason Van movies. The crew shopped here when they needed supplies."

Noor peeked into the shopping bag. "Why did you take pictures of me with the wig?"

Gabriel turned slightly and checked the other side of the street. "I sent your picture to someone Billy knows in London. He'll have a fake ID ready for you at a locker in the train station." His took hold of her hand to cross the street. "Before you ask, it's a cautionary measure."

"What about you? You only bought a ball cap," Noor said.

Gabriel rubbed his chin, feeling the thick bristles of his stubble. "I'm growing out my beard. That and the ball cap are enough. The rest of my disguise is a change in my gait and movement."

Noor laughed.

He raised his brows. "What?"

"You sound like your character, Jason Van."

Gabriel gritted his teeth. "An outcome of my writing."

She gazed up at him, her brows forming deep furrows. "You don't like being compared to your character." It was a statement, not a question.

"I'm grateful to my readers," Gabriel began and stopped. She deserved the truth. A hurricane of images and thoughts tumbled through his mind. Could he tell her about Baran and his selfishness? If Noor knew the truth, would she look at him the way she did today? Or would she turn away in disgust?

An unnamed emotion surfaced in his chest like a beast clawing at its cage. His jaw clenched. *Not now. Not here.*

Gabriel cleared his throat. "I'm trying to make decisions that will keep us alive while we search for Mike and your parents' killers." He rubbed his neck. "I'm not a suave action hero with all the answers."

She opened her mouth to comment and thought better of it. Instead, she took hold of his hand.

The simple gesture calmed the myriad of emotions coursing through him. He sighed.

They walked in silence for a block. Gabriel was about to suggest they stop at a café when a sign by the London Royal Academy of Arts caught his eye. The sign announced current exhibitions and events. One exhibit was "The Essence of eastern mysticism, Attar, Rumi, and Jami."

Noor's mouth curved into a smile. "Do we have time to see the exhibit?"

He checked his watch. "Yes, the train won't leave for two hours." He turned and glimpsed a man with a ball cap. The man had followed them since they left the wig store. "Let's check it out."

London's Royal Academy of Arts was in Burlington House, a lovely structure seated in a cobblestoned courtyard on Piccadilly. The Royal Academy organized an annual exhibition, which allowed artists to exhibit their work during summer exhibitions.

They purchased two tickets for the exhibit and followed the signs to one of the main galleries on the ground floor.

Three massive stone sculptures flanked the entrance of the exhibit. Each sculpture boasted a whirling dervish in different formations of turning. The first sculpture held his arms at waist length. Its head stood straight, staring forward. One foot was extended as if preparing to turn. The second sculpture's head was turned up. Its arms were held wide with palms extended. One foot was anchored to the ground, while the other seemed to push. The third sculpture's face was turned up toward the heavens. Its arms were up, palms facing the ceiling. Its feet posed for circular turns, while its robes billowed around the statue in intricate detail.

Gabriel studied the smooth lines on the statues. The artist had carved "Be with God" on each dervish's robe.

"Those words are the very essence of Sufism," Noor whispered.

The gallery's northern wall offered various works of calligraphy in Persian, Arabic, and other languages. Noor pointed to a series of verses from the Quran. "The term 'Sufi' and 'Sufism' began when spiritual masters began advocating practices for attaining salvation and connecting to God versus traditional Islamic religious practices. They and the masters who came after, believed traditional religious practices to be the basic schooling required for those intent on obtaining higher spiritual education."

Gabriel leaned in to study the calligraphy. "So, the focus from heaven and hell shifted to enlightenment and being with God."

She nodded. "Yes. Two principals were established in Sufism. The first being the Concept of the Unity of Being—Vahdat-e-Vujud. According to this concept, the universe is a manifestation of God's attributes and is not separated from him. The second idea or principle was the chain of Sufi masters—Silsileh. The chain of masters was established to provide guidance to seekers wanting to connect with God." She followed him to a circle of bronze statues. "Many orders of Sufism came into existence. The orders carried through several generations. They would either transform into new orders, or the people of the region would stop going, and it would shut down. Most of the Sufi masters considered the great figures of the Old and New Testament as masters of the path to God. Rumi, for instance, has given many accounts of lessons taught by Abraham, Moses, and Jesus."

Gabriel headed to the western wall. It was covered with miniatures in various sizes. "And while on this journey, one supposedly discovers his or her true self, correct?"

"Yes," Noor said. "It's through this self-discovery we realize God is in all of us."

Gabriel stopped by a miniature of a flock of birds flying

through a desert storm. The plaque above it said "The Conference of Birds." "Tell me about this conference of birds."

Noor's face brightened. "It's an important piece of mystic literature by the Persian Poet and theoretician of Sufism, Attar," she said . "The conference of birds is about a group of birds who realize they are the only kingdom who doesn't have a king. They seek advice from a hoopoe, a colorful bird with a distinctive crown of feathers. The hoopoe tells them they have king named Simurgh, which also means thirty birds in Persian." She leaned closer to the miniature to study the artist's work. "When the birds hear the journey is dangerous, some of them have second thoughts. The peacock being the legendary bird of paradise said he was waiting to go back to heaven. The goose cried that his life depended on being near water. The nightingale said he's in love with the rose and that love is enough. The hoopoe listened to all this and answered each bird either directly or with a story. The conversations allude to humans."

Gabriel nodded. "In other words, humans crave perfection, but we stop the process when there's a sign of change or hardship." He realized he found eastern mysticism fascinating. He'd have to study it. "Do they find their king?" he asked.

Noor pointed to another miniature with a long hallway lined with mirrors. "The birds go on the journey. They face many hardships, and some of them die. Thirty of them make it to the king's palace.

"At the palace, the gatekeeper treats them unkindly. It doesn't bother or offend the birds, for they've been through the worst. They are now tolerant and have empathy for other creatures. They enter a large room lined with mirrors and only see thirty birds." She paused as a smiled hovered at her lips. "They finally realize that by looking at themselves they have found the king, and by searching for the king, they found their true selves."

The gleam in her eyes brought warmth into his chest. Since the success of his first novel, he'd met women from all over the world. None of them had intrigued him the way Noor did. He moved close enough to see the specks of green in her eyes, trying to see beyond her barriers. "What about you? Are you a Sufi?"

She pushed a stray lock of hair behind her ear. "Sufism has a hierarchy. Its system has a master and disciples. The master's word is a command, and all obey.

"History shows Rumi was exposed to Sufism, and many scholars consider him a Sufi master. Others claim Rumi was a scholar and theologian in his own right. He didn't have a master, except for Shams, and Shams didn't have a following. He only mentored Rumi." She chewed on her lip. "I believe in Rumi's doctrine. I believe in the inner journey to enlightenment and in the power of love. But I also believe spiritual growth comes with education, practice, and the use of one's intellect." She blew out a breath. "All this to say I'm not a Sufi. I'm a student of a spiritual university. My mentors are Rumi and other mystics."

A smile hovered at Gabriel's lips. "You're not what I expected, Noor."

Whatever she saw in his expression made her own soften. She stood on tiptoe to kiss his cheek. "Neither are you, Aquaman!"

The hair on Gabriel's neck prickled. He glanced up and noticed the man with the ball cap in the exhibit hallway. Gabriel grabbed Noor's hand. "It's time to go."

CHAPTER THIRTY-TWO

They walked back to St. Pancras International Station. Gabriel stopped by the ticket stand to buy their tickets. He handed Noor hers and bent down to tie his shoelaces. The man with the ball cap stood by one of the newspaper stands.

He led Noor to a giftshop and checked the reflection in the window display. The ball cap man sent a hand signal to his right. Two other men approached the giftshop.

He took Noor's arm. "Let's see what the giftshop has."

She raised an eyebrow but followed him inside.

Gabriel browsed the merchandise. He picked up a magazine and lowered his voice. "We're being followed."

She leaned over, pretending to look at the magazine. "What should we do?"

"Do you see the exit at the other end of the shop?"

"Yes."

"I'll create a distraction. Go through the exit and find a bathroom. Change into your disguise and throw your old clothes away. When you're done, go to the lockers behind the main platform. You know the locker and the code. Grab your fake ID and wait to board the train."

"What about you?" Panic laced her voice.

He gave her a reassuring nod. "I'll catch up with you."

Gabriel browsed a rack of trinkets. The rack had a small mirror at the top. He waited for the man to get close and purposely stumbled, propelling himself forward. Gabriel's shoulder connected with the rack, and he fell to the floor. The rack swayed and crashed into the shelves set up behind it.

Kaboom! Everything on the shelves went tumbling down.

Noor left the shop as two shopkeepers rushed forward to assist him.

"I'm sorry!" Gabriel rubbed his knee. "I tripped on something. I believe it was this." He picked up a souvenir train. People rushed forward to help pick up the merchandise scattered on the floor. "Allow me to pay for the damages," Gabriel offered.

The clerks declined. By this time, more people had come into the store to help.

Gabriel took the exit on the other side and slipped away. He raced to the upper platform. Two men followed him. One wore a Hawaiian shirt, and the other wore a blue cap. Gabriel accessed the first platform and boarded a train. Both men were a few feet behind him. He moved from one carriage to the other until he found a crowded carriage and took a seat in the last row.

Blue cap man took a seat a few rows in front of him, and Hawaiian shirt was in a row to his right.

Gabriel waited until the train announced its departure.

When the final notice for departure sounded, the doors closed. Gabriel jumped out at the last minute.

Blue cap and Hawaiian shirt scampered out of their seats. They were too late. Blue cap stood at the window, glaring menacingly at Gabriel while he dialed a number on his cell phone.

Gabriel put his middle finger in the air. *Two down.* He raced across the platform to the Grand Terrace. He turned a corner and almost collided with a man wearing an old sweater. The man had burn scars on half of his face like Freddie Krueger from the Nightmare on Elm Street movies.

Freddie's look-alike pulled a knife out and advanced toward him.

Gabriel turned back and ran down the stairs to the lower-level platforms. He went through a door on his right and found himself in a corridor for station personnel.

Freddie followed him.

Gabriel was smaller than Freddie, but he was fast. He turned to confront Freddie.

Freddie slashed his knife, and Gabriel turned sideways to avoid the blade. Freddie slashed again. Gabriel ducked and kicked Freddie in the knee. Freddie stumbled and dropped the knife. Gabriel punched him in the jaw. Freddie's head snapped back. He grunted and passed out.

Gabriel jumped over Freddie and dashed across the platform. He headed to the first set of restrooms and peeled off his sweater, grateful he had worn a darker shirt underneath. He pulled on a ball cap and a pair of sunglasses. He hunched over and limped out of the restroom.

He found Noor at the coffee shop close to the Eurostar platform. A cup of coffee sat in front of her while she leafed through a magazine. The wig and dress had altered her appearance, making her look willowy and tall.

"*Attention all passengers for Paris. This is the last call. Please board the Eurostar at Gate thirty-seven A. The Eurostar will leave in five minutes.*"

Noor raised her head and scanned the platform.

Gabriel bit back a smile. She didn't recognize him.

She rose and hastened toward the train.

Gabriel watched Noor board the train and slowly limped toward it. He spotted a woman with platinum blond hair and struck up a conversation with her. Gabriel and the blond boarded the train.

"Well, thank you for helping me find the right train, lass. Akh, I'm excited to visit Paris. It's my first time, ya know."

Noor's head snapped around, and her mouth formed a small *O*.

Gabriel passed through the coach without glancing at her and took a seat two rows behind her.

An hour later, the blond sitting by Gabriel dozed off. He exhaled in relief, grateful for the silence.

How the hell did they find us? Leila's house was being watched. *It's the only logical answer.* He glanced ahead to check on Noor. She held a magazine, pretending to read it. She wasn't turning the pages. Heat coursed through him. What if those men had hurt Noor? She was in danger because of him. He'd have to make different plans. He'd talk to her when they were back in Paris.

He searched the small table in front of him and found a small notepad with a pen. He scribbled a note for Noor and dropped in on her lap as he limped toward the restroom. When he came back, the blond was still asleep. *Perfect!*

CHAPTER THIRTY-THREE

The train arrived in Paris on schedule. Gabriel took the metro, and Noor took a cab. He stopped limping once he entered the hotel's reception area and quickened his pace, eager to see Noor.

He found her pacing the room. She hurled the wig at him. "This will not work." Her face was flushed, and her chest heaved indignantly.

He couldn't blame her. She'd had enough and wanted out of this nightmare. He braced his legs apart and waited for her to tell him she was going home. He told himself it was better this way. At least she would be safe.

Then why did his chest feel hollow?

Her eyes blazed. "I know I promised to do what you tell me to, but it's time for you to accept that I'm not a helpless child." She planted her hands on her hips. "I'm your partner, and I expect you to rely on me, not send me away to hide."

She wants to stay! Conflicting emotions permeated through him. First, warmth spread from his stomach to his chest and all the way to his fingertips. Then, he recalled the image of Asra Madison's torn body, and fear rose like bile in his throat.

Gabriel straightened. "I'm not taking chances with your life."

Her voice shook. "It's not your choice."

His jaw tightened. He forced himself to keep his voice neutral. "I'm trying to keep you safe."

She threw up her hands. "We need to work like partners. That means we both contribute."

"You can contribute without putting your life in danger," Gabriel reasoned.

"I refuse to sit on the sidelines while you risk your life," she said.

Didn't she realize she could get hurt? He opened his mouth to say something.

Noor cut him off. "I don't fall apart when there's a threat, and I'm stronger than you think. I'm not a Navy SEAL, but I can defend myself." She stepped closer to him, hurt laced in her voice. "Have I done anything to make you doubt I'm capable?"

"It's not that." He ran a hand through his hair.

Noor clenched her fists. "Then, what is it?"

"You could get hurt," Gabriel cried. "I can't... not again," He choked, horrified at the tears welling in his eyes.

Silence.

Her expression softened with understanding. "Is that how you lost your friend? The one who gave you the stone?"

Gabriel turned away.

"Look at me," she whispered.

He clenched his fists, trying hard to regain control.

"Please look at me," Noor said.

Gabriel turned around.

A sheen of tears glistened in her eyes. "If you're worried about me getting hurt, how do you think I feel when you put your life in danger?" Her mouth trembled. "I have faith in you. Why can't you have the same trust and faith in me?"

Christ, when she put it that way it made him feel like a jerk. Did he trust her? Could he rely on her?

Yes! The answer came from the deep recesses of his soul and took him by surprise. Maybe there was a compromise. Was he willing to give it a chance?

He cleared his throat.

She held up her hand. "We'll be a stronger team if you treat me like a partner." He tried to speak, but she cut him off again. "I'll also remind you someone murdered both of my parents. I'm more than up to finding these people."

Gabriel took hold of Noor's shoulders and gently shook her. "You're brave, strong, and capable. I'm sorry if I gave you reason to believe otherwise. I was trying to protect you."

It took a second for his words to sink in. She sniffed. "It's not that I don't appreciate your protection because I do. I want you to rely on me like I rely on you."

"I do." Gabriel blew out a breath. "I can't change who I am, but I'll meet you halfway. It's the best I can do."

She considered it and nodded.

Gabriel didn't dare smile. He took her hand and kissed it. "I'm sorry."

She sighed. "What happened?"

"We had three people on our tail. I lost them."

"How did they find us?"

Gabriel massaged his neck. "My guess is Leila's house is being watched."

"Oh, God!" Noor put a hand to her throat. "I should warn her."

"No! The only reason she's safe is she knows nothing. Let's keep it that way."

Her shoulders slumped. "Fine."

Thankful that he'd averted the crisis, Gabriel grabbed a croissant from the tea tray on the table and sank into the sofa. "How about some tea?"

She poured tea into two mugs and took a seat beside him.

Gabriel finished the croissant and stretched his legs. "Okay partner, the next set of clues point to Iran and Turkey. We should go to Iran first."

Noor almost choked on her tea. "You can't go to Iran. It's dangerous."

He narrowed his eyes. "Why would it be dangerous?"

"You're a former Navy SEAL. I'm sure the Islamic Republic would see that as a threat," Noor sputtered.

"I haven't been active for years. Plus, I'm an established writer. My next novel has chapters that take place in Iran. I need to spend time in the country." He couldn't help smiling. "I've always wanted to go back for a visit."

She put her cup on the table. "Did you forget your picture is all over U.S. national news?"

Gabriel grabbed another croissant from the tray. "We're in France, not the U.S."

"What if they don't let you leave Iran?"

He dismissed her fear. "That won't happen. Even if it does, I know someone who can get me out." He hoped he was right. Gabriel made a mental note to contact Sheila.

She rubbed her forehead. "Most people wouldn't have an interest in the country."

Gabriel sipped his tea. "I'm not most people."

She tilted her head, studying him. "No, you're not."

Don't look too closely. Gabriel looked away. "I'll make an appointment with the Iranian consul and ask for an expedited visa. It would help if I told the consul we're engaged."

"That's fine."

He picked up the remote control and turned on the news. Enlarged on the TV screen were his and Noor's pictures.

Noor gasped.

CHAPTER THIRTY-FOUR

"*A confidential source revealed that the man and woman in the photo are prime suspects in the shootings at the Bastille Square. The man is American writer Gabriel McKnight. The woman is an American by the name of Noor Rahman.*" A phone number was listed below the pictures, asking anyone who has seen the couple to call the police.

Gabriel grabbed the clues and shoved some essentials into his backpack. "Put on your disguise and grab your passport. We have to leave now!" He grabbed the ball cap, cursing inwardly while he waited for Noor to change.

She changed in short time and joined him.

"We'll leave through the back door."

They passed through the hotel's courtyard to a small exit at the northeast corner. It opened into a small alley at the far end of Christine Street. Police sirens echoed in the alley. Multiple squad cars parked by the hotel.

"Stay calm," Gabriel whispered.

They stopped by a gift shop and checked the displays. Two men in suits passed by them, checking the area.

Gabriel spotted the bulge of their guns. He tightened his hold on Noor's arm.

The men spoke in French. "Does the woman know anything?"

"I don't know," the second one answered. "We keep them alive."

Noor's gaze met his, and she raised her brows.

"Later," he mouthed and steered her toward the nearest metro station.

Her chin trembled. "Were those men police officers?"

The furrows in Gabriel's brow deepened. "I don't think so."

"Where do we go now?"

He handed two tickets to the conductor. "We'll get off at the next station and go to an internet café. I'll find something on Airbnb."

TWO HOURS LATER, Gabriel and Noor arrived at the Montmartre village. Montmartre was a village built on an iconic hill in Paris. It held narrow cobblestone streets that wound around a hill. Apartments, cafés, gift shops, art galleries, and museums lined the entire area. The crown jewel in Montmartre was the iconic Sacre-Coeur church. The church sat atop the hill with a panoramic view of the city. It contrasted with the bohemian atmosphere surrounding it.

Gabriel and Noor took a narrow road up the hill to a three-story building sitting between a bakery and an art gallery.

Gabriel glanced at his phone. "This is it." He tapped the electronic code installed outside of the building, and the front door swung open.

At the top floor, Gabriel punched the code in the code key and entered the apartment. The place was roomy and furnished in bright colors. A wide window offered a generous view of Paris. The church stood to their right.

Noor sank into the couch and pulled her wig off.

He crouched in front of her. "How are you holding up?"

"I'll let you know when my heart slows down." She ran a hand through her hair. "Are we safe here?"

"Yes."

Her mouth curved into a humorless smile. "This stuff is more appealing in books."

"We must travel to Iran." Gabriel checked his watch. "We're meeting a friend of your uncle's in an hour. We'll get new IDs and take the first flight to Dubai. We'll travel as Iranian nationals."

CHAPTER THIRTY-FIVE

Shiraz Rahman's Journal
Tehran, August 10, 1978
I love to read before twilight during those brief moments when the sun and darkness meet like secret lovers. This is my escape.

Think positive. That's my mantra. For the thousandth time I have imagined a future with Parviz.

"Wherever you are, it must be wonderful."

I opened my eyes. "Parviz! You're home early." I jumped up to greet him.

He pulled me into his arms. "I missed you."

"I missed you, too." I turned my face into his shoulder, breathing the scent of aftershave and what I can only name as the love of my life —my soulmate.

His gazed dipped down to mine. "I want to talk to you."

The slight hitch in his voice indicated his worry. My heart sank. I knew what was coming. I didn't want to hear it. I didn't want to consider it.

The sky was dark now, dark as my mood. The lights illuminating the walking trails glowed in the night, and the scent of night blooming jasmine lingered in the air.

Parviz led me to the gazebo and sat on one of its stone benches, pulling me down beside him. "We can't avoid talking about this. You know what's happening to our country. I want to make sure you and the baby are safe."

I leaned close to him. "We'll be safe with you."

"You're alone most of the time. I can't protect you when I'm not home."

Parviz told me the Shah didn't want to take military action. He planned on sending out a national broadcast, hoping it would stop the riots.

"Do you agree with the King's strategy?" I asked.

Parviz's jaw tightened. "He's our king. I'll support his decisions."

I know my husband. I know what the tightening of his jaw means. "Do you think the riots will settle without military intervention?"

He massaged his neck. "No, baby, I don't."

"I'm not leaving you! I won't do it!" I wiped at the tears trickling down my cheeks, knowing it was a futile effort. Parviz is close to the king. The revolutionaries would hurt me and the baby to get to him. I hate being his weakness. I told him as much.

He cupped my face with his hands. "You're not my weakness. You're my soul, and I'll protect it with everything I've got."

I couldn't control my sobs. "I want to stay with you!"

Parviz had promised he wouldn't ask me to leave the country unless he felt there was a real threat. In return, he wanted me to trust his judgement and leave when he deemed it necessary.

"What about you?" I tried not to shout, but fear clawed at my insides. "What will you do while I'm away?"

"I have training for this." He sounded so damned calm. "I can't focus on my job if I worry for you and the baby."

I hated his logic. I hated that he was right. I hated there were no other options, and what I hated most was that he needed this from me. I had to find the courage to leave without him. It pierced my soul to concede, but I did.

Parviz visibly relaxed. "Thank you. I've made plans for you and the baby."

I threw myself into in his arms, knowing our days were numbered. "I love you."

"And I you," he whispered, holding me tight.

TEHRAN, *September 1, 1978*

My family and friends have left Iran. Mom and Dad are in Spain. Roshi left for New York. Leila took a flight to London. She didn't want to go, but Cameron and Parviz insisted she leave. Cameron leaves in a few days. Moira, Carl, and the twins departed for America last week. Tyler, Mina, and Jonathan will be on tomorrow's flight.

For me, the days pass in a blur. The highlights are the precious moments I have with Parviz. They're brief and poignant like the twilight.

TEHRAN, *September 8, 1978*

I must leave the country. My flight for Paris leaves this evening. My tears flow freely. I can't help it. This is my home. I belong here with Parviz.

Breakfast was a dismal affair. Neither one of us made conversation. After breakfast, we took a walk. I looked over the gardens. They were my heaven and our sanctuary. I wondered if I'd be home in time to watch Tehran dress itself in fall colors.

When we arrived at the gazebo, Parviz pulled me into his arms. "I want you to know that this is hard for me, too. Let's take advantage of the time we have together and turn it into a pleasant memory, one that will carry us through the next few weeks."

How could I argue with that? I lay my head on his shoulder, taking comfort in the moment.

"General! General Rahman." Mrs. Asaad's voice brought us back to reality. She joined us, panting. "There's an urgent call for you."

In the blink of an eye, Parviz transformed from a lover to a soldier. He strode inside. I followed him to his study. He motioned for me to shut the door and picked up the phone.

"Rahman." His eyes hardened. Whatever had happened was not good. "I'll send troops over to help." He hung up. "That was General Oveisi. The riots have escalated to where he's enforced a military curfew. The curfew went into effect for Tehran and eleven cities."

Hope blossomed in my chest. "Does that mean I won't be leaving?"

"No, baby, you will have your own general escorting you to the airport."

Someone knocked on the study door.

"Come in," Parviz called out.

A sergeant stepped inside. "I've brought the daily reports, sir."

Parviz took the file. "Thank you, leave it here."

Parviz receives security reports for the vault twice a day. Very few people know about the vault, and only the king, Parviz, and two advisors know what's in the vault.

I sank into one of the study chairs as Parviz reviewed the reports.

Parviz flipped the pages, then went back to the first page, frowned, and read it again.

I leaned forward. "What's wrong?"

"I don't know." He stroked my cheek. "I must leave for a while. I will check the high-risk areas and the Central Bank. We'll leave for the airport after that. Will you be okay while I'm gone?"

"I'll be fine."

He kissed my forehead. "Try to eat something. You barely touched your breakfast."

I accompanied him to the front door and wrapped my arms around him. I poured everything I felt into a kiss.

Parviz raised his head and smiled. "I'll be back in no time."

"Stay safe," I whispered.

∼

NOOR POURED herself a cup of tea and stared at the view of the Sacre Coeur. She knew how that day had ended. Her heart ached. Mom had been so young and courageous. Mom had shouldered the pain and raised her.

Memories of her childhood were warm and comforting. Mom was funny and kind. She hadn't allowed the past to dim the time they had together. Noor's life had been full of light. *Until someone from Mom's past extinguished it eighteen years later.*

She swiped at her tears, angry at her own weakness. "I'll find the killer."

CHAPTER THIRTY-SIX

Gabriel exited the small park in the eighteenth arrondissement. Paris looked magnificent in the morning. Heck, Paris was always magnificent. One could compare this area to New York's village. The atmosphere was a mix of bohemian and authentic. Under different circumstances, he'd enjoy exploring his surroundings. He wondered if Noor would come to Paris with him when all this was over and stopped himself. *Noor has her own life. We're not a couple.*

Gabriel's bright mood evaporated. He shoved his hands in his pockets and stalked down the hill to the Place Pigalle. He needed dark contacts for his trip to Tehran.

He stopped by a newspaper stand to buy a paper when he heard a hissing sound.

Vzzt. A man fell to the ground several feet to his right. A red stain blossomed on his chest.

Gunshots! Gabriel ducked behind the newspaper stand. He noticed the fallen man had the same height and build he did. He also wore the same color shirt. *Someone mistook him for me!*

"*Mon Dieu!*" the newspaper vendor cried, pointing at the

injured man. Several people, including a police officer, rushed toward the stand.

Gabriel moved to the other side of the stand, searching for the threat.

Another bullet struck the side of the newspaper stand. The vendor shrieked and ran out of the stand toward the main boulevard.

"Wait!" Gabriel called. The fool ran into the Clichy boulevard as a truck came barreling down the road. The truck was going to hit him. The driver swerved the vehicle away from the vendor and crashed into a group of cars parked twenty feet away from him. Smoke and flames burst forward.

A deafening *boom* followed. People bellowed and ran in all directions. A police car skidded to a halt. Armed police officers jumped out of the car.

Vzzt. A man on Gabriel's left hit the ground.

Gabriel dashed to a nearby car and crouched behind it to stay out of the shooter's range. Smoke rose high, creating a thin mist around them. Taking advantage of the distraction, Gabriel sprinted to the metro station and onto an oncoming train.

He exited at the Mirabeau station and threw his burner phone into the first trashcan. Scanning the area to make sure no one followed him, he hailed a cab, then stopped at another metro station. He repeated this several times until he was certain he was safe.

An hour later, Gabriel stopped at a clothing store and bought a new shirt. He pulled it over his own shirt and added a pair of sunglasses to his ensemble. He purchased another burner phone and dialed a number.

Sheila answered on the second ring.

"I need your help," Gabriel panted.

"Are you all right, sweetness?" Sheila's silky voice oozed concern.

"Yes."

"I thought you were looking for Michael," Sheila admonished.

"I am." Gabriel massaged his neck. "The information Mike left me led to—"

"Miss Rahman," Sheila finished. *"Her uncle called me."*

Gabriel stiffened. "You know Morris?"

Sheila snorted. *"I know Morris and Morris's employer."*

"What did they want?"

Sheila tsk-tsked. *"I'm not one to kiss and tell, however, I'll make an exception in this case. Morris wanted to ensure that you and Miss Rahman enter and exit Iran safely. They may have mentioned Turkey."* Sheila paused. *"Miss Rahman is lovely by the way."*

Gabriel stiffened. "Are you in Paris?"

Sheila laughed. *"Sheila is everywhere."* She paused. *"I've accepted Morris's request."*

"Thank you."

Sheila snorted. *"I'd have kept an eye on you anyway. We all root for the hero, and in this case, the heroine."*

Gabriel gritted his teeth. "I'm no hero. You of all people know that."

"Do I?" Sheila murmured. Silence stretched for several moments. She sighed. *"Be careful, Gabriel."* She disconnected the call.

Gabriel knew Noor was safe, yet he felt a sudden urge to get back to her. He took a cab to the foot of the Montmartre hill, knowing it was best to walk up to the apartment. Parisian traffic was atrocious.

He dashed through the winding streets and didn't stop till he arrived at the apartment. He found Noor in the living room. She stood by the window, clutching her mother's journal to her chest.

The tightness in his chest loosened. He exhaled and took two steps toward her. He froze when he saw her expression. "What's wrong?"

Her eyes were rimmed with red. "You were right. Leila was right. My father guarded the vault. Something happened the day

Dad died. Dad received a report and went to check on the bank." Her voice quivered. "He never came back."

Gabriel pulled her into his arms, gaining comfort even as he gave it.

They stood like that for several minutes until Noor sighed and pulled away. "How did your meeting at the embassy go?"

He pursed his lips, wondering how to answer. Best to go with the truth. "I ran into trouble."

She stiffened, and her gaze jumped to his. "What happened?"

Gabriel told her about the shooting.

Noor blanched. "Oh, God." Concern darkened her eyes. "Go home. I'll go to Iran and follow the leads. I promise I'll call you if I find anything related to your brother."

The warmth he had no name for burst from his stomach and went to his chest. He leaned his forehead against hers. "We've come this far. We'll finish it together." He rushed on before she could protest. "A friend of mine will help me leave Iran if we run into trouble." He paused, uncertain how to continue. "Your uncle knows my friend."

"Really?" Noor's eyes lit with curiosity.

Gabriel rubbed his neck. How to explain? "Sit down, and I'll tell you about my friend."

She acquiesced, waiting for him to continue.

He raked a hand through his hair. "I met my friend Sheila when I was in the military. A group of extremists murdered everyone in Sheila's village. Mike and I were searching for survivors when we found Sheila. We took her to the nearest base hospital. By some miracle, she survived and began a resistance against the extremists who hurt women and girls in the Middle East. In time, she gained more power and autonomy. Today, Sheila is a powerful force of justice in the region."

"Wow, she sounds amazing."

Gabriel shoved his hands in his pockets. "The thing is, Sheila doesn't care about laws, and her methods aren't always orthodox. She will save and avenge the innocent, end of story."

Noor raised a brow.

He forced himself to continue. "Few people have heard Sheila's voice, let alone seen her." He stopped and faced her. "Your uncle hired Sheila to ensure we have protection in Iran and Turkey."

Her gaze met his. "Do you trust this Sheila?"

"Yes."

Noor exhaled. "If you and Uncle Morrie trust her, I will, too."

"Sheila was already keeping tabs on us," Gabriel said. "It's her way of making sure we're safe."

She watched him with a gleam in her eyes. "She's protective of you."

Gabriel grunted.

Noor tilted her head. "Why is she protective of you?"

Gabriel bit back a sigh. He should've known she wouldn't let it go. "Sheila believes she owes me her life."

Her eyes took on a gentle glow. "You saved her."

Gabriel clenched his jaw. "I dragged her broken body to the hospital. The doctors saved her."

Her eyes widened. She stood and approached him, her eyes brimming with curiosity.

Gabriel held his breath and waited for the barrage of questions.

When she spoke, her voice was low. "When do we leave for Iran?"

The tightness in his chest loosened. He exhaled. "This afternoon."

CHAPTER THIRTY-SEVEN

"What is separated from its essence longs to return to its source for reunion."
—*Rumi's Masnavi (Rassouli, 2015)*

TEHRAN, IRAN

Noor's eyes fluttered open. A ray of sunlight filtered through the opening of the curtains. It took a few seconds to remember where she was. *Tehran!*

She checked her watch. It was ten in the morning. Scrambling out of bed, she drew the curtains. Sunlight poured into the room from floor to ceiling windows. To her left, the Alborz Mountains surrounded the city like warriors guarding a fortress. Their snowy peaks and rocky terrains soared into the sky. An enormous metropolis rippled from the foot of the mountains and flowed into an endless sea of modern high rises, bridges, and highways. Large patches of green, which she assumed were parks, stood out between the structures. *Manhattan meets the Middle East.*

She showered, changed, and went to find Gabriel. She found him in the terrace.

He stood by the railing, silhouetted against the mountains. His jeans hung loose on his hips. The T-shirt he wore outlined the sleek muscles of his back and arms, and his feet were bare. Face upturned, his attention centered on the mountains. His hands clenched and unclenched the railing. She paused, not wanting to intrude.

As if sensing her presence, Gabriel turned. She caught the fervent flare in his eyes before his expression turned blank.

She smiled and slid the door open. "Good morning."

"Good morning." He glanced up at the mountains. "It's beautiful, isn't it?"

"Yes, it is," she agreed.

"I never forgot this city with its noise and vibrant culture. I never forgot the tree-lined avenues or the scent of Persian Jasmine. And these mountains." His hold tightened on the railing. "Coming back after all these years is bittersweet and incredible." A gentle smile broke across his face like sunrise brightening a landscape .

She wanted to reach out and touch him but didn't know how he'd react. "I understand how you feel. Many would think it strange, but I get it."

His brow wrinkled. "Why? People say they love Italy, or France, or Bermuda. Why would it be different to love Tehran? Loving a country or a culture has nothing to do with politics."

She held her palms up in a gesture of surrender. "Agreed, however, the rest of the world has this image of a country that looks like something from a dystopian novel, populated with a bunch of killers."

Gabriel snorted. "They don't know Iran."

She laughed and nudged him. "Do you want to show me Tehran?"

His eyes twinkled. "Yes. You'll love it."

≈

GABRIEL PULLED out a chair for Noor. It wasn't like him to bare his soul. He didn't know why he'd blurted out what he'd just said. What was it about Noor that made him expose himself?

The terrace door slid open. The housekeeper bid them good morning and carried trays of food to the terrace table. There were platters of freshly baked Persian bread, an assortment of cheese, cutlets, dulmeh, and various pastries.

He picked up a slice of bread known as Barbari and bit into it. *Mmm, delicious.*

Noor thanked the housekeeper. "This is a lovely apartment."

The housekeeper beamed. "Yes. The master likes to keep it in top shape. He remodeled the building last year."

"Master?" Gabriel prompted, wondering if the master was Morris's employer.

The housekeeper bowed her head. "Please let me know if there's anything I can get for you." She retreated to the apartment.

He hadn't expected an answer and let it go for now.

Noor forked a dulmeh onto her plate. "What are you thinking?"

"I was thinking Tehran would be a good place for Mike to stay under the radar."

"Oh? Where would he hide?"

Gabriel picked up another slice of bread. "I don't know." He glanced at his watch. "Are you ready to venture out?"

"Yes. Where are we going?"

"First, we go to the Central Bank. They offer daily tours of the national jewelry collection. Then, we find your mother's friend, Ash."

Noor reached for her cell phone. "I have the number for his gallery. I'll call him this afternoon. There's someone else who can give us information. My parents' former housekeeper, Missus Asaad, kept in touch with Mom throughout the years. She and I have exchanged the usual postcard or two every year. I don't have her phone number, but I have her address."

"Great, we'll check on her, too." Gabriel glanced at her. "You'll need a long shirt and a shawl to cover your hair."

Her smile faltered. "I know. I'll wear the linen shirt and shawl I wore last night. We can buy something more appropriate at a store." She rushed inside to grab the shirt and shawl.

The Islamic Republic of Iran required women to wear form covering trousers or skirts with loose long sleeve shirts that reach below the thigh, and a shawl to cover the hair.

Noor came back wearing a long forest green shirt over her jeans. She placed the shawl over her head and fidgeted with the scarf, tying it securely under her chin. Her hands shook.

He took her hand. "There's no reason to be afraid. I've done my research. You'll be fine."

She cleared her throat. "I'm just nervous."

"I'll be with you the whole time. Have faith in Aquaman."

His quip made her smile. "I do."

The apartment was situated on a steep road like the roads one sees in San Francisco. They walked downhill and turned into the main boulevard. Businesses and shopping centers lined the entire boulevard. People rushed about with their daily routines, modern buildings rose into the sky, and traffic was heavy.

Noor's gazed jumped from building to store to the population milling about. A group of women passed them, chatting happily. A slow smile spread across her face. "The women have taken the Islamic garb and turned it into a fashion statement. They look stunning."

Gabriel squeezed her hand. "Just like you."

They arrived at a shopping center made of steel pipes and colored glass. Sleek with smooth lines and curves, the structure contrasted with the craggy mountains in the background. Curious, they went inside to explore. Bronze sculptures stood on the main floor of the shopping center. A line of shops circled around the sculptures.

Noor stopped by a bakery and pointed to a chocolate éclair. "Do you want to split one of those?"

He grinned and followed her into the bakery. "Sure."

They hailed a cab at the intersection. The cab passed by a modern-looking bridge, crossing an intersection. The bridge held several levels.

Noor's eyes brightened. "That's the famous Tabiat bridge. It's won several global awards."

Gabriel knew about the bridge. At eight hundred and ninety feet, it connected two parks by spanning a large highway. The bridge's curved path had three levels connected via ramps and stairs. "We'll come visit it someday," he promised.

The cab wound through traffic and arrived at a large stone structure with wide pillars gracing its front entrance.

"The Central Bank," the driver announced.

Gabriel paid the driver. "We go this way."

Noor climbed out of the cab and stood rooted to the ground, her face ashen.

Gabriel scanned the area for signs of threat. What's wrong?"

Her voice shook. "My father died here."

Ah hell! He lowered his voice. "I'm sorry. I should've come alone. I'll take you back to the apartment."

"No," she whispered. "I need a minute. I didn't expect it to affect me. After all, I never met my father."

Gabriel's protective instincts were riding him, yet he recalled the promise he'd made in Paris. Compromise was his new mantra. He shoved his hands in his pockets. "He was your father. You didn't have to meet him to care. If this becomes too much, tell me, and we'll leave."

She nodded, rubbing her palms over her jeans.

They entered the building together. The main floor over-flowed with visitors, tourists, and customers. Signs directed them to the museum. They entered a corridor after purchasing the tickets and stood in line to enter the museum's vaults.

Gabriel handed the attendant their tickets.

The attendant beamed. "Mister Michael, you're back."

Noor stiffened.

Gabriel's heart thudded like he'd run a marathon.

The attendant shoved his hands in his pockets. "I told you it would take a few weeks to have the globe and Darya-e-Noor cleaned. You came back in time to see it. It arrived yesterday."

Gabriel glanced at the man's name tag. "Thank you, Mister Mohammedi. I look forward to seeing both pieces."

Mr. Mohammedi straightened his cap. "Would you like another private tour? Our guide is here today."

"Yes, I brought my fiancé with me."

"I'll call Mister Kamali. He was your guide last time." Mr. Mohammedi greeted Noor. "A private tour doesn't mean you go into the vaults alone. You'll have a personal tour guide while you enter the vault with other visitors."

Noor cleared her throat. "I see, thank you for explaining."

"Mister Kamali is the best guide." The attendant picked the phone up and dialed an extension. "He'll be here in a minute."

Noor lowered her voice. "Your brother is alive."

"He was alive a few weeks ago, which increases the odds of him being alive today." Gabriel pursed his lips. "I wonder what he was looking for?"

A lanky man with dark hair and doe-like eyes approached them. He shook hands with Gabriel. "Mister Michael, welcome back."

"Thank you. I brought my fiancé with me this time."

The young man bowed his head. "Please follow me."

CHAPTER THIRTY-EIGHT

"If you walk without sight, it's an error,
Yet leaning on sight is a failure.
You seek monastery and school through convention,
How will you find what's not a location?"
—*Rumi*

Mr. Kamali led them down the stairs to a spacious underground vault. Dozens of mahogany tables sat in neat rows. Rectangular glass cases stood mounted over them. Each case held a historical piece encrusted with priceless jewels. Crowns, necklaces, earrings, dishes, and swords gleamed under the overhead lights.

Gabriel and Noor stopped by the first crown.

"This is the Pahlavi crown," the guide said. "Reza Shah used it for his coronation in April 1926. His son, Mohammad Reza Pahlavi, also wore it during his coronation in 1967."

Gabriel marveled at the craftsmanship and beauty of the pieces. He'd seen pictures of the Shah's coronation. Dad had attended the event.

The next piece was a long handle with a circular end.

Noor leaned closer to the case. "Is that a mace?"

Mr. Kamali nodded. "Yes, it's the Royal Mace of Iran. It's encrusted with diamonds from end to end. The largest diamond is the one at the top. It was Fat'h Ali Shah Qajar's favorite. You'll see him carrying it in several of the portraits down the hall."

Gabriel wandered through the vault, assessing its security systems. The main vault was a combination of several connecting vaults that created one large exhibition area. Dents of what used to be sliding doors marred the spaces in between the exhibits.

Mr. Kamali stopped by a case and beamed. "You missed this last time."

They approached a large diamond mounted on an elaborate frame surmounted by the lion and sun.

"The Darya-e-Noor is one of the largest diamonds in the world, estimated to be one hundred and eighty-six carats." Mr. Kamali circled the case. "Nader Shah brought the diamond from India in 1739. It's set with a frame of four hundred and fifty-seven diamonds and four rubies."

Gabriel studied the display. The diamond was about three inches long and two inches wide. "Incredible." *Why are you interested in this diamond, Mike?*

The guide pointed to another piece. "Here's another impressive piece that was missing last time. This is a geographic globe. At 5.3 kilograms, its stand is pure gold. Fifty-one thousand and three hundred and sixty-six gems cover it. Emeralds show the oceans and seas. Look here." Mr. Kamali pointed at a section of the globe. "Diamonds mark Iran, and rubies mark Europe. Ruby and garnet display North and South America and Australia. Two simple golden lines inlaid with diamonds mark the equator. The lines cross and encompass the globe."

Gabriel noticed a scratch mark on the glass case beside the globe and leaned it for a better view. Someone had tried to get to the globe.

He'd seen a globe like this in a museum in eastern Europe. He gripped Noor's arm and lowered his voice. "Go to the restroom."

Noor nodded and paused. "Mister Kamali, where are the restrooms?"

"Outside the vault toward your left."

"I'll come with you." Gabriel followed her out of the vault.

Once they were out of earshot, he pulled her aside. "The globe we just saw can be opened. I need to see what's inside it."

Her eyes widened. "Why?"

"There are scratches on its glass casing. Mike was interested in the globe. It's important." He checked to make sure no one was nearby. "The museum has several types of security. There are cameras at three of the four corners of the vault. The doors and exits have alarms, and the glass cases have motion detectors. I'll bet each exhibit piece also has a motion detector underneath it."

"Then how in God's name are you going to check the globe?" Noor whispered, wringing her hands.

"I'll create a diversion by tripping the guide. He'll bump into the glass case. That will set off the motion detectors outside of the glass case and under the globe. The alarms will go off. Most vault doors are programmed to close when the alarms go off. When the vault doors shut, we'll be in the vault with the visitors and security personnel. It takes the average security team two to three minutes to assess the threat and reset the motion detectors. Security will remove the glass casing to reset the motion detector under the exhibit. That's when I'll open the globe."

The fine lines around Noor's eyes tightened. "What if there aren't any motion detectors under the glass case?"

Gabriel massaged his neck. "I don't know. I haven't planned that far." He rushed on before she could protest. "This is our best chance at getting the globe."

She bit her lip. "Fine, what do you need me to do?"

Part of him wanted her to go back to the apartment where she'd be safe. The rational side of him knew Noor could help.

Gabriel raked a hand through his hair. "When I reach for the globe, I'll be standing at a certain angle. Stand in front of me so the cameras don't catch me touching the globe. I'll have a short window. The timing must be right."

Noor blew out a breath. "Okay, let's do this."

They went back to the vault. "Mister Kamali,"—Noor motioned to Gabriel—"my fiancé and I have a question. I told him Iran was a diamond on the globe. He insists that it's a ruby. Which is it?"

Mr. Kamali chuckled. "It's a diamond. A famous ruby called Orange-Zib marks Tehran. Here, let me show you." He led them to the globe.

Several visitors heard the comment and approached the exhibit.

Gabriel stuck out his foot. A bulky man tripped and bumped into the guide. Mr. Kamali stumbled and bumped into the glass casing of the globe.

Several things happened at the same time. The screech of an ear-piercing siren filled the vault. Lights flashed on and off, making it hard to see, the vault doors slammed shut, and the security personnel ran toward the exhibit.

One guard checked the exhibit, while another one pulled the man who bumped into Mr. Kamali aside and searched him.

"I-I don't know what happened," the man stammered. "I tripped over someone by mistake."

The last guard swept through the vaults, checking for threats.

Mr. Kamali turned pale. His voice rose over the alarms. "Please stay calm. Everything is all right. The alarms will soon turn off."

Visitors covered their ears, while others covered their eyes from the constant blare of the lights.

A guard spoke into his mouthpiece. "It was a false alarm." The guard paused. "Got it. We'll reset the motion detectors. Once it's done, you can open the doors and reset the lights." The guard's voice boomed over the crowd. "Everyone, please stand back."

Blink, blink, blink, the lights flashed, and dub, dub, dub, Gabriel's heart pounded. His body vibrated with tension. He counted the seconds as the crowd moved back. Two guards lifted the glass case.

Gabriel reached into his pocket and pulled out a stone he'd picked up in front of the apartment. He threw the stone to the floor at the exact moment the guards lifted the glass casing.

A woman shrieked. "A diamond fell off the globe. It rolled under there." She pointed toward the exhibit north of the globe.

Two guards and several people moved toward the north of the globe, blocking one of the security cameras. Mr. Kamali and several others stood by the south and east sides of the globe, blocking the other security cameras. The west side of the globe stood open.

Sweat trickled down Gabriel's back. Time slowed, and his vision gained the kind of clarity that reminded him of his military days. He nudged Noor.

She followed him to the vacant side of the globe and blocked the last camera.

Ignoring the rapid thud thud in his chest, Gabriel reached for the globe. Unable to see the equator line, he ran his hands along the globe's mid-section. *Aha.* He found a dent and pushed.

The top half of the globe slid aside. A piece of paper sat at its center. He snatched it and tucked the sheet under his shirt. Pleased his hands were steady, Gabriel replaced the globe and casing, then rushed to Mr. Kamali, who was wringing his hands and muttering to himself.

The guards found the stone Gabriel had thrown. The shorter of the two picked it up. "It's just a rock."

The guards moved back to the exhibit. Pulling gloves from their side belts, they gently lifted the globe, while the third guard adjusted the motion sensor. Once the glass casing was in place, the lights stopped flashing, and the alarms went silent. Visitors sighed with relief.

It didn't take long for the vault doors to open. Gabriel and Noor followed the visitors outside.

Mr. Kamali's voice shook. "I'm sorry you had a negative experience. You didn't even finish your tour." The guide wrung his hands. "This has never happened."

"Don't worry about it. We'll come back another time." Gabriel tipped the guide, thanking him for the tour.

Outside, he hailed a cab. Neither he nor Noor spoke during the drive back to the apartment.

CHAPTER THIRTY-NINE

"Incredible." Gabriel studied every detail in the document. Noor leaned over his shoulder. "What is it?"

"It's a floor plan of the Central Bank. The artifacts and documents your father guarded were in here. Look." He pointed to the floor plan. "The vault is at the end of a corridor in the bank's basement. There's a lever behind a door. Pull the lever, and the wall moves aside. The interior is lined with shelves. Someone circled the six shelves in the western corner. Whatever was on those shelves was important."

Noor rubbed her temples. "Here's what I don't understand. Mom claimed a guest at her birthday party murdered my father. How can it be if none of the guests knew he was guarding the vault?"

Gabriel snapped photos of the floor plan. "You're assuming none of the guests knew about the vault. Someone in that party knew about the vault. Someone followed him there and killed him." He placed all the clues on the dining room table in chronological order. "There are two time-lapses in our chronology of events. The first is the time lapse between the Iranian revolution and your mother's death. The Iranian revolution took place in

1979. Your mother died in 1997. Why wait eighteen years to kill your mother?"

"I think I have the answer." Noor turned her laptop toward him. "The treasury of national jewels shut down after the revolution. They opened it to the public in 1997. That can't be a coincidence, can it?"

"No, it's not a coincidence." Gabriel rubbed his neck. "The next time lapse is from 1997 to 2019. That's when Asra Madison and Mike worked together. Something sparked Mike's interest in your family's history. We also have three clues we haven't figured out yet—the rose your mother brought from her home in Tehran, the photo of your parents with another Rumi poem, and the postcard of Konya, Turkey. We'll know more when we figure out what the clues mean. We should go visit your parents' home."

"The old house has been turned into a museum. I'll check the museum's visiting hours." Noor yawned and stretched. "I ordered kebobs with salad for dinner. I spotted a bakery down the road this morning. I'll get fresh lavash for dinner. The walk will do me good."

A streak of cold traveled from his stomach to his chest. He didn't want to name or examine the emotion. Not meeting her eye, he scribbled on a notepad. "We have bread left from this morning."

"There's nothing like fresh lavash. I'll be back in no time."

He grabbed her arm. "I'd rather you stayed here."

Her brows rose. "Why? You said no one followed us back here."

He gritted his teeth and prayed for patience. "If you want fresh bread, I'll accompany you."

"Are you accompanying me because you want to take a walk, or is it because you're worried something will happen to me?"

He raked a hand through his hair. "What's wrong with being safe?"

Her eyes flashed. "There's nothing wrong with being safe."

"Then what's the problem?"

She threw her hands in the air. "The problem is you think I'm a helpless person who can't go to a bakery on her own. It's down the road, Gabriel."

"I—"

She didn't let him finish. "This partnership won't work if you can't trust me to be on my own for a few minutes." Her chin rose into what he'd come to know as Noor's "I'm not gonna budge" look.

He sighed. "Take the burner phone."

She nodded and reached for the manteau and scarf. "I'll be back in fifteen minutes."

Noor took the route by the park. The sun had descended behind the mountains. Bright lights lit the park's walking paths. The sounds of urban traffic and the call to prayer mingled in the background, while a warm wind carried the scents of freshly cut grass and summer flowers.

Her thoughts went back to the clues Mom had left. Why was the white rose significant? Why had Mom not told her the truth? She arrived at the bakery and placed her order.

A beaming salesclerk placed the fresh bread into a bag and handed it to her. To her surprise, Gabriel waited for her outside of the bakery. She wanted to admonish him, yet the summer breeze had ruffled his hair, and his aquamarine eyes twinkled, making her heart do a little dance.

She sighed. "I'm glad you came. The weather is lovely."

He gave her a lopsided grin. "I took a break."

She wondered if she'd ever get used to that knee buckling McKnight smile.

Gabriel held out his hands. "Let me take the bread."

She tore off a piece of the bread and handed him the bag. "I do like fresh lavash."

He tore a piece of the bread and bit into it. "Mm. It's delicious."

Noor stood back, taking in the large metropolis. Someday she would explore the city. Heck, she could tour the entire country. The honk of a vehicle snapped her out of her reverie. A car flew down the road and headed straight toward them. The vehicle wasn't slowing down.

Gabriel pulled her aside before the car could knock them off the road. "Careful," he chided.

She stiffened. The touch was unfamiliar. She searched his face, and her eyes widened. "Oh my God. You're not Gabriel, you're Michael!"

A gleam entered Michael McKnight's eyes and his mouth curved upward. "I apologize for the deception, Miss Rahman. Please try not to look surprised. Someone could be watching us."

She forced her features into a neutral expression.

Michael grinned. "That's better. It's good to know my brother can make a lasting impression on a beautiful woman."

She ignored the compliment. "Gabriel and your family have been worried. Why haven't you contacted them?"

Michael scanned the road, then turned back to her. "It's for their own safety. Is Gabe at the apartment?"

"Yes."

He quirked an eyebrow. "Shall we go then?"

She nodded numbly and followed Michael up the steep road. "What do you mean it's for their safety?"

His eyes twinkled. "Uh uh, not until you tell me all about your adventures with Gabe."

"I wouldn't know where to start," she muttered.

Michael pursed his lips in a gesture similar to Gabriel's. "I'd say start at the beginning, but that's such a cliché. Start where you like."

"Okay, how about this? Once upon a time there were these identical twins. One of them showed up on my doorstep pretending to be his brother. He told me he was writing a series, which was not true. In fact, everything he told me was fictitious."

Michael raised his fist in the air. "Right on! I owe you another apology, Miss Rahman. In my defense, my intentions were altruistic. A government agent seeking you out would attract unwanted attention. A writer talking to an editor, there's nothing unusual about that, is there?"

She bit her lip. "I guess you're right."

"I usually am." He grinned. "Am I forgiven?"

Noor bit back a smile. "Yes." She sighed. "You know, a lot has happened since you left. I don't know how I would have figured all this out without Gabriel. He's wonderful, intelligent, and unbelievably courageous."

"Gabriel, huh?" Michael's smile would have put the mischievous elves in one of her clients' novels to shame. "Tell me, Miss Rahman, has it been all business with Gabe? I know my brother's the solemn type, but there's no harm in mixing pleasure with business."

Noor shook her head in mock anger. "You're trouble, Michael McKnight."

"Me?" He feigned innocence. "Not at all."

They arrived at the apartment. The door swung open. "I'm sorry about—" Gabriel stopped short when he saw Michael. He blinked several times. His eyes filled with tears.

Michael dropped the bread on the console and stepped forward. The brothers embraced.

Noor felt her own eyes mist.

After what seemed like an eternity, Michael pulled back. "You got my message?"

Gabriel's voice was hoarse. "I did. What the hell have you gotten yourself into?" He held onto Michael's shoulder as if he was afraid Michael would disappear.

"It's a long story." Michael sniffed. "Do I smell kebobs?"

Gabriel nodded. "They delivered the food."

Michael rubbed his palms together. "We can talk while we eat."

Feeling like an intruder, Noor pasted a smile on her face. "I've ordered plenty of food. Why don't I set the table while you two catch up?" She turned toward the kitchen.

Gabriel took hold of her wrist. "We'll help you set the table."

She kept her smile firmly in place. "It's no trouble. Besides, you and Michael must have a lot to say to each other."

The lines around Gabriel's eyes tightened. He tugged on her wrist while his piercing blue gaze bore down on her. "There's nothing that can't be said in front of you."

Heat tickled her stomach and spread through her body. She stood on her toes and kissed his cheek. "Okay, let's set the table and talk while we eat." She ignored Michael's chuckle.

CHAPTER FORTY

For the first time in months, the cold dread in Gabriel's stomach vanished. Seeing Michael alive and well was like a release valve for the stress and worry of the past months. He hugged Mike more than once before they sat down to an assortment of kebobs and side dishes for dinner.

Gabriel studied his brother. "How did you find us?"

Michael bit into a kebab. "I have a friend who's good with information systems. My friend told me you were on a flight to Tehran. I followed you from the airport."

"Did you know Asra Madison is dead?"

Michael's eyes hardened. "Yes. How do you know about it?"

Gabriel told Michael about the night at Radio City Music Hall and Detectives Robin and Hood.

A ghost of a smile hovered at Michael's mouth. "Robin and Hood, huh?"

Knowing his brother's sense of humor, Gabriel stayed on the topic. "I met with your former director."

Michael's brows rose. "McMillan called you?"

"It was more a case of him summoning me," Gabriel said. He leaned forward. "What the hell is going on?"

Michael gave him a meaningful look.

Gabriel understood what his brother was asking. He nodded.

Michael studied Noor. "Gabe trusts you, so I'll speak in front of you. The information I'll share is highly confidential."

"I understand," Noor said.

He shifted in his seat. "Several months ago, I discovered a steady stream of confidential U.S. information was leaked to our enemies over the course of three decades. An initial investigation pointed to our intelligence and law enforcement agencies."

"Has a terrorist network found its way into our agencies?" Gabriel asked.

"That's what we initially believed. Jonathan assigned Asra and me to find the network. We discovered several leads. One led to a U.S. diplomat in Paris during the Yugoslavian war. Another one led to a U.S. consul in Egypt, and one lead pointed to Tehran just before the Islamic revolution. Asra and I dug into the Tehran leak. Intel revealed top secret information was sent by a fax line registered to Carl McKnight in October nineteen seventy-eight."

Gabriel narrowed his eyes. "Someone was framing Dad?"

"Yes. We looked closer and realized the other leads were also fake. The leaks came from someone who has access to triple zero security information."

"Did you narrow it down based on the agency codes?"

Michael nodded.

Gabriel filled Noor's glass with ice water. "Classified information lives in different security levels. Each level of security has its own serial number. When agencies want to access classified information, they enter a code. The code gives them clearance and access to the classified information. The codes also identify the agency and the person looking at the information. It's a security measure the government uses to monitor who from what agency accesses top secret data."

"I see," she said.

Mike piled his plate with kebobs. "We focused on the Iran

data leak. The informant had sent snippets of information for years. The information wasn't major, and there wasn't a specific time pattern. That changed the last six months of the Shah's regime. The traffic ballooned during that time. We deciphered two pieces of information. The first claimed that General Parviz Rahman was guarding a hidden vault in Tehran's Central Bank. The second piece of information said General Rahman had taken measures to hide what was in the vault. The informant sent details on one of the vault's artifacts to entice the buyer and requested a hefty sum of money."

Gabriel put his fork down. "What was it?"

"A diamond identical to the Darya-e-Noor," Michael said. "I knew Dad was innocent—"

"Wait." Noor touched Gabriel's arm. "I know your father is innocent, but how will you prove it?"

"Easily," Gabriel said. "Our family left Iran in August of 1978. The information sent from Dad's fax was dated October of the same year. Dad was back in Washington in October. Whoever tried to frame Dad was sloppy."

"That." Michael tapped his fingers on the table. "Or someone wanted to capture my attention. I cross-checked the triple zero security levels with our agents in Iran in 1978 and some of the other agencies."

"And?" Gabriel leaned forward.

"There are four people. All four work at CIU, and all four of them are senior level leaders. One of them is Jonathan."

Gabriel whistled.

Michael poured himself a glass of water. "Asra and I dug deeper and learned the informant was selling two pieces of information. The first was the whereabouts of the diamond identical to the Darya-e-Noor, and the second one was a highly confidential document impacting more than our national security." Michael paused. "I took personal time and traveled to Oklahoma City pretending I was you. I wanted to know if Noor knew about the vault. She didn't. When I got back, Asra left me a message. She'd found something important and wanted to meet with me." The furrows in Michael's brows deepened. "I went to the meeting place. Asra wasn't there. I went to her place and couldn't find her. That's when I called McMillan. I was on my way to your movie premiere when two thugs ambushed me."

Noor gasped.

Michael's lips curved into a humorless smile. "The thugs weren't a problem. We made someone nervous. I knew it wouldn't be long before the informant went after my family, so I went dark."

"Is that why you came to Iran?" Noor asked.

Michael grinned. "Beautiful and intelligent. The answer to your question is yes and no. I have two reasons to be in Iran. First, Tehran is a good place to go dark while I try to figure out who the mole in my organization is. The second reason is more complicated." Michael's gaze landed on Gabriel. "Did you get the floor plan from the globe?"

Gabriel smirked. "Yes. Why do you need it?"

"Back in the chaos of 1978, one of the Islamic revolutionaries infiltrated our embassy in Tehran and stole a highly classified document." Michael rubbed his chin. "General Rahman's team intercepted the document during one of their raids. General Rahman was a smart man. He knew the U.S. government would want the document back. He planned to use it as leverage in getting U.S. support against the revolutionaries. He hid the document in the vault." His solemn gaze shifted to Noor. "You father didn't die in some riot. Someone killed him to get to the vault."

Noor stared at her hands. "I know."

"The killer took the document, and it changed hands over the years. I know where it is, and it's in the wrong hands. The second reason I came to Tehran is to get the document." A wicked gleam entered Michael's eyes. "I'll need your help, brother."

"You'll have it."

Satisfied, Michael continued. "You guys probably know that General Rahman hid several of the vault's artifacts before he died."

"Gabriel and I believe that's the reason my mother was killed," Noor said.

Michael was about to say something, then stopped, unsure how to continue. He glanced at Gabriel.

Fury unfurled in Gabriel's stomach. He ground his teeth. "I won't let that happen."

Noor stared at him, then Michael, and back at him. "What are you talking about?"

Gabriel took hold of her hand. "Whoever killed your parents will come after you."

"What? Why?" Her brows furrowed. "I know nothing about the vault."

Gabriel squeezed her hand. When he spoke, his voice was gentle. "The killer doesn't know that. It makes you a target."

A dark blush covered Noor's cheeks. "Let the killer try. I'll be waiting."

Michael raised his fist in the air. "Hoorah!" He grinned. "It's my turn. I want to know what you two have been up to. And"—he motioned to Gabriel and Noor's clasped hands—"I want all the sordid details."

Ignoring the quip, Gabriel recounted everything since Michael's disappearance.

Michael listened without interruption. "Can I see the clues?"

Noor pulled the envelope out of her bag and handed it to him.

He studied each clue, then placed them on the table. "It's interesting your mother put the clues in Rumi's poems. There are many interpretations to his poetry." He tapped on the photo of Noor's parents. "I remember this place. Gabe and I used to swim in the pool when we visited. What happened to the house?"

"It's a museum," Gabriel said.

Michael drummed his fingers on the table. "You should go there. It's where it all started."

The telephone rang. Noor ran to answer it. The tone of her voice belayed her surprise. "It's Ash Kosha, Mom's friend. Mister Kosha would like us to attend a party at his home tomorrow night."

Michael straightened and bobbed his head.

Gabriel raised an eyebrow. Why was Mike interested in Kosha? "Tell Mister Kosha we'll be there."

Noor's eyes widened. She put her hand over the receiver. "Mister Kosha extends his invitation to Michael."

Michael bared his teeth. "I'll be there."

She confirmed Michael would be there and disconnected the call.

Gabriel crossed his arms over his chest. "Please explain."

Michael pursed his lips. "What do you know about Ash Kosha?"

"The basics. He was Shiraz Rahman's classmate and friend. Ash's father was a rich merchant. Ash took over the family business when his father died."

Michael chuckled. "That's the PG version. Ash's father ran a black market for artwork. When daddy died, Ash took over and branched out. Today, he runs the black market for art in the Middle East and Southeast Asia."

Things began to make sense, yet Gabriel didn't want to assume. "What does Ash Kosha have to do with you, brother?"

"Ash has the classified document I'm looking for, and I have something he wants badly." Michael rubbed his hands together. "Boys and girls, we are going to a party."

Gabriel glared at his brother. "What the hell are you talking about?"

Michael leaned forward. "Ash has agreed to hand over the classified document along with all of its copies as long as I give him the floor plan to the hidden vault."

Noor stiffened. "Why does Ash want to know where the hidden vault is?"

Gabriel snorted. "He probably wants to steal something from the vault."

"Not something," Michael interjected. "He wants the twin diamond to the Darya-e-Noor."

Noor gasped. "The diamond belongs to the people of Iran. That's unethical! It's wrong. It's—"

Michael held up his hands. "Hold on. I didn't say Ash will get what he wants." He clapped Gabriel's shoulder. "This is where you come in."

Gabriel nodded. "What do you need?"

Mike's eyes hardened. "I need you to switch places with me. You meet with Ash pretending to be me, while I secure the document."

"Fine, but why?" Gabriel persisted.

"For two reasons. One, Ash is greedy and crooked. He won't give me the original document. I'll break into his safe and steal it. And two, Ash has access to a very special device. It's an enhanced polygraph. He will insist I take the polygraph, and if I pass the test, he'll hand over the document. I know what he will ask, and it's not in our country's interest for Ash to have the answer. I may not pass the test." A Cheshire grin spread across Michael's face. "You don't know the answer to the question. You can take the polygraph and pass with flying colors."

Noor's eyes flashed with emotion. She clasped her hands. "Are you going to give Ash the blueprint?"

Gabriel squeezed her shoulder. "Mike won't do anything unethical. You can trust him."

Noor exhaled, and her shoulders relaxed.

Michael rose and leaned against the balustrade. "We need to plan for the party. Don't worry about clothes. I'll send something over for the both of you." He wiggled his brows. "Partying with the McKnights is an adventure, Miss Rahman."

CHAPTER FORTY-ONE

Noor stood in front of the mirror in the bedroom and studied her reflection. The dress Michael sent her was a silky emerald colored gown. The top half of her gown fit her like a second skin. The gown flared out just below her hips into a pool of fine sheer and silk stopping below her calves. The dress also had a slit on the side, showing a little more leg than she cared for. She let her hair down and applied makeup to her eyes. *This is as good as it gets.*

She knew they were after a killer, yet she wanted to look good for Gabriel. Her inner goddess demanded it. She picked up a manteau and scarf for the drive to Ash's house and went in search of Gabriel and Michael.

She found the brothers in the living room. They looked devastatingly handsome. Both wore matching dark suits. Gabriel had smoothed back his chocolate-colored hair from his face. Michael's hair was unruly. Gabriel's tie was sapphire blue. Michael's tie was silver. They were identical, yet she had no trouble telling them apart.

Both men stood when they saw her. Michael whistled.

Gabriel's warm gaze caressed her from head to foot, and his lips lifted into a smile.

Her pulse quickened, and her body tingled.

"You look stunning," Gabriel said.

"As do you," she replied in a husky voice.

His smiled. "Thank you."

Michael gestured to his face. "I'll say thank you, too, since Gabe and I have the same mug. Now remember, Ash will socialize first to make sure I'm Michael. Then, he'll ask for the polygraph test. We switch places before the polygraph, got it?"

Gabriel nodded.

He rubbed his hands together. "Let's go. We don't want to be late."

The gesture was familiar. Noor tried to recall where she'd seen it and couldn't remember. She let it go.

They drove to a large property west of Tehran. Most of the land was flat except for a large hill north of the property. A winding driveway led to a palatial white structure on top of the hill. Michael stopped in the driveway.

A valet ran forward to park the car. "Please take the elevator to the second floor."

Gabriel put his arm around Noor's waist. "Let's do this."

They took the elevator to a circular foyer with marble columns. A vestibule sat on the left for women to take off their manteau and scarves. A fountain graced the center of the foyer. People mingled in a lounge behind the foyer. On the right, a circular staircase led to an upper and a lower floor. Jazz music floated in background, and waiters circled the rooms with trays of drinks and hors d'oeuvres.

"The view is spectacular," Noor commented when they entered the main lounge.

Gabriel's eyes brushed over her and lingered on her mouth. "Yes, it is."

"Ah, here you are," a nasally voice exclaimed.

Ash Kosha reminded Noor of Colonel Sanders in the Kentucky fried chicken ads. He was a plump man of medium height, with silver hair, a white goatee, and a pair of blue eyes. He even wore a white summer suit with a small black tie.

Ash's eyes swept over her, and his lips turned up, making his cheeks droop. "Goodness, you look like Shiraz." Contrary to Gabriel's praise, Ash's admiration made a chill run up her spine. Ash took hold of her hands. "I'm Ash. Your mother and I were good friends."

"Pleased to meet you." *Ugh!* His touch felt slimy. Noor forced herself to stand still and not pull her hand away. "It's always a pleasure to meet Mom's friends."

Ash's grip tightened. "Shiraz and I went to the same school. I have stories to share with you."

Noor gently freed her hand from his clammy ones. "I'd love to hear them." *So not true.*

Ash beamed at Gabriel and Michael. "The McKnight brothers in person. It's hard to say which one is which."

Michael stepped forward. "Hello, Ash." He motioned to Gabriel, "Meet my brother, Gabriel."

Ash clasped Gabriel's hand. "I'm a fan of the Jason Van series." He rubbed his palms together. "Spot on, as Mister Van says." Ash gurled with laughter.

The lines around Gabriel's eyes tightened. He said nothing.

Ash lowered his voice in a conspiratorial tone. "Is it true that Tehran is the setting for your next novel?"

Gabriel gave Ash his traffic stopping smile. "Tehran will play a special part in my next novel."

Ash giggled. It sounded more like a pig snuffling. "Splendid, splendid. Oh, wait, I have a surprise for Michael." Ash motioned to the crowd, and a tall woman in a skintight black dress and matching ebony eyes joined them. "You remember Sahar, don't you?"

"Of course," Michael said, greeting the woman.

Ash beamed. "Michael and I met Sahar at—" Ash's hands fluttered. "Oh, I forget. It's age, you know." He glanced at Michael.

"We met in Singapore back in 2009," Michael supplied.

Noor didn't realize she was holding her breath until Michael answered. So, this was the test Michael had warned them of.

A man in a dark suit approached Ash and whispered something to him.

Ash rolled his eyes and bowed. "Shahar and I must answer a call." He bowed at Noor. "Will you excuse me, dear?"

Noor masked her relief. "Of course."

Ash tapped Michael's shoulder. "My man will come get you when I'm done with my phone call. Let's meet in my study."

"I'll be there." Michael grabbed an hors d'oeuvre from a waiter. As soon as Ash left, he gestured to the terrace.

Gabriel placed his hand on Noor's back, and the three of them made their way onto the expansive terrace.

Tables sat between exotic plants, and night blooming jasmine covered the terrace. Fairy lights hung over the pillars connecting starlit skies to the terrace, and elegant couples mingled together, enjoying the warm evening.

Noor leaned close to Gabriel. "It's like a celebrity party."

"I wonder what the rest of the world will think if it sees this side of Iran?" Michael mused.

They found a table surrounded by bamboo trees. Once they sat down, Gabriel took his tie off and switched it with Michael. He ran his hands through his hair, tousling it. And just like that, a change came over him. A restless energy took over Gabriel's body. He fidgeted and moved. A smirk replaced his shy smile, and his cobalt eyes gleamed with mischief. The changes were subtle yet so impactful that she wouldn't have believed this was Gabriel.

Michael also changed. He combed his hair back. His devilish smile turned into a solemn one. He stopped fidgeting, and a calm took over his body. He took Gabriel's seat by her and put his arm behind her chair.

Gabriel struck up a conversation with a woman sitting at the table next to him. Within minutes, the two were laughing. He whispered something in the woman's ear, and they both burst into laughter.

Noor wanted to throttle him.

Gabriel grinned at them. "Hey, Gabe, Noor, meet my friend Mojgan." He scooted closer to the woman. "Mojgan, this is my brother Gabriel, and his fiancé Noor."

"Nice to meet you." The woman tittered in a breathless Marilyn Monroe voice.

Noor wanted to gag.

Gabriel grinned. "Mojgan and I were talking about poker. She thinks she can't learn how to play. I was just telling her the only way to learn poker is to play strip poker."

Mojgan giggled. The movement gave her audience ample view of her cleavage.

Michael shook his head. "Be warned, ma'am, my brother is an expert at poker. You'll find yourself without clothes in no time."

"That's the best way to learn poker," Gabriel interjected with a conspiratorial wink. "We should find somewhere to play the game."

The woman whispered something to Gabriel and leaned against him.

Noor's throat tightened.

"Easy sweetheart," Michael cautioned in a low tone. "None of this is real. That's not Gabe, and you know it. Don't give it away by staring daggers at him."

She sniffed. "I wasn't staring daggers at anyone. Besides, he can do whatever he wants to. It's none of my business."

Michael's eyes twinkled. "You don't mean that, and you know it." He pursed his lips. "You know we can have fun with this." He put his arm around her and bent his head to her ear. "I'll bet you anything if I keep whispering in your ear, Gabe will be more interested in us than that woman." Michael kissed her cheek, then pushed a lock of her hair aside and whispered, "In fact, I think he'll kill me."

Gabriel's eyes slid their way and narrowed.

"See." Michael grinned.

Noor's shoulders shook with laughter. She leaned closer to Michael. "You're terrible, Michael McKnight."

"That's better," Michael murmured.

Ash's man found Gabriel and motioned to him.

Gabriel took Mojgan's hand and kissed it. "I'll be back." He walked off with the man.

Michael checked his watch. "We have ten minutes to get in and out. Let's go."

Noor rose and followed Michael toward the foyer.

A waiter stood by the vestibule in the main entrance.

Noor inquired where the restrooms were. The waiter gave her the directions. She thanked the man and as soon as he left, she and Michael ran up the staircase.

Michael pulled a chip out of his pocket and pulled her into a room. He put his index finger on his mouth.

She nodded.

Michael peered outside the room. "Guard," he whispered in her ear. "Stay here." He crept into the hallway.

Noor heard a scuffling sound.

Michael returned, dragging a man inside the room. He lay the man on the floor. "He'll be out for a little while. Let's go."

She followed Michael down the hallway and stopped at a computer room.

A guard sat behind the computer. He rose when he saw them. "What are you doing here?" He reached for the gun in his holster.

Michael smiled sheepishly. "Sorry, I was, uh, looking for a private place to spend time with my fiancé." He slowly approached the guard. "There's no harm done. We'll go back to the party."

The guard hesitated for a moment and reached for his gun.

It happened so fast, if it weren't for the crunch of the bones, Noor wouldn't believe it. Michael punched the guard in the face. The guard hit the ground.

Nausea swirled in her stomach. She was grateful her stomach was empty.

Michael placed the chip in the computer. "This will jam the feed in this hallway." He scanned the different monitors. In one monitor, Gabriel sat in a chair. Ash stood by Gabriel, while a man in a white lab coat read a machine. Gabriel looked relaxed.

"Stay here and watch the monitors," Mike ordered. "I'll get the document. I'll be in the room down the hall. If Gabriel runs into trouble, or if someone comes upstairs, call me."

"Okay."

CHAPTER FORTY-TWO

Gabriel sat in a chair with wires attached to his arms, wrists, and head.

The man beside him had that neutral tone of clinicians. "When is your birthday?"

"January 20, 1974."

"Do you have a brother?"

"Yes."

"Are you here to steal a document from Mister Kosha?"

Ludicrous question. "No," Gabriel answered.

"Are you a threat to Mister Kosha?"

Gabriel raised an eyebrow. "That depends."

To Gabriel's amusement, the clinician looked bemused. He glanced at Ash and cleared his throat. "What does it depend on?"

Gabriel met Ash's gaze. "If he's not a threat to me, he has nothing to fear."

The man nodded at Ash. "It's working."

Ash leaned forward. "Is it one item, Michael?"

"I don't know," Gabriel said.

Ash crossed his arms across his chest. "I will ask one more time. Is it the one item, or is there more?"

Gabriel lifted his shoulders. "I already told you, I don't know."

The clinician checked the monitor and nodded at Ash. "He's telling the truth."

Ash exhaled. "Thank you for indulging me, Michael."

The clinician took the wires off Gabriel, packed the machine up, and left the room.

Ash clasped his hands together. "Did you bring the floor plan?"

Gabriel pulled the sleeves of his shirt back down and put on his coat. "I want to see the document first."

"I want the floor plan."

Gabriel crossed his arms across his chest. "I've shown good-will by sitting through your test. I want to see the document first."

Ash sighed. "I'm sorry, I need more proof. If you get this right, you really are Michael."

Gabriel clenched his jaw. "I'm running out of patience."

Ash raised his hands. "I know, but you didn't mention your brother was coming to Iran. I'm just being cautious. I will ask you a question. Only you know the answer because you told me this. What are your favorite numbers?"

What the...? Gabriel had no idea how to answer the question. Sweat broke out on his brow. He racked his brains trying to find an answer.

Ash watched him closely with one hand on the security alarm.

Gabriel considered knocking Ash unconscious when inspiration hit. "It's 030497." He'd rattled off the numbers Mike had scratched on the whiskey bottle in his apartment.

Ash bowed his head. "I apologize, but I had to make sure it's you." He reached into a drawer and pulled out a key. He walked to a portrait in his study and pushed the portrait aside. There was a safe behind the portrait.

It was all for show. Gabriel knew Ash had no intention of

handing over the document. He glanced at his watch. He had six minutes to kill.

Ash returned with the document.

Gabriel raised an eyebrow. "Don't insult me." He threw the document on the desk.

Ash smiled. "My apologies. A deal is a deal." He went to his desk and punched a series of numbers into the tablet on his desk. A tile on the floor slid back. A safe sat under the tile. Ash placed his thumb on the safe, and the safe opened. He pulled out a document and handed it to Gabriel. "Now can I have the floor plan?"

Gabriel pretended to study the document, knowing it was another fake. He reached into his pocket and pulled out a USB port. "All I have is this copy."

Ash took the USB port. "How do I know you're telling the truth?"

"Do you want me to take your polygraph test again?"

Ash sighed heavily. "No, I believe you." He pocketed the USB and held out his hand. "It was a pleasure doing business with you."

Gabriel shook the offered hand. He still had two more minutes to kill. "How about a drink to celebrate?"

Ash blinked and smiled. "Sure, I have scotch and gin. What will you have?"

"I'll take the gin," Gabriel said. Anyone who knew Mike knew he didn't drink whiskey.

Ash poured two drinks and handed one to Gabriel. "Your brother and Noor Rahman make an attractive couple."

"Yes, they're good for each other." *It was true. Wasn't it?*

"It seems like yesterday when I was in school with her mother. Shiraz was lovely and sweet." Ash's eyes hardened. "She didn't deserve to die like that."

"I heard it was a break-in," Gabriel said, injecting what he hoped was the right tone of disinterest.

Ash sipped his drink. "I was in Paris the day before she died."

Gabriel feigned mild curiosity, "Really?"

"Yes, she owned a bookstore. Can you believe she liked to do mundane work when she could have lived in luxury?"

Gabriel sipped his drink. "Sounds like a unique person."

Ash rubbed his forehead. A dark blush covered his cheeks, and his breathing turned shallow. "I went to the bookstore and had coffee with her. She wanted me to stay in Paris a few more days. She wanted me to meet her daughter. I didn't stay."

"Why didn't you?" Gabriel asked.

Ash's chin trembled. "She still loved Rahman. Shiraz still loved him." Ash rocked back and forth, his eyes filling with tears. "I left for an art exhibition in Malaysia. I should have stayed. She would be alive if I'd stayed."

"What art exhibition?"

Ash didn't answer. He stared at the window, lost in thought.

Gabriel didn't push. Ash Kosha had loved Shiraz Rahman. He rose and left the study, shutting the door behind him. He'd just reached the main entrance when Noor and Michael came barreling down the flight of stairs.

"We have to go now," Michael urged in a hushed tone.

"Something wrong?"

Mike turned to a flight of stairs on the left. "The safe had a motion detector. I disconnected the security system. It's the kind that reboots after six minutes."

They took the emergency stairs down to the private parking area. Michael tipped the valet. They climbed into the car and headed toward the exit. The massive iron gates loomed into their view just as lights illuminated the property and sirens echoed in the night.

"Damn alarm," Michael growled. He pushed the accelerator, and the car jolted forward, barely making it out of the gates. "There's a bag underneath your feet," Michael said. "It has sneakers for Noor and two guns. Get ready for company."

It was close to midnight, yet there were cars on the road. Gabriel thrust the sneakers at Noor, who yanked them on. He handed Mike a gun and kept his eyes on the back of the car. Three motorcycles were pursuing them. "Our friends from the party just arrived."

"What can I do?" Noor cried, rummaging in the bag.

Gabriel kept an eye on the motorcycles. "Keep your head down until I tell you it is safe."

Seconds later, bullets shattered the back windows. Gabriel leaned back and kicked the remaining shards out of the way. He aimed and shot the tire on motorcycle one. The bike flipped over like a toy. *One down.*

The other two motorcycles separated. Each drove to one side of the car, surrounding them. The motorcycle on Michael's side had one driver. The one on Noor's side had two men.

Gabriel didn't wait. He shot the man behind the driver.

The man toppled off the bike. The bikers shot at the car.

"Hold on," Mike cried, turning the car in a full circle. He drove through oncoming traffic and cut into the Shahid Modares Highway.

Gabriel looked back. The bikers were closing in on them. "We have to get out of the car."

"I'm working on it," Mike shouted over the spray of bullets.

Noor reached over and grabbed Michael's gun. She aimed at the second motorcycle and fired. Another biker went down.

"Atta girl," Michael cried.

They approached Tabiat bridge. Michael drove off the highway into a park next to the bridge. He tore his coat and tie off. "You and Noor take a right and go up to the bridge. I'll meet you back at the apartment." He took off in the opposite direction.

Gabriel grabbed Noor's hand and ran through the park.

Crack, crack. Gunshots splintered the bark on the trees surrounding them.

Gabriel pulled Noor behind a tree. He waited a hard beat and peered around it.

One of Ash's men ran toward them. The first level of the Tabiat bridge wasn't far. If Noor could get to safety, he'd take care of Ash's henchman.

He squeezed Noor's arm. "Go to the first level of the bridge and find a café. I'll meet you there."

She shook her head. "I won't leave you!"

"I've got this one. Please go. I'll meet you up there."

She didn't argue. On his cue, she scrambled up the path toward the bridge.

Gabriel fired a few shots to slow the man down, then climbed a tree and waited for Ash's henchman to get close.

When the man was close enough, Gabriel ambushed him, knocking the gun out of his hand. The man rose quickly and barreled into Gabriel.

Gabriel was grateful he hadn't stopped training after his military days. He twisted to avoid the impact. The man turned and threw his leg out to kick him. Gabriel was faster and dodged the kick. The man pulled out a knife and swung it at him. Gabriel stepped aside and tore off his coat, then wrapped it around his arm. The man swiped again. The knife cut through the coat. Gabriel jabbed the man in the nose. Blood spattered everywhere. He did a roundhouse kick, knocking the man unconscious.

"I should kill you," Gabriel muttered in disgust. He raced up to toward the Tabiat bridge, desperate to find Noor.

A vendor stood at the main entrance with a cart of accessories. The vendor's eyes widened when Gabriel approached.

Gabriel noticed the streaks of blood and dirt smeared on his shirt. He smiled sheepishly. "I fell while climbing up the trail."

The vendor studied him with concern. "Are you hurt? Shall I call for an ambulance?"

"No, my pride took a hit. Otherwise I'm fine." He rolled up his sleeves to cover the blood. "I'll take a ball cap and a burgundy shawl." He paid the vendor and ran up to the first level of the bridge. He found a café at the center of the first level.

Noor sat at a table. She spotted him, and her shoulders slumped with relief. "Are you all right?" Her voice shook, and her face was grey.

"I'm fine, it's not my blood." Gabriel handed her the scarf. "Change your scarf with this one."

Noor exchanged the scarves.

"Let's go find a cab."

She straightened. "What about Michael?"

"He'll meet us at the apartment." He took Noor's hand and led her to the nearest taxi station.

CHAPTER FORTY-THREE

"All of the power needed for our life journey is already imbedded in the heart."

—Rassouli, 2015

OKLAHOMA CITY, USA

Morris poured himself a cup of coffee. He'd gone for a long run to clear his head. Gabriel called to let him know Noor was fine. That didn't stop him from worrying. He shook his head. When had he become the worrying type? *Since you promised Shiraz Rahman to keep Noor safe.*

Morris's phone buzzed. He checked the screen and answered the call.

Roshi's bubbling voice crackled through the line.

"Yes. Sure. That's fine." He disconnected the call and sighed. It wouldn't be long before Noor's grandmother and the Russian non-boyfriend showed up on his doorstep. There was no privacy with this lot. He sighed. He'd maintained a careful distance between himself and the rest of the world. How the hell had these people gotten close to him? They cared about him, and much to his own surprise, he cared about them.

The doorbell rang. Roshi had arrived with the food.

"I'm coming," Morris called out. He opened the door and stared speechlessly at his visitor.

"Goodness, Morris, you needn't look so shocked," the Iranian admonished. He waited several moments, looking up and down the street. "May I come in?"

Morris shook himself out of his stupor. "Yes, of course." He held the door open for the Iranian to enter.

The Iranian stepped inside. "There now, that wasn't too hard, was it?"

"This way," Morris mumbled, stomping toward the kitchen. Yep, life as he knew it had changed. He wondered who else would wind up on his doorstep.

The Iranian took a seat on a barstool by the kitchen island and wiped an invisible speck of lint from his trousers. Today's suit was a striped Navy blue. The Iranian paired the suit with a yellow tie. Morris glanced at his own threadbare jeans and a black T-shirt and withheld a smile. They couldn't be more different.

The Iranian glanced at the counters. "This is not at all what I expected. It's very elegant and modern."

Morris gave the kitchen a once over. "Noor and her aunt decorated the place."

"They have good taste." A smile tugged at the Iranian's mouth. "I apologize for showing up unannounced."

Morris shrugged. "I have coffee. Would you like some? Or would you prefer tea?"

"Tea, please."

Morris poured two mugs of tea and took a seat by his employer.

The Iranian picked up a mug. "What have the children been up to? How much have they discovered?"

Morris brought the Iranian up to speed. He was half-way

through his narrative when his phone beeped. Morris checked the text and stiffened. He held out the phone.

The Iranian read the message, and his expression darkened. "Hmm."

Morris growled and paced the room like a caged tiger. "I should have seen this coming. I should have gone to Tehran." He cursed in several languages and paced faster. "I'll be damned if anyone hurts the girl."

The Iranian blinked. "I don't believe I've ever seen you this upset."

Morris's face flushed, and the vein in his temple bulged. "Noor is in danger."

"Morris, do calm down. You're giving me a headache with all the pacing. We will not allow anyone to hurt the child. In fact, that's why I'm here." The Iranian put his mug down. "Sheila is in Iran. It seems like the McKnight brothers are more than capable. They evaded most of the men following them, and Sheila took care of the remaining men pursuing them." He paused. "Sheila said a man named Ash Kosha is behind it. What do you know about Kosha?"

Morris's head swiveled around. "He's an art smuggler and a lowlife who wants to play with the big boys."

"Hm." The Iranian sipped his tea. "I'd like to announce publicly the children are under our protection."

Morris gaped at his employer.

The Iranian waved a manicured hand. "Come, come, Morris, you love the girl. You've become a father figure of sorts to her"—his eyes twinkled—"which makes me her uncle. I believe it's time we let our business associates know the truth, don't you?"

Dumbfounded, Morris nodded mutely.

The Iranian beamed. "Good. We'll start with Mister Kosha."

Morris dialed Tehran.

~

ASH PACED IN HIS STUDY. He had plans for the document. "Damn Michael McKnight. Damn it all to hell!" He poured himself a shot of whiskey. The alcohol burned his throat and did nothing to soothe him.

A knock sounded on the door.

"What is it?" Ash barked.

His head of security came in.

"Well?" Ash growled.

The man shuffled his feet. "I'm sorry, sir, my men are dead."

"You're a bunch of idiots!" Ash hurled the glass into the fireplace, shattering it into pieces.

He was about to fire the head of his security when one of his guards scurried into the office carrying his cellphone.

"I don't want to talk to anyone." Ash turned away.

The guard swallowed. "It's Morris, sir."

"What?" Ash turned around. "Morris?"

The guard nodded.

Why was the Iranian's second in command calling him? Ash grabbed the phone and gulped. "This is Ash Kosha."

"Ash, this is Morris Bertoli. I have a message for you."

Ash struggled to keep his voice neutral. "Of course, I'm listening."

"Leave Noor Rahman and the McKnights alone."

"W-wait a minute." Ash reached for the whiskey bottle.

"No, you will listen and do as I say. You will stop pursuing them right now." There was a pause. Ash heard a voice in the background. *"The Iranian will speak with you."*

Ash nearly dropped the whiskey bottle.

A smooth voice came on the line. *"Mister Kosha?"*

Oh, God. It's him. Ash gulped. "G-good evening. You may not remember me. We've met. I—"

The Iranian didn't let him finish. *"Oh, I remember you. I have an excellent memory."* There was a pregnant pause. *"Mister Kosha, I assume you value your business and your life, correct?"*

"Yes, sir."

"If you'd like to keep both, you will do exactly what Morris says. The children are under my protection. The consequences of not following Morris's instructions will be dire. Have I made myself clear?"

Ash gulped. "Yes, sir, I understand."

"How kind of you. I won't forget your generosity." Click. The line disconnected.

Sweat trickled down Ash's neck. He raised the bottle and took a healthy gulp. Coughing, he sank into the nearest chair. *What the hell just happened?*

The head of his security came in. "Mister Kosha, we know where the girl and her fiancé are staying. I can send a team over there right now."

"No! Leave them alone."

If Ash's head of security was surprised, he didn't show it. He bowed his head. "If that's what you wish."

"It is, now leave me."

The security guard left.

Ash placed the bottle on the coffee table with shaky hands. He had a bigger problem on his hands.

CHAPTER FORTY-FOUR

Gabriel poured tea into three mugs. His gaze strayed to the hallway for the hundredth time.

Noor had been silent on the ride back to the apartment. When they arrived, she'd fled to her room for a shower.

Gabriel handed Michael a mug and glanced at the hallway again.

Michael nudged him. "She needs time to unwind."

"She's been there for forty-five minutes."

He was about to check on Noor when she walked into the kitchen. She'd changed into a pair of loose linen yoga pants and a black sports top. Her damp hair hung loose and fell to her waist.

Gabriel handed her a mug.

She took it and touched his shoulder, thanking him silently. She went to the sofa and sat down. Her eyes were huge, and her complexion pallid.

Michael noticed it, too. He grabbed a bottle of brandy from the bar and poured some into her tea.

"Thank you." Noor cradled her cup in both hands.

She was such a dichotomy—stubborn and strong, yet vulnerable and gentle.

To hell with it all. Gabriel stomped to the sofa and put his arm around her.

Michael grinned. "Okay boys and girls, time for a debrief. I got the document. My part of the mission is complete. How did things go for you?"

Noor shivered.

Gabriel pulled her closer. "Fine. Ash wanted to know if there was only one item, or if there was more. What was he referring to?"

"He was referring to the Central Bank's hidden vault. The informant sent buyers information on one artifact. Ash wants the whereabouts of the other artifacts."

Noor sipped her drink. "You said it wasn't in our country's interest for Ash to know the truth. Why would our government care if Ash or anyone else finds out what was in the vault?"

Michael merely smiled.

"I have a hunch it's one of two things," Gabriel offered. "Either whatever is in that vault will cause serious international conflict, or there's something in that vault that could endanger the United States."

"I see." She burrowed closer to him, trying to absorb his warmth.

Gabriel squeezed her shoulder. "I found out that Ash was in Paris a few days before your mother died. He claims he was in Malaysia when it happened. It should be easy to verify." He turned his attention to Michael. "You can't stay here forever. How can I help you?"

Michael rubbed his chin. "You've already helped. I'll be home soon, I promise."

"Mom wants you home for Thanksgiving."

Michael straightened. "I'll be home before that. Let's get back to you two. What will you do next?"

"We follow the clues," Gabriel said. "First, we will visit the Rahman's home, then we go to Turkey."

Michael nodded. "Focus on Rumi. That's the common thread in all of this."

Hmm. Michael made a good point. Gabriel made a mental note to go over the clues another time.

The telephone rang.

Gabriel rose to answer it.

"*Is Noor okay?*" Morris barked.

"Yes. We're all fine," Gabriel said.

"*Good. Kosha won't be a problem.*"

Gabriel grinned. "Would that be Sheila?"

Morris grunted. "*Pass the phone to Noor.*"

Gabriel handed the phone to Noor. "Your uncle wants you to know that Ash won't bother us anymore."

Her eyes widened. She took the phone and went into the kitchen.

Michael raised his eyebrows. "I've met Uncle Morris. Is he intelligence?"

Gabriel shrugged. "He's helpful. That's all that matters."

Noor laughed. The sound made him smile. When this was over, he'd make sure she laughed often.

Woah, where had that thought come from? It implied a future with Noor in it. To Gabriel's surprise, the thought of Noor in his future didn't make him feel claustrophobic. He wasn't a relationship kind of guy, or was he? He'd have to think about it. He glanced up and noticed Mike's grin.

"Mind your own business," Gabriel growled.

Noor came back before Mike could comment. She sat back on the couch and leaned into him.

Yep, definitely new territory. Gabriel put his arm around her.

"Uncle Morrie says Ash will call and apologize." She shook her head. "Who do you think he works for?"

Michael rubbed his ear. "I'd say he's got an intelligence background."

"It takes one to know one," Noor murmured.

Michael grinned and fisted his hand in the air. "Right on!"

Noor stiffened. "Oh my God!" She glanced at Michael, then at Gabriel. "Michael is Jason Van, the Jason Van of your novels."

Busted.

Her cheeks flushed, and her face grew animated. "Jason fists his hand in the air and says, 'Spot on.' Michael does the same, but he says, 'Right on.' Michael rubs his ear when he's contemplating something and rubs his palms together when he's excited. Jason Van has the same gestures." She leaned in and kissed Gabriel's cheek. "The hero in your stories is your brother. That's sweet."

Gabriel felt his face heat up.

Michael chuckled. "Beautiful and intelligent. Now, imagine my surprise when I read his first book. But then, Jason Van's awesome, isn't he?"

Noor snorted. "He's trouble."

Michael tilted his head. "Yeah, but you've got to admit he's fun."

Noor's voice softened. "I'd say Jason's brother is just as good of a hero."

"Uh uh," Michael admonished jokingly. "My brother doesn't believe he's a hero."

She narrowed her eyes. "I've noticed that. Why don't you—"

"We'll visit your parents' home tomorrow," Gabriel interjected. "Let's focus on that."

Noor tipped her head up and searched his face.

He could see the questions mirrored in her eyes. *Not now,* Gabriel pleaded silently.

She must have sensed his hesitation because she didn't persist. "Mom talked about the old house my whole life. I printed a sky view of the property from Google maps. I'll go get it." She went to retrieve the printout.

Gabriel exhaled and noticed Michael studying him. He glanced away.

CHAPTER FORTY-FIVE

Noor stood in front of the large iron gates of the property that used to be her parents' home. *This is it. This is where Mom and Dad built their hopes and dreams, and this is where it all crashed down on their heads.*

She rubbed her damp palms over her jeans. Her heart pounded, and sweat formed on her upper lip.

Gabriel stood beside her, waiting for her to make the first move.

She straightened her shoulders. "I'm ready." They stepped through the gates.

It was as if she'd stepped back in time into the tranquil, picturesque world her mother had described. Mom's description was accurate. The scents of cut grass mingled with that of jasmine and roses. A road lined with oak trees circled the property, passing through patches of summer flowers, rose bushes, and walking trails.

A large three-story structure sat at the end of the road. She studied her parents' home with interest. The house was traditional with white stone and pale blue shutters. Persian artwork adorned the turquoise shutters and window frames. A flight of stairs led to a wrap-around porch. An old woman with a cane waited by the porch.

Mrs. Asaad was well in her eighties and hunched over. Her face held creases like worn leather, and her snow-white hair stuck out of her scarf like corkscrews. Her bear-like brown eyes glistened with tears. She hobbled forward and spread her arms. "My dear child, welcome home."

Her own eyes misted as she stepped into the older woman's embrace.

Mrs. Asaad's rough hands reached up to her face. "You look just like your mother. You also have your father's eyes. They were the kindest of people, God rest their souls."

"Thank you, Missus Asaad." Noor placed her hand on Gabriel's arm. "This is my fiancé, Gabriel McKnight."

The housekeeper's brows snapped together. "McKnight? You're one of the twins, eh? I remember your parents."

Gabriel bowed his head. "Yes, ma'am, I remember your fabulous cakes. You used to sneak us some before dinner."

The housekeeper cackled and stomped her cane. Mrs. Asaad took Noor's hand. "Come, I will give you a tour." The former housekeeper took them through each room, describing how her mother had furnished the house. Mom's memories and Mrs. Asaad's descriptions gave Noor more insight into her parents' lives.

She saw what used to be her parent's bedroom and pictured her parents reading Rumi in front of the fireplace. They passed another room overlooking the gardens on the east. The room had a wide balcony.

"This used to be Miss Leila's room," Mrs. Asaad said. "How is she doing?"

Noor strode to the balcony. "She's well. She lives in London. We see each other a few times a year."

"The poor child." Mrs. Asaad sighed. "She was happy living

with the general and Missus Rahman, then the young man she loved died."

"Tell me about this young man," Noor said. "Leila never talks about him."

Mrs. Asaad leaned on her cane. "He wasn't vulgar or loud like most of the men his age, and he was very handsome." Her voice softened. "Miss Leila climbed down the oak tree by the window to meet him. She didn't know I saw her. I would have mentioned it if she were in danger," Mrs. Asaad rushed to explain. "The boy was polite, and they were in love."

They arrived at the wide terrace overlooking the gardens.

Mrs. Asaad pointed to a fountain in the middle of the court-yard. "There used to be a swimming pool there." She pointed to a gazebo, and her voice trembled. "The last time I saw your parents together was right there. Your father received a phone call. He left and never came back."

The words shook Noor. *One moment you're living your life, and the next you're living in hell.* She recalled Mom's sudden death, and the bleak days after her funeral.

As if sensing her morose thoughts, Mrs. Asaad patted her arm.

Noor turned to the left. "I'd like to see the gazebo. Why don't you go to the museum's coffee shop? Gabriel and I will meet you there."

Mrs. Asaad bowed her head. "Very well, dear."

Sensing she needed to be alone, Gabriel offered to escort Mrs. Asaad to the coffee shop. "I'll catch up with you." He offered Mrs. Asaad his arm.

Mrs. Asaad took Gabriel's arm, and the two headed toward the café.

Noor made her way to the fountain, which sat behind the gazebo. An artist had carved Persian miniatures into the gazebo's pillars. One side had carvings of ancient Persian warriors. She wondered what the figures represented. She sat on a stone bench.

The fountain sat in front of her. Behind her, a row of rose bushes sprawled across the lawn forming a wall of roses.

The tranquility of the gardens, the scents of jasmine, the bright flowers, and the chirping of birds made her smile. The visit had given her a glimpse of her own history. She worried the visit would overwhelm her, yet it hadn't.

"This was your home, Mom, not mine. I'm glad I visited."

She reached into her purse and pulled out the photo Mom left her. She turned the photo around and read the poem.

From the surface you'll see lifeless faces,
All the way from Rome to Khorasan.
What you refer to, references itself.
To see the human ocean look at yourself.

The poem had come with a white rose. Why? Noor turned around and studied the garden. Behind the summer flowers, there was an older rose bush. She approached the rose bush. It gleamed, heavy with cream-colored roses. She read the poem again. *From outside, you see lifeless faces.* She stood in front of the white rose bush and looked ahead. The only thing she saw was the gazebo. There were no faces sculpted into the gazebo's pillars, were there? Noor ran back to the gazebo and examined the carvings on the pillars. The corner of the western pillar had the faces of a woman and man sculpted into the stone.

Her fingers traced the faces on the stone. *Incredible!* She read the next line of the poem. *Strangers all, from Rome to Khorasan.* "Rome and Khorasan are cities. What was significant about these two cities?" One was in Western Europe, and the other in the eastern part of Iran. *Could it be as simple as that? From west to east?*

Noor's head swiveled toward the east. She spotted a small walk behind the gazebo. The walk disappeared into a cluster of thick trees. She followed the narrow path into the trees.

Oh wow! The path led to a smaller and more secluded garden.

It reminded her of the tales she'd read as a child. Rows of trees and jasmine bushes created a wall around the garden. A stone table and two stone benches stood at the center of the lawn. She approached the table with shaky legs.

"OLD AGE IS A NUISANCE," Mrs. Asaad grumbled, leaning on Gabriel's arm. "In my youth, I ran large households."

"I'm aware of that," Gabriel quipped. "My mother still talks about the feast you prepared for Missus Rahman's birthday."

Mrs. Asaad's mouth lifted into a smile. "I cooked all of Missus Rahman's favorite foods that night."

"It must have been a special evening."

Mrs. Asaad beamed. "Oh, it was. The general wanted it to be a surprise for the Missus. He invited all her good friends. I don't know why they invited that young man. He pretended to be a friend when he lusted after Missus Rahman."

Gabriel narrowed his eyes. "Another man was in love with Missus Rahman?"

The old woman bobbed her head. The action made the corkscrew curls sticking out of her scarf bounce. "Missus Rahman was young and lovely. She loved the general." The housekeeper stopped to catch her breath. "That awful man wanted to seduce Missus Rahman. The Missus never encouraged him."

Gabriel could guess who the young man was, but he asked anyway. "Who was this man?"

Mrs. Asaad crumpled the handkerchief in her hands. "I can't remember his name. He was Missus Rahman's classmate, and he was no good. I saw him sneak into the general's office the night of Missus Rahman's birthday. Someone else followed him there, and they got into an argument." Mrs. Asaad sneered. "Arrogant people never pay attention to the staff."

They stopped in at the foot of the stairs leading to the café.

Gabriel helped Mrs. Asaad climb the stairs. "Do you know what the argument was about?"

"I heard something about timelines."

They reached the coffee shop.

Gabriel chose a table with a view to the gardens and ordered tea and pastries for Mrs. Asaad. "I'll go find Noor."

Mrs. Asaad made shooing motions at him. "Go on, son. I'm fine."

Interesting that Ash was snooping in the general's office. Even more interesting was the argument Ash had with a guest. Gabriel wondered how many of the guests knew the general guarded the vault and feigned ignorance.

He took a shorter path to the gazebo. His stomach dropped when he found it vacant. "Noor? Noor, where are you?"

"I'm here," she called out. "Follow the little path to the east of the gazebo."

Relief washed over Gabriel. He found the path and arrived at a small garden.

Noor sat on a stone bench, her head bent in concentration.

"What are you doing?"

She waved the photo of her parents. "I'm trying to figure out the clue." She told him how she found the garden.

Gabriel examined the small stone table. Persian drawings were carved into the table's stone surface. "What's the next line of the poem?"

"What you refer to references itself."

Hmm. Gabriel leaned closer to the table. The faces of ancient soldiers were carved in the stone. "So, the faces we are referring to are the reference." He studied the faces carved in the stone. A thought struck him. "All the faces on this table are looking at the same direction." He turned in the opposite direction and went toward the wall of thick trees.

He hadn't gone farther than a few feet when the ground gave

way to stone. He looked down. Underneath his feet lay a stone compass. Grass had grown over it, making it hard to see.

Noor ran over to him, and the two of them yanked the grass off the stone. The surface of the compass held carvings of a Persian man and woman. Time and weather conditions had eroded the faces.

Noor read the last line with a shaky voice. "To see the human ocean, look at yourself."

Gabriel ran his hands along the stone. The center of the compass had a circle. He pushed the circle, and the stone compass moved aside. A small wooden box sat in a stone opening. The lid had Parviz Rahman carved on it and painted in gold.

"Who's out there?" a voice called.

Gabriel snatched the box and shoved it in his pocket. He grabbed Noor's hand, and they rushed to the stone table.

One of the museum guards came into the garden. "What are you doing here?"

Noor spread her arms. "We found this little area by chance. It's lovely."

The guard narrowed his eyes. "This area is not open to the public. There are signs all over the property instructing visitors to stay on the main paths."

"We're sorry," Gabriel said. "We were just curious. We'll head over to the main walking paths." He took Noor's hand, and the two of them walked back to the coffee shop.

GABRIEL PLACED the box on the dining room table.

Noor and Michael watched as he gently pushed on the lid. "It's locked. Noor touched the box gently. "This belonged to my father. Mom told me she grabbed everything personal from Dad's study before she left the country."

Gabriel ran his fingers along the box and found a dent at the bottom. He pushed it, and the lid popped open. Two pieces of paper lay inside. The sheets were folded into small squares. He unfolded the first sheet and found two lines of alphabet letters and a date.

Sept. 8, 1978

A B C D E F G H I J K L M N O P Q R S T U V W X Y Z

E F G H I J K L M N O P Q R S T U V W X Y Z A B C D

"It's a code key," he explained. "These were common during the second world war."

Noor picked the sheet up. "Look at the date. It's the day my father died." She examined the sheet. "What do all the letters mean?"

Gabriel pointed to the first row of letters. "On the first line, each letter of the alphabet is bold. These letters are replaced with another letter. In this case, the second line with the letters in italics show every letter of the alphabet is replaced by the fourth letter after it. The letter A, for example, is replaced by the letter E. Leila told us your father was receiving daily reports on the inventory in the hidden vault. He used codes to communicate with his guards."

"If this code is dated, I bet they were switching the codes every day," Mike pointed out. "Based on the date, it's the last code the general sent to his guards."

Noor put the sheet down. "We have the key to the codes used the day my father died, but we don't have the final report on the vault's inventory. We don't even know if Mom ever saw the report. If she saw it, where would she hide it?"

Gabriel picked up the last clue.

"Konya!" They all cried simultaneously.

Mom's friend Banu must know something.

Gabriel reached for his cell phone. "I'll call Morris and see if he can arrange a private flight to Turkey."

Michael rubbed his hands together. "Right on. If Uncle Morris is booking the flight, I'll accompany you to Turkey."

Mike's carefree tone didn't fool Gabriel. "What will you do when we get to Turkey? And don't give me the 'I've got this under control' bullshit."

"I'm not," Mike said.

Gabriel crossed his arms over his chest. "What are you going to do?"

"I have a contact in Konya who can help me. I'll catch a traitor, while you two find a murderer. Maybe we kill two birds with one stone."

CHAPTER FORTY-SIX

Shiraz Rahman's Journal

Tehran, November 15, 1978
So much has changed since my last entry. My wonderful, kind Parviz is
gone! I'll never hear his voice again. I'll never rest my head on his
shoulder. We'll never make love. Why did he have to leave that awful
day? Why didn't I stop him? How do I live without Parviz? Fate, I
hate you!

Tehran, November 22, 1978
I woke with pain. The burn traveled through my body until I could
see red spots behind my eyes. I curled up in bed and gritted my teeth,
not wanting to wake Mother, who slept in the adjacent room.

The pain burned through my chest and worked its way to my
heart. My breath grew labored, while my heart burned.

I prayed for death. I prayed for it to end when I saw a tunnel. It appeared out of nowhere. Its silence and shadows were a contrast to the hurricane of red pain tearing me apart. Did it exist, or was it a trick of my mind? I didn't care. I sunk into its depths. Enveloped in the darkness, I found a sanctuary.

I am a shadow in a still world. I feel no sorrow, no joy, no anger, and no pain. I have no aim or ambition, no stress or responsibility. I am a shadow. I am silence.

TEHRAN, *November 29, 1978*

I convinced Mom and Roshi to leave Iran. I dismissed the groundskeeper and Mrs. Asaad, leaving each of them with a retirement fund. The house is up for sale. There is no reason to live here. The house and its memories belonged to a happy creature, not one who lives in shadows.

I bought a one-way ticket to Paris, and on a late November evening, I packed two suitcases. One held my clothes and some personal items, the other one held every valuable memory of my life with Parviz. It's amazing how two precious years of our life fit into one suitcase.

I took one last turn in the house. I went from room to room, letting the memories imprint themselves into my mind. I went to the gazebo by our favorite rose bushes and relived my last moments with Parviz. It was like looking into a kaleidoscope of brilliant colors and warmth.

I barely heard the thudding in the background. The noise grew louder, penetrating my silent world. I realized it was voices. Voices that echoed.

"Death to the imperialists!"

Hmm, the ignorant mob thought the imperialists were the problem. Well, the country was welcome to the change it fought for. The voices grew louder. The mob banged on the front gates of our home. Fear would've been an appropriate response, but truth be told, I didn't care.

A man stepped out of the trees and ran toward me. "Come with me," he urged.

I ignored him.

He yanked me to my feet. "The mob wants blood, and it won't be long before they break in. You must come with me!"

I laughed. "Let them do it. I've already lost everything."

The man shook me. "Is this how you'll honor the general's memory? By allowing protestors to kill his unborn child?"

I placed a hand on my stomach. Oh God, the baby! How could I have forgotten our baby?

For an instant a streak of colors appeared before my eyes then disappeared. What to do? I ran back to the house.

The man followed me. He glanced at the suitcases in the foyer. "We can only take one." One need not be a genius to figure out which one I chose.

The man ran a hand through his hair. "Hurry! It won't be long before the crowd storms through the gates."

For an instant, hot flames licked my stomach. I ran to Parviz's study. I'd die before I let the mob touch his belongings. I opened his safe and took what was his. I ran back to the foyer and skidded to a halt as a thought occurred. "Who are you?"

The man's eyes gleamed. "I'm Morris. My friends call me Morrie."

I wanted to cry. Parviz had taken extra measures to make sure the baby and I would be safe.

An explosion erupted, and a crash echoed in the property. Flames climbed the trees at the western border of the house.

Morris picked up the suitcase. "We'll leave through the north-east entrance."

I had one more thing to do. I ran behind the gazebo and hid the codes. I came back and picked a cream rose from the rose bush Parviz loved, then turned around and looked back. The house once full of love and laughter stood lifeless and empty, its windows shuttered. The veranda sat bare, the pool drained, the lawns neglected, and the sycamore trees burned in flames. As the voices grew louder, I took one last look at the ruins of my life and walked away.

.   .   .

NOOR CLOSED THE JOURNAL. Tears streamed down her cheeks. Mom had never let her see the pain or the darkness. She'd never shared it with her. For as long as she remembered, Mom was laughter, kindness, and light. It hadn't always been that way. Her heart ached for her parents. She shoved the journal into her purse and closed her eyes, willing herself to sleep.

GABRIEL STRETCHED his legs and glanced at his watch. Thirty minutes to landing.

Michael sat sprawled in front of him, nursing a coke. He raised his can in a salute.

Gabriel glanced to his left. Noor was curled up in her seat, fast asleep. He leaned closer and frowned. Were those tears?

"She read the journal and cried herself to sleep," Mike whispered.

"Reliving the past has been hard for her." Gabriel pulled a blanket over her.

Noor burrowed closer to him.

Mike watched with a ghost of a smile. "You two have something."

Gabriel made no comment.

"She likes you, Gabe."

Gabriel ground his teeth and remained silent.

"What you going to do about it?" Mike persisted.

Gabriel sighed. Mike wouldn't let it go, not until he got an answer. "Nothing for now."

"What about later?"

"Leave it alone," Gabriel mouthed.

"She won't be safe till you find the killer," Michael said.

Gabriel raked a hand through his hair. "I know."

Noor stirred.

Gabriel's eyes followed the ripple of her muscles, noting the curve of her hips, the gentle slope of her neck, her slim waist, her silky skin, and her plush lips. His fingers itched to reach out and touch her. He clenched his fists.

Mike smirked. "Sooner is better than later."

CHAPTER FORTY-SEVEN

"Pain is part of a dervish's existence,
and amidst the pain a true man stands.
They have built monasteries everywhere.
Yes, the whole world is a monastery, it needs real men."
—Rumi

KONYA, TURKEY

Ash stomped down the airplane's stairs. Business required him to travel all over the world. A trip to Turkey, specifically Konya, wouldn't be unusual. He dug out his handkerchief and wiped the sweat off his face. Most people lived on one or the other side of the law. He lived in the grey space between. The people who existed in this realm lived by their own set of rules, and the consequences of breaking those rules were dire.

He spotted a grey SUV with tinted windows. The American waited in the car. Funny how people in this world didn't use names, even fake ones. Ash pursed his lips. He didn't even know if the American was from America. Anyone could fake an accent.

He gulped nervously and climbed into the SUV. The American's blue gaze homed in on him. Ash felt his throat close in. The seconds ticked by.

"Well?" the American snapped. "You whimpered, whined, and begged for this meeting. I'm here. What is it?"

Ash tried not to flinch. "I have a lead on the diamond."

A blond brow raised a quarter of an inch. "Where did you find your lead?"

Ash tugged on the collar of his shirt. "The lead is Noor Rahman."

The American narrowed his eyes. "I thought the Rahman girl knew nothing."

"She's not as clueless as she pretends to be." Ash forced himself to meet the American's eyes. "The McKnight brothers are helping her."

"Plural, as in both brothers? Didn't one of them die recently?"

"No," Ash said. "I saw them both in Tehran. I put pressure on them." He paused and looked away. "We, um, have a problem." Ash wiped the sweat off his forehead. "The Iranian wants me to stay away from Noor Rahman."

The American stroked his chin. "How interesting."

"How do we get the diamond if we can't touch the Rahman girl?" Ash cried.

The American glared at Ash. "Your problem is your inability to think. Get it from her without hurting her."

"But I don't know—"

The American raised a hand, silencing him. "Looks like you have a dilemma. If you hurt the girl, the Iranian will kill you, and if you don't get the information, I'll kill you. If I were you, I'd focus on finding a solution. One that involves a win-win situation."

Ash's chin quivered. "I'll call you once I have something."

The American's eyes reminded Ash of ice chips. "No, I'll call you."

MICHAEL MCKNIGHT STRODE through the bazaar. Like a tourist, he stopped at various shops checking window displays, all the while checking to ensure no one followed him. Caution was important in his line of work. It was the difference between life and death. Michael never let his guard down.

He checked his six another time and turned into a narrow path. His contact was waiting at a small teahouse in the bazaar. Michael entered the teahouse. He spotted his contact instantly and chose a table nearby. A waiter took his order. Michael paged through the newspaper he'd bought.

A woman in an Islamic veil rose to leave. She dropped a piece of paper in his lap and exited the tea shop.

Michael unfolded the note and memorized its contents. He put the note in his pocket and drank his tea. Twenty minutes later, he paid the waiter and rose to leave. He hailed a cab and gave the driver the address scribbled on the note.

The cab dropped him off at a modern apartment complex. Contrary to Gabriel's Jason Van series, agents didn't stay at luxurious apartments when on assignment. However, when the opportunity arose, one took advantage of it. He climbed the stairs to the third floor and knocked.

A woman opened the door and motioned for him to enter. Aliza Cohen worked for the National Security Agency—the NSA. She had a military background and specialized in cyber security and intelligence. She was also what he and Gabriel called a looker.

Aliza's lustrous hair was long and the color of coffee beans. She had compelling golden eyes fringed with thick lashes. Her body was a canvas of lush curves and smooth skin. Picture a taller version of Kim Kardashian. Oh yeah, Aliza was smoking hot.

Most people underestimated Aliza because of her looks. Aliza used that to her advantage.

"Nice digs."

"Thank you." Aliza leaned against the door. "Word on the street is you died jumping out of a helicopter."

Michael spread his hands. "As you can see, I'm alive."

Aliza snorted. "I never believed it."

Intrigued, Michael stepped closer. "Really? Why is that?"

"Because I'm smarter than most people." Aliza tilted her head. Her long hair trailed below her waist. A silky strand fell below her round derriere.

Michael's pulse quickened.

"Why are you here, Mike?"

She wore a simple V-neck T-shirt with jeans. Mm, all that smooth skin. He wanted to run his mouth along her collarbone.

"Mike?"

He swallowed. "Yeah?"

"Why are you here? And please don't tell me it's because you wanted to see where I'm staying at."

He shoved his hands in his pockets. "I need your help."

Aliza raised an eyebrow.

"Someone set a trap for me. I walked into it purposefully," Michael said.

Aliza narrowed her eyes. "Why?"

His nostrils flared. "Because I have someone dirty in-house. I need to find the problem and eliminate it."

"That's quite an accusation," Aliza breathed. "Are you certain the problem's in-house?"

Michael nodded.

"Jesus, Mike, we're talking about CIU."

"That's why I'm here." Michael stared at her fixedly. "Your agency specializes in gathering information. I need to know which CIU employee accessed certain files at the embassy in 1978."

Aliza crossed her arms across her chest. "What makes you think we have access to CIU's files?"

Michael snorted. "The NSA has access to everything."

She threw her hands up in the air. "CIU has access to everything."

Michael rubbed his neck. "I can't look up the information. It'll raise suspicion."

"And it won't raise suspicion if I look?" Aliza glowered at him.

"No, it won't," Michael said. "You're the best. You can cover your tracks."

She tapped her foot on the floor. "Flowery words and phrases won't sway my decision. You of all people should know that." She held up her hand before he could say anything. "I'll help. That doesn't mean I'm confirming my agency has access to your records. I'm just helping, okay?"

"Yes, thank you." Michael took another step toward her. "Were you worried?"

Aliza's eyes softened into pools of warm honey. She leaned up and kissed him. "Not at all."

"Liar." Michael deepened the kiss. Energy zinged through his veins, and his skin felt like it was torched with flames.

Aliza wound her arms around him, returning his kisses with fervor. It was like that with Aliza. One touch, one kiss, and boom. They both combusted.

He kissed his way down her throat.

Aliza moaned. She pulled his shirt up and raked her nails along his back. "I missed you in my bed."

Hallelujah! "I've missed being in your bed." He buried his hands in her hair and pulled her in for another kiss. "Let's remedy that."

Two hours later, Michael lay sprawled in Aliza's bed. Aliza lay draped across his body. Her head rested on his shoulder. Her eyes were closed, and her breathing was steady. He ran his hands up and down her back, enjoying the smooth texture of her skin. He needed one last piece of information to pinpoint the traitor. Once he had everything, he'd bounce the information off Gabriel.

Aliza stirred and peered up at him. "You look like a man with a lot on your mind."

Michael caressed her bare shoulder. "I need to debrief my brother."

Aliza yawned. "I thought he wasn't active."

"He's not, but he's smart."

She leaned up on her elbow. "He's hot."

Michael swatted her backside.

Her eyes twinkled. "He looks like you. That makes him hot."

He pursed his lips. "You know, I just realized Gabe and I have the same taste."

"What does that mean?"

"Gabe's taken the fall. He doesn't know it, but he's serious about this woman. She reminds me of you. In fact, you could be sisters."

"If your brother cares for a woman like me, he has good taste."

Michael leaned down and kissed her. "I wholeheartedly agree."

"So, I have a twin?" Aliza joked.

"Not exactly. She has your height and build, and the same hair. Both of you are strong and independent." Michael kissed the hollow of her neck. "The eyes are different though. Hers are green. Yours are the color of honey." He worked his way up to her lips. "Have I mentioned I love honey?"

Aliza's smile would bedazzle a roaring bull into meek submission. "Have you ever considered retiring?" she asked, resting her chin on his chest.

Whoa, change of subject. Michael rubbed his ear. "Yeah, I'll retire someday."

"I've considered it. I sometimes wonder what it would be like to live a normal life."

Michael raised an eyebrow. "Define normal."

She bit her lip. "My parents died when I was a teenager. I

remember what it was like. You know, a normal job, life in suburbia, and the picket fence." She wrinkled her nose. "Scratch suburbia. The suburbs don't work for me."

Michael chuckled.

Aliza's computer beeped. She jumped out of bed. "That must be the rest of the information." She rushed over to the computer, naked. Aliza wasn't shy or self-conscious about her body. Why should she be? She was gorgeous. She printed out a sheet of paper. "I've manipulated the program. I'm copying it onto this USB port."

Michael took the piece of paper she handed him. He scanned through the document and jumped out of bed, reaching for his clothes. He donned his jeans and reached for his shoes. "I have to go." He folded the document and tucked it under his waistband.

Aliza's eyes widened. "What about the files I'm copying for≥ you?"

He tugged his shirt over his head. "How much longer will it take?"

"Thirty minutes."

"Meet me at the usual meeting place." Michael went to the door, opened it, then closed it and strode back to Aliza. He grabbed her shoulders and pulled her out of the chair. "If you want to retire, I'm in. If you want to try the picket fence thing, I'm in. I have to take care of this problem first." He kissed her firmly on the mouth. "I'll see you in an hour." He rushed out the door, leaving a stunned Aliza standing nude in the middle of the bedroom.

CHAPTER FORTY-EIGHT

"If I realized my own perfection,
I'd shake the dust off my clothes with predilection.
Lightheaded I'd soar to the skies,
Toward the ninth heaven, with my head held high."
—*Rumi*

Noor took in the intricate Seljuk architecture of the ancient mosques and historical buildings. Konya was a delightful blend of old and new. Historical mosques sat beside modern buildings and shopping centers. The dichotomy and overall effect were stunning.

She quickened her pace, unable to help the bubble of anticipation in her stomach. She was visiting Rumi's tomb and would allow herself a few minutes of joy before chasing a murderer. The last thought dampened her enthusiasm.

"Is this your first time in Turkey?" Gabriel asked, distracting her from her thoughts.

Noor nodded. "Yes, I've always wanted to visit." She noticed a mosque with a minaret covered in artwork. "Rumi spent most of his life here. Back then the Muslims called this region 'Rum,' and that's how Molana became known as Rumi, which means 'from Rum.' Konya also has historical importance. It was the base of the Seljuk empire in Persia. The Seljuk's were a medieval Turko-Persian empire that controlled a vast area from what is Pakistan today all the way to the Persian Gulf."

They approached the area close to the tomb.

Little butterflies tapped at her chest. "Did you know this is where the Mevlana or Molana order was established?"

Gabriel shook his head.

"Rumi's son and followers established the order after his death," Noor said. "Rumi's son also created the dance of the whirling dervishes, also known as the *sema*. I've read Rumi my entire life, and I've never seen a *sema*," she mused.

They turned the corner and arrived at the main boulevard in front of the Rumi museum and tomb. A stone wall surrounded the tomb. Wide walkways covered the outer perimeter of the stone wall. The museum and tomb had several domes. At the center, a bluish green minaret stood like a beacon, inviting visitors in.

She took hold of Gabriel's arm. "I'd like to pay my respects to Rumi first."

A ghost of a smile tugged at Gabriel's mouth. He pushed a wayward strand of her hair back. "Let's pay our respect to Rumi."

The atmosphere within the walls of the courtyard was quiet and solemn. Patches of green lawn covered the inner courtyard. Several fountains sat across the property. The main entrance of the mausoleum was half-way through the courtyard.

She glanced up at the green dome. "I can't help feeling that things could have ended differently if I'd stayed home the day Mom died. If I'd made better choices and paid attention, Mom would be alive today."

Gabriel's regarded her solemnly. "I understand how you feel."

They followed a group of tourists to the main entrance. Emotion swelled in Noor's chest. "We're at the grave of a person who moved, transformed, and cured many hearts through wisdom and love. When Mom came here, she was a young widow who'd lost everything she loved. She felt desolate and alone. She didn't know if she'd recover the light that was her essence. She told me her visit to Rumi's tomb was enlightening and life changing." She drew in a breath. "I'm glad I'm here with you."

Gabriel's smile traveled from his mouth to his eyes.

Oh, my! She tugged on his hand, and they followed a group of visitors into the mausoleum.

The temperature inside the mausoleum was cool. The sound of their footsteps echoed through the gallery leading to Rumi's tomb. The floors, walls, and ceiling of the cavernous shrine were all stone. Artwork and calligraphy covered the walls and ceiling.

Rumi's tomb sat beneath the mausoleum's minaret. A large cloth embroidered with gold lay covered the tomb. A green turban lay on top of it.

The melody of a flute—or *ney*—filled the background the way ocean waves lap at the shore, gentle yet present. Farther to the right, a man stood in a corner, reciting Rumi's poems.

> *"Do you know what you are?*
> *You are a manuscript of a divine letter*
> *You are a mirror reflecting a noble face*
> *The universe is not outside of you.*
> *Look inside yourself*
> *Everything that you want*
> *You are already that."* (Shiva, 1999)

Noor bit her lip as a myriad of emotions bubbled up. She bent her head and let the pain she'd been holding since Mom's death flow free.

GABRIEL STOOD at the far corner of the tomb. The combination of the flute and Rumi's poetry was a heady jolt. The old man continued to recite Rumi's poems.

"You think you are alive
because you breathe air?
Shame on you,
that you are alive in such a limited way.
Don't be without love,
so you won't feel dead.
Die in Love
And stay alive forever!" (Shiva, 1999)

Sweat broke out on Gabriel's brow. He of all people knew the power of words, and Rumi wielded them masterfully. The words shook and cornered him. They clawed at his chest, ripping through the barriers he'd erected. Grinding his teeth, he stood stoically in the chamber, while the pain and regret of his past mistake bled onto the mausoleum's stone floor.

He didn't know how long they stood in the mausoleum. He looked up and noticed a woman staring intently at Noor. The woman was tall and middle aged. She circled around to where she could study Noor's face.

Gabriel took a half step and placed himself in front of Noor.

The woman turned toward the exit.

He went after the woman.

Noor noticed his departure and fell into step with him. "What's going on?"

Gabriel lowered his voice. "I have a hunch we'll see if I'm right."

They followed the woman to one of the gift shops outside of the museum.

"That woman was staring at you in the tomb. I'll bet you anything that's Banu."

The woman welcomed them, watching Noor with interest.

Gabriel played tourist and browsed the merchandise.

Noor shot him a curious glance and went to browse the rack of postcards. She selected several postcards and took them to the counter. "How much for these postcards, ma'am?"

"You read Rumi?" the woman asked.

Noor reached for her wallet. "Yes, my mother and I read his poems every night."

The woman's face brightened. "Your mother was a wise woman."

Noor tilted her head to the side. "You said Mom was wise. You knew my mother. Are you Banu?"

The woman's shoulders slumped. "Yes, I'm Banu. It's nice to finally meet you, Noor. Shiraz was very proud of you."

Tears shimmered in Noor's eyes. "Would you have a few minutes to have a cup of tea with me and my fiancé? I'd like to know how you met my mother."

Banu motioned to the young man behind the cash register and spoke in low tones. "Why don't you come to the back? I'll make tea while we talk." She guided them to a small kitchen in the back of the shop.

The kitchen had a large window overlooking a cemetery across the street.

She waved to the small table. "Please have a seat." Banu went to a cupboard and pulled out cups and a tray. "Your mother and I —our paths crossed at university. We were both studying at the Sorbonne. We appreciated Rumi's poetry and struck up a friendship. After graduation, Shiraz moved back to Iran and married the general. I moved back home and married a successful merchant. My husband gave me this giftshop as a wedding gift. I've been close to Rumi ever since." Banu poured three cups of tea and brought them to the table. "My husband and I own other shops in this area. We pay our respect to Rumi every day." She paused. "When your father died, your mother went through a difficult period. A friend helped her leave the country, and she came to me and Rumi."

"Interesting," Gabriel murmured.

"Shiraz was in pain. She couldn't see anything beyond it. She visited Rumi hoping to find answers."

"Answers?" Noor prompted.

"Yes, child, Rumi is more than a poet. His words affect the heart, and his doctrine has guided many throughout the centuries." Banu's expression softened. "I couldn't ignore a sister in need. I took her to the cemetery across the street. I told her to mourn her loss and bury her pain once and for all. She wept all day, well into the evening. I stayed by her side the whole time. We went back into Rumi's tomb and stayed there until closing. When we left, she seemed to have found peace."

Noor took the woman's hand. "Thank you for helping my mother."

Banu bowed her head. "It was the least I could do for my friend."

"Will you take us to the cemetery you took Noor's mother to?" Gabriel said.

"Yes, we can take a shortcut." Banu picked up the empty cups and carried them to the sink. She opened the kitchen's back door. "This is the easiest way to get there."

They crossed the street to the cemetery, then took the main path up a hill toward the far end of the cemetery. A stone and concrete wall enclosed the cemetery. Several feet in front of the wall, a large oak tree stood between two stone benches. The green dome of Rumi's tomb stood in the background.

Banu pointed to the bench on the right. "Shiraz sat here." She smiled. "My prayers are with you. Take your time." She moved toward the graves on the other side of the cemetery to give them privacy.

Noor sat on the bench.

Gabriel took a seat beside her.

Several moments passed in silence before she let out a breath. "My mother was an amazing woman."

Gabriel smiled. "Yes, she was. And so are you."

She dug into her purse. "Here's the last clue."

Gabriel held the postcard up. "The picture on the postcard was taken right here. Look at the angle."

"Mom wrote *Banu will show us the nameless grave*.' Should we look at the graves while we wait for her to come back?"

Gabriel glanced at the cemetery. "It's worth a shot. We can start with the graves that have this specific view of Rumi's tomb. You look at the ones on the right. I'll look at the ones on the left side. Call me if you see anything."

They spread out and began their search.

It didn't take Gabriel long to find it. The grave was farther away from the others. The withered tombstone was a mere few inches from the wall surrounding the cemetery. The writing carved on the stone had blurred to where it was impossible to read. He called out to Noor. She ran over to him.

Gabriel ran his hands along the grave and found a stone square on the ground. He slid his hands along the stone square and felt a lever. He wiped the dirt off the lever. An arrow pointed to the right. Gabriel pushed the lever toward the right. It took a few tries to get the square moved aside. Inside, they found a cylinder-shaped space.

Noor leaned closer to the opening, "What is it?"

"It's a vase holder. This grave must have had a stone cylinder set in the ground to hold flowers." Gabriel pushed up his sleeves and reached inside. "There's nothing in it." He reached in again to check for levers or hidden spaces and found nothing.

Noor sat back on her haunches. "What's significant about the nameless grave?"

Gabriel scanned the cemetery. "I don't know, but I believe

your mother's friend can assist." He motioned to Banu, who was making her way to them, hands wringing and voice hoarse.

Noor clasped her hands together. "Miss Banu, this may seem an odd question, but what can you tell me about 'the nameless grave?'"

Banu lowered her voice. "Have you come for the small box? Is that why you're here?"

Noor stepped forward. "Yes, it's important we find it."

Banu nodded. "Follow me."

They followed her back to the giftshop through a small hallway to an office at the back, where she reached for a safe mounted in the wall. Banu opened the safe and pulled out a small box identical to the one they found in Tehran. This one had the name Shiraz Rahman carved on its lid.

"Your mother came back to the cemetery the following morning. The nameless grave belongs to my ancestor. I had told her about a hiding place in the stone wall behind the nameless grave. Shiraz wanted to hide this box in it. I told her time would ruin it. Besides, other members of my family knew about the hiding space. That's when Shiraz gave me the box and asked me to keep it safe." Tears welled in Banu's eyes. "A week before she died, your mother called me. She told me to give you the box in the event you came to Konya and asked about the nameless grave." She handed Noor the box. "I'm sorry I didn't bring it up earlier, but I wanted to honor Shiraz's wishes. If you didn't mention the nameless grave, I wasn't certain I should tell you about the box. It may not have been the right time."

"Thank you, Banu!" Noor gripped the small box with both hands. "Oh, thank you! You've been a great help."

Banu's lips lifted into a smile. "The box is back where it belongs." She straightened. "Are you free for dinner? If so, I'd like to invite you to meet my family."

"I'm sorry, we can't. We would love to meet your family." Noor bit her lip. "There's something we must do first. We'll come back, and when we do, we'll gather for dinner."

Banu embraced Noor. They exchanged phone numbers and email addresses before saying their goodbyes. After one last thank you, they watched her head back to her shop.

"That woman has a kind heart," Gabriel said.

"Definitely." Noor put the box in her purse.

CHAPTER FORTY-NINE

The hair on Gabriel's neck prickled, causing his muscles to tighten. He turned and scanned the area, searching for signs of danger. His burner phone pinged. He read the text Mike sent him and raised his hand to hail a cab. "We have to go."

Noor gripped her purse. "Great. I want to see what's in the box."

Gabriel took hold of her arm. "We're not going to the hotel."

Noor's eyebrows rose. "Why not?"

A cab screeched to a halt. Gabriel held the door open for her. "We're going to Rumi Culture Center."

Noor gaped at him. "Why are we going there?"

Gabriel nudged her toward the cab. "We're meeting with Mike."

"Why does Michael want to meet there?" Noor asked.

Gabriel shrugged. "I don't know. It must be important, and"—he grinned—"it's convenient because we'll watch a *sema* while we're in Turkey."

She chewed on her lower lip, deliberating between going back to the hotel and watching a *sema*.

"The box has been here for eighteen years. Another hour won't make a difference," Gabriel reasoned.

She capitulated and leaned back in the seat, hugging her purse.

The cab wove through the streets of Konya and stopped in front of large white structure. The Mevlana culture center was an angular white building with large windows facing the entrance. It boasted two domes at the center of the building. The building branched, connecting to an open-spaced arena. It housed art galleries and a well-stocked bookstore. The arena was where the sema—dance of the whirling dervishes—took place.

Gabriel thanked the driver and paid him. They entered the building and followed a group of tourists to the arena. Gabriel chose a pair of seats at the end of the center aisle. The seats offered the best escape route if escape became necessary.

Anticipation lit Noor's face. "Stories say Rumi was wandering in the village one day when he heard the rhythmic hammering of a goldsmith beating on gold. It filled him with so much joy, he stretched out both of his arms and spun in a circle, giving his full attention to God. He felt ecstatic and united with God." Noor studied the arena with interest. "Rumi's son, Sultan Walad, instituted the structured version of the dance several years after Rumi died."

The lights dimmed, and the arena fell silent. Twenty dervishes in white robes made their way to the center of the arena. They moved in unison, forming a large circle. Music flooded the arena. The deep, rich melody of a cello and the gentle notes of multiple flutes washed over the audience. The dervishes raised their arms in the air and rotated their bodies. Their movements seemed effortless, as if they were floating on air. The overall effect was mesmerizing.

Fifteen minutes later, the music died down. The enthralled audience remained silent.

Noor's face glowed.

Gabriel leaned in to tease her when he spotted Michael climbing the stairs at the center of the aisles.

Mike bumped into a woman dressed in Islamic garb. *That must be Mike's contact.* Mike apologized to the woman and continued his climb. When Michael reached their row, he bent forward. "We have company."

The music started up again. Another group of dervishes entered the arena.

Gabriel used their former SEAL gestures. *How many?*

Four. Michael pointed toward the top and bottom rows of the arena.

Gabriel spotted the men. Two stood by the northern entrance, and two climbed the stairs close to the center aisles. To his amusement, Noor followed their hand signals.

Gabriel stayed behind Noor, covering her back while they followed Michael out of the arena.

The two men at the top moved in their direction, and the men from below were getting closer.

Once they exited the arena, Gabriel grabbed Noor's hand and ran. They sprinted toward the parking lot, aware of the echoing footsteps behind them.

Gunshots erupted. Gabriel pulled Noor behind a car in the front row.

Michael crouched behind an adjacent car. He motioned to the front of the parking lot. "I'll distract them while you get the car."

Gabriel nodded. He guided Noor to the back of the parking lot, while Michael ran in the opposite direction.

Gabriel and Noor took cover behind a metal container. The sound of footsteps approaching announced a man creeping toward the metal container, The tips of his shoes pointed out like duck feet.

Ducky neared the container.

Gabriel waited for him to get close, then shot him in the foot.

Ducky hit the ground, cursing in multiple languages.

Bullets rained into the container.

Noor flinched.

Gabriel pushed her behind him.

Ducky's buddy came running toward them.

Sweat poured down Gabriel's face and into his eyes. He wiped it away and waited. His heartbeat echoed in his ears.

When Ducky's buddy stepped around the container, Gabriel shot the gun from the man's hand. As he howled in pain, Gabriel fired again, hitting his leg.

"Arrgh!" Ducky's buddy cried in pain and fell.

"Let's go!" Gabriel gripped Noor's hand, and together they made it to the car. Once inside, he revved up the engine and drove to the front.

Two men circled Michael. He took one down with a round-house kick as the second shot at him. Michael took cover behind another car as gunfire exploded around him.

Gabriel slammed the car into the shooter.

When he hit the ground, Michael snatched the man's gun, then jumped into the backseat.

"Any idea who they were?" Gabriel asked, checking the back mirror.

Michael turned to see if anyone else was in the parking lot. "Several. Did you find your clue?"

"Yes."

The sound of sirens came from afar. Michael tapped on his shoulder. "Let's go. The calvary is coming."

Gabriel pushed the accelerator and made it to the highway. "We have to grab our stuff and leave. The hotel won't be safe." He threw his burner phone to Noor. "There's one number in the phone. Send a text to your uncle. Ask him to have the plane ready."

Noor texted the message. A responding beep came immediately. "Uncle Morrie will have the plane ready to take off in an hour."

"Good." He swerved into an alley. "Let's not waste time." He stopped at the hotel's back entrance. "We go in this way."

Gabriel and Michael checked the suite, while Noor waited in the hallway.

Gabriel motioned for her to enter once he was certain the suite was safe. "Forget your luggage, grab your travel documents and the clues."

Noor ran into her room and came back with a small backpack.

"Our friends from the arena just arrived," Mike announced, peering through the curtains.

Gabriel looked out the window.

Two cars pulled up in front of the hotel. Five men ran inside.

"We can't go downstairs." Gabriel went to the suite's terrace. The terrace was two feet away from the next suite's terrace. There were four terraces on their floor. "We go this way."

Michael took the lead. He jumped onto the next terrace and gave Gabriel a thumbs up.

Gabriel took hold Noor's shoulders. "The space between the terraces is only three feet. It's an easy jump."

Noor blanched. "I don't think—"

He didn't let her think. "Trust Aquaman. He knows best." His attempt at humor worked. Some of the color returned to her cheeks. He kissed her forehead. "You can do it. Don't look down." He helped her climb onto the banister. "Keep your eyes on Mike."

Noor jumped and landed by Mike.

Mike jumped onto the next terrace and waved.

Gabriel climbed the banister and jumped into the terrace with Noor. They continued to move from one terrace to the other.

Gabriel and Noor made it to the third terrace when gunshots bounced off the banister.

"Stay down!" Gabriel cried, pulling his gun out.

Two men stood in the terrace of their suite. The shorter one was a mini version of The Rock. Mini Rock aimed his gun at them. The other one jumped onto the next terrace, making his way toward them. Number two looked like Shrek's scary twin. Scary Shrek was closing in on them.

Michael pulled the gun out of his waistband and shot back.

Mini Rock cursed and crouched.

Noor jumped onto the terrace with Michael.

Gabriel shot at Scary Shrek. The giant climbed the railing and jumped onto the terrace with him. Gabriel kicked Scary Shrek in the crotch. Scary grunted and fell to his knees. Gabriel climbed the banister and tried to jump. Scary grabbed his leg. He kicked Scary in the face. A string of foreign curses ensued.

Gabriel looked down. Another terrace sat a few feet below him. He met Michael's gaze. "Go to the stairwell." Gabriel leaned over and jumped onto the terrace below. He kicked the door open on a terrified elderly couple. "My apologies," he mumbled, running into the corridor toward the emergency stairwell.

Footsteps echoed in the stairwell. Mike and Noor were behind him.

The trio arrived in the lobby and hid in a corridor to the left of the elevators. Noor gripped his shirt from behind. Gabriel peered around the corner. Two men paced back and forth in the lobby. Michael pointed to the restaurant. He held his fingers up for the sign of three, two, and one.

Gabriel and Noor ran to the restaurant.

The restaurant had a few customers. He guided Noor to a door marked with an "Employees Only" sign. They went through the double doors and arrived at a long hallway leading to the kitchen and a flight of stairs staff used to get to the rooms. He pulled Noor into a closet. The sound of footsteps echoed. Gabriel grabbed an iron skillet from one of the shelves and waited. The footsteps slowed. The door burst open, and Scary charged inside.

Gabriel brought the skillet down on his head.

Scary tittered on his feet and fell.

"Let's go." He and Noor dashed to the kitchen and came to a halt.

Ash was there with half a dozen men. *Great!*

Ash smirked. "Hello."

"Are those men yours?" Gabriel growled.

Ash held up his hands. "I don't know who they are. I called your room, but you weren't there. I noticed the men running into the hotel and paid the kitchen staff to wait outside. I am happy to assist you anyway I can."

The doors swung open. Michael came in, panting. He took one look at Ash and growled. If looks could kill, Ash would shrivel and die.

Ash raised both hands in a gesture of surrender. "I travel to Turkey often. When I learned that Noor is in Konya, I came to offer my apologies for the unfortunate misunderstanding in Tehran." He placed one hand against his heart. "My security team is here. Allow me to assist you with your problem."

Gabriel glanced at Mike, who stood with a deceptively calm stance.

Mike shrugged.

Ash rubbed his hands together. "Splendid." He approached Noor. "My dear, I want another chance at getting to know my friend's daughter. Can you forgive me for the terrible misunderstanding in Tehran?"

Gabriel sensed Noor's hesitation and winked at her.

The lines around Noor's eyes tightened. "Very well. We'll put the past behind us."

Ash puffed his chest out. "My driver is at your disposal. He will take you where you wish to go."

A man in dark jeans and a T-shirt stepped forward.

"We're going to the airport," Gabriel said.

CHAPTER FIFTY

Gabriel waited until the jet took off and opened the box they'd found in Turkey. He pulled out a thin sheet of paper folded into a small square. The paper was worn, its color faded to a dull yellow. He placed it on the table beside the key codes. Gabriel used the key codes in the first document to decipher what was on the sheet of paper. "Wow!"

"What does it say?" Noor leaned closer to study the document.

"I know what happened the day your father died." Gabriel pointed to the paper. "The document we found in Tehran was the last key code your father created before he died. The sheet of paper we found in Turkey shows the last report your father received." He pointed to the sheet of paper. "Using the last code yields this message. It's what your father read on September 8, 1978."

HSRCE-I-RSVS HSRCE-I-RSSV
GMKEVEXXI GEWI

"Your father realized there was an error in the codes because he crossed out the last word in the first line and re-wrote the code. Here's what we get if we stick with the original two lines."

Donya-e-Noro
Cigarette Case

Gabriel pointed to the document. "Now look at the words if we use your father's corrected version."

Donya-e-Noor
Cigarette Case.

Noor rubbed her temple. "Leila was right. There is a diamond identical to the Darya-e-Noor. It's called Donya-e-Noor."

"Yes. Your father understood whoever was sending him the codes was also warning him. The date of the first document is important." Gabriel lay down the sheet of codes. "September 8, 1978 was a day of violent demonstrations in Tehran. Law enforcement and military were occupied with the riots. It was an ideal time to break into the vault." He pointed at the codes. "Your father's soldier didn't make a mistake writing the codes. He was warning your father someone broke into the vault by mixing the last two letters in the first line. Your father caught the error and went to check on the bank. He surprised the intruder." Gabriel paused. "You can guess what happened next."

Michael rubbed his ear. "It begins to make sense."

Gabriel placed the clues back into the boxes. "What did you find out from your contact?"

Michael handed him a sheet of paper. "This is what my contact gave me."

Gabriel's brows formed a deep *V*. "This puts Nolan and Jonathan in Tehran in 1978."

Michael's fingers tapped on his thigh. "Both had the same

security clearance as Dad did. Nolan worked from Dad's office until December of the same year."

Gabriel handed the note back to Michael. "You think Nolan's the leak?"

Michael shrugged. "That's what the intel says."

Gabriel knew how Michael's mind worked. "What do you say?"

"I don't know." Michael massaged his neck. "I need to think."

"Are you going to contact McMillan?" Gabriel asked.

"Not yet." Michael ran a hand through his hair. "I need to find the mole first." He paused. "This affects Noor."

Noor stiffened at the mention of her name. "How does this affect me?"

Mike unbuckled his seatbelt and took the other seat beside her. "We're dealing with two different issues—murder and treason. Both are connected to your parents' deaths." Michael glanced at Gabriel.

Noor caught the exchange. "What is it? What aren't you telling me?"

Gabriel clenched his jaw. He realized he was gripping his seatbelt and loosened his hold. "The person or persons who committed the murder, and the person who committed treason against the U.S., were after the artifacts in the vault. Both groups will come after you."

"Because they believe I know where my father hid the diamond and the cigarette case," Noor finished.

The brothers nodded in unison.

Michael glanced at Gabriel warily. "I have a plan."

Noor sat straighter. "What's the plan?"

"We set a trap and catch these people before they get to Noor," Michael said.

Fury unfurled in Gabriel's chest. He loomed over them. "We are not using Noor as bait." He enunciated each word slowly.

Noor tapped her index finger to her mouth.

That she was considering it fueled his anger. "It's not an option." Gabriel rose from his seat and went to the fridge on the other side of the plane. He yanked a bottle of water out of the fridge and took a long sip, trying to cool the fire roaring in his veins.

Noor approached him. "Gabriel—"

Gabriel ground his teeth. "No!"

"Gabriel, please—"

He didn't let her finish. "It's not going to happen."

"It's not your choice!" she snapped and closed her eyes, trying to regain her composure. She lay her hand on his arm. "I want justice for my parents, and I don't want to spend the rest of my life looking over my shoulder. Please try to understand."

Gabriel glowered. "We'll find another way."

"There is no other way." Noor raked her hand through her hair. "I won't lie to you, I'm terrified. However, you'll be there, and Michael and Uncle Morrie will help." She stroked his arm. "It's our best option."

Gabriel wanted to shout. To punch something. To throw her over his shoulder and take her far away from all of it. He shoved his clenched fists into his pockets. Damn it, she was right. They had no other option. This had to end, yet the thought of Noor hurt chilled his blood.

Sweat trickled down his back. So many things could go wrong. She could be killed. *Not if you plan it right.*

He gritted his teeth. "If we're doing this, we must plan it right. I'm not taking chances with your life."

Her mouth lifted into a smile. "Agreed."

Michael nodded in approval and leaned back in his seat.

CHAPTER FIFTY-ONE

PARIS, FRANCE

Gabriel placed two sheets of paper on the dining room table of the safe house. He took Michael, Morris, and Noor through the plan he'd drafted on the flight from Konya.

Morris scowled. "I don't like this plan!"

"I don't either," Gabriel admitted. "It's our only option."

Noor scooted closer to Morris. "Uncle Morrie, I won't be alone. Gabriel and Michael will be there."

Morris turned an ugly shade of red. "I don't care if every U.S. Navy SEAL is there. I don't like the plan."

Noor stared at her hands. "I was hoping you would help."

Morris growled. "Doesn't mean I have to like it."

Michael rubbed his ear. "None of us like it. It's the best way to keep Noor safe."

Morris glared at Michael. "You're doing this for Noor's safety?"

"Absolutely." Michael rushed on before Morris could say anything. "There's a second problem. It's connected to the

Rahmans' deaths. In fact, I believe once we catch the person who killed Noor's parents, we will solve the second problem."

Morris crossed his muscular arms over his chest and stared daggers at all of them.

Gabriel blew out a breath. "Truth is, I don't know how much safer Noor will be if we don't go through with it." He tapped his pen on the table. "We have a common friend who can help. I've called Sheila. Her representative will be here any minute."

Morris banged his fist on the dining room table. "We can't offer Noor up as bait."

The doorbell rang before anyone could comment.

Michael jumped out of his seat. "That must be my contact."

Voices echoed in the hall. Mike came back to the dining room followed by Father Pierre, Mustafa, and Abarron.

Aww hell! Gabriel rubbed his temples as a dumbfounded Michael turned to him for an explanation.

Morris scowled. "Who the hell are these people?"

Noor patted Morris's arm. "They're Mom's friends. I told them we were staying here."

"Do not curse young man!" Abarron tapped Morris with his cane. "I'll have you know that I have impeccable hearing." Abarron hobbled to the closest chair and sat down, giving Morris the once over.

Father Pierre took Noor's hand in both of his. "We've been worried, my dear. The last time we met you were with—" He glanced uncertainly from Michael to Gabriel.

Michael tilted his head in Gabriel's direction.

"Yes, thank you. As I was saying, the last time we met, you were with Mister Gabriel, and we haven't heard from you since."

Noor nodded. "Father, I appreciate your kindness, however, there are things I can't explain. I'm sorry, you must leave. It's dangerous to be here."

"Nonsense!" Abarron pounded his cane on the floor. "If

there's any danger to you, we will help. We made your mother a promise, and we intend to keep it."

Okay, it was time to intervene. Gabriel rose from his seat "Look—"

Mustafa chimed in before he could finish his sentence. "If there is any danger to the child, we will help. Several people helping Noor is better than three people helping her."

"Please," Noor pleaded. "Your lives could be at risk."

"Is Noor in danger?" Father Pierre inquired.

Gabriel met the priest's gaze. "Yes, she is."

"Then it's settled. We will help," the priest replied.

Gabriel counted to five, trying to keep his temper under control. This was getting out of hand. Who was he kidding? It was already out of hand. "You're not trained for this kind of thing." Gabriel's tone left no room for arguments.

Mustafa went to stand by Father Pierre. "People are killing in the name of Allah every day." He paused and rubbed his chin. "I will shock the world and save a life in the name of Allah." Mustafa's deep laughter bounced off the walls.

What the fuck? Michael mouthed.

"Gentlemen," Gabriel said. "We appreciate your offer of help, but you'll put yourselves and Noor in danger. Let us handle this."

"Oh, but we are, my son," Father Pierre added cheerfully. "You make the decisions. We will help wherever we can."

"The three of us are old," Abarron admitted. "However, we are sharp, and we have world experience." Abarron tapped Morris on the shoulder. "Do you see the difference? You wouldn't get anything done if we were three dumb old men. In fact, there's an old saying in my country. We say a wise enemy is better than a simple-minded friend."

"Now Abarron, you know very well that's an old Persian saying," Mustafa interjected.

Abarron waved a hand dismissively. "Bah, the Persians take credit for everything."

Father Pierre coughed. "Let's not get sidetracked. Gabriel, please tell us what is going on, and we will help."

Gabriel's phone beeped. He glanced at the screen. "My guest is here." He excused himself and went to greet his visitor.

Arie, Sheila's assistant, stood in the doorway. Arie was five feet three inches. Her build and features were delicate, reminding one of a porcelain doll. She wore black pants, black boots, and a yellow and black changshan, or Chinese tunic. Gabriel knew Arie carried a dagger under her tunic. He'd seen her use it firsthand. Arie was lethal.

A pair of shrewd eyes gleamed. Arie bowed her head. "Sheila sends her regards."

Gabriel thanked Arie and ushered her into the dining room, where he made the introductions.

Noor rose to greet Arie. "Thank you for assisting us. I am most grateful to you and Sheila."

Arie inclined her head regally. "We are happy to assist."

Mike grinned. "Hey, Arie, good to see you."

The corners of Arie's mouth lifted for an instant. Other than that she showed no emotion.

Mike's phone beeped. "My contact's here. I'll get the door."

Arie took a seat by Father Pierre. Her cat-like eyes sized up each person in the room. Her lips quivered slightly when she saw Mustafa and Abarron sitting side by side.

Michael came back accompanied by a stunning brunette. The woman moved with a natural grace that was both captivating and sensual. Her honey-colored eyes surveyed the people in the room. Every man in the room fell silent. A knowing smile tugged at the woman's mouth. The goddess knew her own allure.

Gabriel caught Noor watching his reaction. He winked at her.

Michael smirked. "Everyone, this is Aliza Cohen, a friend. Aliza, meet Noor Rahman. She's hosting this, uh, meeting. The mug mirroring mine is my brother, Gabriel, and these people are their friends."

"Nice to meet you." Aliza took a seat between Morris and Michael.

Morris pursed his lips. "You're NSA, right?"

Aliza bowed her head. "And you're Interpol, correct?"

The question surprised Gabriel. He knew Morris had some formal training, but he hadn't considered the International Criminal Police Organization, otherwise known as Interpol.

Morris shrugged. "A long time ago."

Aliza's eyes rested on Arie.

Noor made the introductions. "Aliza this is Arie." Noor glanced at Gabriel, unsure how to proceed.

"Arie works for Sheila," Mike offered.

Aliza's golden eyes gleamed with interest. "How interesting. I thought Sheila's a myth."

"It will please Sheila to know her efforts are recognized," Arie said in a musical tone.

Mustafa watched the interaction with interest. "Who is Sheila, and why is she a myth?"

Aliza didn't take her eyes off Arie. "Sheila is the hand of justice. She protects women and children from drug dealers, terrorists, and human traffickers. Her punishment is swift and harsh. She's impossible to track because no one can identify her. Her own employees have never seen her."

Father Pierre stroked his chin. "Judgment is for God, not humans."

"I disagree, Father." Arie's voice hardened. "There are crimes committed against innocent women and girls every day. No one has raised a hand to help them. No government, no international entity, not even your God. The only person who cares is Sheila. When these abandoned women and children pray to Sheila, they know Sheila will respond before your God does."

"There is but one God," Mustafa chided gently. "If you call out to him, you will receive his blessing."

Arie tilted her head. "Why bother God when Sheila takes care of the problem?"

Aliza crossed her legs and faced Mike. "There's never a dull moment around you."

Mike bowed his head. "I do my best to please."

"Careful, McKnight," Aliza huffed. "Pleased is not how I feel considering the way you left back in Turkey."

Noor gasped. "You were in Turkey? What happened?"

Aliza tapped her fingers on her leg. "Let's see, I was naked in bed when Mike rushed off hardly saying goodbye."

Noor blinked, blushed, and swallowed a chuckle.

Abarron slapped his forehead, Mustafa shook his head, and Father Pierre sighed.

Gabriel raised an eyebrow. "Looks like you're losing your touch, bro."

"The circumstances were exceptional," Mike protested.

Noor smirked. "Jason Van would never leave a gorgeous naked woman in bed. Would he, Gabriel?"

Gabriel grinned. "No, he wouldn't."

Michael threw his hands in the air. "There were lives at stake. That ought to count for something." He reached out and took hold of Aliza's hand. "I promised to make it up to you, didn't I?"

"Which is why I will give you another chance," Aliza leaned over and kissed Michael's cheek.

Aliza's reaction didn't surprise Gabriel. Women loved Michael. It was his brother's besotted expression that took Gabriel by surprise.

"No, no, no, child!" Abarron pounded his cane on the floor. "You will do no such thing. Why would he buy the cow if he gets the milk for free? This is a lesson I teach young people." He shook his finger at Noor, Aliza, and Arie. "Do not engage in any sexual activity unless you have a ring on your finger. Do you hear me? You will not secure a husband if you offer the milk for free!"

Aliza and Noor broke into peals of laughter. Arie's eyes glinted with humor.

Gabriel raised his hand. "As interesting as this discussion is, we are running out of time. Looks like Father Pierre, Abarron, and Mustafa insist on offering their help."

Aliza's eyes narrowed. "Wait a minute, I'm here because Mike needs help in a matter regarding national security."

Abarron rested his chin on his cane. "We are here to help keep Noor safe. We can also assist you with your security matters. Go on, son." He motioned graciously to Gabriel.

Aliza crossed her arms and glared at Mike.

Gabriel cleared his throat. "I will give you a quick rundown of what we're dealing with. Then, we can walk through the plan."

For the next thirty minutes, Gabriel took everyone through the events of the past weeks, beginning with Michael's disappearance. He pulled out two sheets of paper and set them on the dining room table. "Here's what we are thinking." He pointed to the drawing on a sheet. "We need someone to keep tabs on these people."

"Sheila will take care of that," Arie said.

Morris rose from his seat. "We can't offer Noor up as bait."

"Uncle Morrie, stop right now!" Noor's tone didn't allow room for argument. "I'm a grown woman capable of making my own decisions. I will do this, and it's not up for debate." She kissed him on the cheek and softened her tone. "Your help, however, is appreciated."

Arie smiled for the first time.

Morris ran a hand through his hair and sat back down. He drew a line on a name. "You can count Roshi out. I checked her alibi years ago. She's not the killer. I wouldn't allow her to get close to Noor if she wasn't clean."

"We will definitely rule her out, "Noor said. "Aunt Roshi is family."

"Fine," Gabriel said. "We'll rule her out for now." He handed a sheet of paper to Aliza. "We'll need your help with this. Can you get what we need approved?"

Aliza read through the document. "Yes."

Gabriel made notes on the sheets of paper. "That leaves Father Pierre, Abarron, and Mustafa. We first need to find you a place to stay."

Mustafa raised his hand. "I texted my attorney while you were talking. He'll buy three apartments in Oklahoma City by the end of the week."

Everyone stared at Mustafa. He lifted his shoulders. "I'm financially secure. It's no trouble."

Gabriel folded the sheets of paper. "Seems like we have a plan. I'll send everyone timetables and a phone number. Use the number to let me know when things are in place on your end."

Abarron rose. "We should go plan for our trip."

Father Pierre and Mustafa also rose to leave.

Morris placed his cup on the tray and rose. "I'll keep in touch."

"Uncle Morrie, won't you stay here?" Noor offered.

"My flight leaves tonight. I'll see you back in Oklahoma City." Morris gave Noor a one arm hug and left.

Arie rose to leave.

Noor reached out and took hold of her hands. "Please be careful. I will never forgive myself if you or anyone else gets hurt."

Arie's opal-colored eyes softened. "You are kind and brave, sister. Don't worry. Sheila is careful as am I." Arie bid Noor goodbye and turned to Gabriel. "Sheila sends a message. Try to not get killed." Arie left on that note.

Noor went to Aliza. "Mike and Gabriel are staying at the safe house. Why don't you stay here while you are in Paris?"

Aliza beamed. "Thank you, I'll take you up on your offer."

"Great. You'll be comfortable upstairs." They wandered off together.

Gabriel found himself alone with Mike. He rubbed his

temples. "Christ, what a motley crew. The rabbi, the priest, and the Muslim scholar, check. The shady uncle, check. The unpredictable vigilante, check. The civilians, check."

Michael smothered a laugh. "We'll make it work. They won't get to Noor."

"No, they won't," Gabriel said.

Mike glanced around and lowered his voice. "Can you ask Dotts to look into something for me?"

"Sure, what's going on?"

"I have a hunch. I need Dotts to research someone."

CHAPTER FIFTY-TWO

TEHRAN, IRAN

Ash Kosha stood by the window of his office, staring at the rocky terrains of the Alborz Mountains. He'd taken the first step in getting close to Noor Rahman. He didn't have much time to get the information he needed. The American was losing his patience, and his business associates were questioning his capability.

A knock sounded on the door. His assistant stepped in and placed the mail on his desk. A white satin envelope peeked out from the stack of mail.

He looked at it curiously and opened it. "Finally!" He was so pleased, he wanted to roll around on the thick carpet. Instead, he dialed a number.

"I told you not to call," the American snarled.

Ash's cheer fizzled. His mouth went dry. "I have good news. Noor Rahman invited me to a jewelry exhibition hosted by her aunt. Noor is a sponsor. She's letting me in her circle."

"Good, get the information, and don't mess up." The American disconnected the call.

WASHINGTON, D.C., USA

Moira McKnight poured herself a cup of tea and racked her brains for something to do. *Please, let my boys be all right!* She'd repeated the silent litany since Michael disappeared. She didn't know where Michael was, and now Gabriel was on the other side of the world with Noor, trying to find answers.

Maintaining a daily routine under the circumstances was the hardest thing to do. She'd cleaned her house from top to bottom and reorganized the kitchen twice. She'd redone the garden and knit multiple sweaters for her grandson. "I'll do yard work," she said to the empty kitchen.

Some days, the fear of bad news paralyzed her. Then, the warm glow that came with the birth of her children flickered in her heart. It gave her hope. Moira rubbed her chest. "Mike's alive, and I'll hear from Gabriel soon."

Determined to get through the day without crying, Moira powered up her laptop. She hadn't checked her email in two days. It wouldn't hurt to check it again. She found an email from Noor in her inbox.

Hello Moira,
I went to Tehran after all these years, and I'm enchanted with the city. I visited my parents' home and went to the bazaar you recommended. I bought a pair of twin cobalt stones from an antique jeweler. They're in great shape. I leave Tehran tomorrow. Let me know if you need anything from Iran. If not, I hope to see you and Carl at Roshi's exhibition. You will receive the invitation shortly. All is well here. I hope all is well with you.
Noor

Moira sat as if glued to her chair. She read the email again.

Swiping at her tears, she rushed to Carl's study and flung the door open.

Carl rose from his chair. "What's wrong?"

Moira flung herself into his arms. "They're all right," she sobbed. "Gabriel and Michael are all right."

Carl took her by the shoulders. "How do you know this?"

Moira laughed between the tears. "That wonderful girl, Noor, sent me an email. She said she bought a pair of twin cobalt stones and they're in great shape. We never talked about jewelry. She's trying to tell me Gabriel and Michael are all right. Come see for yourself." She took Carl's hand and dragged him to her office.

Carl read the email and turned to her, opening his arms. Moira went to him. "Thank God," he choked into her hair. Carl kissed her. "The way Noor worded her email suggests Mike's still in danger.

Moira wiped at her tears. "Noor wants us to be at Roshi's exhibition. It's important. Have you checked the mail for an invitation?"

Carl went to the stack of mail he'd placed on the kitchen table. He sorted through the pile and pulled out a white envelope. He tore the envelope open. "We're invited to the opening of a jewelry exhibition next week. Tell Noor we'll be there. I'll make the arrangements."

Moira grabbed her laptop and replied to Noor's email.

WASHINGTON, *D.C., CIU Headquarters*

Jonathan Smith sat brooding in his office. The phone call with Michael McKnight put him on edge. "What a clusterfuck!" He planned to retire in six months. Treason wasn't a small administrative oversight. He tapped his fingers on his desk. He had to fix the problem before it turned into a nightmare. He'd get involved.

He noticed the envelope sitting on his desk. Noor had invited him to Roshi's jewelry exhibition.

It all circled back to Noor Rahman. The girl had become a target overnight. Problem was, she knew nothing. *Or did she?* There was only one way to find out.

He dialed his assistant. "Book a flight and hotel accommodations for Oklahoma City please. I plan on staying for a week."

LONDON, England

Leila put the final touches on the last piece of jewelry. She examined her work critically. This piece was the highlight of the exhibition. It was a rendition to the old days in Iran.

Creating the piece had come with a heavy price. Images from the past filtered through her mind, tormenting her. She rubbed her temples. *Memories, so many memories.* She heard the wind rustling the leaves on the oak trees in her uncle's gardens. The scents of summer roses and night jasmine filled her senses.

She saw the old house in all its glory. She remembered the parties, the music, and Tehran's starlit skies. Then came the image of two lovers planning the future. *Cameron!* She wiped the sweat from her brow. "I won't think of the past. The past is gone."

A knock sounded on the door. Mrs. Forrester entered the workroom. "Do you want me to book a hotel, ma'am?"

Leila waved her hand. "No, thank you. I'm staying with Noor."

NEW YORK CITY, New York

Benita sat in her studio, working on her latest set of plates. A ghost of a smile tugged at her mouth. She was proud of her online business. People loved her art, and she appreciated the solitude of her work. It was a win-win situation. Trust was for the naïve. She'd learned that the hard way.

Benita finished the last plate and went to the kitchen to pour herself a cup of tea. The doorbell rang, making her jump. She cursed and placed her cup back on the counter.

No one knew where she lived. She ran into the bedroom and grabbed her pistol. She checked the peephole.

Larry, the postman, stood outside the door with an envelope in his hand. Why was Larry at her door?

"Who is it?" she called out, her heart pounding.

"I have a letter for you," Larry announced.

"Leave it in my mailbox."

Larry scratched his head. "It's certified mail, ma'am. I need your signature."

Her mind raced. If she ignored Larry, she wouldn't know who sent the letter. She could tell Larry she didn't want the letter, pack her bags, and hit the road. She never stayed in one place for long, but she was tired of running. She liked New York, and she liked her beautiful apartment.

Benita squared her shoulders. "Who's it from?"

Larry glanced at the envelope. "There's no first name, ma'am. It says Rahman."

Benita drew in a breath. Lightheadedness took over. She took a few calming breaths to control the shaking in her limbs. She unlocked the door and opened it a few inches.

Larry's eyes widened.

She wondered what he thought of the scar. It didn't matter. The physical scar wasn't the one that tormented her.

Benita signed the paperwork. She jerked the envelope out of Larry's hand and shut the door, bolting the locks. She stood behind the door, chest heaving.

She waited for the rapid thumping of her heart to settle. Once she gained her composure, she laid the envelope on the kitchen table and poured herself a cup of tea. The envelope beckoned and taunted. Benita ignored it and went back to work.

She pulled out another plate and picked up the delicate paint brush. Her hands shook violently. She put the paintbrush down. "Damn it!"

She went back to the kitchen and tore the envelope open. "No, no, no!" She'd done everything humanly possible to forget the past. That was the problem with the past. It came back to haunt you.

The memories surfaced like a stampede of elephants. She was back in Tehran. Demonstrations littered the streets. The pungent odor of human sweat. The acrid stench of gasoline and smoke, and people smashing property with no thought to whom it belonged to. The frenzy of the crowd, and the onslaught of fear. It all came tumbling down on her.

Her breath grew labored as images of Shiraz Rahman's birthday clouded her mind. The beautiful home and heavenly gardens. The candlelit living room, the sickly-sweet smell of jasmine, and the muffled conversation in the background. Shiraz blowing out the candles. The conversation at the dinner table and the slip no one noticed except her. She knew her death was imminent.

The sound of shattered glass jolted Benita back to the present. She'd broken her special tea glass. Panting, she wiped the sweat off her forehead and grabbed a broom from the pantry. *No more!* She was tired of hiding. It was time to finish it once and for all. The Rahmans were dead, but their daughter lived. She glanced at the invitation. *I'll go to Oklahoma City. I owe it Shiraz, and to myself.* She threw the shards of glass into the trashcan and grabbed her laptop.

≈

WASHINGTON, D.C.

Mina Delany grabbed the mail and unlocked the front door. She threw her coat, purse, and keys on a chair and sifted through the stack of mail. She spotted the white envelope and tore it open.

Her eyes narrowed. Suddenly, Gabriel McKnight was close to the Rahman's daughter. Michael McKnight disappeared in the Persian Gulf, and Asra Madison was dead. Iran was the common link in all of it.

The Rahmans are the common link. Sweat broke out on her forehead. She recalled Shiraz Rahman's birthday party. She'd come in from the gardens and was looking for Tyler when she heard the voices in the study. She recognized Parviz and Tyler's voice. She didn't know who the third person was.

Mina took the envelope to the kitchen and poured herself a glass of wine. Tyler would be home any minute. She needed the truth.

It wasn't long before Tyler sauntered into the kitchen. "Hi, sweetheart." The smile on Tyler's face froze. "What's the matter?"

Mina glared at him. "Do the McKnight's know anything about the argument you and Parviz had the night of Shiraz Rahman's birthday?"

Tyler paled. "No. I've told you this before."

"You're sure?" Mina asked.

"Yes."

Mina crossed her arms over her chest. "What are you hiding from me?"

Tyler looked away.

"Tyler, it's time to tell me the truth. What did you argue about that night?"

Tyler went to the cabinet and poured himself a shot of scotch. He sat on a barstool and stared out the window. When he met her eyes, his filled with tears. "I made a big mistake, Mina." His jowls shook. "We're not the only ones who knew."

"What are you talking about?"

Tyler wiped the sweat off his forehead. "We're not the only ones who knew Parviz was guarding the vault."

Mina scooted her chair closer to him. "Tell me everything."

Tyler did.

Mina picked the white envelope up. "Noor Rahman invited us to her aunt's jewelry exhibition. I'll book the tickets."

Tyler nodded. "Fine."

Washington, D.C.

Gabriel waited outside of the police station. He'd spent the entire morning in a meeting with McMillan and Michael.

McMILLAN HAD INSTRUCTED him to hold off on talking to the police until he and Michael had made the necessary arrangements. Gabriel's phone beeped. He read the text and turned toward the police station.

He asked the officer at the front for Detective Hood. The police officer's eyes widened when Gabriel gave him his name. He took Gabriel to a conference room with pale walls and an old metal table. He told Gabriel to wait and went to find the detectives. Several minutes later, Detectives Robin and Hood marched into the conference room.

Robin wore his perpetual scowl. He opened his mouth to speak or snarl.

Gabriel didn't want to know. He raised his hands. "I didn't kill Asra Madison, and I can prove it, but I need your help."

Hood tilted her head. "Why should we believe you?"

A slow smile spread across Gabriel's face. "Because I came here on my own. Because your gut tells you I'm innocent, and you want to catch the real killer. Help me, and you will."

CHAPTER FIFTY-THREE

OKLAHOMA CITY, OKLAHOMA

Gabriel zipped across Park Avenue. He'd changed out of his usual attire of jeans and a shirt into a suit and tie. The private opening for Roshi's exhibition was held at the Oklahoma City Art Museum. The museum invited a hundred and fifty people to the exhibition. Amongst the guests were the Mayor of Oklahoma City, the Governor, heads of multiple corporations, Middle Eastern families who lent pieces to the exhibit, and the press.

Noor was at the museum helping Roshi finalize details for the evening's reception. She was safe for now.

Gabriel crossed over to Couch Drive and found himself at the main entrance of the Art Museum.

The Oklahoma City Art Museum was no Smithsonian, yet it had an old-world charm. The atrium lobby was transformed into an elegant reception area. A group of musicians stationed themselves below the main staircase, warming up their instruments. A small bar was set up at the northwest corner of the atrium lobby. The lobby's main attraction was a magnificent glass tower made by Dale Chihuly. It stood at fifty-five feet, filling all three floors of the atrium. The glass tower held twenty-four hundred pieces of blown glass in various shades of blue, yellow, gold, and green. Sunlight bounced off the tower, transforming the atrium into a haven of color.

He tapped at the small listening device in his ear. "Can you hear me?"

"Affirmative," Billy answered.

"Ditto," Michael confirmed.

"Good. I reception starts in thirty minutes. I'll keep the mic on."

Noor stood by the entrance, talking to Roshi and Leila. Her eyes lit up when he approached them.

"Gabriel!" She kissed him on his cheek.

Gabriel put his arm around Noor's waist. "I was looking forward to the event." He greeted Roshi and Leila, congratulating them on the exhibit.

Leila batted her eyelashes. "I keep telling Noor I'm glad she found you. What good is life with no play?"

"I consider myself a lucky man," Gabriel said.

Roshi tapped his shoulder with her fan. "You're also a smart man."

The first set of guests arrived. Seven women in dark blue burka's greeted Roshi. Their security stood at a discreet distance.

"They're Saudi royalty," Noor whispered and went to greet the women.

Gabriel hung back and mingled with the guests. Every so often, Noor's eyes would seek him out. He winked at her and turned to the entrance.

By five thirty, the atrium lobby was packed with guests.

Mom and Dad arrived. Dad gave him a questioning look asking if Michael was okay.

Gabriel nodded.

Dad's eyes filled with tears.

Mom came forward and hugged him. She leaned up and whispered, "Is your brother all right?"

"Yes, he'll be home soon," Gabriel said.

Mom's face radiated joy. "I love you, Gabriel. I love you, too, Michael," she whispered in his ear for Michael to hear. Mom took hold of Dad's arm and went to mingle with the guests.

"Jesus, your mother's scary," Dotts muttered.

Michael chuckled.

Jonathan arrived. He greeted Roshi and leaned in to whisper something in her ear. Roshi burst into laughter. After talking to Noor, Jonathan approached Gabriel and clapped him on the shoulder. "Good to see you, son. I'm sorry your Paris trip turned up nothing."

"It was worth a try," Gabriel said.

Jonathan declined the drink the waiter offered him. "I have men posted around the museum. I couldn't do much for Noor's parents, but I can help keep her safe."

"Thank you, sir."

Jonathan lowered his voice. "I talked to Michael. I'm glad he's alive. Do you know when he's coming back?"

Gabriel maintained a stoic expression. "No, sir."

Jonathan nodded. He spotted Gabriel's parents and waved. "I'll go say hi to your parents. Stay alert."

Gabriel waited until Jonathan was out of earshot and tapped on his microphone. "You didn't tell Jonathan you're back."

"No, we find the leak first," Michael answered.

Tyler and Mina Delany arrived. Mina greeted Noor and Roshi. Tyler headed straight to the bar.

Gabriel waited until Mina joined Tyler and pulled them aside. "Let's talk."

Mina nodded gravely and tugged on Tyler's arm. The trio moved away from the bar.

Gabriel chose a corner where he could keep an eye on Noor. "General Rahman had an argument with Missus Rahman's friend on the night of her birthday. There was a third person in the room. That was you. What was the argument about?"

Tyler tugged on his collar.

Mina nudged Tyler. "Tell him everything."

Tyler gulped. "I was a young diplomat when we were stationed in Tehran. Mina and I had student loans." Tyler rubbed his forehead. "Iran was in complete chaos, and Ash wanted to smuggle Persian artifacts out of the country. He'd doctored the paperwork and had a list of buyers. Some of them were reputable museums." Tyler's jowls shook when he spoke. "I had diplomatic immunity. Ash wanted me to get the artifacts out of the country. It was tempting, and I almost gave in." Tyler paused. "I couldn't do it. It would ruin both our careers." His hand moved between himself and Mina. "I backed out." Tyler took a handkerchief out of his pocket and wiped his forehead with it. "The general found out and threatened to have Ash arrested. Ash pleaded and begged. He said he wouldn't do it again. The general gave Ash a reprieve. He told Ash he'd keep a close eye on him.

"Your father was my supervisor. Carl has a strict moral code. He would have sent me packing if he'd found out about it. The general said he wouldn't tell your father so long as I stayed on the straight path. We left Iran a month after Missus Rahman's birthday."

Mina elbowed him. "Tell him the rest."

Tyler gulped. "The general was guarding a secret vault holding priceless artifacts and documents the Iranian government hadn't disclosed. Ash knew about the vault, and so did several of the senior level diplomats." Tyler raised his palms. "That's all I know, and I have done nothing unethical since then."

Gabriel turned to leave.

Mina squared her shoulders and took hold of Tyler's hand. "Tyler retires in a few months. This could ruin his years of service. Are you going to tell anyone about this incident?"

"No." Disgusted, Gabriel turned away.

Ash Kosha arrived. He strode up to Noor and hugged her. The man took slimy to a whole new level. He stood by Noor for several minutes and moved away when more guests stepped up to speak with her.

Noor grimaced when Ash turned away.

Two women approached Gabriel. A skinny blond with heavy makeup batted her eyes. She reminded him of a racoon. "You're Gabriel McKnight, the author."

Gabriel bowed his head and greeted the woman. He shifted to keep Noor in his line of sight.

"I made a bet with my friend, Lauren." Skinny blond stepped into his space. "You're Jason Van. The stories are about you, aren't they?"

Gabriel stepped back, putting distance between them. "Sorry to disappoint you ladies. Jason was born from my imagination. We have little in common."

The one name Lauren giggled. "I don't believe that. Will you take a picture with us?"

Gabriel took a picture with them and extricated himself.

"I can't see them. Are they hot?" Michael asked.

"Yeah, are they hot?" Billy repeated.

Gabriel ignored their questions. He was about to join Noor when a woman approached him. A large scar ran from her left temple over her face and disappeared behind her neck. On any other person, the scar would mar the beauty. This woman's delicate appeal shone through it.

"You're one of Moira's boys, aren't you?" Her voice was lyrical and husky.

"Yes, ma'am."

The woman studied him. "Which one are you?"

"I'm Gabriel, ma'am. And you are?" She looked familiar, yet Gabriel couldn't place her.

"Your parents are good people." The woman pursed her lips. The movement made the scar on her cheek more pronounced. "I've been watching you. You're protective of the Rahman girl."

Gabriel stiffened as recognition hit him. "You're Benita."

The woman flinched. "Benita no longer exists. My name is Julie." Her eyes darted around the lobby. "I need to get out of here."

Gabriel lowered his voice, not wanting to scare her. "You disappeared years ago, why?"

Benita—Julie—shook her head. "How far are you willing to go to keep Noor Rahman safe?"

"Look, Miss Julie, if you know of any threat—"

Benita's chest heaved. She lowered her voice. "Answer my question."

Gabriel met her eyes. "As far as it takes."

Approval shone in Benita's eyes. She leaned up and whispered something in Gabriel's ear.

He listened in astonishment.

Benita turned and disappeared into the crowd before Gabriel could question her further.

Gabriel tapped his earpiece.

"I'm on it," Mike growled.

"Fa, I have the information you need," Billy announced.

Gabriel listened, and everything fell into place. Cold sweat trickled down his neck. "I have to warn Noor." He looked over by the bar.

Noor wasn't there.

What the hell? Where did she go?

Gabriel walked through the Matisse exhibition. She wasn't there. He ran up to the Chihuly exhibit. A man in a dark suit followed him. Gabriel wove through the crowd and went to the jewelry exhibit. Noor wasn't there either. He took the stairs and went back to the lobby, hoping she'd returned. She was nowhere in sight.

Gabriel sought a waiter. "Have you seen Miss Rahman?"

The young man pointed toward the entrance. "Ask the event planner. Missus Robsen may know."

Gabriel thanked the waiter and rushed toward the entrance. He found the event planner. "Have you seen Miss Rahman?"

"Yes." The event planner tilted her head toward the stairs. "She went to the fourth floor. She said she'll be back in no time."

"Who was she with?" Gabriel's heart almost stopped when he heard the answer. He took the stairs leading to the Matisse exhibit, conscious of the man following him. He wove through the main galleries and turned into the stairway on the right. He ran up the stairs. The *clank, clank* of footsteps came from above. A sharp *crack* followed.

Gunshots. Gabriel turned and took the first exit. He turned and realized he was at the museum's theatre. He darted inside. *Where the hell is security?*

The theatre was dark. Gabriel took cover, crouching behind the rows of seats, and waited.

Two men entered the theatre. One man searched the aisles, while the other one moved toward the stage area.

Gabriel crept around the aisles until he was behind the first man. He reached up and pulled the man down. The man struggled. Gabriel had the advantage. He twisted around and pulled the man into a choke hold. The man passed out. Gabriel lowered him to the ground and searched through his pockets. He found a gun and grabbed it.

The second man heard the scuffle and ran toward them. Gabriel ran through the aisles, ducking as the *thuds* of a silencer echoed in the theatre. He headed toward the back of the theatre and reached out, searching for the light switch. *Yes!* He turned the stage lights on. The glare of the lights blinded the man, giving Gabriel a chance to escape. He ran out of the theatre into the hallway.

He was running down the corridor of the main landing when

another *crack* splintered the wall panels. Gabriel turned a corner and hid behind a pillar.

The edge of the corridor had a quarter dome acrylic mirror. Gabriel could see his assailant's movements through the mirror. He took a coin from his pocket and aimed at a large metal vase sitting below the mirror. His aim was true. The coin hit the base of the vase and bounced off, creating a loud ping.

Muffled gunshots ensued. Several seconds passed. Through the mirror, Gabriel watched the man approach the corner of the hallway. He fired several shots. The man went down. Gabriel checked the gun. *Great, no more bullets.*

He ran back up the corridor. His heartbeat echoed in his ears, drowning out all other sound.

A museum employee stood by the elevators.

"Call security!" Gabriel cried, running to the staircase.

"I've called the police. They're on their way." Dotts's calm voice echoed in his ear.

Please let her be alive, let her be alive! Gabriel climbed the stairs two at a time. He arrived at the fourth-floor landing and burst into Roshi's office. It was vacant. He checked the other offices. They were vacant. He looked around and spotted a museum janitor. "Have you seen Miss Rahman?"

The man pointed to the staircase on the right. "She was with a friend. I believe they went to the roof terrace."

Gabriel sprinted to the staircase. He arrived at the roof terrace and inched the door open.

CHAPTER FIFTY-FOUR

Noor enjoyed talking to Mrs. Preston, one of the exhibit sponsors. Mrs. Preston was an avid reader of Rumi and a kind woman.

"I didn't know you collected old copies of Rumi's *Divan-e Shams*," Noor said. "I have an antique copy. Would you like to see it?"

"Yes, I'd love to look at it. Do you have it here?" Mrs. Preston asked.

She glanced over her shoulder. Gabriel was talking on his cell phone. It was all for show. He was talking in his earpiece. He winked at her and continued his conversation. Her heart fluttered. Gabriel looked hot in a suit. Scratch that, Gabriel looked hot in everything. Gabriel was hot, period, dot, end of story. She turned her attention back to Mrs. Preston. "I have it here. I'll go get it."

Noor scanned the crowd. The McKnights conversed with Jonathan and her grandmother. Uncle Morrie was chatting with Aunt Roshi. Ash flirted with some blond, *poor woman*. Leila was busy with a group of jewelry experts, and the guests seemed to be enjoying themselves. Once again, she sought Gabriel. He was in deep conversation with a woman who had a scar on her face. She decided not to bother him. She would run upstairs, grab the book, and come back before anyone noticed.

She took the stairs up to the fourth floor and went into the temporary office assigned to Aunt Roshi. The book sat on the desk. She picked up the old book and slid it out of its box cover. A memory flashed in her mind. She was a child helping her mother pack for a trip to New York. Her mother took the book out of its cover. *"This is Rumi's Divan-e-Shams. I love this book because your father gave it to me."*

She closed her eyes. "Why didn't you tell anyone you were in danger that night in Paris? Why did Dad hide the Donya-e-Noor and the cigarette case? Where did he hide them?" Noor sighed heavily. "So many unanswered questions."

She stroked the bottom of the leather box. Her hand froze. There were carvings in the leather. How odd. She'd never noticed them before. She tilted the box and held it up to the light. The carvings were uneven, as if someone had hastily carved them on the leather. Noor reached for a piece of paper and covered the bottom of the book. She drew her pencil over it as if coloring the entire area. Verses appeared on the sheet of paper. "It's another Rumi poem."

Seek the science that will untie a tangle.
Seek it as long as you have life to handle.
Leave that unimportant that looks like it's precious.
Seek that important that looks like it's worthless.

Another clue! What did it mean? When Mom died, she left two necklaces along with Rumi's volume of poetry in the safe at the apartment. Everything else was in the bank. Why not leave the necklaces and the book in the bank?

She reread the poem.

"Leave that unimportant that looks like it's precious.
Seek that important that looks like it's worthless."

"So, the poem wants me to ignore the necklaces and focus on something that doesn't seem to have value." Unlike the necklaces, the *Divan-e-Shams* wasn't worth much. Noor ran her hands along the book just as Gabriel had done a few weeks ago. She traced the whole book and found nothing. She ran her hands along the outside of the cover and found nothing. She ran her hands along the inside and felt nothing.

She put the book down and raked a hand through her hair. What was it that Michael said? The common factor in everything was Rumi. She picked up the box cover and studied it again. A small dent marred the box's spine. Noor held her breath and pushed on the dent. A small compartment at the back of the box slid open. A large pink diamond and a golden square case fell into her hands.

Oh, God! She picked them up with shaky hands. The diamond sitting in her palm was magnificent and huge. The cigarette case was thin and made of gold. A peacock graced its surface. The peacock's feathers were encrusted with diamonds, emeralds, and rubies. Noor put them back in the in the box and pushed on the spine to hide them. She had to find Gabriel. Placing the book back into its box cover, she was about to leave the office when her cell phone rang.

"Hello."

"Hello sweetness." The woman's timber voice was enticing and hypnotic. *"You shouldn't be alone, it's not safe."*

Noor's breath caught in her throat. "Is this Sheila?"

"Yes, sweetness."

"H-how did you know I'm alone?"

The woman's laugh reminded her of summer meadows. *"Sheila sees everything, and she doesn't see you in the lobby."*

"You're here?" Noor gasped.

Sheila didn't answer.

Noor bit her lip. "I'll go right now. Thank you, for everything."

"The pleasure is mine." The line disconnected.

"I knew I had to keep an eye on you. Shiraz would never leave this world without giving her precious daughter the whereabouts of the Donya-e-Noor."

Noor's head shot up. For a moment she couldn't believe her eyes. Leila stood in the doorway with a gun in her hand.

"Leila, w-what are you doing?"

"What does it look like, sweetie?" Leila waved the gun. "Shiraz loved that damn book. I was certain she'd left you an answer in there."

Noor gaped at Leila, dumbfounded.

"Don't give me the doe eye look," Leila snarled.

"You... you killed Mom and Dad?" A streak of pain traveled through her chest. "No, that's not possible."

Leila raised her brows. "Oh, but it is."

Noor couldn't comprehend it. Her chest hurt, like an invisible hand was pushing down on it. "But why?"

Leila motioned to the door. "Let's go to the rooftop where we can talk in private."

Shock turned Noor's legs into rubber. She stood rooted to the floor. *Leila killed Mom and Dad! Leila is the killer?*

Leila walked around the desk and shoved the gun into her side. "Move."

An onslaught of contradicting emotions flooded Noor. Fear came first. Leila would have no qualms killing her. Then came pain. It gripped her insides until she wanted to cry out. This woman whom she'd loved had killed her parents mercilessly. Finally, there was the burn of rage. It kept her upright.

She clutched the volume of Rumi's poems and steadied herself. *Gabriel will come for me.* She'd buy time by distracting Leila.

Leila pressed the gun into her back. "You think I don't know what you're doing? Move."

Noor forced her legs to obey.

They arrived at the rooftop terrace. The terrace was vacant. At the far left, a pavilion covered a bar area. Tables and chairs sat stacked on top of each other. The rest of the terrace had beams sitting two feet apart in a circular pattern.

Noor stopped by a beam. "Why did you kill my parents?" She hated she couldn't mask the hurt in her voice.

Leila stepped closer to her. "Where is the diamond?"

Noor tightened her hold on the volume of poetry. "I don't know."

Leila slapped her so hard she felt tears gather in her eyes.

Noor squared her shoulders. "If I die today, I want to know why you killed my parents. You owe me the truth."

Out of the corner of her eye, Noor saw the door to the terrace inch open. *Gabriel!* She kept still trying not to show the relief flooding through her.

CHAPTER FIFTY-FIVE

Gabriel crept onto the terrace and took cover behind a wooden beam. Noor stood farther off to his left. Even from a distance, he could see the haunted expression on her face. Leila had a gun aimed at her. Anger clawed at his insides like a wild beast clambering to break free.

Noor's voice shook. "How could you do it?"

Leila sneered. "Your father asked the same question before I shot him."

Gabriel wiped the beads of sweat off his forehead. The gun had no bullets, and the terrace offered no cover. *How do I get her out of gun range?*

He scanned the terrace. The pavilion was his best bet. It stood on the right side of the terrace between Leila and Noor. He needed to get to the pavilion.

The door to the rooftop muffled and creaked. Abarron hobbled on to the rooftop with Mustafa in tow. "See, I told you she's on the rooftop." Oblivious to Leila, Abarron shuffled over to Noor. "Some of your guests are leaving. They want to say good-bye, child." He stopped short when he noticed Leila.

"What the hell is this?" Leila snarled.

Abarron tilted his head. He leaned on his cane and cupped his ear. "Huh? I can't hear you. I have terrible hearing, and my eyesight isn't great either." He moved closer to Leila.

Mustafa had followed Abarron onto the rooftop. His smile froze when he saw Leila holding a gun. He squinted at Leila. "Why in God's name do you have a gun, child? Put the gun down before you hurt someone." He paused. "Are you a Muslim girl? Please tell me you're not Muslim. God help us if someone films this. There will be another story about Muslim shootings." Mustafa inched closer to Noor and waved his hands animatedly. "I don't know why the media doesn't film us doing something harmless like gardening or baking a cake. I, for example, bake excellent cakes. I learned from my wife, God rest her soul." He rubbed his chin. "Hmm, maybe I can change that perception." He fisted his hands on his hips, partially blocking Noor with his own body. "Abarron, we should give the world a better understanding of the Muslim culture. What do you think about that?"

"Huh? I can't hear you?" Abarron cupped one ear and limped closer to Leila.

Mustafa stepped closer to Noor. "What do you think about a video of me baking a cake? We can post it on social media. I don't know how it works, but your grandson knows social media, doesn't he?"

Abarron scratched his beard. "I have a better idea. The two of us can record a podcast on friendship and acceptance. We'll call it baking cakes with the rabbi and Mustafa. After we show the young people how to bake a decent cake, we will talk about life."

"Great idea!" Mustafa beamed at Leila. "You can put the gun down, child. We will discuss whatever is bothering you on the first episode."

Thank you, Rabbi and Muslim scholar. Abarron and Mustafa had provided enough of a distraction for Gabriel to get to the pavilion. He moved fast, running from one beam to the other until he reached the pavilion.

"Shut up!" Leila waved the gun back and forth. "Stand where you are, or I'll kill all of you."

Abarron glowered, yet he obeyed Leila's command.

Mustafa shook his head, forehead wrinkled.

Leila glared at Noor. "Your parents loved you. You weren't even born, and my uncle was making plans for your future. I wasn't as lucky. At the tender age of six, my parents went on a work trip to Isfahan. I begged my mother to stay, but no, she had to accompany Daddy. She told me it was for two days." Leila snorted. "My idiot parents died in a car crash, and I was shipped to my uncle's home."

Gabriel climbed the stone pillar of the pavilion and landed silently on the roof.

Abarron's dark eyes flicked his way, then settled back on Leila.

Leila's chest heaved. Her eyes like those of a feral animal scanned the rooftop. "I loved my uncle and Shiraz!"

"Then why...." Noor began.

Leila's voice rose to a crescendo. "I gave them my love, and they betrayed me!"

Noor spread her palms. "Explain how my parents betrayed you."

Leila shook her head. "You're trying to stall for lover boy to arrive."

"No, I'm trying to understand what my parents did that warranted their deaths."

"Your father was out trying to control the crowds," Leila said. "A lot of good that did. The people wanted the monarchy gone, and nothing but a revolution would satisfy them. I begged my uncle to leave the country with us, but no, he had to defend a country and a doomed monarchy." Leila beat her chest. "He preferred the monarchy to his own family. He abandoned us!" Leila took a deep breath. "Uncle Parviz planned to ship me off to

England. He dropped me off at the airport. I waited until he left and took a cab to Cameron's house. Cameron and I loved each other. He wanted the stupid cigarette case, and I wanted the diamond. We devised a plan.

"We met in the gardens of my uncle's home. The stupid housekeeper knew and kept her mouth shut thinking she was protecting young lovers. I snuck out at night, pretending to meet Cameron. I sat outside of my uncle's study and wrote the codes he gave his soldier for the following day.

"Cameron and I hit the hidden vault on a day of mass demonstrations. Cameron paid off a guard. It should have been an easy job." Leila's voice faltered. "That's when everything went wrong. Cameron developed a conscience. He claimed he wanted the cigarette case because it didn't belong to Iran. He wanted to return it to its rightful owner. He tried to convince me to leave the Donya-e-Noor. We argued at the bank, and I killed him. He betrayed me." Leila aimed the gun at Noor. "Your father arrived at the bank after I killed Cameron."

Gabriel inched closer to the edge of the pavilion's roof. Noor stood below him to his immediate right. Mustafa was beside her. Abarron wasn't too far off, and Leila stood below him at his far left. He gauged the distance between himself and Leila. He couldn't jump the distance to knock the gun out of her hand. His best bet was to jump in front of Noor. If he twisted his body at the right angle, he'd survive the bullet. *Yeah, and pigs can fly.*

Leila's movements grew more animated. She fidgeted from one foot to the other. "I gave my uncle one last chance. I begged him to give me the diamond. My uncle refused. He believed it belonged to the people of Iran. Can you believe that? The selfish, stupid, ungrateful people of Iran? That was my uncle's ultimate betrayal. He deserved to die!"

Noor's eyes filled with tears. "And Mom? Did Mom deserve to die?"

Leila's eyes darted from Noor to Abarron, and from Abarron

to Mustafa. "I told you I loved Shiraz. I was patient with her. She never got over Uncle Parviz's death. I waited to approach her. She seemed clueless at first, but time was running out."

Noor nodded as understanding dawned. "The Islamic Republic of Iran re-opened the National Jewelry Collection. You knew it was a question of time before they found the second diamond, correct?"

"Exactly," Leila confirmed.

"You were the surprise visitor at Mom's bookstore back in Paris," Noor said.

Leila bobbed her head. "I timed it with Roshi's visit. I didn't want Shiraz to be suspicious. I talked about the hidden vault and casually inquired if Shiraz knew where my uncle hid the Donya-e-Noor and cigarette case."

Noor rubbed her temple. "Mom knew Dad told no one about the diamond. She put two and two together."

"Yes, Shiraz realized the truth. I confronted her the next day. I was certain she would give me the location of the diamond. She didn't. Shiraz claimed the diamond belonged to the people of Iran. She claimed she didn't have it."

"Did it occur to you she told the truth?" Noor clenched her fists. "Did it occur to you that Mom didn't know where it was?"

"No!" Leila raised her chin. "Shiraz knew where the diamond was. She wouldn't tell me. She betrayed me like everyone else I've loved. I had to kill her!" Leila stepped closer to Noor. "Which brings us to the present. You're the last living person I love. I'll ask you one last time. Where's the diamond?"

"Love?" Noor repeated. "You only love yourself." She lifted her chin. "My parents were right. The diamond belongs to the people of Iran. I don't know where it is. If I did, I'd never tell you."

Mustafa inched closer to Noor. "You shouldn't take what isn't yours."

"Shut up, old man." Leila's arm rose.

"You're angry at me, keep the gun pointed at me," Noor cried.

Dotts' voice rang Gabriel's earphones. "The police arrived at the museum."

"I'll kill all of you." Leila raised her arm to fire the gun.

Knowing they were out of time, Gabriel gritted his teeth and leapt in front of Noor.

CHAPTER FIFTY-SIX

Several things happened at the same time. Abarron threw his cane at the beam closest to Leila with surprising force. The beam's bulb shattered, throwing the terrace into semi-darkness. A gunshot echoed in the night. Mustafa threw himself over Gabriel and Noor, shielding them with his large frame, and Leila let out a blood-curdling scream.

It took a second for Gabriel to realize he wasn't shot. He rose and grabbed Noor by the shoulders, searching for traces of blood. "Are you all right?" He couldn't control the tremor in his voice.

"Yes," she whispered.

"You?" he asked Mustafa.

Mustafa nodded, rising. His cap lay on the floor beside him. He picked it up and stared at it with wide eyes. The bullet had gone through the cap.

Light flooded the rooftop. A man stood by the doorway. His obsidian eyes flashed with anger. Tall, lean, and elegant, he could have been a movie star. Gabriel could see the headline. *Bond, the latter years.* The man moved with grace, exuding the kind of confidence that came with power. He waited for Leila to notice him.

Leila's mouth fell open. "No, it's not possible! You're dead. I killed you."

The man's smile was more a baring of teeth. "You were always a cruel and selfish woman."

Leila backed away.

Morris moved behind Leila and drew a gun. Gaze homed in on Leila, he spoke calmly. "Gabriel, take Noor downstairs. Take them all downstairs."

Noor rushed forward. "Uncle Morrie, no! I don't want you to go to prison."

The other man, Bond Senior, appraised Noor. "Don't worry, my dear. She will not die. Killing her would be a merciful act. She'll suffer. I'll make sure she loses everything. I've notified the French and the Iranian governments we've located a murderer and a thief. Leila will spend the rest of her life in some Godforsaken prison." He pursed his lips. "Preferably one in Iran."

Leila let out a guttural laugh. "Really? You told the authorities on me? You were with me when I broke into the vault in Tehran. That makes you an accomplice, Cameron."

Bond Senior spread his palms. "Cameron, whom you killed, was my brother. On the day of September 8, 1978, I made a formal presentation at Stanford University. Over a hundred people witnessed it. I believe the university filmed it. Even I can't be in two places at the same time."

Realization dawned. Gabriel shook his head. One more piece of the puzzle fell into place.

The door to the rooftop burst open. Jonathan Smith ran to the terrace with five of his men. *Great, the cavalry's here.* Jonathan's gaze scanned the rooftop. His eyes rested on Gabriel and Noor, making sure they were all right. Once he was certain they were unharmed, his eyes traveled to the group on the rooftop. "What the hell is going on?"

Gabriel waved in Mustafa and the rabbi's direction. "These two gentlemen are with us."

Jonathan glared at Morris. "Why is he carrying a gun?"

"I have a permit," Morris muttered, keeping his eyes on Leila.

"He was protecting us. Leila's the killer," Gabriel explained.

Jonathan blinked. "Parviz's niece is the killer?"

Gabriel nodded. "She was going to kill Noor."

Jonathan shook his head. "The police are here. You and your friends need to leave. I'll give them a statement. They can reach out to you tomorrow."

Unperturbed by the government agents with guns, Bond Senior tilted his head in Leila's direction. "What happens to her?"

"The police will deal with her," Jonathan said.

Leila's eyes darted between them like a caged animal.

Bond Senior and Morris exchanged a look.

Bond nodded.

Morris lowered his gun.

The moment Morris lowered his gun, Leila ran to the edge of the roof and jumped off.

"No!" Noor covered her face with both hands.

The sickening thud made Gabriel grimace.

Jonathan ran toward the edge of the roof terrace and looked down. "Jesus!" Mustafa shook his head and whispered a prayer. Abarron patted Noor's shoulder while she wept. Gabriel put his arm around her shoulders and led her inside.

CHAPTER FIFTY-SEVEN

G abriel accompanied Noor to the parking lot behind the museum. "Noor, I know this is difficult—"

Her eyes flashed. "No, you don't! Someone you trusted didn't murder your parents—didn't betray you!" Her shoulders slumped. "Oh, God. I must go to Grand-mere and Roshi. The police rushed them out of the building when... when...." Her voice broke.

"Noor!" He gripped her shoulders. "I understand you're grieving, but it's not over."

"What?"

"Michael is looking for a traitor, remember? The traitor will come after you because he or she believes you know the location of the vault's treasure."

"You're wrong." Her voice wobbled. "Leila and that man's brother, Cameron, were the traitors. They—"

"No!" Gabriel kept his voice steady. "Leila couldn't have framed my father. I'm asking you to trust me. Please!"

She rubbed her temples with her hands. "I—"

He didn't give her time to think. "Your uncle gave me his car keys. We must finish this, or you'll never be safe."

She looked like she was going to argue, then the fire left her eyes. "Fine."

He guided her to the car, and they headed to her house. Gabriel wanted to hold her, console her, but there was no time. His hands clenched the steering wheel. Noor was hurting. Nothing he said would undo or lessen the pain of betrayal.

It was dark when they arrived at her house. A pitch-black blanket covered the sky, and the streetlamps threw warped shapes on her lawn. The leaves of a whispering willow rustled, warning him of impending danger.

Gabriel's skin prickled. "Stay in the car and lock the doors."

"There's no need—"

He didn't let her finish. "Mike asked Billy to research the whereabouts of Jonathan, Mina, and Tyler during the last months of 1978. They all claimed to have left Iran by October of the same year. They all lied. One of them is the traitor, and that person will come for you." He forced himself to remain calm. "Mike is working with a high-level government agent. They have a plan to catch the traitor. Here's where we come in." He told her about the plan.

"Gabriel." The hollow look in her eyes tore at his insides. "There's no need for this. Leila had the codes. She was the one sending information about the diamond."

He ignored her comment and handed her the burner phone. "It'll be over soon."

Her face was ashen, and her lower lip quivered, but she nodded.

He exited the car and waited for her to lock the doors.

Keeping to the shadows, he crept toward her house and entered through the back door. The house was dark except for the glimmer of light coming from the lamp above the kitchen stovetop. A shuffling sound came from the kitchen. Gabriel crept toward the sound, then crouched behind the center island, ready for Mike's signal.

Something struck him from behind. Everything went dark.

NOOR GRIPPED the burner phone with both hands. She didn't want to think about Leila and past betrayals because thinking about it right now would break her. She pushed the pain to the recesses of her soul—somewhere deep to bring out and examine later. Instead, she turned her attention to the house. *Why did I go along with this? Leila was the killer, the destroyer of lives. End of story!*

Leila had spied on Dad. She knew the codes and shared them with others. She wanted to sell the diamonds. She clutched the phone to her chest. Gabriel was paranoid, and she was tired of sitting in the car.

She reached for the door handle but paused as a thought occurred to her. Yes, Leila had the codes, and yes, she planned to sell the diamond. But she didn't have access to the U.S. Embassy, hence she couldn't have framed Gabriel's father. She also didn't kill Asra Madison. Noor knew this because Leila was at London's annual gala for jewelers when Asra died. She'd emailed the newspaper article to Noor.

An icy shiver ran down her spine. "Oh, God, Gabriel's right! There is a traitor." She glanced at her watch. He'd been gone for a while. She unlocked her door, then crept out of her car. Mimicking Gabriel's moves, she stayed away from the streetlamps and crept toward her house. The pounding of her heart made it hard to hear anything. Where was Gabriel? She raked a hand through her hair. Whoever killed Asra Madison wouldn't hesitate to kill Gabriel. Noor squared her shoulders.

I won't let anyone hurt him!

She ran to the garage and punched in the code to her safe. It popped open. Reaching in, she pulled out the gun Uncle Morrie had insisted she purchase. Circling the house, she wondered which of the three was a traitor—Jonathan Smith, Mina, or Tyler

Delany? They were all at her mother's birthday, and based on what Gabriel shared, all three had access to the Embassy's classified documents.

The dim glow of lights made her pause. Gabriel wouldn't turn on the lights. Who was in the kitchen? She inched the door open and peered inside.

A figure loomed by the kitchen counter, pointing a gun at Gabriel.

THE AMERICAN CREPT into Noor Rahman's backyard. He'd waited patiently to claim the prize. The one problem was the Iranian, and a solution had presented itself for that, too. Ash Kosha reached out periodically, seeking an alliance. The American had neither planned nor intended to form an alliance with the fool, yet the timing of Ash's call was right. Hence, Ash became the perfect distraction for the Iranian.

Rahman's niece also proved to be useful. He bit back a laugh. Yes, between those two, the Iranian had been misdirected.

The American had planned everything meticulously, down to the very last detail, including attending the jewelry exhibition. An opportunity presented itself when Noor left the reception. He'd followed Noor up to the roof terrace. The damned Iranian and his half-brother were there, Rahman's niece lay in a pool of blood, and police officers and government agents surrounded the building. Rage had consumed the American, but he was good at improvising. He picked the lock to Noor's back door. It gave way easily.

GABRIEL FLOATED BACK TO CONSCIOUSNESS. He reached up and winced. His head throbbed. Where was he?

Realization dawned. He was slumped behind the island in Noor's kitchen. The house was dark except for the dim lighting from above the kitchen stove. Gingerly, he moved into a crouch. The cool marble at his back helped with the nausea. A rustle sounded in the kitchen. He peered around the corner.

Noor stood at the stove with her back to him. She was pouring hot water from an electric kettle into a cup.

"I'm sorry, Noor. Your night is just getting worse," a familiar voice said.

Gabriel froze. He knew that voice. How had he not figured it out?

The man on the other side of the island pulled off his wig and beard. Mina Delany grimaced. "You must believe I never meant to hurt Parviz or Shiraz. That was all Leila. I should have never left Leila in the vault that day."

Noor bowed her head, not bothering to turn around. "Why?" her voice sounded husky. Mina would think it was because of what she'd been through. Gabriel knew better. His heart thundered in his ears, and nausea made him dizzy. He counted back from five, then forced himself to move.

"Why?" Mina repeated, irritation clear in her voice. "Imagine life as a public servant or agent if you want to give it a grand title. They send you to Godforsaken countries. You risk your life day in and day out. You work with the locals for years, promoting democracy. Then, the regime changes, and years of hard work goes down the drain. Not once but every Goddamn time. What do people like me get out of it? Nothing! We get nothing." Mina paused and drew in a breath. "Iran was in turmoil, and our government wasn't backing the Shah. It was a question of time before an anti-U.S. regime took over. My thanks would have been a bullet in the head.

"When I discovered there was a hidden vault in The Central Bank of Tehran, I realized it was my golden opportunity." Mina started pacing. "Tyler had racked up gambling debts, and the

Shah was sick with cancer. No one knew about the vault, or the bags of priceless stones sitting in it. One less bag wouldn't have made a difference to Iran. It was payment for the hard work I had put in. Surely you can understand that."

"Why did you frame Gabriel and Michael for Asra Madison's death?" Noor asked.

Mina smirked. "You figured that one out, didn't you? No matter, you won't live to tell anyone. After Leila killed Parviz, we had to leave the vault. She helped me drag Parviz's body to Jaleh Square. It was the best cover. Problem was, we couldn't get back into the vault. I thought I lost my one chance until rumors surfaced that Rahman hid the Donya-e-Noor and a cigarette case. I waited for years, then expedited the process. I had a side business of sorts."

Noor placed both of her hands on the counter. "You sold your government's secret documents to buyers and manipulated Tyler into doing the same, correct?"

"Yes," Mina said. "Mind you, it was little things, nothing that hurt our country. It was a lucrative side business, plus I had something to keep Tyler in check." Mina stepped closer to Noor. "I planted a trail leading to Carl McKnight and made sure Michael McKnight saw it. I knew he'd chase it and find the diamond. Unfortunately, Michael asked Asra Madison for help. Asra figured out the truth and had to die. I killed Asra and framed the McKnights." Mina waved the gun. "Enough talk, where is the Donya-e-Noor?"

"Are you going to kill me?" Noor asked.

"Yes." Mina's mouth tightened into a firm line. "Your lover boy is unconscious. I'll kill you both. I left false evidence on Jonathan's computer. I'll tell the authorities Jonathan hired someone to eliminate you and Gabriel. I figured it out and came to save you. I was late. You were already dead." Mina unlocked the gun's safety. "The authorities will be too busy trying to pin the deaths on Jonathan. Tyler and I will sell the diamond and leave the country."

Noor hung her head. "How will you kill us?"

"I'll give you a sedative. You'll go to sleep, then I'll shoot you. It will be quick and painless. That's the best I can do." Mina stepped around the island. "Show me the diamond."

Noor made a choking sound.

Gabriel crept behind Mina and kicked the gun out of her hand.

Mina stumbled and whirled around. She blinked several times. The woman standing by Gabriel wasn't Noor.

"Miss Delany, my name is Aliza Cohen, and I work for the NSA. I'm wearing a wire. Jonathan Smith, assistant director of CIU, my supervisor, and local law enforcement, heard everything you said. You are under arrest for treason and multiple murders."

"I was playing a practical joke on Noor," Mina sputtered. "You can't prove anything."

Aliza pursed her lips. "We can prosecute you for treason and attempted murder. Do you remember Benita Varoujan? She's the young woman you tried to kill years ago in Tehran. She found the last fax you sent from the Embassy in 1978. She's alive and ready to testify against you."

The back door to the kitchen swung open, and Michael and four agents entered the kitchen.

Gabriel's head pounded. Before he could move, the cold steel of a gun's barrel pushed against his spine.

"Stand back or I'll kill him," Tyler growled.

Gabriel groaned inwardly. The damned headache had put him off balance. He hadn't noticed Tyler's approach.

Aliza pulled a gun and aimed it at Tyler. "I wouldn't do that if I were you."

"Put the gun down." Michael's steely voiced boomed in the kitchen. He, too, aimed a gun at Tyler.

Droplets of sweat poured down Tyler's face. His beady eyes

rolled in his head as his gaze bounced from Gabriel to Aliza then Michael before finally landing on Mina.

Gabriel's body tightened. He knew the look. Tyler and Mina would react the way all cornered animals did. His own gaze met Michael's questioning one. Gabriel dipped his head.

The move was barely perceptible. The lines around Michael's eyes tightened. He blinked instead of nodding.

Tick!

The grandfather clock in Noor's hallway announced the passing of time. Gabriel's muscles brows rose like wound up springs.

Tock!

Gabriel's vision cleared. He angled his body to the right, ready to elbow Tyler. Before he could react, the blast of a gunshot filled the kitchen.

"Aargh!" Tyler's body twisted as the gun fell from his limp arm.

Michael and an agent reached for Tyler, while Aliza and the other agents went for Mina.

Noor stood in the hallway. She lowered the gun with steady hands. The movement was a contrast to her ashen face and glistening eyes. She never looked more beautiful to Gabriel.

CHAPTER FIFTY-EIGHT

Gabriel opened his arms.

Noor's gun clattered to the tile, and she ran to him.

He held her tight. "It's over. You're safe." He didn't know who he was consoling, Noor or himself.

Michael stepped over Tyler and took Aliza by the shoulders. "Are you okay?"

"Yes." Aliza peered over his shoulder. "Is he dead?"

One of the agents checked Tyler's pulse. "No, he'll live."

"This is all a misunderstanding," Mina cried while agents handcuffed her. "I'm a federal agent. You can't do this."

The agents dragged her out of the kitchen.

"Did you get everything?" Aliza asked.

The man behind Michael straightened, and his mouth parted into a wide smile. "Yes. It's all on record. Nice work, Miss Cohen."

Aliza smirked. "Thank you. See what happens when you play nice with the NSA."

Michael kissed her on the mouth. "I love playing nice with the NSA."

A police officer poked his head into the kitchen. "An ambulance is on the way, sir."

Michael glared at a sniffling Tyler. "Stay with him."

The officer nodded.

A man and a woman stepped into the kitchen. Several police officers followed them. The man was tall, broad-shouldered, and wore a pressed suit. The woman, slight and petite, was dressed in Chuck Taylors, leather pants, and a "Punk Rocks" T-shirt.

Gabriel was about to make the introductions when Michael rubbed his hands together. "You must be team Robin Hood. Gabe told me about you. Let's talk."

Gabriel bit back a sigh. Keeping his arms around Noor, he made the introductions. "Detectives, this is my brother, Michael McKnight."

Detective Robin scowled.

Detective Hood tilted her head and studied Michael. A smile tugged at her mouth. "Yes, let's do that."

GABRIEL AND NOOR walked hand in hand to Morris's house. He unlocked the door and guided her to Morris's kitchen.

Noor leaned her head on Gabriel's shoulder. "I'm not ready to see my family yet. Tell me about Benita. What happened to her?"

Gabriel guided her to the kitchen and pulled a chair out for her. "Benita was an administrative assistant at the U.S. Embassy in Tehran. She and Jonathan were an item. She discovered Mina was corresponding with an enemy cell in the Middle East and confronted her about it. Mina made up a story about an operation to draw our enemies out, and Benita believed her." Gabriel took the chair beside her. "Benita accompanied Jonathan to your mother's birthday. At the party, Mina feigned ignorance when Leila mentioned your father guarded the treasury of national jewels. Benita knew that wasn't true because she'd heard Mina discuss it with Jonathan the same day.

"The day after the party, Mina invited Benita out for tea.

Benita didn't want to raise Mina's suspicion. She went with her. Mina drove Benita to the outskirts of the city and attacked her with a knife. She left Benita's body on the side of a road. A local couple found her and nursed her back to health. Benita left Iran and changed her name. She's been hiding from Mina ever since."

Noor raised her head from his shoulder. "How did you find her?"

"Dotts, I mean Billy, found her. He uncovered the truth while he was looking into Jonathan, Mina, and Tyler's backgrounds."

Noor shook her head. "So many people hurt by greed." She suddenly straightened. "Oh, gosh. I forgot." She reached for her tote bag and pulled out her volume of Rumi. "I have something to show you." She put her hand on the spine of the box cover and pushed. The cover slid aside. A pink stone and a cigarette case fell out.

Gabriel gaped at her. He picked up the diamond, held it in his palm, then picked up the golden cigarette case. "How did you find them?"

She told him about the poem. "I was going to find you, but Leila cornered me." She shuddered at the memory.

He put his arm around her shoulders. "It's over."

"Not entirely," a cultured voice trailed into the kitchen. Bond Senior and Morris stood at the threshold of the kitchen.

Gabriel rose, surprised he hadn't heard them arrive.

Morris dipped his head toward the hallway. "I have an underground entrance to this house."

Bond Senior pulled a chair from the kitchen table and sat across from Noor. He broke into what Hollywood would call a million-dollar smile. "Miss Rahman, please forgive me for not introducing myself to you back at the museum. My name is Cyrus Rohan, and I'm sorry for everything that has happened to you."

Noor held the diamond and the cigarette case in her lap. "You and Uncle Morrie helped us back at the museum. Thank you!"

Bond Senior waved her thanks away. "My brother and I were more than happy to help."

"Brother?" Noor's brows furrowed.

Bond Senior smiled. "Yes, Morris is my brother."

Noor's gaze traveled from Bond Senior to Morris then back to Bond Senior.

Bond's eyes twinkled. "The resemblance is uncanny, isn't it?"

Gabriel snorted. The two men looked nothing alike.

A dark hue covered Noor's face. Uh oh. Gabriel knew that look. She marched up to Morris and jabbed him in the chest. "You had a brother and never told me?"

Morris raised both hands in a sign of surrender. "It never came up."

Her eyes flashed like hard chips of glass. "I have been through enough! There will be no more secrets in my life. Do you hear me?"

Gabriel winced. Could Morris hear her? The entire neighborhood could hear her.

Noor's shoulders slumped. "I just can't handle anymore secrets."

Morris shuffled his feet. "Yeah, okay." He patted her on the shoulder. "You have my word."

Noor glared at him. "Is this gentleman your brother?"

"Yes," Morris said.

"That's not enough," Noor snapped.

Morris raked a hand through his hair. "My father was a wealthy Iranian businessman. My mother was an Italian teacher. They met in Munich and had an affair. I'm a result of the affair. My father went back to Iran intending to divorce his wife. He realized his wife was pregnant. He broke it off with my mother and stayed married to his wife. He had two children from his marriage, and me. I grew up spending most of the year in Italy and summers in Iran. When my father died—" He glanced at Bond.

"When our father died," Bond corrected. "My brother and I learned we had another brother. We searched for Morris and made him our business partner."

Noor crossed her arms across her chest. "If there are three of you, where is your other brother?"

"His brother was the man your mother knew as Cameron Jahan," Gabriel said. "Cameron was your identical twin, wasn't he?"

Bond Senior bowed his head. "Yes, Mister McKnight."

Noor jumped out of the chair. "Your brother tried to kill my father?"

Bond Senior held up his hands. "No, my dear. Neither Cameron, Morris, nor I wanted to harm anyone, least of all your family members. When Cameron dated Leila, I warned him against it. He didn't listen, and against my better judgment, allowed Leila to become part of our plan." Bond's eyes blazed. "She killed Cameron." Bond let out a deep breath and pressed his palms together. "Miss Rahman, you must believe me when I say our intentions were honorable."

Noor narrowed her eyes. "You broke into a private vault. You tried to rob the vault."

"No, Miss Rahman, you're mistaken. We weren't robbing anyone." Bond motioned to the chair in front of him. "Please sit down."

Noor went back to the chair.

Bond held out his hand. "Will you please give me the cigarette case?"

Noor hugged the cigarette case to her chest. "It belongs to the people of Iran."

Bond bowed his head. "I agree wholeheartedly."

"You can trust him, Noor," Morris interjected.

Several seconds passed. Noor handed the cigarette case to Bond.

"Thank you." Bond opened the case and pulled out a thin

sheet of paper. "The cigarette case belongs to the people of Iran." He handed the case back to Noor and pocketed the piece of paper. "This note does not."

Noor's eyes widened. She put the diamond and cigarette case back in the book box's spine.

"May I ask you what you will do with the diamond and the cigarette case?" Bond asked.

Noor didn't hesitate. "I will return them to the Iranian government."

Gabriel grinned. *That's my girl.*

CHAPTER FIFTY-NINE

"My mind told my heart because of your ignorance,
you're deprived of glory, do you know it, pray?
My heart replied you are mistaken.
I already have glory, you're the one who's gone astray."
—Rumi

PERE LACHAISE CEMETERY, PARIS, FRANCE

Gabriel paced Avenue Gambetta and checked his watch. Mike and Aliza rushed out of the metro station.

He kissed Aliza on the cheek and glared at Mike.

Mike clapped him on the back. "Sorry, we were, uh, delayed." Judging from the satisfied smirk on Michael's face, Gabriel guessed what the delay was.

Michael scanned the cemetery. "Do you know where to go?"

"Yes, I took Mom and Dad up there," Gabriel said.

Aliza glared at Mike. "Your parents are there? You didn't tell me your parents would be there."

Michael grinned. "There was no time. We were busy."

Aliza brushed a hand through her thick hair.

Mike grabbed her hand and kissed it. "Relax, they'll love you." He tugged on her hand. "Come on. Gabe won't forgive me if we're late."

Aliza shook her head and turned her attention to Gabriel. "How did Noor pull this off?"

"When she returned the Donya-e-Noor and cigarette case to the Iranian government, she received a formal appreciation letter from the Iranian President," Gabriel said. "The Islamic Republic of Iran offered her a reward for returning the items."

Mike's eyes lit with curiosity. "What was the reward?"

Gabriel turned right and took a lane that traveled uphill. "She declined the reward and requested the transfer of her father's remains to Paris. She went through red tape with the French government and got it approved."

They arrived at the top of a hill. A group of people stood around two tombstones. Noor's grandmother and Boris, the non-boyfriend, conversed with the buff blond guy who worked for her. Roshi was in deep conversation with Bond Senior and Morris. Mom and Dad were talking with Father Pierre, Mustafa, and Abarron. Noor stood farther off, staring at the tombstones.

Mike grabbed Aliza's hand and strode ahead. "Come on, I'm not up for another lecture from the Rabbi."

Aliza laughed, allowing him to lead her away.

Noor spotted Gabriel, and her eyes brightened.

Father Pierre cleared his throat. "We are ready to begin."

Everyone gathered around the tombstones.

Noor addressed the group. "Thank you for joining me today. We're gathered here to honor my parents, Parviz and Shiraz Rahman. Some of you knew both of my parents, some knew only one, and some of you may not have met them, yet they've somehow touched your lives." She paused. "As you know, my father died before I was born. That didn't stop Mom from making sure I knew him. My father lived his life with a strict moral code. Honor, integrity, and kindness were his core principles. He was

General Rahman to his colleagues, Parviz to his friends, and to us he was family. No matter the relationship, anyone who met my father will say he adhered to these principles in both his profession and his personal life."

Gabriel noticed his own father's nod of approval.

"My mother." Noor's voice faltered. "Mom was kind, generous, and brave. Mom believed that love was God's greatest gift to mankind. She once told me she'd found the other half of her soul in my father." She turned and faced both graves. "Mom and Dad, you loved each other dearly. I know you're together wherever you are. Today, your physical remains are beside each other. I'd like to end the memorial by reading lines from Rumi."

"Don't be without love so you won't feel dead.
Die in love and live forever!" (Shiva, 1999)

Gabriel had heard the words before, yet they shook him. He knew he stood at a major crossroad, and whatever he decided would alter his future. He remembered what the poet Robert Frost had said about the road not taken. *And that has made all the difference!*

In the silence of the Parisian cemetery, he had an epiphany. Gabriel raised his head and found Mom watching him. He averted his gaze. Nothing flew past Mom.

The group scattered. He waited for Noor to bid everyone goodbye and approached her. "How are you feeling?" What a lame question. What did he expect her to say? Just peachy.

Noor stared at the graves of her parents. "You know how people say the truth unburdens and sets you free? I don't feel free. I don't—it's not...." She bit her lip, unable to continue.

Gabriel shoved his hands in his coat pockets. "I'm sorry."

She rubbed her temples. "I loved Leila, and all along she was a murderer. Doesn't say much for my judgment, does it?"

Gabriel stepped closer. "Don't do this to yourself."

She bowed her head. "I had Leila buried in a plot near my parents."

He searched her face. "Why?"

She chewed on her lower lip. "I must accept what I can't change and take control of what I can. Leila was broken and"—her voice shook—"she broke my family." Noor paused and let out a sigh. "It was the right thing to do."

Her words tugged at Gabriel's heart. He wanted to gather her in his arms. He wanted to tell her the truth. He swallowed the words lodged in his throat and ran a hand through his hair. "I'm dining with my parents. Mike and Aliza are coming. Will you join us?"

She looked away. "I'll take a raincheck. I'm not the best company right now."

"I understand."

She lifted her bright green eyes to his. "Thank you for everything, Gabriel."

Gabriel forced himself to keep his distance. "I should thank you."

She opened her mouth to say something, then changed her mind. "Have a safe trip."

Gabriel felt his throat close in. "Thanks. I'll be in touch."

CHAPTER SIXTY

"Stationed by the road, you pursue the road.
Enveloped by the moon, you pursue the moon.
Imprisoned you pursue Joseph's allure,
You are love and Joseph, you are him for sure."
—Rumi.

EIGHT WEEKS LATER, GEORGETOWN, WASHINGTON, D.C.

Gabriel typed furiously on his laptop. He stopped and reviewed the draft. *No, not good enough.* The tone had to be right. He heard someone talking to him in the background. He shut out the noise, focused on the manuscript. This was unfamiliar territory. It had to be perfect. He made edits, then reviewed his work. *Much better.* He hit the print button.

The aroma of Italian food made Gabriel's stomach rumble. His desk watch told him it was one in the afternoon. When was the last time he had eaten? He looked up, surprised to find Michael standing in the doorway of his office.

"Good to see you're back in the real world."

Gabriel stretched. "What the hell are you talking about?"

Michael crossed his arms over his chest. "I've been here for a whole week. I've tried to talk to you. God knows it was a futile effort. You type, crawl into bed, get up, and type."

Gabriel raised an eyebrow. "And your point is?"

Michael threw his hands in the air. "You risked your life to save Noor. You looked at her like you'd found salvation. Why are you here, typing on the damned laptop, when you should be with her?"

Gabriel yawned and scratched his chin. Woah, his stubble had grown into a full beard. "Just because you and Aliza are engaged doesn't mean everyone else should head into marital bliss. Where is my future sister-in-law?"

"She's in Singapore for business. She'll be back tomorrow night." Michael studied him. "What gives, Gabe?"

Gabriel's stomach growled. "Let's eat first."

The brothers clambered into the kitchen.

Gabriel took in the massive amount of food, and his mouth watered. "You ordered from Little Italy?"

"Yep." Michael grabbed a plate and dug into the cannelloni. "Billy wanted to stop by. I told him you were in one of your writing marathons. He said he'd stop by later." Michael scowled. "That's Billy code for 'I'll stop by when he's sane again.'"

Gabriel ignored the jibe and piled his plate with food. He bit into the savory pasta. Creamy flavor exploded in his mouth. *Mm, delicious.* He reached for two slices of Italian bread and spread butter on them. They ate in silence, then cleared the kitchen table. Gabriel poured tea, while Michael placed a plate of Italian pastries on the table.

Gabriel grabbed a pastry. "We'll have to run extra to make up for this."

Michael bit into the pastry. "So, we'll run extra." He took a sip of his tea. "Okay, your stomach is full. Talk to me."

Gabriel stared into his tea mug. "I've called her twice, Mike."

Michael snorted. "You've called her twice in two months.

Each time you've talked to her less than a minute. The effort you put into seducing your woman is legendary, bro."

"She's distant. She's been distant since she realized Leila killed her parents." Gabriel sipped his tea. "I'm giving her space. Plus, I have things I need to do first."

Michael put his cup down. "It's been two months, Gabe. Whatever you need to do can wait." He held up his hand before Gabriel could comment. "Let me ask you something. Would you rather be here talking to me, and yes, I know I'm phenomenal company, or would you rather be with her right now?"

Gabriel ground his teeth. "It has to be perfect. The timing, the—"

"No, it doesn't." Michael banged his fist on the table. "All you have to do is tell her you care about her." He leaned forward. "Trust me, I know how you feel. Tell her before it's too late. Tell her before you lose her."

Good point. *Hmm. Mikey, the life coach.* He could use that for his next Jason Van novel. He reigned in his train of thought. His mind had the tendency to wander when he was under stress.

Michael was right, it was now or never.

He leaned over and gave Michael a one arm hug, then grabbed his mug and rose.

"Where the hell are you going?" Michael cried.

"I'm taking your advice. I've got to do something first," Gabriel called over his shoulder.

GABRIEL CLIMBED the stairs to the front porch of the Victorian house. He rang the doorbell and waited.

Arie opened the door. "Come in. Sheila is expecting you."

Gabriel followed Arie down the hallway to a living room overlooking lush green forest.

A figure in a blue burka rose. Sheila was tall at five feet eleven inches. The burka covered her entire frame. The only thing Gabriel could see was Sheila's hazel eyes. "Hello, sweetness, where's Miss Rahman?"

"I came alone," Gabriel said.

"It's safer for her," Sheila mused. "I guess I won't need this." Sheila pulled the burka off, and the man who grinned back at Gabriel could have easily been on a GQ magazine. He was in his early thirties with a slim athletic build. Thick ebony hair was combed back from his face, emphasizing his cheekbones and firm jaw. He wore a pair of jeans and a long-sleeved black shirt. Hazel eyes twinkled as he pulled a small device from his mouth.

"Good to see you, Gabe." A deep baritone replaced Sheila's melodic one.

"It's been a while, Amir."

Amir moved with the grace and ease of an athlete. "I trust all is well with Mike."

Gabriel shook Amir's outstretched hand. "Yes, Mike sent his regards and thanks. We're both grateful for your help."

Amir waved the thanks away. "Sheila protects the good people." He motioned to the chairs overlooking the forest. "Sit down."

Gabriel plopped into an armchair. "How long are you going to keep this charade up?"

Amir crossed a jean-clad leg. "For as long as it takes. Innocent women and children pray for justice every day. Governments are either too corrupt to help, or they're bound by red tape. Sheila makes a difference, and you know it."

Gabriel leaned forward. "You're a law professor for God's sake. It'll ruin the life you've worked hard to build. You'll become a target. You could get killed."

Amir's voice hardened. "We all die, Gabe. What's important is how we live our lives while we're on this earth."

Gabriel rose and paced the room. He stopped in front of Amir and looked him in the eye. "You can't blame yourself for Baran's death. Baran died because of me. I was selfish and careless. I know it's inadequate, lame, and late." His voice shook. "I'm sorry. I'm very sorry."

Amir's eyes widened a fraction. You didn't kill my sister. Terrorists did."

"You were just a kid." Gabriel swallowed the lump in his throat. "It was my fault."

Amir tilted his head to the side. "Do you remember that day, or do you remember her death? I remember that day as clear as if it were today. I was with Baran when your note arrived. You told her to stay behind. You stressed it wasn't safe, yet she went to the wedding. Do you know why?" Amir leaned forward. "Because Baran believed in freedom. She believed in making a difference, and she stood against the radicals. My sister knew there was a price to pay, and she chose to fight. No one forced or coerced her. Don't dishonor her memory by making her a victim. Remember Baran as she was—bright, intelligent, and courageous." Amir rose and put a hand on Gabriel's shoulder. "You've never talked about Baran. I'm glad you finally are. So, hear me loud and clear. Baran's death was not your fault. You weren't responsible for her decisions, and you're not responsible for mine." He paused. "If it makes you feel better, every one of those men paid dearly for their actions. Sheila made sure of it."

Finding himself unable to say anything, Gabriel merely nodded.

Amir hugged Gabriel. "Aside from me and my father, you were the only person who didn't treat Baran like a pariah. You cared about her, and you saved my life. You're family, Gabe."

Arie stepped into the living room with a tea tray, took one look at them and turned back. She came back with a bottle of whiskey and two glasses. She set the tray beside them and left the room.

Amir poured the whiskey and raised his glass. "Let's drink to Baran, an incredible woman."

Gabriel lifted his glass. "To Baran, an incredible woman." They sat for hours, reminiscing about the past and honoring Baran's memory.

It was close to midnight when Gabriel rose to leave. He reached into his pocket and pulled out the lapis lazuli. "Baran gave me this stone before she died. I've kept it with me. I think you should have it."

Amir took the stone and held it against his heart. For an instant, Gabriel glimpsed a shadow of the little boy he'd met in Afghanistan two decades ago.

CHAPTER SIXTY-ONE

OKLAHOMA CITY, OKLAHOMA

Noor ran another lap around the Oklahoma River. *Gabriel likes to run,* the voice in her head whispered. She ignored the voice and completed her lap. The sun was up, sending rays of warmth to the kayakers paddling along the Oklahoma River. She wondered where Gabriel was. Was he jogging, too? Did he have a woman in his bed? *Get a grip, Noor!* She slowed down and headed back to her car.

An hour later, she walked into her office with a latte in hand. Coffee was her poison of choice these days. She reviewed the chapters a client sent her and glanced at her watch. It wasn't even mid morning.

Noor turned the heat up in her office and stared at the window. Ever since the day at the cemetery, she felt cold. It was as if a winter frost had settled inside her bones. She wondered if it would ever go away.

Gabriel! She missed him with every fiber of her being. He understood her, and she understood him. *Or so I thought.*

Gabriel had called twice. Their conversations were brief. She needed space after Leila's death—space to process and accept the truth. Gabriel had given her that space. And more.

She stayed in touch with his family. Lily, Gabriel's sister, called her often, and she congratulated Mike and Aliza on their engagement. Moira McKnight called her once a week. Noor never inquired about Gabriel, and his family members didn't bring him up.

She shook off her morose thoughts and turned back to her computer. Her cell phone rang. The number was blocked. Curious, Noor answered the call.

"Hello, sweetness," a husky voice purred.

"Sheila?" Noor almost jumped out of her chair. "Is Gabriel all right?"

Sheila's husky laughter was more like a melody. *"I'd say he's as good as you are."*

Noor bit her lip. "You've seen him?"

Sheila didn't answer the question. *"I'm not one to offer relationship advice, precious. However, there's a first for everything, so here goes. The past is powerful. It defines who you are today. You must accept and respect it. That said, don't give the past too much credence, or it will rob you of your future. You and only you should define your future."*

Silence.

She considered Sheila's advice. Why hadn't she reached out to Gabriel? Was it because she feared rejection? No, she believed her family history was too much for him. Well, that was too bad! Noor raked a hand through her hair. "You're right. What happened in the past is the past." She rose and paced the room. "Gabriel's an idiot!"

Sheila chuckled. *"That's more like it. Now, go tell him that."* The line disconnected.

Could Gabriel put the past behind him? If she was willing to do it, he could, too. Hope streaked through her, and a trickle of warmth traveled from her stomach up to her chest. Noor wondered if she should call Gabriel. Her pulse quickened at the thought of hearing his voice. Gabriel's voice was intoxicating. *I won't call him. I'll go to him.*

Determination and irritation brought a flush to her face. She went back to her computer and searched online for plane tickets. She was checking her calendar when the door to her office flung open.

Brodie walked in and paused. "May I ask what brought the fire back into your eyes?"

Noor didn't look away from the monitor. "I'm going to Washington, D.C. to beat some sense into Gabriel. I'm so mad at him."

Brodie's eyes twinkled. "How exciting. Let me save you time and money. Your Romeo is standing at the reception area right now."

Noor swiveled around. "Gabriel's here? Now?"

Brodie smirked. "All six feet and something inches of him. Oh, and his identical hottie and the sexy babe from Paris are here, too."

Her head spun. *He's here.*

"Quit moping and look sexy." Brodie put his hands on his hips and studied her. "The little green dress is perfect. Your hair, however, needs attention." He pulled the elastic band out of her hair.

Her hair tumbled around her shoulders.

He combed it with his fingers. "There, now you're perfect. See ya later." He scrambled out of her office.

Noor rose, sat down, then rose again. Her knees trembled. She tried to compose herself. *Play it cool, Noor, play it cool.*

The door to her office swung open, and Gabriel walked in.

GABRIEL GLARED at Mike and Aliza. "Explain one more time why you two followed me to Oklahoma City."

Mike clapped him on his shoulder. "Moral support, brother. Noor cares about you, but it won't stop her from breathing fire when she lays eyes on you."

Gabriel's rubbed his chin. "What makes you think she'll be angry?"

"Because that's how I'd feel," Aliza chimed in as they entered Noor's agency.

The receptionist recognized Gabriel and jumped to his feet. "Mister McKnight, welcome back. Are you here to see Miss Rahman?" The receptionist's eyes widened when Aliza and Mike joined Gabriel.

"Yes, but I don't have an appointment," Gabriel said.

The kid adjusted his glasses. "Let me call Miss Rahman." He picked up the phone and dialed Noor's office. "Mister McKnight is here. Do you have time to meet with him?" He put his hand on the receiver. "Will the other gentleman and lady be joining you?"

Mike chuckled. "No, we'll stay here in case my brother needs help getting to the emergency room."

The receptionist blinked in confusion.

Aliza elbowed Mike.

"Ignore him. I do," Gabriel reassured the kid.

The kid opened the door to the back offices. "Go ahead, sir, she's waiting for you."

The walk down that corridor was the longest walk of Gabriel's life. His heart pounded so hard, he worried it would burst out of his chest. He passed a series of offices. Noor's employees stared with open curiosity.

He tried not to feel self-conscious while he walked toward her office. He raised a clammy hand to knock on the door when Brodie stepped out and shut the door behind him.

"Good to see you, Mister McKnight." Brodie's tone was pleasant.

"Likewise, thank you." Gabriel had no patience for small talk.

Brodie blocked him. "She cares about you. Don't hurt her again."

Gabriel reached for the door.

Brodie stepped in his way. "I won't be nice next time."

Gabriel nodded. "Your warning is duly noted. Please move."

Brodie moved away.

Here goes. Gabriel opened the door and stepped inside.

Noor stood by the window. She wore a little green number that showed off her figure. Her silky hair fell loose around her shoulders.

Gabriel's mouth went dry. He took a step forward and stopped.

Her eyes darkened into a deep green.

Aw hell! Mike was right, Noor was furious.

She lifted her chin. "Hello, Gabriel. This is a surprise. What brings you to Oklahoma City?" She looked and sounded composed.

Gabriel knew better. He was treading on a minefield. One false move, and he'd mess it up. He spread his palms. "I came for you."

Noor crossed her arms over her chest and raised an eyebrow.

"You needed space, and I—"

She didn't let him finish. "Yes, I needed time and space to heal. God knows I walked around like a zombie for weeks, and I don't know if the pain will ever go away." She glared at him. "You gave me what I needed and more. In fact, it seemed like you were more than happy to keep the distance."

"Noor—"

She went on as if he hadn't spoken. "It's why I didn't call you. You seemed content."

Gabriel stepped closer. "You're wrong." He raised a hand to stop her from interjecting. "I know this theme. Man and woman meet. There's conflict, and the entire time it's a prelude to a relationship. The man falls in love and panics. He puts distance between him and the woman he loves. He tries to move on. He fights the good fight and eventually loses the battle. Realizing he's an idiot, man comes back to beg for forgiveness and another chance at happiness." He raked a hand through his hair. "That's not why I'm here. I mean it is." He read the confusion in her face and took another step toward her. "It was different with us from the start. We clicked from the first moment we set eyes on each other, Noor. I knew you were the one for me when we left Tehran. Problem was, neither one of us was ready." Gabriel wanted to reach out and touch her. He knew once he touched her, he wouldn't stop. He forced himself to forge on. "We each had a journey. In my case, finding Mike was the trigger. I'd drowned myself so deeply in guilt that I couldn't see the strength of a strong Afghan woman. I used my guilt as a cloak to distance myself from everyone." He looked into her eyes, and his heart clenched. "I learned a lot about love and personal growth from you.

"Your journey was finding the answers to your past and accepting the truth. You were so focused on your past, you went through life not knowing what you want." Gabriel blew out a breath. "That day at the cemetery, I promised myself I'd give you time to grieve. I didn't run. I knew what I wanted then, and it's what I want now."

She searched his face. "What do you want, Gabriel?"

"You." He gestured between them. "Us." There, he'd said it plain and simple.

Her eyes glistened with tears. "You had to say the right thing, didn't you? Now I'm not even angry."

Gabriel stood still, waiting for her reaction while his heart thundered.

She closed the distance between them and came into his arms.

Hallelujah!

He wrapped his arms around her and inhaled the scent of flowers. Okay, no more patient guy, no more talk. He grabbed a fistful of her hair, tilted her head up, and kissed her. It wasn't a gentle coming together of lovers. It was hungry, hard, and desperate. He poured everything he felt into it.

Noor's reaction was strong. She wrapped her arms around him and kissed him back.

Coherence fled, and hunger mounted. His hands wandered all over her body, caressing silky skin everywhere he could touch. She was all generous curves.

Noor ran her hands up and down his back. He rained kisses down her throat and onto her shoulder, then took her mouth again. He lost his sense of time and place. The only thing that mattered was the woman in his arms. He was about to rip the fabric covering her when the sound of someone clearing his throat broke the silence. Laughter ensued. It annoyed him, making him want to growl like an animal.

"Aha! See what I mean. It's a good thing we're here to watch over the child." The voice was familiar. Gabriel couldn't place it, and frankly he didn't care. His focus was on the sweetest pair of lips he'd ever kissed.

A deep voice chuckled. "I guess that depends on the individual's point of view."

"Maybe we should give them a minute," another voice suggested.

More laughter.

Gabriel's brain cells started to function. Sanity returned in bits and pieces. *Christ, we're in Noor's office.* His hand came away from under her dress, and his mouth eased its hungry grip from hers. Gently, he lightened the kiss, then pulled away. He rested his forehead on hers, trying to get his breathing under control. They were both panting. He lifted his head. Noor's hair was tousled, her lips swollen, and the zipper on the back of her dress was down half way. He pulled it back up. The buttons of his shirt were open down his chest. He started to close them, then noticed the crowd standing in her doorway.

Abarron glared at him. Mustafa and Father Pierre were beside him. One looked away, while the other rubbed his chin, eyes twinkling. Everything amused Mustafa. Aliza and Mike stood to the right, and Brodie was at the far left. Mike and Brodie sported identical grins. Aliza's smirk reminded him of a cat who'd caught a juicy mouse.

Noor blinked several times, swallowed a laugh, and hid her face in his shoulder. "Oh, God."

He kept his arm around her waist. There was no reason for embarrassment. He wasn't some teenager caught kissing a girl.

"No, no, no, child." Abarron hobbled toward Noor. The tap of his cane echoed on the wood floor. "Haven't you listened to anything I've taught you?"

Gabriel glared at his brother.

Mike spread his hands. "I told the gentlemen that Noor was busy. They insisted on seeing her." He flashed his teeth. "Besides, you've already heard the whole why buy the cow when the milk is free lecture."

Abarron stomped his cane on the floor. "I was right. Look at your friend." He pointed to Aliza. "She has a ring on her finger."

Mustafa, who had been affable until now, sobered. He lay a hand on Gabriel's shoulder. "Noor is like a daughter to us. What are your intentions?"

"I thought his intentions were obvious," Brodie muttered, fanning himself.

Michael threw his head back and roared with laughter.

Gabriel opened his mouth to berate his brother when Father Pierre straightened his shoulders. "Are your intentions honorable, son?"

The entire room fell silent. Everyone held their breaths.

Noor tried to speak.

Gabriel tightened his hold on her waist. "Yes."

Michael beamed and rubbed his hands together. "Okay, folks, you heard the man. Let's give the young lovers some privacy."

Abarron scowled. "I don't see a ring on her finger."

Mike was adamant. He steered the crowd out.

Gabriel found himself alone with Noor once again.

She lay her head on his shoulder. "Let's go to my place."

"Are you kidding? Your grandmother, your aunt, and God knows who else will show up on your doorstep. We're going to my hotel."

CHAPTER SIXTY-TWO

Gabriel yawned. Sunset arrived, and rays of orange and purple fell across the bed.

Noor lay naked, sprawled across him. Her leg rested on his thigh, and her cheek lay against his heart. They'd made love most of the day and dozed in between.

Gabriel grinned and caressed her back. He could get used to this.

She slit her eyes open. "Hello, Aquaman."

He grinned and leaned down to kiss her. "Hello, yourself. Are you hungry?"

She stretched and sat up. "I am."

He leaned up on his elbows. "I'll order food. We can eat here and crawl back into bed, unless you want to go out."

A smile tugged at her lips. "Let's stay in. I'll go take a shower."

He wondered if Noor was the shy self-conscious type that hid her body.

She rose from the bed and padded naked across the carpet. *Guess not.*

He leaned back to enjoy the view.

Noor's batted her eyelashes playfully. "You can't look at me like that, Aquaman. At least not for now. I'll have to hold off on jumping you."

Gabriel spread his arms. "Jump me all you want."

Her laughter sounded like pure joy. Gabriel knew because he'd felt the warm sensation all day.

"I need energy. Feed me first," she said.

He picked the phone up. "Do you have a preference?"

"No, I'll have what you're having," she called out over her shoulder.

He ordered dinner and followed her into the bathroom.

She sat amidst a tubful of bubbles, hair pulled back into that knot-thing women do. A ghost of a smile lingered on her mouth. Water and bubbles poured down her breasts. A droplet hung on one nipple. Her lips parted. "I was hoping you'd join me."

He grinned and stepped into the tub.

An hour later, they were at the dinner table wearing large bathrobes. Dinner comprised of chicken bites with Thai-style peanut sauce for appetizers, pan-seared salmon with crispy potato wedges and asparagus for their main meal, and a triple layer chocolate cake for dessert. They devoured the food.

Noor sipped her tea. "You know how to show a girl a good time, Mister McKnight."

"I'm delighted you approve, Miss Rahman." He paused, not knowing how to broach the next subject.

She angled her head to the side. "What's wrong?"

He cleared his throat. "I want to ask you something."

She put her cup down. "Okay, what is it?"

Gabriel took a deep breath. "Do you remember when we first met? You thought I was writing a new series?"

Noor smiled. "Yes."

He ran a hand through his hair. "After we came back from Iran, I thought Mike's idea wasn't bad. I had a few ideas and put them on paper. I liked the outline and wrote the story." He paused. "It's different from the Jason Van series. The main character is an average guy with all the flaws of your average guy. The series covers multiple cultures and is character driven. Harvey suggested we partner with you for this series. That is, if you're interested. I'll understand if you don't want to since we're together. I thought I'd ask you first."

Noor gaped at him. "You're writing a new series?"

"Yes, I brought the first fifty pages of my manuscript," Gabriel said.

She squealed. "You have it here?"

Gabriel rubbed his chin. A slow smile was forming on his face. "Do you want to look at it?"

"Yes, please." She jumped up from the table and followed him to the closet.

Gabriel pulled out the packet and gave it to her.

She hugged the envelope. "Gabriel, I'm honored you and Harvey are trusting me with this." She reached into her purse and pulled out a pair of glasses. After shaking off the robe, she sat cross-legged on the bed. "Will it bother you if I read it now?"

Gabriel snorted. "Are you kidding? A gorgeous naked woman reading my manuscript. It's my private fantasy come true."

She blew him a kiss, then turned her attention to his manuscript.

He went to the small kitchen and made tea. He placed a cup by the small table beside the bed.

She murmured a thank you, not taking her eyes off the manuscript.

He sat on the small armchair by the window and watched her read his work. He wasn't nervous when it came to his writing, but her opinion mattered to him.

After what seemed like an eternity, she raised her eyes to his. "Gabriel, this is great. It's brilliant and edgy. I have a few suggestions, and I know it will become another hit series. How far along are you? Can I read the rest?"

Relief coursed through him. "I'm halfway through the first book. Yes, you can read the rest."

She leaned forward. "I want you to know that I'll be an excellent consultant. I also want to say no matter where our relationship goes, it won't affect the work we do together."

He felt that warm sensation in his stomach and closed the distance between them. "I will say this once and only once. I'm in this for the long haul." Gabriel took his own robe off and climbed onto the bed. "I must warn you, I'm a hands-on author." He pulled the manuscript out of her hands and placed her glasses on the small end table. "Very hands-on." He leaned down and kissed her.

GABRIEL AND NOOR were in Noor's kitchen when the doorbell rang. *The cavalry is here.*

Roshi stomped into the kitchen with Morris trailing in behind her. She put her hands on her hips and glowered at Gabriel. "What the hell took you so long?"

Gabriel glanced at Morris.

Morris lifted his shoulders in a *'what do you want me to do?'* gesture.

Gabriel put his arm around Noor's waist. "I gave her time to grieve. I didn't leave, and I'm not going anywhere."

The answer pacified Roshi. She snorted. "That's the problem with men. They never have the right timing." She cupped Noor's cheek. "Are you happy, sweetheart?"

Noor hugged Roshi. "Yes."

The doorbell rang again. Noor ran to answer it.

Mrs. Navid and Boris joined them.

"Grand-mere, please don't. Gabriel finished explaining to Aunt Roshi he was giving me space. Everything is okay."

Mrs. Navid patted Noor's cheek. "I know, baby. Your young man called me before he came to see you."

Noor's startled gaze met his.

He lifted his shoulders. "Family's important."

She stood on tiptoe and kissed him.

Roshi walked over to the counter and poured herself some coffee. "Morris has an announcement."

Morris almost choked on his coffee.

Gabriel guessed what was coming. He leaned back against the counter and crossed his arms over his chest.

Morris looked at him for help.

He lifted his shoulders, mimicking Morris's action.

Morris scowled.

Noor raised her brows. "Uncle Morrie?"

Morris cleared his throat. "You know your aunt, she loves you, and, uh, you see we—" He glanced at Roshi.

Roshi threw her hands in the air. "Oh, for heaven's sake, Morris and I are having sex. We've been at it for a while. We've just made it official." She sniffed. "Now you know."

Noor gaped at her aunt, then at Morris, and bent over in laughter. "That's wonderful!" She hugged her aunt, then kissed Morris. "Sneaky man, how did you hide your relationship?"

Morris's cheeks sported two spots of red. "It wasn't too hard."

Roshi punched Gabriel in the arm. "It's your turn to spill the beans, lover boy."

Gabriel sighed inwardly. Close-knit families were a blessing and curse. "It was a surprise."

"What surprise?" Noor turned her face up to his.

Gabriel leaned down and kissed her. "Since Morris and your aunt are official, they won't need two houses."

"I'm not moving out of my house. I've just finished my garden," Roshi interjected. "Please continue."

"I bought Morris's house," Gabriel announced.

Noor blinked. "You what?"

"I can write anywhere," Gabriel explained. "I'll keep the house in D.C. because I love it and because my family is there. I figured I'll spend some of my time here with you, and you can come to D.C. to spend time with me."

Noor's brow furrowed. "You can stay here with me. You didn't need to buy a house."

Gabriel laughed. "Yes, I did. Now that my family knows we're together, they will visit Oklahoma City all the time. They can stay at the house while I stay here."

Noor put her arms around his waist. "You're an amazing man, Mister McKnight."

"You're amazing yourself, Miss Rahman."

Mrs. Navid stepped forward. "It's my turn to make an announcement." She raised a hand. "No, I'm not getting married, and no, I'm not in a relationship. I talked to Gabriel's mother. The McKnight family is coming to Oklahoma City for Thanksgiving. We will celebrate Thanksgiving at Gabriel's new house."

EPILOGUE

THANKSGIVING DAY, OKLAHOMA CITY

The kitchen in Gabriel's house bustled with activity. He was grateful for the large space since everyone had gathered there.

Mom, Lily, and Roshi pulled casseroles out of the two large ovens and transferred them to the dining room table.

Noor and Aliza were putting final touches on the side dishes.

Ethan held his son's hand as the baby tottered around the kitchen.

Bond Senior carved the turkey, while Dad carved the ham.

Morris and Michael took trays of drinks to the dining room table.

Mustafa and Father Pierre were lining desserts on the dessert table, and Mrs. Navid, Borris, and Aunt Shahla discussed politics with Abarron.

Gabriel had invited Amir for Thanksgiving. Amir declined. Sheila had business in Iran during the holidays. He promised to visit them later.

Gabriel told Noor about Baran and her brother. He didn't share Amir's secret. It wasn't his to share.

Noor looked forward to meeting the Afghan-American law professor.

When they all settled around the table, Father Pierre raised his hand. "I've always believed everyone should adopt the tradition of Thanksgiving. It's not about the turkey, or the food, or the holiday. It's appreciating life's blessings and the people you share your life with. Let's take a moment to be thankful." He raised his glass. "A toast to family and friendship."

Everyone raised their glasses.

Noor leaned close to Gabriel. "It's wonderful, isn't it?"

Gabriel looked around the table. Yep, it was the classic hallmark scene. He leaned down and whispered in her ear. "Aren't you glad I bought the house?"

MIDNIGHT

Michael and Aliza drove downtown. Michael turned into Oklahoma Avenue and stopped at what looked like an old commercial building. He parked the car and held the door for Aliza.

"Are you certain the information is accurate?"

Michael's mouth flattened into a firm line. "Yes, McMillan confirmed it. He wants me to look into it."

Aliza buttoned up her coat. "How the hell did this slip by our agencies?"

"I don't know." Michael spotted the small security camera situated between the red bricks of the building. He waved his hand in front of the camera. The front door buzzed open.

They entered a garage. A freight elevator stood at the center. They took the elevator to the third floor and stepped into a large loft.

The Iranian had furnished the loft with modern furniture and artwork. It was classy and understated.

Cyrus Rohan, the Iranian to business associates, greeted them. "Michael, Aliza, welcome." He gestured for Mike and Aliza to follow him to the living area.

Morris sat on a couch, sipping tea.

"Would you care for a drink?" Cyrus offered.

Michael put a hand on his stomach. "No, thank you. I'm still full from the day's festivities."

Cyrus's eyes softened. "Yes, that was fun. Wasn't it?" He crossed his legs and picked imaginary lint off his trousers. There were several moments of silence. Cyrus steepled his fingers. "I'm pleased you are both here. Your unique skills will be a great help to us. Morris and I made the mistake of working with the wrong government agents in the past. That is a mistake we will not repeat." He took a deep breath. "I must ask. Are you going to continue with your careers, or do you plan to settle down and start a family?"

Michael glanced at Aliza, and his mouth turned up. "We'll settle down at some point. For now, we both agree our government needs us."

Cyrus nodded. "Very well." He reached for the folder sitting on the coffee table. "I have the information we discussed." He handed Michael the folder.

Michael pulled a sheet of paper out of the file and held it between himself and Aliza. He whistled. "Who else knows about this?"

Cyrus's eyes hardened. "There are rumors circulating the community as we speak."

Michael rubbed his chin. "We've just scratched the tip of the iceberg."

Cyrus leaned forward. "It's important that we keep this amongst ourselves for now."

Michael handed the document back to Cyrus. "That's not a

problem. Gabe's smart though. It won't be long before he figures it out. When Gabriel figures it out, Noor will know, too."

Cyrus sighed. "I'm aware of that. When they figure it out"—he spread his hands.—"they have us to assist them."

GABRIEL FLOATED BACK TO CONSCIOUSNESS. The fire's cheerful warmth had died down. He untangled himself from Noor and rose from the bed. He added a few more logs to the fireplace. Warmth and light spread across the room. The antique volume of *Divan-e-Shams* sat on the loveseat. He read Rumi with Noor every night and was enjoying his education in Persian literature. They were on this journey together. He sat on the couch and pulled the book onto his lap. A sheet of paper fell out.

It was the piece of paper with the two lines of code naming the *Donya-e-Noor* and cigarette case. Luckily both items were back in Tehran where they belonged.

He lifted the sheet of paper. Something about it bothered him. Why write two lines of code on a whole sheet of paper? Why not leave a small note? He held the paper under the light. *Something's not right.*

"What are you doing?" Noor sat up and rubbed her eyes.

"I'm trying to solve another puzzle."

"Come back to bed, Aquaman." She pulled the cover aside. Her hair fell around her like a silk halo, and firelight illuminated her generous curves. She looked like a goddess from another world.

He put the sheet of paper back in the book. He'd worry about it later.

THE END